Elsie Silver is a *USA Today* bestselling Canadian author of sassy, sexy, small-town romance who loves good book boyfriends and the strong heroines who bring them to their ⸻ she lives just outside Vancouver, British Columbia, ⸻ husband, son, and three dogs and has been voraciously reading romance books since before she was probably ⸻ to.

⸻ loves cooking and trying new foods, traveling, and ⸻ time with her boys—especially outdoors. Elsie has ⸻ a big fan of her quiet 5:00 a.m. mornings, which ⸻ most of her writing happens. It's during this time ⸻ can sip a cup of hot coffee and dream up a fictional ⸻ of romantic stories to share with her readers.

Website: elsiesilver.com
Facebook: authorelsiesilver
Instagram: @authorelsiesilver

ALSO BY ELSIE SILVER

WILD LOVE

ELSIE SILVER

PIATKUS

PIATKUS

First published in 2024 by Bloom Books,
An imprint of Sourcebooks
First published in Great Britain in 2024 by Piatkus

5 7 9 10 8 6

A CIP catalogue record for this book
is available from the British Library.

ISBN: 978-0-349-44163-4

Printed and bound in Great Britain by Clays Ltd, Elcograf S.p.A.

Papers used by Piatkus are from well-managed forests
and other responsible sources.

MIX
Paper | Supporting
responsible forestry
FSC® C104740

Piatkus
An imprint of
Little, Brown Book Group
Carmelite House
50 Victoria Embankment
London EC4Y 0DZ

An Hachette UK Company
www.hachette.co.uk

www.littlebrown.co.uk

For all the women who've figured out that good enough isn't actually enough. And for those of you who are still looking for more. It's out there. You'll find it. And if not, don't worry. There's always Ford Grant.

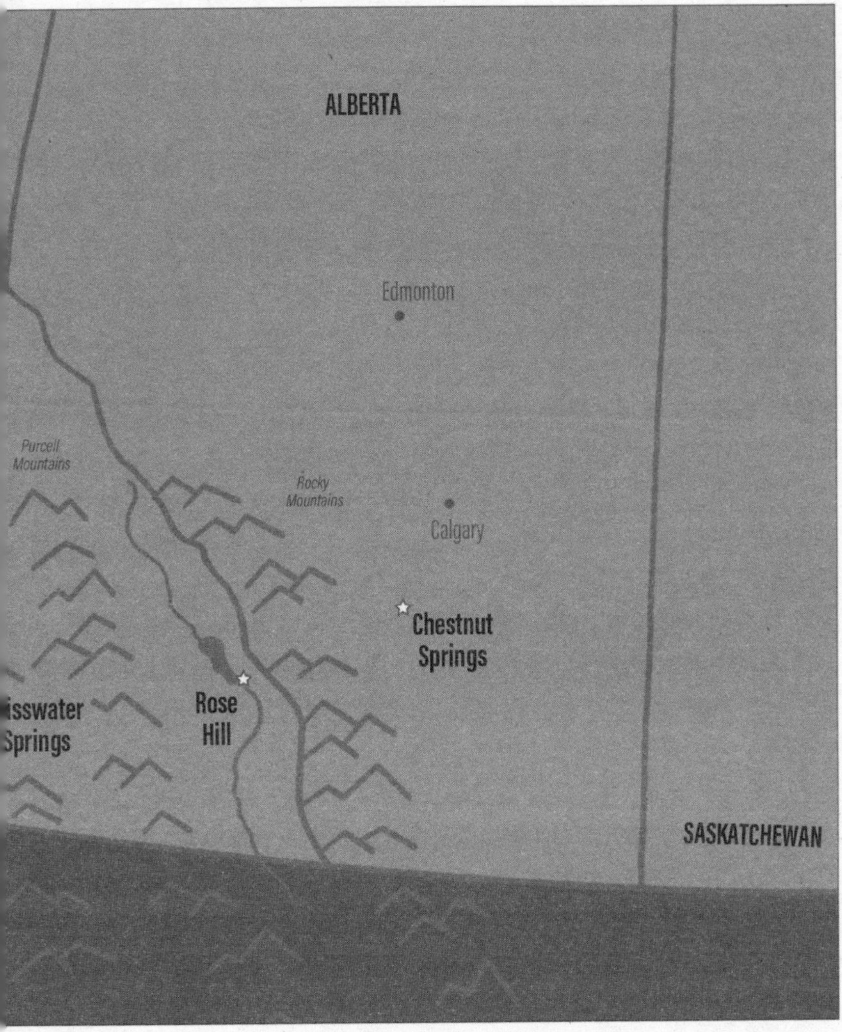
ALBERTA
Edmonton
Purcell Mountains
Rocky Mountains
Calgary
Chestnut Springs
isswater Springs
Rose Hill
SASKATCHEWAN

CHAPTER 1

Ford

"Dude. *Forbes* named you the World's Hottest Billionaire." My best friend, Weston Belmont, announces the title with extra flair to mock me. He makes it sound like I'm a stripper about to take the stage.

I ignore him and focus on unpacking the box of cleaning supplies at my feet.

"Ford." He shakes the glossy magazine at me. "This is crazy."

My eyes slice toward West, and I give him the blankest look I can muster. He lounges in the high-backed chair with his boots kicked up on my desk. Dirt crumbles off the bottoms, making this place an even bigger mess than it already is.

"It's crazy all right." Propping my hands on my hips, I turn to survey the old barn that will be the head office for my new recording studio and production company. I'm calling it a barn, but it's more of an empty, dusty outbuilding.

Rust-colored holes in the floor lead me to believe there were stalls in it once upon a time. Now, it's mostly a big, messy open space with a small kitchenette area near the front door that's separated by a long narrow hallway.

Either way, it sits just a short walk from the main farmhouse on a massive plot of sloped land, right on the edge of Rose Hill.

And when you open the old barn doors, the view is nothing short of spectacular.

The lake butts against the bottom property line, pine trees frame either side making it feel like a private oasis. The edge of the small mountain town is a mere five minutes down the road. Beyond that, it's all jagged mountains that stretch back into miles upon miles of pristine Canadian wilderness.

The spot is beautiful. But everything on the property has fallen into disrepair. It all has so much potential though. I can see it clear as day. Guesthouses for the artists. Antique furniture. Spotty Wi-Fi. No paparazzi.

Rose Hill Records. Named after the town I've come to love.

I've produced *one* successful album, and now I've got the itch. I want to do it again and lucky for me, an influx of artists want a turn too. I'm excited to be creative every day. Listen to music every day. Make songs come to life every day.

Especially *here*.

Rose Hill is the perfect place to make a home and start the business I've always wanted.

A personal haven where I don't have to wear a stuffy suit or report to shareholders who don't care about anything but the bottom line or get hounded by the press about being "the World's Hottest Billionaire," like it's some sort of crowning achievement.

"It says here you declined to comment."

If they named West the World's Hottest Billionaire, he'd milk the hell out of it.

Me? I decline to comment and take off to a small town where I can start a brand-new business venture by myself. I hate the attention.

"Actually, I gave them one comment before saying I officially refused to comment."

West snorts. "Oh, this ought to be good."

My cheek twitches. He knows. He knows me better than almost anyone.

"I told them I'm barely a billionaire and just happen to be more attractive than the 2,500 other people on the list. They want to write an article about the least interesting aspect of my life. So, no comment, because this accomplishment doesn't deserve one. Conventionally handsome, rich guy says no fucking thank you."

"So weird they didn't want to publish that charming one-liner from you, Ford. A real head-scratcher."

I shrug and ignore the jab. Talking about money makes me uncomfortable. I've had an abundance of it my entire life and have now spent an awful lot of time around people who make my childhood look meager. I have never found it to be an especially impressive trait about any one person I've met. In fact, it's kind of the opposite. When you have a lot of money, people act differently around you, and if you let yourself get too obsessed with your own money, you can turn into a real piece of shit.

Why would anyone want to read an article about how rich some guy is?

I've also never flourished in the spotlight. The attention makes me snappy and sarcastic, and what I've been told is *rude* or *out of touch with social cues*. Though I'm not sure I'd take it that far. I'd call it direct and say other people get offended too easily.

Unlike West, I don't come off as likable. I'm aware of the perception, but I'm not particularly bothered about changing it. Anyone who knows me knows better. And I'm not losing sleep over the opinions of those who don't.

I bend down, scoop up the hand-held duster, and make my way across the room. My lace-up boots thud on the scuffed hardwood floor as I trudge over to the vintage cast-iron stove in the corner. Cobwebs and partially burnt logs fill the space beneath it, and I wonder how long they've been there, who put them there, what story they might tell. If they weren't such an eyesore, I'd leave them. To be frank, I feel a bit like a yuppie intruder barging in to make everything all shiny and new.

I could pay a person to do this grunt work, but hiring someone I can trust feels like a mountain too steep to climb. Plus, there's a certain allure to building something with my own hands. Yeah, I've got the money, but I don't *need* to spend the money when I'm perfectly capable. When I've got the ambition and the dedication.

Hard work—that's how I ended up owning one of the

busiest bars and premier live music venues in Calgary. That's how I ended up founding a music streaming app that catapulted my bank account into an obnoxious stratosphere. My dad had plenty of money, plenty of connections, and he could have set me up easily—but he didn't. He was hell-bent on my sister and me learning the value of money.

But what will all my successes from here on out be chalked up to?

Money. Connections. *Luck*. And I don't believe in luck.

"What even is this picture of you?" West holds the magazine up from across the room. "You look like you're hiding behind the popped collar of your jacket."

"I was."

"Why?"

Bless him. His furrowed brow and tilted head betray his genuine confusion. To someone like him, it makes no sense why I wouldn't bask in the notice. He's larger-than-life, fun, a big fucking showboat—and I love all of that about him. West also has a good heart and is trustworthy as all get-out. He's genuine in a world of so many people who aren't. He found me reading by the lake as a kid and started talking to me like he knew me. Hasn't stopped since then, unlikely of friends as we might be. There's something about us that has just… stuck.

For twenty years we've stuck.

"Because I didn't want my picture taken. Don't like it."

"Why? Do you need me to tell you how handsome you are?"

I scoff. "Because I was walking down the street to meet my sister for coffee, not at a photo shoot."

He chuckles. "I mean, would it have killed you to smile?"

"Yes." I stare at the fireplace, duster in hand, trying to figure out how the hell I'm going to do everything on my list.

"You're gonna need a shovel for that oven. Not a duster."

"Thank you, West. I'm so glad you're nearby to lend your opinion."

He lets out an exaggerated sigh. "It's gonna be like the old days. Just you and me getting into trouble."

"You got into trouble. I watched."

"I remember Rosie tagging along, just fucking shit-talking you the entire time. God, nothing made me prouder of her."

My body stills at the mention of his sister. *Rosalie*. I haven't laid eyes on her in a decade, but my shoulders get tense all the same.

I turn to face West. "Doesn't she have her master's and some fancy job in Vancouver now?"

I already know she does. I look her up from time to time—just to make sure she's happy, of course. West mentions her when we talk, but never in detail. It's all generalities, surface-level updates. But then, why would he tell his best friend anything more in-depth about his baby sister, who took off to live in the city?

It's better I don't ask.

He waves a hand, like Rosie slinging jabs as a teenager is the most impressive feat to him. "Those were the best summers. I was always such a sad fucking panda when you went back to the city for school."

I hated it too. Back to the city, back to school with kids who—unlike West—treated me like I was different from them. Back to the pressure of being the son of one of the world's most recognizable guitarists. Rose Hill was my favorite escape as a child, and it would seem nothing has changed for me as a thirty-two-year-old man. It's like time stands still here. No one here treats you like you're rich or famous or even particularly special. Everyone just goes about their business. That fresh mountain air must give everyone the perspective that city people seem to lack.

But my attachment to this area is more than just that. I'm drawn back to this place on a much deeper level. To the memories it holds.

"Well, this year you won't have to cry about it, West. You're officially stuck with me."

I toss the duster back into the box, coming to terms with the fact I might need to hire someone to help get this place up and running if I want to record here anytime soon. The main house is now livable—fully updated it myself over the winter—but this building is so much worse.

"Fuck yeah. I'm going to get you on my bowling team."

"No. Absolutely not. You told me it's dads' night out, and I'm not a dad." I kick my toe at what I thought was a dead bug but am now certain is mouse droppings. "Except to maybe an entire herd of mice."

"I don't think mice roam in herds."

"Whatever they are, I don't think they qualify me as a dad."

"That's fine. It's really just Sebastian and me, assuming he's in town, and then we've got you—"

"You haven't got me—"

"And then we've got Crazy Clyde."

"Who's Crazy Clyde? I don't think you can just roll around calling people crazy anymore."

"He's the dude who lives on the other side of the mountain—pretty much a hermit—because he believes in every conspiracy theory known to man. His stories are my favorite. And he'll introduce himself as Crazy Clyde, so I'll let you be the one to correct him."

I blink at my friend. This sounds like my nightmare.

"I'm not fucking bowling with you, West."

He scoffs and dismisses my words with a hand flick. "You say that now. But you always said no to my shenanigans as a kid too. And then you'd be there. Emo hair in your eyes, pushing those oversized glasses up the bridge of your nose." He grins at me, perfect white teeth flashing bright next to his rough stubble. "Moody scowl on your face. Probably some obscure book of poetry clutched under your arm."

I can't help but snort out a laugh at his accurate description as I shake my head. "Get fucked, Belmont."

"Look at you now—"

My pointer finger aims straight at him. "Don't even say it."

As he speaks, his hands make sweeping, dramatic movements through the air. "World's Hottest Billionaire."

"I hate you."

"Nah. You love me. I'm the sunshine to your grumpy."

My brows pinch together. "What?"

"It's a thing in romance books—"

A knock at the door cuts him off, and we both turn to look across the barn, toward the rickety front door down a narrow hallway that turns sharply into the kitchenette.

"Who would be here?" West whispers like we're in trouble.

Maybe we are. I've only been in town for a short while, working on the main house, so I have no idea who it could be. My sister Willa would barge in unannounced. My parents would call. My best friend is sitting across from me.

Truth is, I have no one else in my life who cares about me enough to drive all this way.

I keep my circle tight and trust few. The allure of Rose Hill is that the paparazzi don't want to spend all day driving to *maybe* get a shot.

"I don't know." I shrug and West's eyes go wide as an owl's as he shrugs back.

Another knock.

"I can hear you whispering in there," a feminine voice I don't recognize calls from the other side of the wooden door.

My head goes to Rosie first, but this voice sounds too young to be hers. So, with a heavy sigh, I stride toward the door and yank it open.

Before me stands a girl. She's wearing black ripped jeans. Black Chuck Taylors. An oversized Death From Above 1979 T-shirt—one of my favorite bands. The garment boasts a few intentionally distressed holes across it. Her pitch-black hair is tied in two braids, one down each shoulder, complemented with straight bangs in a slash across her forehead. All of this is topped off with an unimpressed expression on her face. The top loop of a JanSport backpack dangles from her fingers.

I don't know how old she is. Young. Looks like that awkward, confusing age just before you become a teenager—based on her sullen stare and the sizable zit on her chin. She crosses her arms and drags her gaze from my face down to my feet before making her way back up.

"Who are you?" I don't mean to sound like a dick when I say it. After all, she's just a kid.

Her lips flatten, and she blinks once, slowly. "Your daughter, dickhead."

Now it's my turn to blink slowly. I hear West's chair roll across the hardwood and his heavy steps as he approaches.

"Pardon me?" I say. I heard the words, but my brain is not processing their meaning.

"You're my dad," she says and rolls her eyes. "Biologically speaking."

But there's no way. There's absolutely no way. The mere statement puts me on the defensive. It's laughable.

One stupid *Forbes* article about my bank account and the cockroaches crawl out. I know this story all too well. I almost feel bad for the girl. She's too young to pull this off on her own. Someone *must* have put her up to it.

"Listen, whatever your name is, I'm not sure what you're after from me, but I can take a guess. And you're barking up the wrong tree."

"My name is Cora Holland. Your name is Ford Grant Junior, and you're my biological dad."

"Oof, leave the junior off," West murmurs from behind me. "He hates that."

I don't spare my friend a glance. Instead, I stare down at the snarky little kid spouting total bullshit right to my face.

She's got a lot of nerve. I'll give her that. "That's impossible. I never fucked Morticia Addams."

Her head tilts and her eyes roll again. She barely reacts. "Really original, nepo baby. Never heard that joke before." She rifles through her backpack. Black, *of course.* With a flourish, she pulls out a sheet of paper emblazoned with a logo I recognize.

The company I submitted DNA to so I could complete a family tree as a gift for my mom.

"What about a paper Dixie cup?" she continues. "A petri dish? A sterile tube? You fuck any of those for a few bucks at any point in your life?"

I feel every drop of blood sink down to my feet as my stomach turns and my head spins.

Because yes, in fact, I did.

West slaps my shoulder, giving it a firm squeeze as he edges past me and out the door. "Right, well, see you at bowling, I guess."

And then I'm left here.

Alone.

Staring at a young girl who may well be my biological child. And feeling like what I might actually be is the World's Most Unprepared Dad.

CHAPTER 2

Rosie

I SMALL BACK AT THE BOARDROOM FULL OF PEOPLE.

My boss.

My boss's boss.

My boss's boss's boss.

I wanted so badly to nail this presentation. I think I did. No, I *know* I did. But you wouldn't think so based on the blank looks and absent nods. It's not like I expected a standing ovation, but a couple of pats on the back might have been nice.

Instead, it's borderline awkward.

"And, well…" I wipe my hands down the front of my pencil skirt, a sign of how nervous I am. "That's my take on the acquisition based on the research I've done."

More blank fucking looks.

"So, uh, thank you for coming to my TED Talk." I laugh at my own joke, but it comes out shrill and desperate and makes me cringe internally.

I glance over at Faye, my favorite member of the admin team, who's taking meeting minutes. She presses her lips together to stifle a laugh and gives me a discreet thumbs-up.

At least Stan, the company president and also my boss, pities me enough to chuckle lightly. But he laughs at almost everything I say. Then licks his lips and stares at my tits.

So, with one more brief smile, I snatch up the stack of papers from the table in front of me and hustle back to my seat at the boardroom table. The solid pressure from the backrest of my chair has me sighing as I relax back into it.

As someone from accounting takes their turn, Stan leans in toward me, probably to complain about how buying another gravel pit will cost the company money while completely ignoring the fact it will also make them more money.

"You were great. Such a smart girl."

My lips tug back as I try to swallow a wince. *Such a smart girl* makes me want to hurl all over his expensive tan slacks. But I swallow my vomit and force an awkward smile onto my face like I'm flattered by his condescension. "Thank you, Stan."

The meeting drags on in a boring blur of people talking, spreadsheets on projectors, and me trying to convince myself I'm going to love this job eventually. I have too many student loans to let myself think otherwise.

This is the best job ever!

I repeat the sentiment in my head, thinking about my sizable paycheck. How grown up I'll feel when I'm debt free. I'm the most educated person in my family. Working in the city at a Fortune 500 construction materials company.

Living the dream.

Before I know it, the meeting has ended and most people have filed out of the room—Faye whispered "you killed it" in my ear before departing—but not me. I'm still the newest employee in the room, which means I'll be the one cleaning up after the production meeting. As I'm tidying the room, Stan, who is still lingering at the table, gestures me toward him.

"I need you a moment, Rosie."

"Rosalie," I correct. Because Stan doesn't know me well enough to call me Rosie.

He just chuckles, like my request is amusing.

Stan is the best boss ever!

If I think it enough times, maybe I'll believe that too.

"Can you come show me on this map exactly which property you were talking about?" he asks. "The one that borders our current pit?"

"Of course."

When I come to stand beside him, he has a satellite image map on his laptop screen, zoomed all the way out like he can't even figure out which country we're in.

"May I?" I ask, pointing at his mouse. He nods and lifts his hands, leaning back in his chair but not getting out of the way.

I brush it off and bend down, maneuvering the map to where it needs to go. With a few clicks, I zoom in and shift over until the outline of the property in question comes into view.

"Right there." I point at it just as I feel a hand on the top of my ass.

His hand.

I freeze, shocked by the contact and by the absolute gall of this man. He could have claimed he was touching my tailbone or something equally ridiculous, but then he slides his big, meaty palm down over the curve of my butt. His fingers trail over the middle, about to dig in, when I turn abruptly and slap his hand away.

He has the audacity to give me a set of wide, little-boy eyes, like he's innocent. It pisses me off.

He pisses me off.

I transform from friendly Rosie into I'll-fucking-kill-you Rosie. After all, you don't grow up the only sister to a guy like Weston Belmont and enter adulthood without a scrappy side at least partially intact.

My shoulders go rigid and ice hardens my voice. "Stan, if I wanted you to touch me, I would tell you."

"Rosie—"

"But now I'll have to tell HR instead. You're a pig."

He looks stunned by my words, by the abruptness with which I scoop up my belongings and storm toward the door.

You'd think he'd apologize, beg for mercy, but instead, he says, "HR is gone for the day. You'll have to wait until tomorrow."

"You look tired."

Ryan stumbles from our bedroom and gives me a dopey smile. I wait for the swirl of butterflies to crash around in my stomach, but they don't come.

"I am," he says, immediately heading for the coffeepot.

I'm not sure where he was last night. I came back to an empty apartment after a session of late-night stewing around the office while I finished up some work. HR really was gone for the day——I know because I went past their offices multiple times, which just added to my anxiety.

When I got home, I cracked open a bottle of wine and stared out over the city. Under the pitch-black cloud-covered sky and the endless West Coast drizzle, cars weaved through the wet downtown streets of Vancouver with a gentle whooshing sound that was almost soothing. After that, I'd eaten a bowl of popcorn for dinner and contemplated my life.

Most girls would have been worried about their boyfriend's whereabouts. They'd probably blow up their phones and demand to know where they were and who they were with. But I was struck by no such inclination.

I like Ryan. I've always liked Ryan. Since the first day he flopped down next to me and flashed me that signature lopsided, boyish grin in the first finance course of my master's program. Everything about our relationship after that was easy. Friends and study buddies, roommates, and from there… more.

Then I just never left.

Sometimes I wonder if it was all just a little *too* easy. We grew from roommates to partners in a way that seemed simple and obvious. Now, we're feeling like roommates again, and I wonder what changed and how I never noticed it happening. I wonder if sweet, lovable Ryan has noticed or if I'm the problem.

I wonder… do you feel yourself fall out of love? Or do you just wake up and realize it one day?

"What'd you get up to?" I ask. "I didn't even hear you come in."

He pulls out the second seat at the island in our sleek two-bedroom apartment. "Yeah. Didn't get back until like three and you were out cold. Some bigwigs from the head office took the guys and me out for beers after work, and one thing led to another."

He chuckles good-naturedly and ruffles my hair. Some days that might feel sweet. But after what happened to me yesterday, it feels… condescending.

I give him a brittle smile and smooth my hair. Ryan is a good guy. I remind myself of this all the time, over little things. I feel guilty those little things are irritating me, and I feel guiltier for what that irritation might mean.

He's like a golden retriever. Happy and chill and unbothered all the time. And sometimes when he accidentally drools on me or gets hair on my black shirt, like some sort of big, happy idiot, I want to snap at him. But he's so well-meaning that I don't.

I ignore it because our lives are too damn busy for me to worry about that right now. Ryan is everything I should want and I don't want to throw away a multi-year relationship with a nice guy, all because I'm overworked and on edge.

That seems rash. It could be a phase. I could regret it. I've always been the responsible child in my family. I don't make thoughtless moves.

"Fun," I add without feeling. Because a bunch of oil

industry guys going out on the town doesn't sound any better than a bunch of construction industry guys doing the exact same thing.

They both sound like prime ass-grabbing situations.

My cheeks heat as I recall the feeling of Stan's hand over the curve of my body. I've always thought I'd be able to brush something like that off. When I ride the SkyTrain, people bump into me all the time. But with him it's the intention—the path his touch took.

It felt *wrong*. And I stayed awake for a long time thinking about it. Realizing I had heard the sharp, ragged intake of his breath behind me as his fingers dug in.

That little gasp is what spurred me into motion.

That little gasp plays on repeat in my ears. It makes my skin crawl. It makes me not want to show my face at work. It seems like it shouldn't bother me this much, and yet it does. I'm not sure who I trust enough to tell. I could tell West, but I know how he'd react, and I don't want him to go to jail.

So, I opt for Ryan. Sweet, lovable, reliable Ryan.

"I have something I was hoping I could get your opinion on."

He pauses from scrolling on his phone to peek up at me, a reassuring expression on his face. "Yeah, babe. Of course."

"So yesterday, at the end of that big meeting I've been prepping for—you know the one?"

His eyes stay glued on the screen, but he nods. "Yeah, of course. You've been walking around muttering that presentation under your breath for at least a week. I bet you nailed it."

"Right. Yeah. That's the one. And it went well. But,

so…" My fingers twist in my lap, cup of tea forgotten on the counter before me. I have my full attention on Ryan as I try to muster the courage to get this out. But Ryan has his attention on what appears to be a video of a raccoon taking a bubble bath.

"At the end of the meeting, I was showing my boss, Stan, something. And he touched me. Well, he grabbed my ass."

My throat feels tight as Ryan jerks his head up in my direction. "Oh shit," is the first thing he says, but there's an edge of amusement to it. Like this is somehow funny.

"Yeah. Oh shit."

Ryan straightens at my terse tone, finally looking concerned. "Do you think he meant to? Like, was it on purpose?"

The bridge of my nose stings at that being the first thing he asks. "Yes, it was very much on purpose."

"Dang. Are you all right?" He puts the phone down and gives me his full attention, though I'm finding I wish he hadn't. I thought I wanted his attention, but now I'm squirming under his gaze. Turns out this was easier to talk about without him staring at me.

I nod briskly, assuredly, to cover for the fact I don't know if I actually am all right. "I told him I'm going to take it to HR, but they were gone already. So now I'm kinda gearing myself up to walk in there and let them know."

He blows out a loud breath and shifts on his stool, placing a hand on my leg before saying the worst thing he's ever said to me. "Shit, Rosie. I'm sorry. I know how important this job is to you. Do you think it might be better to pretend like it never happened? These big companies"—his fingers graze my thigh before squeezing it, and I feel myself recoil from his touch—"they stay as far away from scandal as possible. And it's still a relatively new position for you… I'd hate to see that jeopardized."

I'm stunned into silence. I blink back at the man I've lived with for the past two years, a mixture of fury and devastation twisting inside of me.

My mouth moves and so does my body, but not in conjunction with what I feel inside. "Yeah. For sure. Wouldn't want to jeopardize anything."

I nod as I pat his hand, which is still on my leg. But I'm uncertain who's reassuring who here.

All I know is that Ryan's reaction isn't what I wanted from him.

Which is why I take his hand and remove it from my body.

"I'm glad you agree. I think I'd just carry on with my work if I were you."

If I were you.

"Mm-hmm," is all I can muster as I pull away from him.

"I know, babe. I know." He tries to squeeze my shoulder reassuringly and a wave of discomfort washes over me. I don't want to be touched. "Once you've been working in the industry as long as I have, you'll learn we have to look past some things if we want to be successful."

In response, I scoff and make an internal note to look past sexual harassment in the future. It's an especially obnoxious sentiment coming from someone who was out all night getting wined and dined by the bigwigs at his company. I know Ryan thinks what he just said is well-meaning and supportive, but it makes me want to punch him square in the face.

Sweet, professional, MBA-toting Rosie Belmont doesn't hit people though, so I swallow the urge and mumble, "Thanks," before walking away.

The disparity between our experiences is a lance through my heart, but not one I necessarily want to take out on Ryan at this moment. I can't afford to be reckless.

But the fact he doesn't even seem upset? That smarts.

I didn't need someone to go in there and beat the shit out of Stan, but I'd be lying if I said I wouldn't have liked it. It might have been nice to feel like the man I share my life with has my back. That he'd defend my honor—lame and old-fashioned as that might sound. Even the tiniest spark of ferocity over my safety, the injustice of it all, would have sufficed.

Hell, I'd have settled for a hug.

I get neither.

When I go to leave later that morning, Ryan offers me a thumbs-up and says, "Go get 'em, tiger," from behind the glass shower door.

I feel sick on the train the entire way to work.

I begin to shake on the elevator ride up to our floor.

I keep my eyes down, knowing that if I can just make it to the privacy of my tiny office, I'll be able to regain my composure behind a closed door.

But I'm intercepted by Linda from HR. She has an apologetic expression painted all over her face before any words even crest her lips. "Good morning, Rosalie. Once you're settled, can you come to my office?"

"Yes, of course." My voice cracks as I nod.

We exchange matching forced smiles, but when I turn away from her, a big, fat tear rolls down my cheek. Because I know exactly what's coming.

CHAPTER 3

Ford

CORA AND I HAVE SPENT THE LAST HOUR ON THE FRONT steps of the dilapidated barn, looking over our Kindred DNA results. While I scoured the internet for reliable assessments of Kindred's testing accuracy, she sat quietly beside me, waiting. I saw her eyes roll when I typed the same question, only worded differently.

In my defense, *how accurate is Kindred testing?* might bring up different results than *is Kindred testing ever wrong?*

"So you're pretty sure I'm your biological dad?" The question sounds stupid to my own ears, but I'm having a hard time processing this news.

"Pretty sure." Cora fiddles with her shoelaces, and I stare at the scribbles she's made in black marker over the white toe of her sneakers. I used to do that too. "Just recently found out my parents used a sperm donor. And this links us."

Am I supposed to hug her or something? Seems kind of

creepy, considering I don't know her at all. I opt to find out more information instead.

"Are you… Do you…" I run a hand through my hair, frustrated by my loss for words. "Do you have a home?"

Her responding sigh is so dramatic, so exasperated, I feel my lips twitch. It reminds me of my sister, Willa.

"So you came to find me—"

"Yup. And I found you. Your name is in the news because of your new production company and shit. Kids these days are pretty good with the internet."

"I just… I'm sorry. I'm having a hard time processing this. I didn't expect, well, you."

Her chipped, black-polished nails trace the scribble-covered rubber toe of her shoes. "You donated sperm. What did you expect?"

"To walk out of that building with a much needed one hundred dollars in my pocket."

An awkward silence descends between us. And guilt creeps in. I need to rein in my attitude, not be a dick to a child. "I was nineteen. Wasn't really thinking beyond that. Never imagined there could be a kid out there."

She scoffs. "Did you forget donating?"

I shrug, elbows propped on my knees. "Sort of." My eyes slice in Cora's direction. "Sorry."

Her eyes roll again, but her cheek hitches up for a beat too. "It's okay. I thought you were loaded or some shit. Your dad is a famous rock star. Why did you need a hundred bucks?"

A chuckle rumbles in my chest, and I drop my head. "I

was dying to see Rage Against the Machine on their reunion tour. But my dad, rich and famous as he might be, didn't fund my—or my sister's—lifestyle. He was big on teaching us life lessons and avoiding the silver-spoon effect. At that point, I'd just started university and was broke. My tuition was paid, but I worked at a bar to pay rent and eat." I shake my head as I think back on that conversation with my dad. "He wouldn't spot me the hundred bucks for tickets. Told me that hardworking people prioritize necessities and sometimes go without the extras."

Her lips twitch, and she looks away. "Wow. You really showed him."

I don't respond to that as it hits me—I'll have to tell my parents about Cora. I think? I'm not sure why she's here or what she wants.

"It's almost like Zack de la Rocha played a part in my conception, and I guess that's pretty cool. And they haven't been on tour since, so who can blame you, really? Decent investment."

I laugh now because how can I not? "I appreciate your logic on that one."

Cora cracks a smile, but it's a sad one. She told me she's twelve. But she seems wise beyond her years, world-weary in a way a twelve-year-old shouldn't be.

My voice comes out rough when I say, "Okay, let's pretend I really am your biological parent. What brings you here to my doorstep?"

"What doorstep? This place is a dump," she mutters sullenly, and I glance over my shoulder to confirm that it is indeed a dump without a doorstep.

"Actually, that's the house." I point to the craftsman-style house beyond the barn. It's not perfect, but it's close. New and rustic all at once. The barn though? Yeah, it needs some work.

But I know it will be worth the effort. The view of the lake, the smell of pine on the breeze. Spring is in the air, and as soon as everything greens up, this place will be impressive.

"My dad died."

That one sentence stops me in my tracks. Her fingers are still fidgeting, eyes still downcast, but I'm motionless as I watch her.

"I'm sorry for your loss." God, that sounds so fucking lame. This kid's dad died, and I turn into a clichéd Hallmark card.

But she doesn't seem to care. In fact, she shrugs again. Apparently, it's her signature move. "He was sick for a really long time. He had ALS, so we knew it was coming, ya know? Not like it was some big surprise."

I swallow roughly, deciding to let her talk rather than insert myself into what clearly isn't my story.

"My mom…" She sighs, her entire torso rising and falling with the heavy exhale. "My mom isn't coping well without him. They were high school sweethearts but had me later in life. Trouble conceiving and all that. And we don't have anyone to help us."

Pressure crushes hard and heavy against my chest. It feels like someone's booted foot is holding me down and they're putting more and more of their body weight onto my lungs. I struggle to keep my breathing even, but Cora doesn't seem to notice.

"I think she needs to go live somewhere with… some support." Now her head wobbles, and I can see her weighing her next words carefully. "Been doing some research, and I'm pretty sure she's clinically depressed. Like… bad. So I started searching up different places for her, ya know? Maybe an inpatient center. There are a few around. Talked a bit to the counselor at my school about it too. But with me being a minor, she said I'd probably get moved into the foster system unless we could arrange a kinship placement. She's doing me a solid right now by not calling social services already."

Now it's my turn to drop my head and trace the toes of my boots, so I have something to do with my hands. I wonder how we must look right now, sitting side by side, mimicking one another's movements.

"Turns out you might be my only living family. Well, besides my mom."

Fuck.

"No aunts or uncles or grandparents? Someone you might know better than me?"

She sniffs and I give her the courtesy of not looking her way. I don't know the kid, but she seems like the type of person who wouldn't want me staring at her while she cries.

I know I wouldn't. Maybe it's hereditary.

"Nah. Both parents were only children. Grandparents are dead."

"Okay." I nod, still staring at our shoes. "Okay."

"Okay, what?"

"Okay, let's take you home. Maybe talk to your mom."

From the corner of my eye, I see her turn to stare at me. "Just like that?"

I straighten and lean back against the rickety steps behind me. Internally, I'm freaking out. I'm not equipped for this shit. I don't even know what kinship placement means. What it looks like. What's required. But if I'm the only thing standing between this girl and the foster system, then fuck, how would I sleep at night if I said no? Deep down I'm too damn soft for this shit.

"Yeah. Just like that."

She's twelve. She doesn't need to worry about the details. That's what the adults will do. My lawyer. My lawyer, Belinda, who is going to *kill* me for this.

I can practically hear her now. Her voice sounds like she smokes a pack a day. She'll probably berate me for always being such a raging asshole and then choosing the most inopportune times to have the biggest bleeding heart.

She won't be wrong.

Then I'm up, locking the front door to the "dump" and jogging toward my Mercedes G-Wagon. "Let's go, kid," I call back as I wave a hand over my shoulder. "Need a bathroom? A snack? We can grab a burger on the drive." I need to move. Get going. I need to push myself far enough down this path that I don't think too hard about it and come up with more reasons I shouldn't.

Because in my heart, I know this is the right thing to do. No matter how fucking insane it seems. I'm trusting my gut.

Cora isn't far behind me. She slides into the passenger seat, and I can feel her staring at me. Probably confused by how I went from comparing her to Wednesday Addams to whatever the hell I'm about to do now. "I would never say no to a burger."

As I check my pockets for my wallet, I ask, "Are you tall enough to sit in the front seat?"

"I'm twelve."

I sigh and press the start button, the hum of my SUV filling the otherwise quiet cab. "It seems like kids these days stay in car seats until they can legally drink, so just trying to be safe or whatever."

She snorts and clicks her belt into the latch. I catch myself staring at her profile, trying to pick pieces of myself out in her. The snarky one-liners are mine for sure. Possibly the great taste in music. The black laces. Maybe even her heavy brows that make her look like she's scowling.

We travel off my property in silence, and it's not until I hit the end of the long, tree-lined driveway that I realize I don't know where I'm going. "Wait. Where do you live?"

She glances down, hiding beneath a wince. "In Calgary."

"That's… that's over three hours away."

She bites at the inside of her cheek before peeking up at me. "Yeah. Sorry."

"How did you get here?" My signal light is on, but I haven't made the turn yet.

"Bus. Took all night with the stops."

"Your mom let you take the bus all the way here overnight?"

She turns her head and stares out the window. "I think she probably slept through me leaving and still hasn't gotten out of bed."

We pull up in front of a typical split-level home on a street full of similar houses. There's a school just down the street. A hockey net sits on the side of the road, sticks and gloves stacked on top like some kids got called away midgame for lunch.

It looks like a perfectly normal family neighborhood. One with tidy driveways and middle-of-the-line cars.

The only thing that appears different about Cora's property is the lawn. It's mowed like all the rest, but the lines aren't quite straight. There's something disheveled about the place compared to the houses next to it. The partially drawn curtains in the middle of the afternoon make it seem almost shut down, like the people who live here are away on vacation.

But I know they're not.

Cora hops out of the vehicle and slams the door harder than necessary, then strides up to the front door. I follow, glancing around to see if anyone is watching. It's surreal, pulling up with a kid I didn't know existed, to a house I've never visited, and meeting a woman who… used my sperm?

I scrub a hand over my stubble as I approach the front door.

"Sorry about the mess," Cora mutters as she presses a sequence of numbers on the lock and pushes into the house.

And she wasn't kidding. I stand at the entryway and take in the open-concept home before me. My office may be a dump, but this house feels like a dark, stale cave. The TV is playing a news station, just loud enough that I can hear the anchor mumbling something while the ticker runs across the bottom. The kitchen needs cleaning. There's a pizza box on the cluttered counter. Milk left out beside it. Dirty dishes stacked in the sink.

Nothing smells rotten—yet—but it smells stagnant.

"Make yourself at home," Cora says. "I'll go get Mom." Then she darts around the corner, shoes on, feet thumping up the stairs.

I remain standing awkwardly in the entryway—I don't know how to make myself at home here. What I'd like to do is clean and open the windows, but that feels like overstepping.

It's funny how being the World's Hottest Billionaire doesn't prepare you for something like this. It was a stupid title to win, and now I have proof. Cora wasn't especially forthcoming during the drive. Any time I asked about her mom, she'd turn and stare out the window before mumbling the least detailed answer possible. I get the sense she's protecting her mom, shielding me in her own way. Avoiding the conversation.

I recognize the move because I do it too. But this time, it has me walking into a situation that could play out in so many different ways. It could all blow up so spectacularly.

I pull out my phone to check the time. I wait another ten minutes before checking my phone again.

Then I hear murmurs and two sets of footsteps, and before I know it, I'm facing a woman who appears to be in her late fifties—she can't be that much younger than my mother. Though the comparison to my mom ends there. I thought Cora looked tired, but this woman looks *stricken*.

She approaches with a dazed expression on her face,

forcing a smile to her lips as she lifts her limp hand to take mine. "Hi, I'm Marilyn."

"Hi, Marilyn. I'm Ford," I reply softly, taking in the baggy clothes, tangled hair, and creases on her cheek—presumably from sleeping. Having just checked my phone, I know that it's not even 2:00 p.m., not a typical time of day to be asleep on a Tuesday.

Come to think of it, Cora should have been in school today.

"It's nice to meet you," I add as I step back from the woman.

She nods, hitting me with another smile. This time it's watery. It matches her quavering voice and the stray tear that rolls down her cheek. It matches the words she says next. "Cora tells me you're here to help us out."

With one look down at Cora's protective expression while she clings to her mother's limp hand, I realize I've headed down a path where there's no turning back. By now, I should have learned to guard myself more. But apparently I haven't learned my lesson yet because I already know I'm invested enough that I'm not walking away.

"Yeah, Marilyn. I'd like to help in any way I can."

CHAPTER 4

Rosie

My teeth strum along my bottom lip like a pick on a guitar string. I grip my steering wheel as my eyes remain locked on my brother's house, also our childhood home.

After two weeks of moping around, jobless and directionless and brimming with self-pity, I'm officially back in Rose Hill. The town where I grew up. The town I rarely come back to. The town I didn't realize I missed until I desperately needed the comfort of coming home. A safe place to land while I nurse my wounds and figure out my life.

I just drove up the steep gravel driveway, the same one I fell down as a small child. With scraped knees and blood all over my brand-new white sneakers, I cried as my brother hosed me off like I was a horse. I'd been devastated, but today I chuckle as I recall it.

It's funny how a moment that felt so low can eventually make you smile.

My gaze drifts over the farm which sits on the west edge of town. Cliffs above the property separate our land from the highway. That main thoroughfare was literally blasted through the mountains long ago and now a chain-link fence attached to the rock keeps loose pieces from tumbling onto the road—or us.

On the left, I see the picturesque lake. It takes me back to all-day tubing and teenage keg parties on its shores in the summer, skating, ice fishing and snowmobiling in the winter.

I look right and see my parents' house much farther up the hill. Just the peak of the roof pokes out of the trees. When West took over the farm, they moved "away," or so they claimed.

The truth is, they've spent their entire lives worrying about West, and I'm not sure they can handle having him too far out of sight.

Glancing back at my brother's place, I suck in a deep breath to give me the guts to walk in there and pretend I'm doing *so great*.

Right before I ask if I can crash for a bit.

"Fuck it, Rosie. Get your ass in there," I mutter before shoving my car door open and striding toward the front porch. I don't bother locking my car. If someone has the balls to hike onto our land to steal my shit, then I applaud their fortitude.

Honest to god, I'd ask them where they get it because I am fresh out.

I don't think I've taken a single breath since that deep

one in the front seat. Now I'm just holding it as I reach up to knock and get this over with. Just before my knuckles make contact, the door swings open and all that breath I've been holding is sucked right out of my lungs.

By Ford Grant.

My stomach drops to my feet with the most unsettling lurching sensation.

I have to tip my head back to meet his emerald gaze. He's always been tall, but now he's just... *big.*

"Ford."

He stares at me, and the weight of his gaze has my heart thundering against my ribs.

"Hi."

His dark brows furrow, and I can't help but notice his hair, which used to be more auburn, has darkened in adulthood. It's a deep brown now, the russet tone only shining when the light hits it just right.

Neatly trimmed stubble frames his high cheekbones. The tan skin on his throat flexes as his Adam's apple bobs above the V of his khaki-colored tee.

God. It has to have been at least a decade since I last saw him. You'd think he'd have grown less awkward in that time but apparently not. Because he's standing stock-still, staring like he's never seen me before.

So, I stick my hand out and quirk one side of my lips up. "I'm not sure if you remember me. My name is Rosalie Belmont. We used to spend July and August shit-talking each other while trailing after my brother, Weston Belmont."

He shakes his head, face impassive, when he steps onto

the porch and reaches out to me, his warm hand enveloping mine. "Right. Rosalie. I must have gotten so good at tuning you out that I forgot you entirely."

A laugh lurches from my chest and unwanted tears gather in my eyes.

Teasing has never felt so good. So comforting.

"Ah, the good old days." The words are a whisper as I drop his piercing gaze and rub the tip of my nose.

I don't want to look at him because, for all his biting words and bored facade, I know Ford is a good person and he'll see right through me.

He was there when Travis Lynch broke my heart. Picked me up from a party on the other side of the lake and drove me home, casting glances my way as I scribbled vile, immature things about Travis in my journal. And then stayed silent when I rolled down the passenger side window and chucked it into the trees on a dark, winding road.

We never talked about that night. There wasn't much to say. My older brother's best friend, who antagonized me at every turn, witnessed my total meltdown over a guy who peaked in grade 10 before dropping me off at my parents' house without another word.

But. I know he saw the gutted look in my eye that night—know he stared just a little too long. And I know if I meet his gaze now, he'll see it again.

"Auntie Rosie!"

Thank you, Lord. The voice of an angel. Saved by hell on wheels with blond pigtails. "Emmy!"

She shoves past Ford and launches herself at me with

enough force to knock the wind from my lungs a second time along with one fat tear from my eye. I quickly swipe it away. But over Emmy's shoulder, I catch sight of Ford glaring at the traitorous tear's path like it personally wronged him somehow.

I roll my eyes at him and turn all my attention to the little girl in my arms. Warm and wiggly. "Dang, girl, knock it off with all this growing business." I heft her up with a grunt. "Soon I won't be strong enough to lift you."

She cackles and lands a sticky kiss on my cheek. I try not to cringe. I love my niece, but I draw the line at messy faces and runny noses. Makes me want to hose them off the way West did me.

Still waiting for that maternal gene to kick in, I guess.

"What are you doing here?" Emmy pushes back to look at me, one pudgy, *sticky* palm on each of my cheeks.

"That's my question too," my brother announces, startling me as he wanders up from behind Ford.

I squeeze Emmy tighter. I'm not above using a six-year-old as a shield against these two men. "Surprise?" I squeak at my brother with a totally over-the-top grin on my face.

Thankfully, West isn't one to dig. He's not big on sharing feelings—unless it's with his fists—so he smiles and forges ahead until he's hugging me too, squishing his little girl between us.

"You need to bathe this hellion, West. She's sticky and smells like orange juice."

"Orange *freezie*," she corrects solemnly.

"Before dinner?"

"Whoa, whoa, Rosie Posie. You don't get to show up outta the blue and judge my parenting. This is my week. Mia is always on my ass, so I don't need you to pile on too."

I arch a brow. "Maybe Mia is onto something more than your ass?"

Emmy giggles maniacally, clearly amused by us tossing the word *ass* around so casually.

Now it's my brother's turn to roll his eyes. Their marriage may not have worked, but he and Mia are excellent co-parents, and I admire the hell out of them for that.

West ignores my jab and carries on with his questioning. "You just drive out as a surprise, or you staying for a bit?"

Before I answer, I put Emmy down and watch her tear back into the house, announcing to her brother Oliver that I'm here. My eyes cut to Ford again. Arms crossed and chin dipped low, he's staring hard enough to unnerve me. "What are you? His bodyguard?"

"Ha!" West barks out a laugh. "I don't need a bodyguard. And if I did, I wouldn't hire the World's Hottest Billionaire."

My eyes bulge, and I have to press my lips together to keep from laughing. I saw the article—picked it up and even read it—but I don't want to give Ford the satisfaction of knowing that.

"Ford Grant is a *billionaire*? Do they mean junior or senior?"

West laughs, but Ford groans and shakes his head. "I'm going back inside. You two assholes have fun out here."

I watch him walk away, probably a little too closely.

Definitely a little too closely, based on the way my

brother gently punches my shoulder. "You better not be checking him out."

I let out a playful scoff. "Whatever. It's not every day you get a clear shot of… what was it? The World's Hottest Billionaire?" I make sure I say it loud enough that Ford hears me.

West chuckles. "Playing with fire, sis. What would Ryan say?"

My shoulders tighten, and I swallow before turning my eyes back up to my brother's, the same shade of blue as my own.

Then I tilt my head from side to side four times.

West nods three times.

And that's about the entire conversation we'll have about that.

It's exactly what I wanted. Exactly what I needed. I'm not ready to decide a single thing about Ryan until I clear my head and can make a rational decision.

"So, dinner?" my brother asks. "Spare room or bunkhouse?"

"Yes, to dinner, and I'll take the bunkhouse, please."

He turns and I follow him. Relief floods my system. I knew I could count on West to save me from myself. What I didn't count on was Ford fucking Grant with his eagle eyes and billion-dollar ass.

CHAPTER 5

Ford

"Here, let me show you. I have a plan," Cora says from where she's sitting on the couch beside Oliver. She's showing him how to build a Nether portal or some shit in Minecraft. The terminology is lost on me. He says nothing, as usual, but I can tell by the look on his face that he's enthralled. Emmy has squeezed herself in on Cora's other side, crunching on what has to be her third freezie of the day.

Me? I feel like I'm living in a madhouse.

After weeks of getting everything in order, I'm on day one of being Cora's official kinship placement. My lawyer hates my guts for making her do this, and my financial advisor thinks I've lost it. Maybe I have.

I've done nothing to get the recording studio up and running, which is making me squirrely. The never-ending list of things I need to do keeps me up at night. I need flooring, walls, paint, heating, air conditioning, upgraded electrical, some semblance of curb appeal from the outside. The entire place needs a facelift, and that's not including the booth itself.

And now Rosie fucking Belmont has waltzed into the scene with her smart mouth and suspiciously watery eyes. And all I want to do is demand to know who hurt her so I can fix it.

Carrying a secret torch for this woman is nothing new, but it's been a decade. I never expected every teenage feeling to come barreling back in full force the minute I laid eyes on her again. But god, she's grown up. Her eyes are still the brightest, most impossible shade of blue. Almost crystalline against the golden hue of her skin—and still just as expressive as they used to be. They darken with anger, they twinkle with mirth, and today they swam with emotion. Her hair was always long, but now it's longer. Layered and wavy, framing her heart-shaped face in a wild tumble. The same dark blond I remember now artfully painted through with strokes of bright gold and the odd pearlescent streak. It's messy, yet intentional. It suits her.

That's what I'd thought as I stood there at the front door staring at her.

All it took was one look—one heartbeat—and I was eighteen all over again.

"All right!" West claps his hands behind me, and I start. "What's for dinner?"

"Freezies!" Emmy shouts back with a fist in the air. She appears borderline feral, and if I'm being honest, she scares me a little bit. She's a miniature West and raising her is cosmic payback for the shit he put his parents through.

"Absolutely not, you little nut bar. You get vegetables and more vegetables. Everyone else gets…" He trails off as he rifles through the fridge.

Much like my main house, West's home is a craftsman-style farmhouse. Big baseboards, narrow windows, sort of a cottage feel with all the bedrooms upstairs and a glass-paneled veranda out front. His is yellow, while I had mine stripped down to the original boards and layered with exterior glaze to give it a more rustic feel. Mine is mostly modernized inside; his is a little more out-of-date.

"Well," West sighs. "We might be ordering a vegetable pizza because Emmy has snacked me straight out of food."

This is so West, always flying by the seat of his pants. I close my eyes and smile. On the back of my lids I see Rosie and replay the way words failed me as I soaked her in earlier.

And when I open my eyes, I see Rosie too. She's standing in the doorway to the kitchen, gawking over at the couch. She must have just returned from setting herself up in the bunkhouse, and when I follow her gaze, I realize she's staring at Cora. And Cora is staring right back.

I'm a dick for not having introduced them yet, but the entire exchange on the front porch threw me off.

"Hey." Rosie tips her chin at Cora. "I'm Rosie. West's sister."

"Hey." Cora mimics the motion. "I'm Cora, Ford's daughter."

I wince. Not because I hate the sound of it. We just haven't talked about… I don't know. Titles?

Rosie reels backward as she takes that in, then she turns

her baby blues on me and not-so-subtly whispers, "*Wow. Congratulations on finally losing your virginity.*"

All I can do is stare at her. We really are right back to where we were as teenagers in a matter of minutes. As in, she's still funny and beautiful and completely off-limits, and I still feel transported back to the dumbstruck boy who is awkward as hell around her.

It's only a matter of time before I say something mean to keep her at arm's length. And she'll retaliate by saying she hates me before coming back with something equally snarky.

That's our customary vicious circle.

"Oh, well, he was a sperm donor to my parents," Cora spouts matter-of-factly. "So, for all I know, he could definitely still be a virgin. Your whisper wasn't very quiet, you know."

I shut my eyes and massage my temples. This girl is too smart, too snippy, too take-charge. She's going to be the death of me, and I'm the one who signed on the dotted line to take her under my wing. I'm in way over my head.

"What's a sperm donor?" Leave it to Emmy to fixate on that part.

West chuckles and tries to rescue me with, "Emmy! Ollie! Let's mind our business and go wash up for dinner. I'll make the order."

I'm grateful for his intervention as I hear their little feet pattering away.

When I finally open my eyes, Rosie is staring at me. Baby blues wide, glossy pink lips popped open in a perfect O shape.

"What?" I snipe, knowing she has a snarky comment ready to fire at me. She always does.

She smirks, never one to back down at my barking. "The genetics are strong with that one. I like her."

It's Cora who groans. "I'm right here. It's rude to talk about a person like they aren't present."

And I sigh.

Because it's going to be a long-ass night.

"So, this is your room." I glance down at Cora, who stands woodenly beside me. It's her first night with me, and I'm floundering rather spectacularly in an attempt to make it less awkward.

"I know. You showed me already."

I'm pretty sure I'm failing.

I give myself a silent pep talk to pull it together. I'm a grown-ass man. I shouldn't be this nervous around her. I don't know what the hell I'm doing, but I should at least be equipped to fake feeling prepared for this.

"Right, well, I was just about to say that there is also a guest room on the main floor if you'd rather not stay on the same floor as me. But it doesn't have an en suite bathroom, and I wake up early, so it might just be disruptive."

"Why would I care about staying on the same floor as you?"

I grimace. "Just want to make sure you're comfortable."

She doesn't move. Her arms are crossed, but her eyes slice over in my direction. She's full-on side-eyeing me. "You know, my mom may be out of it, but she ran every criminal check she could on you."

"Fair. I don't blame her."

"I wish I hadn't told you I have no family left. The threat of a long-lost uncle in the mafia might have been good safety insurance."

I snort. She's funny. "We can pretend if you want."

Now she snorts too, and I feel a flicker of success at having almost made her laugh.

Quiet footfalls lead her into the center of the room. I watch her turn in a slow circle, taking in her surroundings. It's pretty much her color palette—pale gray walls, and a bedframe made of black wrought iron.

"Is the room okay? I went ahead and got you the basics. But we can… decorate or something? If you want? Art? Bedding? Books?"

"I really want black sheets."

My brows furrow as I take in the simple, dark purple bedding I opted for. I thought dark purple would be dark enough.

Apparently, I thought wrong.

"Okay. I'll see what I can find." I run a hand through my hair, internally chiding myself. I don't know how to talk to a twelve-year-old. Plus, she feels more like twelve going on twenty.

"Are you hungry? Are there specific snacks you like? I didn't know what to get, so I figured I'd wait and see what your favorites are. But the house is stocked. I want you to… make yourself at home."

She nods, finally glancing back my way.

"I can get you a boiled egg."

Now it's her turn to scrunch her nose up. "A boiled egg?"

I never thought I could feel so judged by a child. But here I am. Justifying the nutritional merits of boiled eggs. "It's a great snack. High in protein. Helps you sleep well."

Cora looks full-on disgusted.

"There's also cereal."

I get a quirked brow for that one. "What kind?"

"Oatmeal?"

Her lips pull back in a teasing expression as she shakes her head.

"Lucky Charms?" I try again. I bought them against my better judgement. The sugar content is terrible, but they seemed like something a child would like based on what I've seen with West and his kids.

For that suggestion I get double finger guns, an almost-smile, and a "Now we're talking."

We head downstairs, and I watch Cora eat her cereal at the kitchen island while I'm hit with the full impact of what I've agreed to do. Nerves creep in. Doubt creeps in. And later, when she says goodnight and shuts her door, I decide to go online and find some black sheets so I don't totally blow this entire thing.

CHAPTER 6

Ford

"WHAT ARE YOU DOING HERE?"

Rosie flips her head around from where she sits at the end of the dock, clearly startled by my arrival. "Enjoying the view."

I wanted peace and quiet to clear my head tonight. I know that with Rosie here I'll get neither. I look beyond her at the darkened lake. Without the scattered glow from the solar lights dotting the pillars, it would be pitch black out over the water. But I know the view well, given that this dock sits near the property line between my and West's houses. Even though there's nothing visible on the horizon right now, I can envision it almost perfectly.

"What are you doing here?" she asks.

I stay standing, not sure how to act around her. *Still.* Even though I'm now a perfectly successful and independent thirty-two-year-old. "I came to sit on my dock and escape the new realities of my life in the dark, by the water, where it's quiet. Except you're here, and it's never quiet where you are unless you're plotting someone's death."

She snorts, but it's half-hearted. Then she turns back to the still body of water again. "First, this isn't your dock. It's my family's. I would know, because I've been coming here for years. Second, I don't plot people's deaths."

I stride toward her and opt not to tell her that, according to the land survey, this dock does, in fact, fall on my property. "Fair, you're more of a crime-of-passion type. But I've spent years thinking you planned Travis Lynch's death out in detail on the pages of that diary."

She laughs, but it's not light and airy like I remember. There's a heaviness to Rosie now that doesn't match my memories of her. She may be three years younger, but she always kept up with us through her teen years. West never excluded her, and she was always the "it" girl in Rose Hill— popular to the point of being beloved—if that's a thing.

As someone who was more of a loner, she always seemed that way to me anyway. I only got the summer experience of Rose Hill as a kid though. Now and then, we'd come for Christmas, or the odd weekend getaway, but my family's life was in the city. My mom's practice, my dad's band. He'd go on tour, and Willa and I would go to school. But the summer was sacred. My parents built it that way on purpose. We spent those two months based here in Rose Hill and it was the best escape.

It wasn't until I was an adult that I started spending more time here just because I wanted to. It wasn't until the city became too fucking much that I decide to move here permanently.

"Yeah. I'm fairly sure I wrote an entire paragraph weighing whether it would be more humiliating for him if I cut off his penis or his testicles."

"Dark. What did you settle on?" I crouch down, placing a hand on the wooden boards to take a seat. Several feet separate us, but our legs dangle over the edge as we sit side by side, taking in the view of lights from homes dotting the other side of the lake.

"I forget."

"That's a shame. I saw him at the grocery store the other day."

"Yeah?" She doesn't look my way, but I can tell by the change in her voice that she's entertained. "What does it say about me that I hope he's aged poorly?"

"It says you can take the girl out of the small town, but you can't take the small town out of the girl."

At that, she sighs.

"And that you're still just as mean as you used to be," I add.

Now she laughs. It starts out as a soft hiccup and grows into more. It grows into the laugh of a younger Rosie. The one who took up every inch of space in a room just by breezing in and smiling.

"Ah, Ford. Thank you. Being insulted by you just feels so right. Please don't tell me what *that* says about me though."

My lips twitch and my legs swing in time with hers as I search for what to talk about next. "So, how's city life?

Seems like you moved away and stayed gone. Job. Boyfriend. Condo. What brings you back now?"

"Oh yeah? Do you come back here often? I thought you bought a bar and founded a wildly successful music streaming app. Figured you'd be something of a city slicker yourself."

I just shrug. Gramophone is the app she's talking about. It started as a university project I made with a group of friends—until it blew up into so much more.

It blew up in more ways than one.

"I did all those things, yeah. I thought buying the bar where I worked through college would give me a passion project. And it did for a while. Then the app came along. And that scratched the itch for a bit too."

"But not now?"

I shrug. "Gin and Lyrics became more successful than I banked on. I was bored, so I hired more people. Put more parameters in place. Now the bar practically runs itself. I started off only booking bands I liked, but when we got busy enough, I started booking groups other people like to keep the crowds coming."

"Bands you don't like."

"Yeah. Business over my personal preference, but that's okay. That bar doesn't feel like it belongs to me anymore, even though my name is on the deed. I'm happy that it makes other people happy. I'll always be proud of that place."

She nods, body swaying back and forth gently. "And the app?"

"Gramophone started out the same way. But of course, it

wasn't just mine. I had partners. And it became more about the personal fame and fortune than it was about the music."

"Not a fan of that vibe I take it?"

I sigh heavily. This one hurts. More than the bar. I don't especially like talking about it.

"I find that when a person's obsession with money outweighs their commitment to integrity, I no longer want to spend my time around them."

Rosie hums thoughtfully at the bite in my voice. But she doesn't press for more. She falls back into teasing me—and it's a welcome reprieve.

"So now you're going full recluse on the abandoned land next door? You gonna bury chests of money here? Is this some elaborate eccentric-billionaire thing where you leave a treasure map behind?"

"No. It's an eccentric-billionaire thing where I open my own recording studio and only work with musicians I like or believe in. I've got the capital to launch artists who can't afford to get their foot in the door, and the connections to help the ones who need a place to do something without their shitty labels meddling. With the internet and streaming services distribution isn't the challenge it once was."

"And your dad?"

I sigh. Cora called me a nepo baby, and as much as I hate it, she's not wrong. Separating my success from Ford Grant Senior and his globally renowned rock band, Full Stop, has been next to impossible. "His name carries clout. I'd be an idiot not to have him come in and guest-produce something at some point. Though we'll probably clash at every turn."

"Adorable. And has he met his granddaughter yet?"

I go still. I feel like *I've* barely met her myself. West knows about her and now Rosalie does too. I looped Mr. and Mrs. Belmont in too, only because they figured it out themselves after snooping around. After years of having to suss out West's antics, they've developed a sixth sense for any sort of drama.

"It hasn't come up yet."

"What?"

"They're traveling. I was thinking I would tell him and my mom when they get to Rose Hill. They're spending the summer here, at their place."

"Ford." She sounds genuinely horrified.

"What? I've barely had a minute to wrap my head around this development. I'm drowning in emails and calls and promises I made to people to have this place up and running. I didn't imagine this being my life. I planned to renovate the house and office here on my own, but now I've got Cora registered in school. She needs support. And I don't even know for sure how long she'll live here."

"Will she be here full time?"

"No one planned for this. Her mom's in deep depression after losing her husband. That's how the sperm donor thing came to light, I guess. Which is why Cora tracked me down."

Rosie chuckles softly. "Resourceful kid."

I sigh and dip my chin. "Marilyn was devastated when she realized the way Cora had been covering for her. We talked with her doctors and her and I had a heart-to-heart. She doesn't want to drag Cora through the ups and downs of her early treatment—doesn't want Cora seeing her that way anymore. She asked me to let her work on getting better for a month. So at least that long. And they just… they really have no one to help them, you know? No family at all."

"Shit, that's heavy," Rosie mutters as she kicks her feet.

All I do is nod and continue venting.

"Yup. And I can barely stay on top of buying snacks and trying to find the black sheets she requested. Snacks for children are loaded with an absurd amount of sugar and every black bedding set I find looks all shiny, like it belongs in a porno. Trust me, I just spent the better part of an hour scouring the internet."

She groans and covers her face with her hands, but I can see her smiling. "You still need to tell them."

My molars clamp as I weigh how much I really want to divulge tonight. Then I tell her anyway, because I don't like the thought of Rosie judging me for my decisions.

"A fan went to the press when Willa and I were younger, claiming my dad was the father of her child. It wasn't true, but it was messy. I remember my parents arguing and him having to go to court. I remember the way they talked about that woman—about that baby. He was furious, and my mom was hurt. It all worked out in the end, but I don't know how they'll react to this."

Rosie's eyes are wide, her tone hushed. "I don't remember that."

"You wouldn't. It was just before we started coming to Rose Hill. That one event changed the way they parented us. His touring stopped, and they got their place out here to get us away from the media."

"They might need a heads-up. Processing time."

I groan. *I'm* the one who needs processing time. Processing time without my dad going off about this, calling in lawyers and private investigators to discredit Cora and her mom.

I'm his son, and he'd do it to protect me. Just like I'm withholding this information to protect Cora.

Rosie pushes though. She's always pushing on my sore spots. Needling me. "You can't just spring this on your family, Ford."

And unfortunately, I've always been snippy with her. That's been my defense mechanism where she's concerned for years. And it's all too easy to fall back into old habits.

"Oh, like the way you just showed up on West's doorstep with tears in your eyes and zero explanation for what was going on?"

Her head whips in my direction, and I take in her face on the dimly lit dock. Dark blond strands tumble out of her high ponytail and skim over high cheekbones that narrow in on a heart-shaped face. Her lips are shapely but delicate. Eyes bright. Nose slender but perfectly straight. She complained about her nose as a teenager. She'd say it was too big, too strong. But to me, it's always been one of her most striking features.

To this day, she remains the most beautiful woman I've ever seen.

"These things are not the same. I don't owe West an explanation of what's going on in my life. I'm an independent adult. And he's my brother."

"An independent adult with a car full of suitcases and

bags, who's crashing in her brother's bunkhouse with no expected departure date."

Her jaw tenses, and her eyes narrow. "I don't owe you an explanation either, Ford. And I sure as shit don't need your approval. Shouldn't be throwing stones, not when you're sitting in a glass house."

I consider her words, realizing my concern for her probably came off condescending.

"I'll talk about it when I'm ready," she continues. "But rest assured, this isn't how I imagined my life either."

I want to tell her I feel the same way about my situation, but she doesn't give me an opportunity. "Thanks for the chat." Then she's up and walking away. The boards rattle beneath me as she goes, but then her footsteps cease and all I hear is the gentle lapping of the lake beneath me.

"Actually," her voice cuts through the night and I feel her head back in my direction. "*You* leave. This is *my* dock, and I want to be alone."

I smirk into the night because that feels exactly like something Rosie would say. Exactly like a stupid fight she'd pick with me. The type of fight I'd always let her win.

And the more things change, the more they stay the same, because with that smirk still plastered on my face, I push to standing and she moves past me, her body brushing against mine on the way.

She takes her seat, smack dab in the middle of the dock, like she's staking her claim. All she needs is a flag bearing a family crest that she can nail to a board.

I'm about to walk away, but I allow myself one last glance

in her direction. Shoulders tense, her nose tipped up high. I've pissed her off, but not *that* badly. Not enough that it stops me from reverting to my teenage self.

I bend down and reach out to wrap my fingers around her high, bouncy ponytail.

I give it two firm tugs, watching the way the light hits the column of her throat. She growls with annoyance, but it doesn't scare me.

"Goodnight, Rosie Posie."

"Fuck you, Junior. I hate you." The old insult flies so easily from her lips, but it does nothing to wipe the smile from my face. "I thought I told you to get off my dock."

I relax my hand, and the silky strands of her hair slip through my fingers. I hear the soft whoosh of her breath as I let go.

And then I turn and walk away.

This may not be her dock, but if she wants it, she can have it.

CHAPTER 7

Rosie

I SLEPT IN THE OLD BUNKHOUSE, WHERE WE USED TO HIDE out during a thunderstorm or have group sleepovers as kids. It smells like damp wood. The bottom bunk is only slightly more spacious than the top. The sheets are cheap flannel. And even though a bullfrog croaked away outside as I drifted off, I can't remember the last time I slept so well.

Being back in Rose Hill feels like stepping out of the city-girl meatsuit I've forced myself to wear day in and day out, hoping I'd get used to the new me. But now I've shed the costume and I feel like I can breathe again.

It's as though I had this idea in my head of what success looks like. I could see my life so damn clearly—the most vibrant scene right before my eyes. So real I could almost reach out and touch it.

But every day I spent inserting myself into that scene, I grew more and more uncomfortable. More and more dissatisfied.

I questioned why winning didn't bring me greater satisfaction. I kept trying to convince myself I needed time to adjust to the way winning felt. After all, I'd finally gotten what I thought I wanted.

As I stand just a few steps out the door of the bunkhouse, soaking in the wild beauty that surrounds me, it hits me full force—I don't miss the city at all.

The sun is shining, the air is crisp, and the lake sparkles like a sheet of infinite diamonds. Even the crushing burden of my student loans and debilitating lack of income feel more tolerable in this peaceful setting.

This. This is what I missed. This is what I needed.

From my left, I can hear Emmy up and tearing around the farmhouse. Farther up the mountain, smoke curls from the chimney of my parents' new build. I know I need to make the trip up there and fill them in—shit, even just say hi—but I'm dreading it down to the tips of my toes.

I don't want to admit to them how thoroughly everything has fallen apart. West is the one who always had to come clean about making mistakes. Getting arrested. Crashing his car while drag racing. Knocking someone up. Getting injured. It's only since he had kids and started his horse-training business that he's taken a break from turning their hair gray.

But me? I'm the good one. The one who flies under the radar and handles her shit by herself so that no one needs to worry.

But as much as I hate to admit it, I'm tapped out on handling my own shit. All of a sudden, it dawned on me that

I am monumentally tired of having it all together. Which is why after two weeks of moping around and sending out résumés that get no response—or that require a reference—I told Ryan I was going home to see my family. I couldn't meet his eyes when I told him I didn't know how long I'd be gone.

That was nearly twenty-four hours ago, and I have one lone text from him asking if everything is okay with me. It almost made me laugh when I saw it on my phone. He's so agreeable. He didn't even ask me to stay.

You do whatever you need to do was all he said.

We've probably been done for a long time, but we like each other too much to actually pull the plug. I don't hate Ryan. Quite the opposite, in fact.

But I don't miss him. And I don't burn for him. And I'm acutely aware that like is not love.

Those thoughts stick with me as I make the short drive into town. While I navigate through the winding cliffs that lead to the hill descending into the main drag, I mull over why I should go back to the city at all. Without a job and without a partner, what's there for me?

My friends are his friends.

My condo is, in fact, his condo.

It's depressing if I let myself think about it for too long. The things that are truly mine are this car and a couple of postsecondary degrees, which go hand in hand with a mind-boggling student loan balance.

Rosie Posie is really winning.

Pulling up in front of my favorite spot in town is a balm though. What I need is tea from the Bighorn Bistro. Café by day and farm-to-table restaurant by night. And the best tea ever brewed. No one can compete with Tabitha's handpicked blends.

The door to the bistro jingles when I tug it open. It smells like warm croissants and rose petals when I walk inside. The interior is an oasis, with leafy green plants, twinkling lights wrapped around wide wood beams, and massive skylights that let in all the light you could want. Long raw-edge lumber tables fill the dining area—everything here is family style. Something locals grumbled about when Tabitha first opened, and something they flock to now. It's quite possibly the only "nice" restaurant in town, but the quality and attention to detail is better than anything I've seen in the city.

I doubt Tabitha's here this morning, but I make a mental note to reach out while I'm in town. She's a couple of years younger than me, but we played on the volleyball team together in high school and she roamed around with me and my friends in the summer. And like I summoned her with my thoughts, she rounds the corner, wiping her hands on a white apron, dark hair in a messy braid falling out around her face. She even has a smudge of flour on her cheek.

"Rosie!" Her eyes go from tired to lit up when she sees me, and I can't help but do the same. Tabitha's the kind of person with whom I can waltz in and pick up exactly where I left off.

We've always been kindred spirits, in a way. Both of our families expected us to be the "easy" children, though where West was a little rough-and-tumble, her sister was truly down-and-out. She was *that* small-town story.

"Hi, Tabby. Surprise?" I offer a shrug and a small wave. "How've you been?"

She huffs out her breath and the loose hairs around her face fly away. "Tired."

I chuckle. It feels like a normal part of adulthood that we all universally complain about how tired we are. So, I go with it. "I hear that," I reply, eyes roaming the selection of beautiful pastries behind the glass.

"No. Like I am next-level tired. Remind me to never have a baby."

My eyes snap up to her face. "A baby?"

"Erika." She says her sister's name with a hard look in her eyes, like that alone answers the question. And it does.

"She doing okay?" I feel awkward asking, but not asking seems worse.

"If okay means living in the city, getting knocked up, and constantly leaving a toddler with me while she takes off to do god knows what, then, yeah. She's fucking fabulous."

"A toddler?" I know little about small children, but I do know you don't just up and leave them all the time. But Erika has been struggling for years. Last time I talked to Tabby, she'd paid for her sister's treatment program herself and had set her up with a safe place to live in the city. My heart hurts to think it may not have worked out.

Tabitha wobbles her head back and forth. "Okay, well, he's two. That saying about terrible twos is no joke. Luckily three is on the horizon. Do you know they call them threenagers then? Trying to convince myself that sounds better."

A dry laugh sticks in my throat because I don't know

what else to do. "What about your parents? They don't help?"

She grimaces, and I recall her mentioning that her parents were thinking of cutting all ties with Erika. My heart hurts even worse now.

"Rosie, you don't need this drama in your life. You need tea, am I right?"

I can tell Tabitha is trying to change the direction of the conversation, so I go with it. "Yeah. Tea and a croissant. But why don't we grab a drink sometime when you're not working or on toddler duty? My treat. You can tell me all your drama and I'll tell you mine."

Her entire body sags in relief. "Yeah? I would love that. So much."

"It's a date," I say brightly.

"How long are you in town?"

My teeth clamp down on my bottom lip. I've been avoiding looking at this reality too closely. Telling myself that after a brief break I'll be able to head back to the city refreshed. Keeping my blinders on has been a decent strategy so far.

But this morning I answer her before I even think about it—before I can lie to myself or overthink the consequences.

With the stunning view from the bunkhouse in my mind, I say, "Indefinitely."

Then I glance down at my receipt, realizing I just put a dent in my bank account by simply buying tea and a croissant.

I need to get a job.

The thought hits me—I could get one here, in Rose

Hill. That's what a girl with only double digits left in her bank account would do. She'd woman up and go find herself a job.

I decide on the spot that I'll take a walk down the main drag after this and see if any workplaces in town jump out at me. Any type of job would do really. I'm proud of my education, but I've never felt above any sort of employment. I'm a hard worker, and now, more than ever, the draw of a paycheck is my biggest motivator.

Someone behind me clears their throat impatiently startling me into action, so I smile apologetically at my girlhood friend as I back away from the till. "Thanks, Tabby. Catch you later," I say with a friendly wave before turning away.

Then I step out into the crisp spring morning, feeling alarmingly at peace with the prospect of getting a job *here*.

When Ford steps out of his SUV, I swallow hard.

Faded black jeans.

Faded black shirt.

Gold aviators perched on his strong nose.

It's like the shiny new version of him, without the mullet and wire-rimmed glasses he sported as a kid. Back then, he was tall and skinny. His arms swung at his sides and made him look like Gumby when he walked.

He doesn't just walk now though—he *strides*. All it took was a decade to go from dorky, endearing Ford to Big Dick Billionaire Energy Ford.

I take him in from where I'm loitering near the front

door of what I assume will be his office, based on West's description of the property last night.

I've never felt uncomfortable around him, but I'd be lying if I said watching him round the front of his SUV with a scowl on his face doesn't send a thrill through me. The kind that makes my legs a little weak, makes my cheeks a little hot.

Then he has to ruin it all by talking.

"What do you want? Cora is finally in school, and I have a pile of work to get done. I'm too busy to take a torturous stroll down memory lane with you right now."

Yep, that'll do it. Hot Ford transforms into Dickhead Ford so damn easily. I'm about to toss my lukewarm tea in his face just to surprise him, but I remind myself I'm here with an idea.

A great idea.

An idea that I *really* need to work because as it turns out job openings in Rose Hill are few and far between.

"I have a proposition for you."

He lifts his sunglasses onto the top of his dark, mussed hair and furrows his brow in my direction as he breezes past.

"That sounds terrifying," he mumbles as he slides a key into the worn wooden door's deadbolt.

"No, it's perfect." I follow him into the dusty, dank building. "Trust me. It's a business proposition. And you can't say no."

That has him turning to face me, his notable height causing me to come to a screeching halt in the entryway. He pulls his sunglasses off his head and gently chews on the plastic bit at the end of the metal arm.

It should be gross.

But I find it appealing.

"You hungry or something?" I cross my arms and cock a hip out. I feel like a bratty teenager around him. It's annoying that he brings out this side of me.

Except the way his eyes rake over my body feels nothing like when we were teenagers.

His face stays impassive while mine heats to an inferno.

"I can't say no?" He ignores my dig and bites down on the plastic again. "That doesn't sound like a very smart business decision."

I swallow again, but this time my throat is entirely dry, and it makes my mouth feel like it's full of cotton. "Oh, no, trust me. This will be a very smart business decision."

"Right. You'd never trick me. Would you, Rosalie?"

I roll my eyes and note the cobweb in the corner when I do. "Please, I'm not a kid anymore."

His eyes drag down and back up my body again before he sighs and looks over his shoulder at the stack of files on the rough-hewn table serving as a makeshift desk. "Don't I know it."

Everything he says sounds so snarky. It immediately gets my hackles up, but I can't go back to ragging on him until I get this locked down.

"I have an MBA. I wouldn't corner you into making a poor business decision."

His dark green eyes are back on me now, assessing. "Okay."

I blink a few times. "Okay?"

"You told me I couldn't say no." A charming dimple pops up on his left cheek, but just a flash. There for a moment and gone.

Standing taller, I step toward him and take a deep breath, eyeing his scuffed boots until I draw my gaze up to meet his forest-green stare. His scent wraps around me. Cedar. No, sandalwood. I'm not sure. Trees. Wood. The scent of the incense I burned during my hippie phase. And something fresher, brighter.

With a shake of my head, I blurt out my plan. "You should hire me."

He blinks and slowly pulls his sunglasses from his mouth as his eyes bounce between my own. I lift my chin high and stare back at him, refusing to back down.

"I can be your assistant. Or whatever. Something? I'll clean up the cobwebs. I'm a wizard in Excel. Good—no great—with budgets. Who knows, maybe I can make you into a trillionaire? Or I can help with Cora! Busy frowning and staring at your bank account balance? No problem! I'll pick her up from school."

He continues to stare, his features giving nothing away. I should have been nicer about my offer. Maybe. No, definitely. Time stretches, and my tongue darts out over my bottom lip as my confidence wanes and nerves set in.

His gaze follows the tip of my tongue almost in slow motion.

His throat bobs, and he repeats the best word in the world. "Okay."

"Okay?"

He shrugs and crosses his arms, biceps bulging against the thin fabric of his worn shirt. "Remember the part where you *just* told me I couldn't say no?"

I nod. "Still expected you to be a dick and do it anyway."

His lips tip up and he shakes his head as he turns and moves away from me. "Rosalie, when have I ever said no to you?"

And I just stand here, stunned.

I need a ride home from this party.

I want to be alone.

I need a job.

Because try as I might, no matter how big of a dick he's been, I can't come up with a single instance of Ford ever telling me anything other than *okay*.

CHAPTER 8

Rosie

I LEAN AGAINST THE SIDE OF MY CAR IN FRONT OF ROSE HILL Middle School. It's not quite warm yet in early spring but leaning against black paint in a direct sunbeam is a fantastic way to fool myself into feeling like it is.

When Ford mentioned pickup time, I immediately offered to head out. That barn fucking stinks, and when I suggested he might want to hire a professional contractor to bring it into this century, he stopped talking to me. Like the sulky boy I remember. Even though he knows I'm right.

That's why I couldn't wait to get out of there. Too much tension. A knot in my stomach that's making me second-guess my qualifications for this position. The memory of how my last job ended—that maybe I wasn't hired for my capabilities at all. I needed some room to breathe. Away from Ford. Breathing is always harder around him. Which is also why I'm here early.

My phone vibrates in my back pocket, and I pull it out to find Ryan's name flashing across the screen. With a heavy sigh, I swipe to answer.

Maybe the warm sun will make this conversation feel better.

"Hey."

"Babe. Hi. How's the family visit?" he says, sounding totally distracted. I know he's probably at work right now, scanning emails or reviewing his formal invitation to the Old Boys Club. Something crunches, and he's clearly chewing. It shouldn't annoy me—everyone needs to eat—but the sound is like nails on a chalkboard.

Probably because I took off on the heels of something that clearly upset me, and he seems completely nonplussed about the entire thing.

"Yeah. It's good. Gonna head up to see my parents for dinner tonight."

"Nice. Say hi to them for me."

Yeah. 'Cause that won't be awkward.

"Will do. So, listen—"

"When are you thinking you'll head back?"

"Right, so… that's the thing. I sort of… I got a job here." The crunching finally stops.

"You got a job there?" He sounds floored, and I instantly feel guilty.

"Yeah." My lips roll together, and I look out over the field where I grew up playing soccer. "Kinda just fell into my lap. And well, you know I've been trying to find a job."

"Yeah. But *there*?" He says it with a scoff that rankles me.

Has me standing up just a little bit taller. Feeling defensive of this place. I'm allowed to rag on Rose Hill—it's not perfect, but it is *mine*. He's not from here, though, and it rubs me all wrong that he thinks he's allowed to shit-talk my town.

"Yeah. It's a great opportunity. And I need the space."

"Space?"

I wince. I can imagine him now. The air of boyish confusion on his face as he turns that word over in his head.

Space.

"Yeah. Space."

I'm met by silence at first. "Is that figurative or literal?" he says, finally. "Like the space around you that you get out there? Or space from me?"

I swallow, regarding all the parents waiting to pick their children up. They chat happily, and I get the odd curious glance. I grew up here, sure. But I don't come back often enough to register for most people.

"I think both," I say in a hushed tone.

More silence.

"I'm sorry, Ryan. I'm just… I want to be straight with you."

"Is there someone else?"

I think of all the dirty looks Ford shot me this afternoon. And the way he tugged on my ponytail last night.

I shake my head. "No. There isn't."

His heavy sigh tells me he's relieved. That flash of jealousy after him seeming so disinterested lately catches me off guard. *Too little, too late.*

"Okay, good. Listen. I—can I come visit you there? I'd

love to just sit down and really talk this over. See what we can do to give this our best shot."

I want to tell him no. I want to tell him I'm done. I want to say it's not me, it's him. I also want to ask him why he was so damn comfortable brushing the Stan situation under the rug.

But I also don't want to talk about that at all—to anyone. And I don't want to be *mean* like Ford told me I am. I don't want to make such a final decision when I already feel so lost. And I don't want to be the kind of grown woman who dumps a long-term boyfriend over the phone.

"Yeah, sure. Of course."

"Okay, great." I can hear the smile in his voice and the creak of his chair as he adjusts himself in it. "I'm looking at my calendar now. Would the second weekend of next month be all right for you?"

My mouth hangs open so wide that a fly *and* its entire family could move in. "Next month?"

"Yeah. I have some really important projects right now. Workload is impossible to get out from under."

Really important.

His matter-of-factly scheduling to woo me four weeks from now strikes me silent. If the situation wasn't so painfully lackluster, it might be funny. If I wasn't so offended, I might laugh. He should be dropping everything and rushing here. To talk. To apologize for not rubbing my back when I told him about what happened to me at work. For not sharing my rage when HR served me with a bullshit dismissal letter detailing my subpar performance—which conveniently followed one of their company presidents sexually assaulting me.

The bell rings and I am saved by it, literally. Because with more peace and quiet and warm sunshine, I might have said something *mean* to him.

And I know I'm not perfect. I know I haven't pulled my weight in making things work between us lately. But I can also see that neither of us wants to pull our weight. We're just here because we're comfortable. *Safe.*

The doors blast open, and the squeals of happy children fill the air.

"Sure. I'll check my calendar," I mumble.

And then I hang up. Agitation courses through me, followed by a deep sense of shame that I've never felt before.

Shame because I'm too embarrassed to do anything about Ryan and my old job. Shame because my boyfriend of two years feels no inclination to take up for me over the whole debacle. And shame because I shouldn't be letting it bug me this much. I'm happy, funny, good-time girl, Rosie Belmont—but I feel like a dulled-down version of myself.

I feel how Cora looks as she trudges toward me in a pair of clunky Doc Martens with a deadly scowl on her face.

I almost laugh, because she looks just like Ford did this afternoon. Moody and temperamental—and wearing black from head to toe.

"Cora!" I call out, raising my hand in a wave. "I'm your ride today!" I feel the weight of more than a few gazes on me, but I ignore them.

Her eyes roll and she hikes her thumbs beneath her

backpack's shoulder straps. "You don't have to yell," she grumbles as she approaches.

"Want me to dance next time so you can pick me out of the crowd?" I give her a teasing elbow nudge as she walks past me.

With a glance over her shoulder, she shakes her head and juts her chin out at some of the waiting parents. "No. These pervy small-town dads would like that way too much."

Oh boy. I remember this phase. Thinking you're all cool and grown-up, when in reality, you're chock-full of teenaged angst and every mood known to man. A bittersweet pang hits me as I watch her climb into the front passenger seat. Maybe she and I aren't so different after all.

Which is why I plaster on a grin and yank the driver's side door open before sliding in next to her.

"I meant the chicken dance, not a striptease," I say with mock disappointment as I crank the key in the ignition.

She doesn't respond, but when I peek over at her, I swear I see her lips twitch.

"What are you doing?"

Parked in front of Ford's shitty office, Cora stares at me with her forehead all scrunched up. She even looks like him when she does that.

"Thinking." My hands twist on the steering wheel of my Subaru.

"You look like you're going to pop a blood vessel," she says casually, right as she pops a stick of Juicy Fruit into her mouth.

"That's an accurate depiction of how I feel inside too."

"Is it Ford?"

I slump back in the seat, flattening my hands against the wheel. "It's my entire life. You know?"

She nods, and I'm about to say something like, *of course you don't know, you're a fucking twelve-year-old*, but the look in her eye tells me perhaps she does.

"My job. My current living situation. My boyfriend. Having to tell my parents about all the above. A popped blood vessel would be a literal cherry on top."

She perks up at the mention of *boyfriend*. It's subtle, but it's there. The way she leans incrementally forward and inspects me a tad more closely.

"You have a boyfriend?"

I huff out a breath and shake my head. "Great question. I keep asking myself the same thing."

Disappointment fills her responding sigh.

"Do *you* have a boyfriend?"

She scowls at me.

"What? It's not like I'm going to run and tell your dad about it—or sorry, Ford. Fuck, sorry. What are we calling him?"

"Boss?"

I snort. She's funny. "Personally, I'm partial to Junior."

"I heard he really doesn't like that."

I lean close and give her a conspiratorial wink. "Exactly."

Her eyes search my face like she's not sure what to think of me. I'm positive I don't give off the maternal vibe she's probably used to from older women. I'm too much of a mess for that right now. And I'm too old to be her sister. Maybe more like a cool aunt. One who appreciates not having sticky freezie juice hands all over her.

Cora's company is a breath of fresh air, and I'm not sure I'm ready to leave it yet. I'm also not above admitting she might make what I'm about to do next a little less tense.

"Hey, wanna come to my parents' house with me instead of watching Junior storm around and clean up a building he could easily pay someone to clean up for him?"

She smirks, turning to look out the window. "Sure. Greta and Andy seem cool."

"Oh, you've met them?"

"Briefly. Once. They definitely give off grandparent vibes."

"Probably because that's what they are."

She gives me a sour glance, and my lips twitch. Let's hope they continue to give off sweet grandparent vibes when they find out Rosie "the good girl" went off the rails and blew her chance at the job, the house, the guy, and the two-point-five kids in one fell swoop.

I hate letting people down.

Anxiety churns in my gut, but I force a thin smile in Cora's direction. "Go tell Ford so he doesn't worry about you. I'll wait."

Then she's bounding out of the car, a little skip in her step that has her backpack bouncing. It makes her seem younger than the scowls and mouthiness would imply. I smile after her, hoping I get to pick her up from school more often.

Within moments, she's back.

With Ford in tow.

She doesn't spare him a backward glance, though, as she hurries back toward the car and into the front passenger seat.

"Why is he here?"

She shrugs. "Said he wanted to come with us."

Ford draws up short, watching her buckle up with a look of confusion on his handsome face. His head turns slowly as he eyes the back seat, and I can barely keep from bursting out laughing. I doubt he remembers the last time he sat his fancy ass in the back of anything that wasn't equipped with a privacy divider and a bucket of ice.

I hit the button to drop the back passenger window and call out, "Want me to come hold the door open for you, Junior?"

The way his head tilts. The way his arms cross. The way his eyes slice to mine from over the top of Cora's headrest. It all drips with disdain.

And yet, I smile.

Without another word, Ford steps forward and tugs the back door open. When he folds his tall frame into the back seat, I *almost* feel bad. My Impreza hatchback is practical and fun to drive, but it's not made for men of his stature to ride comfortably in the back seat.

"Don't worry, sir. It's not far. And if you're feeling peckish, I suspect I've left a partially melted Clif Bar in the pocket behind that seat."

He continues to give me his best bitchy look through the rearview mirror while Cora plays Pokémon GO on her phone, trying to pretend she doesn't think I'm funny.

Then Ford reaches forward. He pulls out the Clif Bar, which has to be expired, rips it open, and takes a huge bite, all while holding my gaze. His square jaw moves, dark stubble drawing my eyes to his lips for just a beat before they tug back up. "Thank you, Rosalie," he deadpans. "This is delicious."

CHAPTER 9

Ford

Rosie takes a deep breath before raising her hand to knock on the door to her parents' house. I'm not sure why she's knocking. Seems more like her to just barge in and announce herself. I reach out to squeeze her shoulder as reassurance, but years of practice kick in, and I force my hand back down while internally reminding myself that I'm her boss—not her boyfriend.

Still, it's impossible to ignore that something is off with her. I just can't figure out what. She's herself, but also skittish. At least my eating a past-it protein bar made her laugh. That was worth it, even if I can't get the taste of stale oats out of my mouth.

"Rosie, baby!" Greta Belmont shakes her head and blinks a few times, like her eyes might be fooling her. "What are you doing here?" She recovers enough to wrap her daughter in a tight hug.

"Hi, Mama." Rosie hugs her back. Hard.

"What are you doing here?" Andy says from just behind his wife, a thread of suspicion weaving its way into his tone.

Greta turns around to smack him in the chest, one arm still looped over Rosie's shoulders. "Give your daughter a better welcome than that when she shows up to surprise us!"

Andy arches a brow at his daughter. The man is all bark, no bite. He's got a big, soft heart, but he isn't known for being warm and fuzzy. "How are you, Rosie Posie?" he asks, eyeing her carefully before stepping up to give her a gentle hug. His blue eyes are just like Rosie's, and his hair is thinning just a little on top.

"I'm good, Dad." There's a hitch in Rosie's voice though. One she covers by clearing her throat and adding another, "I'm good," before pulling away.

Her mom finally turns, catching sight of the rest of us who got dragged along on this expedition. "And you brought Ford and Cora with you!"

Greta looks happy to see me.

Andy looks confused as to why I'm here.

To be fair, I am too. Maybe it was the way Cora stared at her chipped nails when she announced, "I think Rosie is having a mental breakdown. Also, I'm gonna go to her parents' house with her. See you later."

I wasn't about to let her have a mental breakdown alone.

Rosie glances over her shoulder at me, cheeks pinking slightly before she turns back. "Yeah. I meant to just bring Cora, but Ford invited himself." She brushes her hands down the front of her jeans like she's wiping dust off her hands. "So here we are!"

"Well, come in. Come in. Let's have some tea." Greta hits me with a wink. "Or a beer? I seem to remember you and West getting into those when you were younger."

Andy regards me carefully. He's not quite scowling, but there's nothing welcoming about his expression either. I suspect his spidey senses are tingling too—like he knows there's something not *quite* right about his fiercely independent, by-the-book daughter showing up out of the blue.

"Tea is great."

Greta smiles and slings an arm over Rosie, pressing her daughter tight against her side. "Perfect. Tea is Rosie Posie's favorite."

I bite the inside of my cheek as we move indoors. I guess Mrs. Belmont hasn't seen her daughter sling back a gin and tonic like there's about to be a worldwide shortage the way I have.

We follow Andy into the living room, and I can't help but notice Cora taking in her surroundings. The Belmonts' new home resembles a large concrete box, modern from top to bottom. Except their furniture.

They relocated their old farmhouse pieces straight into their new place. You'd think it would clash with the modern stainless-steel appliances and slate-gray walls, yet there's a certain eclectic charm to the place. I don't think it's intentional, but it's there all the same.

The furnishings have character. Each cushion on the floral-print velvet couches sags slightly in the middle. The coffee table has a glass slab on top of an ornate wrought-iron base. Beneath it, the Persian rug exudes a relaxed vibe, its white base accented with pink and blue and a minty green. Even the bookcases have a sort of vintage-cottage style to them.

Greta settles into the flower-print love seat, close to her daughter. Cora and I take opposite ends of the couch facing them—the same couch I passed out on after too many beers as a teenager, I'm sure. And after setting a tray with a teapot, cups, and a plate of shortbread cookies in the center of the coffee table, Andy takes the navy-blue leather La-Z-Boy chair, possibly the only piece of furniture from this decade.

"No Ryan this trip?" Greta asks as she leans forward to pour the first cup.

"No," Rosie says quickly, eyes flitting up to mine as Cora homes in on the cookies. "Not this time."

"Oh my god. This cookie is so dry," Cora whispers so only I can hear, holding it in front of her face like it could be a specimen in a lab.

"Is he doing well? That boy works too hard."

Rosie's lips roll together, and I can't help but feel like she's avoiding my gaze. "He definitely works a lot."

"Too much?" Andy pipes up. He poses it as a question, but his eyes make it feel more like a statement. Like he *knows* something.

Greta sends him a silent reprimand while Rosie dives for a cookie and shoves it into her mouth, like it might keep her from having this conversation. "Probably," she mumbles, quickly wiping a crumb from her lip.

"What?" Andy says, still looking at his wife. "She shows up out of nowhere, unannounced, with Ford at her side? We always expected this would happen."

Rosie's eyes go comically wide, and then she coughs like the dry-as-dust cookie she's just thrown back has gone down the wrong tube. Her mom slaps her back, which does nothing but knock dry crumbs violently out of her mouth.

Fuck me, this is the world's most awkward tea party.

With one hand on her throat and one on her mom's knee—a silent plea for her to stop beating on her spine—Rosie struggles to catch her breath.

"Maybe you should give her the Heimlich," Cora provides, unhelpfully, from her end of the couch.

Rosie shakes her head. "No, I'm fine." She swipes the back of her hand over her mouth and then glares at her dad. "First, you always expected *what* would happen?" Then she looks at Greta. "And second, good god those cookies are so dry, they might as well be a mouthful of flour."

Cora nods before blurting, "Accurate."

Me? I lean forward, prop my elbows on my knees, and rub my fingers at my temples. Perhaps I can conjure up a strictly platonic reason I felt the need to accompany Rosie to this meeting like some sort of dickhead knight in shining armor.

Except all the reasons that pop up in my mind are ones that don't belong there. Ones I could never give voice to. There's nothing platonic about the way I feel when it comes to Rosie. And I'm happier than I have any right to be that she's back in town.

"I mean, it's the way the two of you always bicker—"

"Dad, I'm going to stop you right there. There are three reasons you're wrong. One, Ford is West's best friend. Two, he's my new boss—"

"What?" Greta sounds shocked.

Andy appears more and more suspicious. "What about your fancy big-city job?"

With a defeated sigh, Rosie draws herself up and looks him in the eye. "It didn't work out, Dad."

They stare at each other for a few beats, like they're having some sort of silent conversation.

Then Andy nods firmly.

Rosie offers the same back.

The rest of us just watch in confusion.

"So anyway," Rosie carries on, waving in my direction with one hand. "I've taken a position as Ford's personal assistant."

Personal assistant. Is that what she thinks? I'll admit, I wasn't much of a conversationalist today. Something about having her in my space set me on edge. I felt like I was constantly orienting in her direction, like my gaze was pulled to her against my will.

It was unsettling.

And it kept me from telling her what I really imagined her doing for the business.

"No," I say, and she starts at the one word that cuts through the room. "I'm hiring Rosalie as my business manager. Right after we have a formal interview tomorrow, where we lay out some ground rules, and I get a chance to view her résumé."

"She has her MBA," Andy says proudly.

I nod and look him in the eye. "I know, sir. I've seen her LinkedIn profile." My eyes move back to Rosie, like they always do. She's too stunned to say anything snippy, which is unusual, to say the least. "And she has a hell of a mind for business, I'm sure. That's why I'll have her help with getting Rose Hill Records up and running. Then I can focus on the creative side, knowing the numbers are in good hands."

Rosie blinks, mouth slightly ajar.

"And what about when she goes back to the city?" Greta just comes up and kicks me in the hypothetical gut for no good reason. Hits me with what I know is probably true. My stomach drops hard and fast, just like it did when Rosie left town the first time.

She has a life in Vancouver. A *boyfriend*.

I know she's not going to stay in Rose Hill for long.

But I also don't like to think about that. I'll never admit it to anyone, but I'm feeling awfully sentimental about having her so close again.

Rosie Belmont took off to start her life ten years ago and has barely been back. It crushed me then when she left.

I don't even want to think about what it might do to me now.

"I'm sure she could work remotely." I force a smile, then peek at Rosie before adding, "If that's what she wants."

Cold water sluices over my skin as I turn my head to suck

in a harsh breath. My arms move in long, slow strokes while my brain runs wild. A swim usually helps clear my head, but today, on the heels of that tea party, it's not working.

I think about Cora.

I think about the mold I found in one wall of the office today when I tried to replace a light switch.

I think about the artists who are filling my email, wanting to work with me.

I think about not having an opening date in sight.

But most of all, I think about Rosie.

Which is why her voice stops me dead in my tracks during my evening swim.

"Are you stalking me, Junior?"

I come to a screeching stop as I draw in a breath and use both palms to push my hair off my face.

At the end of the dock, Rosalie is snuggled up in a Navajo blanket, enjoying a bag of chips. Staring at me like I'm an idiot—as usual.

"What?"

"You keep swimming past my dock. I've been watching you. You just go back and forth between this post and that buoy, over and over again. Like a lion pacing in its cage. Or like a weirdo trying to catch sight of me."

To be fair, I feel a bit like a lion pacing his cage. And I'd be a liar if I said I hadn't considered catching sight of her.

"And it's fucking cold out. You don't win any sort of hero award for swimming in the lake before June."

My legs kick and my arms trace the top of the water as I stare back at her. "I just like it. Clears my head. Tires me out. You should try it sometime. It might make you more agreeable."

She pops another chip into her mouth, legs swinging off the end of the dock. "I'm good. Watching you exercise makes me feel like I'm almost experiencing it myself. Plus, we both know I'll never be agreeable with you and that water is glacier-cold this time of year. It would just make things worse. No, thank you, sir."

"It's good for my metabolism," I reply simply, treading water and staring back at her.

When her eyes wander over my shoulders, I look away, gooseflesh popping up on my skin, heart pounding just a bit harder.

"If you're cold, I'll let you sit on my dock. Might even share my chips with you. No point in having a good metabolism if you can't eat fried potatoes whenever you feel like it."

I smile. It's a small one, but it's a smile all the same. "Let me get this straight. You're going to let *me* sit on *your* dock and eat *your* chips?"

She shrugs and grins back. "Yeah. I need to be somewhat nice to my new boss."

I give my head a shake, but I also don't say no. Instead, I swim to the shore, grab my towel and shrug on my robe, and walk along the dock toward Rosie, plunking down a safe distance from her.

Her head tilts. "I won't bite, Junior. That's too far to share chips. Or am I supposed to throw them at you? Because I'm not opposed to that plan. Open wide and I'll pretend I'm aiming for your mouth."

I grumble and push up on my palms, edging closer toward her. Close enough to eat chips but far enough to keep things professional. Or familial. Or whatever the fuck my best friend's little sister is supposed to be to me.

She holds the bag out, still looking out over the water.

"Still only eat Old Dutch sour cream and onion?"

I'm met with a soft giggle. "I can't believe you remember that. But yeah. They're getting harder and harder to find in the box though. Sometimes I have to settle for the bag." She sneers at her snack.

"Does it matter?"

"The box is more charming. Tastes better too, I think."

"You think so?" I pop one into my mouth and it's like instant déjà vu. While Rosie has been eating these chips her entire life, I've never eaten them with anyone other than her. Sunburnt shoulders, freckles on our noses, wet towels, an entire pack of kids here for the summer pushing each other off the dock.

"Yeah, it's like Coke out of a glass bottle—superior in every way."

I wobble my head as I reach for another chip. "You're not wrong."

She smiles, satisfaction painting her features. "Music to my ears, Junior. Haven't heard how right I am in a while."

The comment is offhanded enough, but it still gets my gears turning. Rosie is studious and bright, and even though she's a grade A shit-talker, she's an exceptional human. I know she is. Who the fuck has been telling her she's anything other than right?

"Where's Cora?" she asks between crunches, clearly not giving a shit about looking prim or polite in front of me. And that's special—someone who treats me like I'm *me*. She treats me like I'm just a regular dude and not the planet's sexiest bajillionaire or whatever the fuck that stupid article was called.

I don't want to be him, and with Rosie I don't need to be.

"Writing frantically in her journal. I asked her if she wanted to come down to the lake with me, and she shot me a dirty look."

"Ugh. I should really start writing in a diary again. So cathartic. Probably will need to if I'm going to work with you all day, every day."

I scoff and run a hand through my hair, watching the water ripple beneath the spring breeze. "I don't know what I'm doing with her. I mean, I've got a roof over her head and food for her to eat, but we're strangers. I don't know how to be a dad."

"I don't think she needs you to be her dad. She has one of those—or had. She just needs you to be there for her in whatever way works for the two of you."

"This whole thing is fucking weird, and we both know it."

Rosie nods, lost in thought, still kicking her feet in an almost childlike way. "Yeah. It is. But sometimes we're just doing the best we can, ya know? Like this is brand-new for both of you. There's going to be an adjustment period. And I remember being her age, so full of angst and hormones and thinking I knew so much more than I did. You need to find a common ground with her, something you can do together that doesn't feel like… like homework or something. Clearly, she doesn't enjoy swimming, but what does she like?"

I snort. "The color black."

"Black is a great color."

"Rosie, black isn't a color. It's a shade. And that's rich coming from the girl who's been wearing pink almost exclusively since I first met her at nine years old."

She laughs. "You're such a nerd. And I don't *only* wear pink. Currently my bra and panties are bright red."

I freeze for a beat and then wipe my face with an open palm. I huff out a beleaguered sigh, pretending like I'm exasperated by her when I really just need a moment to regain my composure.

And to keep myself from imagining Rosalie Belmont in bright red lingerie.

A soft laugh filters over from her. "Calm your tits, Junior. It was a joke."

With that, she… throws a chip at my face.

Her eyes widen like she can't believe what she just did, and then she laughs with a subtle shake of her head. "I swear I revert to a bratty twelve-year-old when I'm around you."

I chuckle, look down at my hands, and… throw my chip at her face.

"Ford Grant. I know you did not just do that." She gasps the words out, struggling to keep it together. Her cheeks pull up into round, rose-colored apples. If I have to throw chips at her to make her laugh like this—the kind of laughter that hurts your stomach and gets you kicked out of class—so be it.

I'll throw chips at Rosie Belmont every damn day.

All I do is shoot her a wink and toss another one, which hits the bow of her top lip, leaving a dusting of sour-cream-and-onion powder in its path.

She throws her head back and laughs, that long pony-tail cascading farther down her back. A little moisture leaks from the corner of her eye as she pulls a chip from the bag, but before she can throw it at me, my hand whips out. I'm laughing too when my fingers curl around her dainty wrist.

We're both laughing when I playfully tug her closer and reach for the chip gripped between her fingers. She tumbles into me, and it crumbles all over us as we fall and fight over it like two children over a toy. The bag of chips gets discarded on the other side of her.

Her free palm lands between the thick lapels of my terry cloth bathrobe, on my bare chest.

And that's when the laughter stops.

Her eyes fall to where her skin presses against mine. All the immature playfulness between us bleeds away, dripping between the boards of the dock and washing away in the lake.

When my eyes snap back up to hers, I get the full experience of watching Rosalie Belmont lick her lips while the tips of her fingers curve lightly into the indent just below my collarbone. She's taking a good, long, blatant look.

And I'm too stunned to move. Too weak to stop her.

"What the fuck are you two doing?" West's voice, cutting through the golden twilight air, has her gaze flying up to meet my own.

We both shoot up to a sitting position as if we've been caught doing something wrong.

I've barely gotten my bearings when she pats my shoulder like she's consoling a child and whispers, "Sorry."

With no warning, she shoves me off the end of the dock and into the lake to the sound of her brother's laughter. I only drop below the water for a moment before I burst back above the surface.

"Taking a walk down memory lane," she calls back to West as he strolls down the dock in heavy boots.

Both Belmonts laugh while I wipe the water from my eyes and look up. I point at Rosie, not sure what just happened, but certain of one thing for sure...

"You're going to pay for that one, Rosie Posie."

CHAPTER 10

Rosie

WHEN I WALK INTO THE MILDEW-SCENTED BUILDING WE'RE calling an office, I'm ready to face the day.

I toned down my regular work attire, but my blazer is a dusty rose—pink, I guess—and that makes me happy. I've paired it with a plain white tee, baggy boyfriend jeans, and a pair of suede, beige boots with chunky heels—hopefully, they'll hurt when I kick Ford's ass for being so utterly bewildering.

The hair tug. The way he went eerily still at my red underwear joke. The way he dragged me closer to him. The way his chest peeking from beneath his robe stopped me in my tracks.

The way he let me touch him with no hesitation.

Yeah. I'm gonna kick his ass all right.

Ford is already here, sitting at the old desk, phone propped between his shoulder and ear. He looks relaxed—arms crossed, feet kicked out, so he's leaned back. I can faintly hear someone talking on the other end, and while he listens, I try not to stare at him or what I now know is a hard chest under his cable-knit sweater. Beaded bracelets stacked on top of a watch that is just shiny enough to draw your eye.

Mussed hair. Scuffed boots. His stubble a little longer than it was yesterday.

He's basically a flashing red light. There are so many reasons I shouldn't let my brain proceed.

My brother. My maybe boyfriend, maybe roommate. I need to keep my eyes on my work and not on whatever transformation Ford has gone through in the past decade that has left him oozing sex.

I steel myself as I offer him a firm wave and turn away with a new sense of direction. Or at least a new sense of which side of the road to avoid veering off into.

But when I actually look at the space, I come to a screeching halt. Straight across from Ford's desk, approximately twenty feet away, is another desk. With another chair. Facing him.

Basically, my own personal torture chamber. Am I supposed to spend all day working while facing Ford? No fucking way.

I storm toward the desk but come up short when my eyes catch on what's sitting on top.

The book cover has a pattern of butterflies in a field of flowers. They dance along the tops of the blooms. The hard cover was shiny once, but it's a little water-stained now. A little dirty in one corner.

I place my hand on my chest, rubbing it in slow, firm circles as I stare back at my diary. The same one I threw out the window all those years ago. The steel clasp is broken, but the heart-shaped lock still clings to the two rings meant to hold it shut. But now, it might as well be wide open.

If someone wanted to go through it, they'd be in for a wild ride through my unfiltered thoughts and feelings. In fact, if I remember correctly, the first page says something along the lines of "Read at your own risk. I might have talked shit about you in here."

With a few steps forward, I'm standing right above the book and trailing my fingertips over it. Feeling where the cover changes from glossy to matte.

My eyes well with tears, and I'm not sure why. Possibly because I'm coming face-to-face with a lost artifact from my girlhood.

I turn my head, chin grazing my shoulder as I peek over at Ford.

His eyes are already on me, and he doesn't bother dropping my gaze as he responds to the person on the phone, "That's a great plan. Why don't you run it past them and get back to me?" He hangs up without saying goodbye. To some people, that might seem rude, but I'd be willing to bet that, in Ford's head, it's just efficient.

"Did you put this here?" I point at the diary as I turn my entire body to face him. I don't pick it up yet. I'm not sure I'm ready.

"I did." He tips forward to toss his phone on the desk

before returning to his leaned back position, lifting his arms and linking his hands like a hammock behind his head.

My throat goes dry. "Where did you get it?"

"From the side of the road. You managed to clear the ditch and land it between a fallen log and a poplar tree."

My face scrunches up in confusion, because not a single part of this makes sense. "It was still there after all these years?" Even as I ask, I know it's the wrong question. It wouldn't be in this condition after ten years spent on the forest floor.

"No, I went there the day after you threw it and searched for it." His head tilts as if he's considering his next words with extra care. "It took me a few trips."

I blink, trying to wrap my head around his words. "Are you saying you went back more than once to look for my diary?"

He shrugs. A silent affirmation.

"Why?" I can't for the life of me understand why he'd do that. The time. The effort. All spent on his best friend's little tag-along sister, who spent every summer doing her best to annoy him.

Then it hits me, and I point an accusing finger. "You wanted to read it, didn't you?"

He stares at me blankly, and I walk toward him, delighted I've found a brand-new thing to tease him about. "Did you read my journal, Junior? Was it juicy—"

"I never read it." He sits up straight and pulls himself toward his desk. Without sparing me a glance, he flips his laptop open dismissively. "I wouldn't do that to you. But I figured you might want it one day. You'd left for college by the time I tracked it down, and I just forgot about it. Haven't seen you since then anyway."

"You've seen West."

He nods, still avoiding my gaze. If I didn't know better, I'd say Ford was nervous right now. Embarrassed even.

"You could have given it to him."

"I could have," is his impassive reply.

And suddenly, I'm the one who feels nervous. This man did something sweet—tender, even—a really long time ago, and I have no idea how to respond.

He clearly didn't want anyone who might read it to have it. And West would have definitely read it because he's that type of shit-disturber. Probably would have made a hit list of every guy mentioned in it too. Or cracked an awkward inside joke at Christmas dinner.

"Wow." I comb my fingers through my carefully curled hair. "You really wanted to guilt me about pushing you into the lake last night, huh?"

That gets me a twitch of his cheek and a coy peek from below heavy brows. "Is it working? Do you feel bad?" His eyes flit back down to the screen on the heels of his question.

It's my turn to stare back at him with a blank look on my face. Because after this revelation, Ford makes me feel a lot of different things..

And *bad* doesn't top the list.

Speechless.

Affected.

Confused.

Ford breaks the silence without glancing my way. "When you're done gawking at me, can you look for a contractor that won't dick me around on gutting this place? Oh, and I'd like to see your résumé, mostly so I can say I didn't lie to your parents."

And I decide I don't feel bad about pushing him into the lake after all.

Not even a little bit.

Cora looks like an adorable storm cloud stomping out the front doors of the school. Ford was adamant that, as his business manager, I didn't need to pick Cora up. I pushed back and said it makes it easier for him to work through the afternoon. But the truth is, this daily excursion gives me the break I need from feeling the weight of his gaze on me while I work. And I like Cora. I enjoy her company. She makes me laugh even when I don't feel like it, so picking her up feels like a treat, not a task.

When she catches sight of me, I lift both hands like I'm about to wave. But instead, I fold my thumbs and fingers together and begin the chicken dance.

When she figures out what I'm doing, her eyes bulge and her steps quicken.

I hook my thumbs under my armpits and start flapping my arms, but Cora is so close now that I can't hold back my laughter. I don't know her well enough to tease her like this, but hey, we have to start somewhere.

Someone nearby must be watching us, because right

before she draws up in front of me, her head snaps to the side. "What do you think you're looking at?"

Her eyes narrow on the man, but me? I get the giggles. I don't recognize him, but I don't recognize many people in Rose Hill anymore. This place has gone from charming lakeside retreat to bustling mountain town in the past ten years.

"Hi, Cora," I say calmly as I watch her trudge around the car and practically fall into the passenger seat.

"Hi, Rosie."

I get in, buckle up, and start the engine to pull out of the parking lot. "How was school today?"

"Fine, until you did the chicken dance at pickup."

"Do you think all the kids will talk about me tomorrow?" I cast her a teasing look, and I know she's amused because she does the sullen tween thing of clamping her lips together and turning away to stare out the window.

"You remind me of my dad sometimes. That's something he'd have done."

When I realize she doesn't mean Ford, I pause for a beat but decide there's no point in tiptoeing. "Yeah? He sounds cool."

"He was," is her soft reply as she stares out the glass.

"What was his name?" I ask as I turn out of the pickup loop and head onto the quiet neighborhood street.

"Doug."

"Well, if Doug would have approved of my chicken dance, I'll keep doing it."

Now I get a snort. "Oh yeah. Ford is more like my mom. You're the Doug in that relationship."

I point at her. "Except there is no relationship between

Ford and me. Just childhood frenemies turned boss and employee."

Cora gives me a look that says she thinks I'm an idiot. It's one of her best, most well-practiced expressions, and I admire that about her.

"Frenemies?"

"Yes. It's the perfect description for us." My eyes slice in her direction, and she's back to staring at me like I'm the dumbest person alive.

All it does is make me smile.

"School was actually good, though? You making some friends?"

She shrugs. "Yeah."

Okay, we're in one-word-answer territory. We'll circle back to that another day. Or I'll take a casual stroll down the halls and see for myself.

"And how about things with Ford?"

He annoyed me today. I thought we were having a moment, a little heart-to-heart over my journal, but then he shut down. And when I gave him my résumé, he scrutinized it thoroughly. Brows drawn low, red pen in hand as he tapped it against his lips. I watched him from my desk. Okay, I glared at him from my desk. Then he literally wrote "HIRED" on the top, walked over to me, and dropped it on my desk with an obnoxious smirk.

Cora shrugs again. "He's cool."

"Yeah?" I can't keep the amusement from my voice. *Cool.* I love that she sees him that way. So many people never did. He was too cerebral, too quirky. People labeled him a lot of things in this small town, but cool was not one of them. Although I would have never said it, I always thought he was.

She nods. "Yeah. We don't like…" Her hand swivels before her as she searches for her next words. "Talk a lot? I guess." A shrug. And silence. I can tell she's thinking, can practically see the words on the tip of her tongue, so I don't say anything. I just let her digest.

"But I love Gramophone. I listen to all my music there. And this morning I overheard him talking with Ivory Castle. She was this lame teenybopper pop star, you know? But then she recorded with him, and he gave her this whole new sound. Have you heard the new single from that album? It's all smoky and gritty but mainstream enough that people with bad taste in music will still like it. She plays the guitar and everything. She's great. You know, if you can just pretend those other sellout albums don't exist."

I bite down so hard on my inner cheek that I swear I taste blood. Behind all her snark, I somehow missed the serious case of hero worship this girl has going on with Ford.

"That is pretty cool. Does he know all this?"

She bats a hand through the air like she's swatting at a fly. "Nah. He mostly just stares at me like I terrify him."

I feel a twinge of sympathy for Ford—he truly is unprepared for this.

"I don't want to make his life harder, so I don't push my luck. He's busy and important."

Now I feel a sharp pang of sympathy for Cora. Because that is so fucking relatable. I tried so hard, for so long, to fly under the radar with my family that I now recognize all the ways I missed out on a deeper connection with them. I don't want to say that I resent my parents for letting me become the invisible child, but it certainly taught me not to rely on them… not to confide in them. And in a lot of ways, I did it to myself. I saw the anxiety they had around West and decided I wouldn't add to that.

As I think back on it, it made me feel very alone. And I don't want that for Cora—or for Ford.

"He's not as bad as he comes off sometimes," is what I offer back. "You can't take him at face value—and I know that's tough sometimes. Trust me, I do." Because it's true. For all my stomping and huffing about the guy, I know he's a good one. And I know the way he works. "But you don't make his life harder, I promise you that. Don't make yourself into an inconvenience when you aren't one. He may not know you well yet, but he wants to, and he just isn't sure how to do it."

She nods sternly and we fall into a comfortable silence. As I turn up the radio for the short drive back to Rose Hill Records, I shake my head with a small smile on my lips.

He looks at her like she terrifies him. And she looks at him with stars in her eyes.

But they're both too alike to say a single word to each other.

It's adorable.

CHAPTER 11

Ford

"I told you I'll eat anything." On a stool at the kitchen counter, Cora is absorbed in reading a book. She doesn't bother looking up to answer my question about her dinner preferences. She just keeps reading. While I flail around trying to find out what she likes to eat so I can make it for her.

We just tried calling her mom at the treatment center, but Marilyn wasn't available, and it took the wind out of her sails—even if she won't admit it. She's trying to be cool, but I can tell she misses her mom, and I don't blame her at all.

That's why I'm trying to make it better.

"If I could cook you anything in the world, what would you pick?" I try to clarify my question as I stare into the refrigerator. Admittedly, not everything in the world is in here. But if she would tell me what she actually likes, I could try something similar. I mean, shit. I could have it brought in.

"Anything." I see her shrug out of the corner of my eye and wonder if this is how I was growing up. I'd know if I bothered to tell my family about this situation. My mom, my dad, my big-mouth sister. They'd all have something to say about it. I'm sure they'd all have good advice too. But they'd also come with criticisms. I worry they'll tell me I shouldn't have done this with Cora. That it was impulsive. That I'm putting myself at financial risk. That I'm under no obligation to help in this situation.

And they'd be right. But the truth is, I'm feeling startlingly protective of Cora.

Any critical comment or advice that I do less than I already am could make me go borderline feral. Like full papa bear mode. And it's an unfamiliar feeling. One I'm still grappling with. One that's keeping me from seeking outside advice.

"So, frog legs?"

Her hazel eyes pop up over the top of the book. "Sure."

"Liver?"

"I love it."

"Caviar?"

"Your rich kid is showing."

Fuck me, that was funny. I wipe a hand across my mouth to hide my smirk.

"Hot dogs?"

She gives me a confused look. "You know, that's actually the most offensive food on that list. Do you have any idea what's in them?"

I reach into the fridge and inspect the package. "Meat trimmings."

Cora just nods. But she's finally not ignoring me for whatever Stephen King horror shit she's reading in an attempt to be as anti-stereotypical as possible.

"Are they less offensive if we roast them over a fire?"

For a moment, her eyes light up before she goes back to trying to look cool and unaffected. "Do you have stuff for s'mores?"

I'm a thirty-two-year-old bachelor workaholic. Of course I don't have stuff for s'mores. But I only say, "I don't."

She probably thinks she's unreadable, but I don't miss the way her shoulders fall.

"I can go grab the ingredients."

"No. It's fine. Hot dogs on a fire sound great. I'll go grab a sweater."

After she stomps up the stairs, I get to problem-solving. Because if that girl wants s'mores, she's going to have them.

A quick swipe across my phone's screen pulls up Rosie's contact information, and I hit call.

"I knew you were stalking me," she answers.

I roll my eyes, standing in my big, empty kitchen, and cut to the chase. "Do you have the stuff to make s'mores?"

"Dude. Have you seen the bunkhouse? I have a hot plate, a toaster oven, and a kettle in the corner. I'm living on the wrong brand of sour cream and onion chips because the grocery store here doesn't stock Old Dutch."

"Okay, never mind—"

"*Of course* I have the ingredients for s'mores."

"You're a hot mess, Rosalie."

"All I heard was that you think I'm hot."

I say nothing to that. There's no safe answer. Especially not when my neck gets all red at the mere mention.

"Can I swing by and grab the ingredients?"

"No."

"No?"

"Why would I share them with you? You're a bajillionaire."

"That's not an actual term."

"I know, but it has a more satisfying and ridiculous ring to it."

I try one last time. "They're for Cora."

Rosie goes quiet and then, "Oh. Well, why didn't you say so? I'll bring them over."

Then she hangs up on me.

"You know how to start a fire?"

Cora stands at my back as I arrange the sticks and newspaper at the bottom of the fire pit.

"I do."

"I'd have thought you had a butler to do it for you."

I sit back on my heels, kneeling as I look up into Cora's snarky little face. "Man. Did you and Rosie make some sort of evil plan to mock me mercilessly today?"

A small giggle I've never heard from her tumbles out. "No. But I wish we had."

"You women are going to give me a complex," I say, dusting my hands clean. "You wanna light it?"

"Me?"

"Yeah. I feel like adding pyromania to your personality profile would be a good fit."

Cora doesn't laugh. She stares at me, considering my words. I wonder if I shouldn't have said them. Probably shouldn't be ragging on a twelve-year-old.

My twelve-year-old *daughter*.

But then she says, "That was funny."

"Yeah?"

Another small giggle. "Yeah. And I want to light it. Show me how."

"You've never done this before?"

She shrugs. "My dad had ALS."

I know as much, but I'm missing how that has anything to do with lighting a fire.

"So, like… he just became more immobile every year, for most of my life. My mom took care of him. I tagged along. We didn't do camping or anything. Or maybe we did when I was too young to remember."

Without hesitation, I decide this is what we'll do—all the things she never got to. Simple things. Childhood things. Things that include her.

This is what Marilyn wanted for her.

"Well, believe it or not, my parents loved to camp. Before they bought their cabin here—when I was your age, actually—we went camping all the time. Hell, we still went camping even when they got their place."

"Your parents have a place here?"

I nod while reaching for the long-arm lighter I brought down from the house.

"Can I meet them sometime?"

Her question catches me off guard. People usually just want to meet my dad because he's, well, him. Famous. "You want to meet my parents?"

Another shrug. I swear her traps must be extra strong with all the unaffected shrugging she does. "Yeah. I never got to do the whole grandparent thing. Might be kind of all right."

I blink a few times, trying to process that she wants to meet my parents for the grandparent experience. She should be careful what she wishes for because after seeing them with my sister's kids, I know how over-the-top they are.

"Okay. Yeah. I'll find out when they'll be here." I don't tell her I haven't told them about her, and I suddenly feel sick that I haven't.

"I brought beers and s'mores!" Rosie announces, popping my bubble of guilt as she walks up from the lake.

The fence line between the two properties doesn't extend to the water, so it's more direct to walk over than to bother driving around. Still, her presence surprises me. It takes me back to when we were kids, ripping around town on our bikes like the little gang of misfits we were. Showing up at each other's houses unannounced. Messy hair, dirt under our nails, sun-bleached hair.

Not a care in the world.

Rosie looks nothing like that anymore. She's wearing an oversized, bright-white, fuzzy fleece that reminds of a blanket. Her hair is drawn up in a high pony, held in place with a neon-pink velvet scrunchie. And she's rounded the ensemble off with plush socks, Birkenstocks, and a pair of black leggings.

Some people might think she looks like a hot mess, as I told her earlier. But I think she's just plain hot. Blazers and high heels all day, then *this* at night. I think what I find appealing about the dichotomy is she clearly just wears what she wants—what she feels like—and looks good in it all.

I don't get the sense she gives a single fuck about what I think of her, and I find that refreshing as hell.

The longer I watch her, the more a heavy tightness takes over my chest. I press my palm there to ease the ache. Willing myself to not think too hard about my body's reaction.

"Hi!" Cora welcomes her so brightly that I almost do a double take. The enthusiasm at seeing Rosie is unexpected, but also… same.

"Hello, my little storm cloud," Rosie says as she places her drinks and food on the grass.

My little storm cloud?

She makes her way to the firepit where we're crouching and ruffles Cora's black hair affectionately. Cora rolls her eyes but smiles shyly down at the ground. Leave it to Rosie to blast through any walls or tendrils of discomfort. That's her gift. The ability to walk into a room and make everyone like her without even trying.

She's the sun, the rest of us are just dumb rocks orbiting her.

"Hello, my big storm cloud," she says to me, before turning her knuckles onto my scalp and giving me a noogie.

"Very professional, Rosalie."

I don't let myself look at her, but I freeze when I feel the nail of her index finger trace along the shell of my ear. I know she's being playful, but I suck in a sharp breath all the same.

One I hold when she leans down, face close enough to really be unprofessional. Her breath fans across my neck when she whispers, "We're not at work right now, *Junior*."

I glare at her from the corner of my eye, but Cora interrupts me.

Laughing.

"He really does hate that, doesn't he?"

I know they mean the nickname, but I'm still caught up in the feel of Rosie's fingers on my skin. I didn't hate that part at all.

Rosie steps away, ending the contact. "Oh yeah. Always has. I brought you a soda since you can't drink beer." Rosie wobbles her head like she's thinking that one over. "Yet. You can't drink beer *yet*. When did we start, Ford?"

"I only remember you drinking gin and tonic."

She sighs wistfully and flops down onto an empty stump as her seat. "God. I love gin and tonic. Panty remover."

I cough, but Rosie forges ahead, ignoring me. "Anyway, Cora, I ran to the store and got you this root beer they make at the brewery in town."

"You ran to the store?" I ask, urging Cora closer so we can get the fire lit.

Rosie shrugs. "I mean, yeah. I wasn't going to show up without something for Cora."

Cora kneels beside me, and it makes me realize that for all her big attitude she is still really very small. Her legs next to mine. Her hands as they wrap around the lighter.

I stare at her, struggling to push up the safety lock while also igniting the flame. It hits me how young she is, how alone she is, that she's been here for days, and I've spent that time being awkward as hell around her.

"Here." I reach my arm over her shoulders. "I'll do the safety. You squeeze the ignition and light the paper."

Cora nods and captures her tongue between her lips in concentration. It seems like a simple enough thing, using a lighter. I think back to her sitting in the kitchen earlier, reading her book, staying out of the way, being perfectly agreeable, and I realize she's adapted to be amenable to *anything* just to make things easier on her parents.

"There! It's lit! It's going!" She squeals in excitement while I find the bridge of my nose stinging as I watch her get excited over a simple flame.

"Okay, easy now," I say as she holds the flame to the crumpled newspaper. "You're going to blow on it gently."

"Won't that put it out?"

"No, just gently enough to spread the flame."

She doesn't look at me, but she hands over the lighter and then places her palms on the bricks surrounding the pit, blowing gently. When the flames brighten, so do her eyes. So does everything about her, and I *finally* feel like I'm doing something for this girl other than just being her legal guardian.

I find myself smiling too. But I'm not watching the flames.

I'm watching Cora.

And when I glance up, Rosie's eyes are also alight. Except she's watching *me*.

CHAPTER 12

Rosie

I can't ignore the burning urge I feel the minute Ford walks away to get Cora settled in for the night. My hand dives into my pocket and I pull my phone out immediately and fire off a text to Ryan.

> **Rosie:** Hey, I know you're probably at work right now. Wondering if your schedule is still looking as full or if something has opened up. I feel like we need to talk. This weekend maybe?

I stare at the lit screen of the phone, and within a minute, I see three gray dots start to roll. They start. And they stop. Several seconds pass and then they start up again. This pattern continues for much longer than is necessary for a simple answer. But I find myself sitting there waiting for words to pop up all the same.

Ryan: Hey babe! Wish I could. Heading out on the road
to do some sight visits so I'm not even gonna be
in town. Busy right now. Call you when I get home
tonight.

I have a momentary urge to tell him that it's *site visit* not
sight visit. But that urge is overrun by my absolute indiffer-
ence. I don't bother responding. Instead, I shove my phone
back into my pocket with an eyeroll and go back to enjoying
the crackling heat of the fire in front of me.

I'm entirely lost in watching the flames dance when Ford
settles on the stump next to mine. "Here," he says gruffly as
he wraps a blanket around my shoulders. It catches me off
guard that he brought a blanket down from his house just
for me.

But I opt not to pester him about it. The food coma has
me feeling more mellow than usual.

"That was fun. Thanks for inviting me." He's tall enough
and the stumps are close enough that our legs line up and
press against each other.

But I decide it's better if I don't fixate on that.

He chuckles, low and raspy, while we stare at the roaring
fire. The lake shimmers in the dark beyond us, and an owl
hoots somewhere in the trees over the crackling logs.

"I didn't invite you. I asked to borrow ingredients, and
you invited yourself."

I smile at that. "Hey, at least I brought beer."

He reaches for his and takes a deep swig. Somehow, the
sound of him swallowing is hyper-masculine. "You could

have shown up empty-handed, and we'd have been happy to see you."

"You mean Cora would have been happy to see me." I nudge him with my elbow, trying to steer this moment back into playful territory. Because there's something different about Ford now.

Ten years ago, his intensity was awkward. Kind of endearing, really. Now that intensity is... I don't know. It makes me squirmy, like I can't handle having his full attention on me without my skin itching.

"No. I'd have been happy to see you too."

It's my turn to take a deep swig of the pale ale I brought from the brewery in town. It's not especially cold anymore. The heat from the flames has warmed the can, and it's lost a bit of its fizz. But I swallow that shit like I'm parched in the desert.

"You're different," is all I come up with to say.

He leans closer, bumping his shoulder against mine. "So are you."

"Probably a good thing, eh?" I tease, bumping him back. "Didn't like me much when we were kids, if I remember correctly."

His lips lift in a smug smile, gaze still latched to the fire he built with his daughter. Then he turns and looks me dead in the eye. "You're not remembering correctly, Rosie."

My heart pounds. I don't know what to say to that, so I pretend it never came out of his mouth. I think I assigned a deeper meaning to it in my head, and that's why it made my stomach flip. I likely exaggerated the way my body felt when the words met my ears—the way his voice rumbled deep enough that I could feel it in my chest.

"I think she had fun tonight." I force the words from my otherwise parched throat, just as I realize all our joking elbows and shoulder nudges have brought us a hell of a lot closer than we should be.

Neither of us moves to pull away. Instead, I find myself face-to-face with him. His dark forest eyes almost glow, like the sun through a broad green leaf in the summer.

I lick my lips and his gaze drops.

"Cora?"

"Yeah. She ate. She laughed. She talked a bit about music. I think…" My gaze races over his face, and I wonder when he got so damn handsome. If he changed bit by bit or if it happened overnight.

Or maybe I'm the one who changed.

I hung around with lots of West's friends. Hell, I even had crushes on some of them. But with Ford, it was different.

The pull to him was less physical. Something deeper. He was alluring to me. A specimen I'd never encountered. He was intellectual and introspective, but there was a debonair quality about him, even as a gangly teenager.

He was challenging. Smart and cutting and always watching just a little too closely.

A mystery wrapped up in an enigma.

He felt *nothing* like the boys in this small town.

And now? Now he feels like no man I've ever met.

"Rosie?" He gives me a verbal nudge and I realize I trailed off while staring at his chiseled, manly features.

I clear my throat. "Yeah. Sorry. I think music might be a good common ground for you guys. She talked a bit about it today when I picked her up. I think she needs to feel like she's not a burden to you."

He nods and continues staring at me.

My skin does that awful itching thing, and I wonder if I'm allergic to Ford Grant. His proximity gives me a rash.

I touch my palm to my cheek and his eyes follow.

Apparently, a fever too.

"Why are you looking at me like that?" My words are a whisper in an already hushed night.

His gaze meets mine, and this time he's the one who licks his lips.

I watch the motion before adding, "You should stop."

His dark brows drop low on his forehead, two small lines popping up between them like he's concentrating. "I know."

My fingers press into the sides of the aluminum can in my hand hard enough that I hear it crinkle. It draws my gaze down. I can't handle staring at him anymore anyway.

"Are you single?" The second the words leave my lips, I hate myself for saying them. They're enough to make him draw away ever so slightly.

I hear the bristling of his stubble against his palm as he scrubs a hand over his mouth.

"Yes. Are you?"

I keep my eyes low; my breathing feels labored. Like it's hard work to keep from collapsing under the weight of his stare.

"I don't know."

And it's true. I've spent so long being a people pleaser—avoiding making any waves—that I'm terrified of disappointing the people I care about. But I know I'm done. I've finally come to terms with it. But telling Ford before I tell Ryan would be shitty. Where Ford and my personal life are concerned, vague is better. *Safer.*

He stands, calmly unfurling his powerful body, before stepping right in front of me and bending down to my level. His lips are a breath away, his eyes so deep and searching I can't hold his gaze.

Slowly, his hand comes up to grip my ponytail—just like he did the other night. But tonight, with one slow tug, he guides my head back so I'm forced to look at him. "Next time you ask me that, make sure you are."

Then he turns and walks away. Leaving me stunned and reeling even more out of control than I already was.

And when I get back to the bunkhouse, I'm too amped up to sleep. I thought the walk back would clear my head, but it only gave me time alone to fixate on our interaction. So, I pull out my old diary and hunker down for a walk down memory lane. Ryan never calls and I barely even notice. I'm far too invested in reading my teenaged musings on Ford Grant.

I laugh, I cry, and I fall asleep with the journal in my hand and my bedside lamp still lit.

CHAPTER 13

Ford

"I had fun last night," Cora announces in the quiet car.

"Me too."

"Can we do it again? Cook on the fire?" She peeks up at me, almost shyly. Like she's not used to asking for what she wants. Or like she thinks I might say no.

"Of course."

"Would you show me how to build the little pyramid thing with the paper and sticks?"

"Should I be at all concerned about your sudden interest in lighting fires?"

She scoffs and looks out the window. "It was nice. Cozy. It felt very… I don't know. Country?"

I turn into town, heading toward the junior high school. I know exactly what she means. Surrounded by wilderness. Water. Stars. You can have a fire in the city, but it just isn't the same. Too tidy, too sanitized. "I love that feeling too."

"Can we try my mom again today?"

"Of course," I say, resolving to call the facility *first* and make sure we call at a time that guarantees success.

She nods. And then I nod. But today, the silence isn't awkward. In fact, I feel like I made some headway last night. That we forged a small connection in what is otherwise a really fucking weird arrangement.

"How late did you and Rosie stay up last night?"

Rosie. Try as I might, I can't stop thinking about whatever that moment was last night. The tortured expression on her face as she watched my lips while telling me I shouldn't be looking at her like that.

Cora asks me the question casually enough, but I see her fingers fiddling with the straps of her backpack as she stares out the window.

"Not for much longer. She headed home. Work night or whatever. You'll see her after school."

She turns now, casting a suspicious glare my way. "Good. I like her."

"Me too."

"It's possible I like her more than you."

I bark out a laugh. "I don't blame you. She is far more likable than me."

"Pretty too."

Good lord. We're edging into dangerous territory. And all it takes is one quick glance to know that Cora is staring at me too hard for the comment to be offhanded.

I shrug. "She's Rosie Belmont," I say, like that explains the way she looks. The way she is. The way she always has been. "And my best friend's baby sister."

Then I change the subject right as we pull into the drop-off line. "Wanna listen to some samples with me this weekend? I've had a bunch sent to me since I announced the new company."

I can tell I've shocked her. But I can also tell that Rosie was right—a spark of interest flares in her hazel eyes.

Her oversized black hoodie has holes where she's pushed her thumbs through. She points at me and then at herself. "You want to listen to music with me?"

"Yeah. Thought it might be fun."

"Yes, please," she says simply. And then she opens the door and steps out, but before she goes, she swings her backpack over one shoulder and turns back to me with a smug smirk on her lips. "And just so you know, all the perv dads at pickup have noticed she's"—her fingers curl into sarcastic air quotes—"*Rosie Belmont*, too."

She smiles and slams the door in my face.

Leaving me stewing over the fact I now feel the need to accompany Rosie to the school for daily pickup.

"Pleeease," Rosie whines as she spins in her chair, staring up at the ceiling. There's something childish about the entire scene. The tone of her voice, her dramatic begging. But it's the way her hair trails behind her that has me staring. Brown, gold, silver—it's like every strand is a different color, and all darker at the root. Some come from the salon, no doubt, while others have probably changed in the sun.

I dated a girl who wouldn't go out in the sun without a

hat because she swore it ruined her color. I couldn't tell. But I liked her for more than her hair.

Too bad she liked me for my money.

"No, listen. The pay will be solid. Just come look at the place. You did a terrific job with my parents' house. On time, under budget, the whole thing. You're the cream of the crop for contractors."

She continues spinning, and I can just make out the dull, deep voice of someone on the line.

"I know there are other contractors in the area, but you beat them by a country mile. No comparison. You're a cut above."

Another turn in the office chair.

Rather than watching her, I really should work my way out from under the pile of emails I need to respond to. And I've got a metric fuck ton of sound equipment to order.

"I am not full of shit. Ask West—he'll tell you this is a great gig. And if you get called out for a fire, that's fine. We'll make do."

She finally catches sight of me, my shoulder propped against the doorway, and stops twirling. Her eyes move down and back up, taking me in with no shame. Likely as payback for what I said to her last night. "Yeah, I know West thinks that's a good idea. But West also thinks racing on a road with no guardrails and a cliff on one side is a smart idea. And you should see this guy. He's wearing a Rolex. And he styled his hair to look like it's mussed when it's not. He isn't going to join your bowling team. You wouldn't want him."

With a quick glance down at my wrist, I catch the glint

of my Rolex. The one I bought to celebrate having a million dollars in my investment account. All money I earned *myself*. It was the first stupid, frivolous thing I bought with my own cash.

I fucking love this watch.

And my hair *is* mussed because I was stressed while driving back here, worried what kind of footing I'd be on with Rosie after my moment of insanity last night.

I've really gotta stop pulling this girl's hair.

I jut my chin at her. "That's the contractor?"

"Yes, the contractor I like and trust," she says, raising her voice pointedly for the contractor's benefit.

I hear the guy mumbling something through the receiver on her cell.

"He says he'll do your office if you join the bowling team."

"Jesus. What is with these guys and their stupid bowling team?"

Her hand snaps up to cover the phone like I've said something downright sacrilegious. "Ford, that bowling team is like Fight Club or something. Invite only. Other dads don't get invited. It's *prestigious*." She sighs heavily and whispers, "I don't know why, but they take it seriously, so you'd better get your game face on if you're planning to join."

I've been mocking West's bowling team for almost two years now. And not being a dad has kept me safe from any invites. But now?

Now I don't have an excuse. I live here. And technically, I'm a dad.

I rake a hand through my hair, mussing it further. "Okay, tell him fine. Tell him that—"

Rosie opens her mouth to speak, but then pulls her phone away from her ear to look at the screen. "He said, 'See you tonight at seven,' and then hung up on me."

"Who is he?"

"Sebastian Rousseau."

"Do I know him?"

"Nah. He moved here a while back. He's an airtanker pilot. Came to town to fight a bushfire and loved it too much to leave. He works summers and picks up construction gigs when it's not fire season. He's kinda scary. But also nice."

"Why's he scary?"

"Cause he's a grumpy asshole."

"You tell me I'm a grumpy asshole."

"Well, next to Bash, you're a teddy bear."

I roll my eyes. "Well, call him back and tell him I can't do it tonight. I need time to find someone to watch Cora. I'm not leaving her alone when she just got here."

Rosie tosses her phone down on her desk. "I'll hang with her."

"You're going to spend a Thursday night hanging out with a twelve-year-old?"

"Why not? Is it somehow more badass when you do it?"

I bristle. I'm trying to play it cool, but I was looking forward to hanging out with her tonight. While stressing about Rosie on my drive back, I was also brainstorming dinner options.

"I told her we'd cook over the fire again."

"I'll ply her with pizza and a chick flick. She's young. She'll bounce back. Take one for the team, so we don't have to work in a place that smells like mold. You're not in the city anymore, Dorothy. Good contractors are not a dime a dozen. You can click your five-hundred-dollar Frye boots together all you want—these guys don't just pop up out of nowhere."

I give her a dry glare and walk over to my desk. As I toss my phone and planner down, a sheet lifts as the air wafts beneath it.

I pick it up and note the messy, loopy scrawl that fills the page. When my eyes catch on the date, I realize what I'm holding. The torn edge, the pale gray lines. Eighteen-year-old Rosie sat in my passenger seat writing on this exact page.

I turn to look at her, and her eyes are already on me. Amusement twists her lips.

"Did you rip this out of your journal?"

"Sure did." She crosses her legs, tall, black leather boots ending just below her knee.

"Why?"

"Because we touched on this exact entry the other night. You gonna read it? Or just stand here looking for something to disagree with me about? You'll love it. I was horribly malicious and judgmental as a teenager. Like, even I'm horrified by my own word choices."

I drop my eyes to the paper and read the first lines.

Dear Diary,

Travis Lynch is a piece of human garbage.

I glance at Rosie. "You sure I'm allowed to read it?"

She crosses her arms and her loose knit sweater stretches over her breasts in a way I should not be noticing. "Would be weird to put it on your desk if you weren't."

This is so us. We try to be nice to each other, and just end up exchanging verbal jabs. I shake my head in frustration and gaze down at the page.

> *Dear Diary,*
>
> *Travis Lynch is a piece of human garbage. Tonight, I showed up to the party at his place unexpectedly, and I walked in to find him with his dick down the throat of some summer vacation slut. I heard that broccoli makes cum taste bad, so I hope Travis has been eating all those greens he loves so much.*

I stop to peek up at Rosie, who is watching me raptly. "Does broccoli really make semen taste bad?"

With a light laugh, she shrugs. "Dunno. Never put that theory to the test."

I chuckle and keep reading.

> *Ford (who is usually a total dickhead) drove to pick me up when I called him crying. The drive should have taken him twenty minutes, but he was here in ten. Means he must have been out already, so I feel less bad*

*about ruining his Friday night. Based on the
way he won't look at me right now, I think he's
pretty pissed. I should feel bad, but I kind of
like pissing him off. So, it actually feels like a
bright spot for tonight.*

I glance at Rosie, shaking my head. "Some things never change. Huh, Rosalie?"

"Rosalie. So formal," she teases back.

I scoff, about to go back to reading, when I decide this might be the perfect moment to create some distance between us after last night. Lay down some ground rules. Formality isn't a bad thing between a boss and his employee. Especially when my control around her is shit, and she doesn't know if she has a boyfriend.

So, I focus on the journal page while the words tumble out, almost unbidden. "We're at work, and I'm technically your boss. We should keep things professional. If we were going to fuck, I'd call you Rosie. But we're not, so let's stick to Rosalie around the office and at any future business functions."

From the corner of my eye, I see her flinch. Unfortunately, I've always been awkward and abrupt around her—that's another thing that hasn't changed.

"Oh good, you're *still* a total dickhead," she mutters with a scoff.

My stomach turns, and I know what I said came out harsh. Way too fucking harsh. But I'm too chicken to look at her. If I look at her, I'll take it back. I'll look

at her like I did last night. I'll tell her things I shouldn't.
Reveal the thoughts and feelings I keep a padlock on. So
I let the charged silence hang between us and keep my
eyes latched onto the page as I finish the journal entry.

> *Cutting off Travis's dick for embarrassing*
> *me like that could also be a bright spot. Or his*
> *balls. I wonder which would be worse. If I cut*
> *off his dick, he'd be dickless. But I think losing*
> *the balls would make his dick not work, and*
> *that's probably worse.*
> *Anyway, this is pretty incriminating.*
> *I wonder if Ford will bail me out.*

That's where it ends. That's where she growled and tossed
the diary out the window. When I chance a peek back up
at her from across the office, she's glaring at me. I know the
expression well. That's the thing about Rosie—I can be a
total prick and she just gives it right back.

"Did I offend you?"

Her brow arches. "You've been offending me for years.
If you were too nice to me, I'd worry one of us was terminal
or something."

That makes my lips twitch.

"Plus, I'd never fuck you. I hate you too much."

Ah. There it is.

It shouldn't make me smile. But it does. She knows
exactly how to get under my skin, bring out the worst
in me.

I slide the page back across the desk toward her. "I like this one. It shows how truly unhinged you were."

"I still am. Better watch your back, Mr. Ford Grant Junior."

Oh yeah. I've pissed her off all right. But the thing about knowing how to piss each other off is that we also know how to confuse each other.

That's what last night by the fire was.

Mutual confusion.

And I must want more of it because I flip open my laptop and toss out, "That journal entry is fascinating, but all wrong. I was at home when you called that night. And I broke every speed limit to get to you."

CHAPTER 14

Ford

I REGRET THINKING IT WAS A GOOD IDEA TO WORK DIRECTLY across from Rosie all day. Keeping my eyes off of her is torture. Every sigh she lets out—and there are a lot of them today—draws my gaze.

But she never looks back, her focus entirely on the laptop before her. It's not even natural. I know she's refusing to look at me. And the only things she's said to me were work-related. She hasn't mocked me once.

So, I guess that's why we start emailing, even though we're both stuck here, facing each other.

Good morning, Mr. Grant,

I'm creating a budget for the renovation. How much do you have slated?
Please advise.

All my best,

Rosalie Belmont

Business Manager at Rose Hill Records

Hi, Rosalie,

Whatever it takes.

Ford Grant

CEO and Producer at Rose Hill Records

Mr. Grant,

I need numbers if I'm going to make you a budget.

And you need to add a closing greeting to your email signature. Otherwise, people will know you're a total dick.

All my best,

Rosalie Belmont

Business Manager to His Royal Dickness at Rose Hill Records

Hi, Rosalie,

I don't especially care if random people think I'm
a dick.

Numbers are attached here.

Have a happy day!

His Royal Dickness

CEO and Producer at Rose Hill Records

I hear a light chuckle when that one lands in her inbox.

Then we work in silence. She hums now and then, and I chew on my pen as I try to schedule sound engineers around a constantly moving timeline. I field an inquiry from a record label on the album I did with Ivory Castle. I scroll through more and more inquiries from interested artists as news of the new company spreads. A country starlet with a PR problem catches my attention. I've seen Skylar Stone in the news—everyone has. But that one email piques my attention all the same.

I've got a thing for rescues.

My pulse ratchets up when I see another email come in from Rosie.

Good afternoon, Dark Lord,

Attached is a spreadsheet with my anticipated
budget for the office and recording studio
renovation. One tab is budgeted, the next is

projected. I will work with the contractor and subcontractors to complete the latter.

Please advise on the feasibility and feel free to point out any issues you might find since I know how much you love to create problems where none exist.

All my best,
Rosalie Belmont
Business Manager at Death Eater Records

P.S. I'm hungry and leaving for lunch. You have a free hour to harvest souls or whatever while I'm away.

She's up and walking out the door when I fire off:

Rosalie,

Thank you for this. Lucky for you, I can multitask eating souls for lunch at my desk while I work.

Have a happy day!
Tom Riddle
CEO and Producer at Rose Hill Records

I know she has her email hooked up to her phone, so I'm not surprised when I hear her laugh from outside the door. Then she shouts, "It's really the *have a happy day* that gets me."

And I shake my head because it's hearing her laugh that gets me.

I wasn't lying when I said I don't care if random people think I'm a dick.

But Rosie Belmont isn't random people.

I'm snapping photos of the outside of the barn-slash-office so I can send them to the designer I used in the city for my bar. The goal is to maintain the mountain chalet feel of this place by preserving the barn's old wood.

I don't want it to look shiny and new and cookie-cutter.

I want *character*. I want music with character and a space that inspires it.

I'm imagining charming, matching cottages nestled in the trees where artists can use this space as a retreat. Mountains, lake, wilderness—a serene space to calm their minds and focus on their art, away from the glitz and glam of what can be an ugly industry.

The quiet out here. It's… profound. And I didn't realize how badly I needed it until I got here.

That's why the piercing sound of the office line ringing from inside makes me wince as it slices through my moment of peace.

Then it stops.

Then, "Hello, Ford Grant Junior's office."

My molars clamp down at the use of my name. I love my parents, but seriously, fuck them for keeping with that tradition.

"Oh my god, the *real* Ford Grant?" Rosie lets out a fake little squeal, and I freeze.

"Mr. Grant! It's been too long. How are you?"

My legs carry me over the craggy grass that surrounds the building and I march up the front steps, skipping one here and there to get inside faster.

When I fling the door open, I'm met with Rosie's wide, blue eyes, her hip cocked against the desk. It's brisk out today—it feels less like spring and more like winter—which is probably why she waves a hand at me to shut it.

"Oh, *baby* Ford? He's good. Working hard on this place and his scowl, as the case may be."

A beat of silence as her eyes wander over my features.

"I'm sure he's not ignoring you. Just—well, no, I'm here because he hired me."

Her lips press together, and I rake a hand through my hair. My dad means well, but he's fucking bossy sometimes, and we've butted heads many times.

"I hear what you're saying, Senior. But Ford's a big boy now, even though he sometimes acts like a little one, and if he requires your input, I'm sure he'll ask. He's a smart, responsible man, so we gotta trust him to make wise decisions. He's not actually dumb, even though he's pretty, ya know?"

I feel like my jaw is about to unhinge. Rosie stares down at the desk, twirling her finger, like she didn't just pay me two compliments and jump to my defense all in one breath.

"Are you and Gemma going to be out here this summer? Sure would be nice to see you guys. Been too long. Plus, rock stars age one of two ways: Sting or Keith Richards. Which way are you headed? I'm curious."

I hear my dad laugh through the phone. Not a single fucking boundary in Rosie's mind. In her head, he's not the world-famous guitarist from Full Stop. He's the dad from down the road.

"You're not as old as them? Well, shit. Isn't it funny how, when you're a kid, you view middle-aged people as super old?"

She nods and hums along with whatever he's saying.

"Sounds good. I'll let him know. Bye, Senior." Then she places the phone back on the receiver and looks me straight in the eye. "You owe me one."

I swallow roughly and nod. "Why'd you do that?"

She seems tired when her shoulders sag and her chin dips down. "Sometimes we need a minute to get our bearings before we have the big conversations, yeah?"

I'm not sure what to make of that. I'm not sure if we're talking about her or me.

Or us?

I brush that thought away. There is no us. Except in a work capacity.

"Plus, I'm allowed to rag on you, but I don't really like it when other people do it."

That sentiment should satisfy me. After all, she and I are nothing more than coworkers and reluctant friends. Or at least that's all we *should* be.

It's with that rule in my head that I round my desk only to stop when the sound of paper tearing fills the quiet office.

A quick glance up confirms that Rosie is striding toward me, diary in one hand, ripped page in the other. She drops it on my desk and taps her fingers on the sheet twice before she says, "I owed you one," and then spins on her heel back to her desk.

I watch her walk away, fingers itching to reach for the page. And when I do, I'm taken back to a day I remember well.

Dear Diary,

I'm having a bad day. Not as bad of a day as West. But it still feels pretty fucking bad to me.

I decided to take chemistry by correspondence this summer. Thought it would be cool to have a spare next year by getting ahead. And chem is hard. For some reason I thought doing it without all my other homework would make it easier. But I was wrong and now I realize that maybe I'm just a big, dumb masochist.

I failed my final. Failed the entire course. Had a big cry about it by myself. Partly because I'm disappointed in myself and partly because I'm dreading having to tell my parents because the report card requires their signature. I hate letting them down.

I almost did it too. Walked into the kitchen with the failing grade sheet in one hand and a pen in the other. Fully ready to apologize profusely for blowing it so badly.

Only to find them sitting at the table talking in very serious tones to West. There was a bag stuffed full of pot right in the middle of the table and Ford was standing in the corner looking like the human embodiment of a cringe.

I'm no chemistry genius. But I'm smart enough to piece together what was going on.

Still, my parents treated me like a baby. Asked Ford to take me out of the house because I "didn't need to hear about this stuff." And he's such a goody two-shoes that he just nodded and obeyed.

We sat on the dock in an uncompanionable silence. Him waiting for West, and me waiting for my parents. I guess he got bored because he finally asked me about the paper in my hand. And I was feeling just sorry enough for myself that I decided—fuck it, I'll just tell him. I've got nothing to lose.

So I did.

I expected him to make fun of me. God knows he probably hasn't failed a single class in his life. But he didn't say a word. Instead, he took the pen and paper and forged my mom's signature with alarming accuracy before sliding the sheet back across the dock toward me.

I just sat there staring at him like the slack-jawed idiot that I am while he gazed *out over the lake looking debonair and intelligent.*

Me staring must have gotten to him because eventually he said, "Sometimes we need a minute to get our bearings before we have the big conversations."

I bet he read that in one of his high-brow poetry books along the way. But I still said thank you before I left. Even though he refused to make eye contact.

Pretty sure he was only nice to me because he feels bad about how dumb I am.

But at least I can give my parents a break before I deliver more bad news this way.

My chest twinges. I hate that she felt as though she had to swallow her disappointments just to make things easier for everyone else.

"I never thought you were dumb," I announce, lifting my head to face her across the office. "And I knew your mom's signature from watching West practice it so he could forge it on similar notices."

All Rosie offers to that is a conspiratorial wink before focusing back on her computer screen.

"Did you ever tell them about the test?" I press.

Now she smiles but doesn't meet my gaze. "Nah. That one's our secret, Junior. I took it again the next semester and passed. Never did get that spare I was dreaming of though."

It strikes me that she's always been so committed to not letting anyone down that she may never have really learned to put herself first.

So that's exactly what I tell myself I'm doing when I tag along to school pickup. Keeping her company, putting her first, and keeping the "perv dads" from getting the wrong idea.

Because Rosie might think she knows what our secret is, but mine is that I loved sitting on that dock with her even back then.

CHAPTER 15

Ford

"My sister is babysitting for you?"

West sounds disbelieving as he turns the steering wheel of his truck with his palm.

"She's not babysitting. Cora is twelve. And Rosalie offered. They're having pizza and watching *Legally Blonde*."

He snorts. "Rosie never offers to babysit for me."

"That's because one of your kids is feral and—" I stop what I'm saying, realizing I've stepped in it.

West just chuckles. "Don't be weird. You can say it. One is feral, and the other doesn't talk."

"I mean, he talks to you and Mia."

"Doesn't much help a babysitter, though, does it?" His tattooed fingers rap against the steering wheel. "Fine by me. Smart kid. He'll do it when he's good and ready. Then we'll all be wishing he'd shut up."

Leave it to West to be totally nonplussed by his son's

selective mutism. Where I'd be giving myself anxiety and researching the hell out of every option out there, West just goes with it, following his son's lead.

"Ollie is lucky to have you."

West grins almost maniacally. "Nah. I'm lucky to have him. That kid has taught me a lot about life."

And I don't doubt it. Becoming a dad changed West. Put him on a different path. He and Mia may not have been written in the stars, but he and those babies were. I think they might have saved him, actually. It wasn't until they came around that he stopped doing crazy, dumb shit.

"You missed the turnoff," I say when we blow past the bar on the lake. The one that has a bowling alley in the basement. Arcade games. Pool tables and a restaurant upstairs.

West scoffs. "No, I didn't. That's where the tourists go. Rose Valley Alley is where Dads' Night Out happens."

Fuck me, this is cheesy. "Do you really call it Dads' Night Out?"

"Yeah. What the fuck else would I call it? 'Grown men who have children meet at a bowling alley one night every other week'?"

Every other week?

"Yeah, man. It's a league. Ladies' Night is one Thursday, Men's Night is the next. We take a short break between seasons. This is spring season."

"I thought it was once a month or something."

"Dude, you're lucky it's not once a week. In a bigger town it would be."

I gape at my friend. We've always stayed in touch and

met up here or in the city. We may not have always been based in the same place, we may even be opposites, but West is my longest-standing friend. And absolutely my most loyal.

But this bowling obsession? I don't know what to make of it.

"Lucky. Right."

West laughs at my clear dread, and before I know it, we pull up in front of an old building on the side of the highway. Drilled onto the top frame, at the roof, is a large cut-out of two bowling pins and a bowling ball, creating an unusual silhouette against the setting sun and the mountains' peaks. Neon signs flash out front, advertising everything from "OPEN" to "NEON BOWLING" to "WINGS N BEER."

We park and follow a dock-like wooden walkway to the front door.

Inside, balls crash against wood and the sign out front didn't lie—it indeed smells like wings and beer. A piece of cardboard taped to one post near the front desk proclaims, "Welcome to Men's League," and I can't help but laugh.

This is so… small town.

"Weston, how ya doin', pal?" a large man with pink cheeks and a bright smile calls out from behind the till.

I try not to stare at how the buttons on his striped bowling shirt look ready to burst.

"Just great, Frankie. Got a fourth for the team here. Can we do all the registration paperwork after?" West hikes a thumb toward the lanes, where people are milling about. "I'd rather get him introduced to the gang."

"You bet. You're on six tonight," the man replies before shifting his attention to me. "What's your shoe size?"

"Thirteen? Do bowling shoes fit differently?"

The man chuckles and pulls out a pair of shoes, tossing them on the countertop. "Here ya go, big fella. They should fit."

I grab them and follow West farther into the alley, feeling like a nervous kid heading to a brand-new school. I think of Cora. Her fearlessness. If she can waltz into a new town and a new school and a new house with a dude she barely knows, I can join a fucking bowling league.

"Here we go." West slaps my shoulder as he gestures me forward. "Guys, this is Ford."

A man with close-cropped dark hair, a few streaks of gray in it, glances up from where he sits tying his shoes. He's got dark eyes, an unfriendly face, and where he's not as tall as I am, he's got a bulk that I don't. He looks like he hates me, and I haven't even opened my mouth yet.

"That's Bash," West says. "Or Sebastian. But the full name is a mouthful, ya know?"

Oh good. My new contractor.

"And this here"—West pushes an old, wiry man toward me—"is Crazy Clyde."

Crazy Clyde is wearing a dirty trucker hat with the Rose Valley Alley logo on it and a suspicious glare on his face. It still seems like just calling him Clyde would be less of a mouthful.

"Who's this?" The man's watery eyes narrow.

"My friend Ford," West explains. Again.

"Fords are shit cars. Can't trust 'em."

"Well, good thing I'm not a car." I smirk back at him.

West laughs. But no one else does.

"Where you from?"

"Calgary originally, I guess."

The man makes a spitting motion. "City folk. Can't trust 'em."

"Clyde, shut up." It's the first thing Bash says as he finishes tying his shoes.

"Don't trust you either. I told you the Denver airport is the Illuminati headquarters, and you went there anyway. And you…" He spins on West. "You're too fuckin' happy. Jokin' around all the time. It's like you don't even care that the government is tracking you on that phone you carry everywhere."

West pulls his phone out and waves it in front of Clyde. "This one? They can go ahead and track me. They'll get real bored, real fast." He turns to me. "Clyde lives on the other side of the mountain with no electricity or running water. But he makes an exception for beer on tap every other Thursday."

Clyde grumbles something that sounds an awful lot like *you mouthy little shit* before he turns away to take a sip of his beer. I don't know whether to laugh or just stand here in stunned silence. Clyde is truly a walking, talking mountain-town stereotype.

I turn wide eyes back to West and blurt out the first thing that comes to mind. "Does Rosie know about him?" She'd have a blast talking to this guy.

West snorts and waves a server over. "She knows about him but has yet to meet him. That would be quite the showdown."

As West orders us a couple of beers, another man approaches. He's tall. Taller than me, which is unusual at six foot three. But this guy does it. Long legs, long arms, even his neck appears to be unusually long.

Bash stands, coming to my side to face him. He crosses his arms and says nothing. He'd look tough if not for the two-tone bowling shoes on his feet.

"Hi. I'm Too Tall," the man says. "The team captain for the High Rollers. We'll be playing each other tonight."

He sticks his hand out, and I laugh as I shake it because that was a weird introduction.

The tall dude doesn't laugh. And neither does Bash. They stare off like this is fucking serious.

"I'm Ford. I don't think you're too tall at all. What's your name?" I ask as I draw my hand away to the sound of West's snicker behind me.

"Too Tall."

I blink. This guy can't be serious. He wants me to call him Too Tall as his actual name?

"Right, but what's your big-boy name?" That gets me an amused grunt from Bash and a sneer from *Too Tall*.

Without telling me his real name, he turns and walks away, tossing a parting snipe over his shoulder. "Good luck tonight. You're gonna need it."

That's all it takes. One petty sentence, and I'm suddenly very invested in this bowling league. Because fuck this guy and his dumb nickname and his high school attitude and his bowling shirt, which matches all the guys he walks back over to.

West hands me a beer and laughs. "I fuckin' hate Too Tall."

Bash nods.

"Can't trust 'em. Neck is unnaturally long," Clyde grumbles.

And me? I hold my beer up, a toast to the opposing team. "Thanks, Stretch! Appreciate it."

"Stretch." Bash huffs out the word, and it *almost* sounds like amusement coming from him. "I like that."

We don't beat the stupid High Rollers in their stupid matching outfits, but I have a hell of a lot more fun than I thought I would.

CHAPTER 16

Rosie

CORA YAWNS SO WIDE THAT I WONDER IF IT HURTS. HER
hands curl into fists and her dark lashes flutter shut. I smile
softly at her, propped up against the opposite arm of the
couch. For all her sarcastic one-liners and no-nonsense per-
sona, she looks very young right now.

I wonder when she last got a hug. The last one I got was
from my dad when I pulled up unexpectedly at my parents'
house.

"I liked this movie," she announces, settling into the
couch as we bask in Elle Woods' victory.

I push my feet, clad in fuzzy socks, under her blanket
and give her legs a slight nudge. "It's all the pink isn't it, my
little storm cloud?"

She scoffs and rolls her eyes, nudging my legs back with
her own. "I don't hate pink."

I curve a teasing brow at her.

Her eyes flash up to the neon scrunchie in my hair. "I think it looks nice on you."

"Thank you."

"But you're pretty. It makes sense."

My head tilts as I regard her. We had a fun night. It was wholesome. We ate too much pizza. I did up root beer floats for us. We made fun of Ford behind his back and laughed. She even told me about school, where she's found two other little storm clouds to roam with. And I love that for her.

What I don't love is what she just told me.

"*Anyone* can wear pink, Cora. And you? You aren't just pretty, you're beautiful. Inside and out. And that has nothing to do with the colors you wear"—I wave a hand over her—"or in your case, shades. You could wear pink if you wanted."

Her eyes drop and her fingers fiddle with the blanket as the credits roll across the screen.

"Do you ever feel like you… like you… I don't know. Just want to re-create yourself?"

God. Damn. Talk about an unknowing punch to the gut.

"You're talking to the girl who freaked out and fled her life less than a week ago. So yeah, I know that feeling. I've done it successfully a few times."

Cora nods, a question on her face as she rolls her lips together.

This time, I rub my foot against her leg to reassure her. "Hey, Cora."

She lifts her eyes to look at me.

"Pink and black go great together. If you want to wear pink, do it. Ten out of ten you can pull it off. I mean, come on. You've got the genetics of the World's Hottest Billionaire."

At that, she huffs out a giggle, dropping her chin shyly.

"If anyone says anything, just scowl at them and say, 'Do you even know who I am?'"

Now she laughs.

"I'd milk the hell outta that title if I were you."

"You could too, if you wanted." Her eyes dance with amusement, and my gaze flicks back and forth between them.

"I don't think I look young enough to convince people that Ford is my daddy."

I broke every speed limit to get to you.

That fucking sentence has played on repeat in my head all day. I've thought about it countless times, to the point I'm not sure it holds any meaning anymore.

Except... the fact I'm obsessing over it does mean something.

But did it mean something coming from *him*? Or was it off the cuff? Was it even true, or was he fucking with me?

Right back down the rabbit hole I go.

"Are you going to go back to the city?" Cora's question drags me out of my spiral.

"Sorry?"

"Are you going to move back?"

"Wow. Most people get to warm up with simple kid questions before they get hit with the hard-hitting ones."

"Sucks to be you," Cora says with a snotty little shrug.

I can't decide if that makes me want to laugh or cry, so I

prop my head back on the couch and stare up at the wooden beams stretching across the ceiling. "I don't know. I feel this pressure to live that city life. Ya know? I'm the first person in my family to go to university. Staying here in Rose Hill would have been simple, but I made it out. I did the thing. It feels counterproductive to come back here in some ways. And yet…"

"And yet?"

My lips quirk. This girl should become a journalist with all her hard-hitting questions.

"And yet I love it here. It feels like home. The condo in the city doesn't. That life doesn't. It feels like I'm in a race that I don't give a flying fuck about winning. One I'm signed up for just to say I took part."

"What about your *boyfriend*?" She says the word with a dose of disdain I didn't see coming.

Next time you ask me that, make sure you are.

That's the sentence I obsessed over last night. That sentence is the reason I stayed up all night reading my journal. Trying to affirm to myself that I have all these entries that prove Ford and I hate each other the way we've always said we do.

But now, as an adult, I'm not sure they read that way at all.

I went looking for proof there's nothing between us, and all I found was evidence to the contrary. I feel like one of those cartoon characters with stunned eyes and question marks circling above their head.

"Ryan?"

"Yeah."

I'm starting to think he's avoiding me. I messaged him today. Told him that if he couldn't make it out here sooner, I wanted to come back for a visit next weekend. I left out the part about how by visit I meant break up. But apparently, he's going to be away with work. *Again.*

"You asked me about re-creating yourself, and I think that he and I both have. We've changed, our lives have changed. Sometimes you grow together, and sometimes you grow apart. If I go back, it won't be for him—it will be for myself."

It's the first time I've given voice to that realization. I've thought about it a lot. Maybe I've been dragging it out longer than necessary, paralyzed by feelings of obligation. But you don't just blow up a two-year relationship with a decent person without sleeping on it—without being sure.

Somewhere along the way, I've come to realize I wasted a lot of years chasing a life I thought I was supposed to have. Spent a lot of time checking off milestones I thought I was supposed to reach. Achieving goals I thought were supposed to make me feel like I'd finally accomplished something.

I was chasing a fantasy that was supposed to satisfy me. And Ryan was part of that fantasy—the one I was supposed to want.

But now, I know I don't want what I'm supposed to. And there's no coming back from that. I'm going to look him in the eye, say it to his face, and give him a hug when I end it. I respect him enough for that.

"That's very mature of you." Cora nods like she's impressed, and I clear my throat to cover a laugh.

"Thank you," I say simply. "And you know, if I move back, you don't have to worry. Ford was adamant about coming with me to pick you up today, so he knows what to do. You're in good hands."

Cora snorts and hides behind her hands as she bursts into a fit of girlish giggles. "That's not why he went with you."

My face scrunches in confusion. "What do you mean? Of course it is."

"No." Cora grins, mischief dancing in her eyes. "It's because I told him about all the other perv dads eyeing you up."

I scoff. "Ford doesn't care about that."

"Don't re-create yourself as someone oblivious, Rosie. It doesn't suit you." She pats me on the leg like I'm dumb, hops off the couch, and gives me a quick and borderline awkward hug. "Thanks for tonight. I had fun. Even with all the pink."

Then she's off to bed.

And I'm left spiraling, just like I have been for the past twenty-four hours.

I wake to the feel of calloused fingers gently pushing my hair behind my ear. A corduroy pillow, both velvety and ribbed, rubs against my cheek. The smell of fried chicken, beer, and sandalwood swirls in my nostrils.

When I pry my eyes open, I'm faced with Ford looking rugged and heart-stopping as he sits on the coffee table watching me. Broad shoulders straining against his brown leather jacket, strong thighs filling out a pair of faded blue jeans. Even his stupid, expensive leather boots are still on his feet.

Like he saw me lying here when he walked in and came straight for me.

I broke every speed limit to get to you.

"Hey," I murmur as I sit up. "Sorry. I fell asleep once Cora went to bed. Not before—I swear I was responsible."

He smiles softly and reaches forward as if to stroke my hair again, but he quickly withdraws and props his elbows on his knees. "I know you were."

"How was bowling?" I ask, pulling in a deep breath, trying to wake myself up.

The grin he hits me with is almost blinding, especially since he usually keeps it hidden behind a scowl.

"Are you drunk?"

"No." He rakes a hand through his hair with a raspy chuckle. "I just… I had fun. It was stupid, but also… relaxing? Social?"

I'm suddenly aware of how dim the light is, how quiet the house is, and how close we are.

I'm suddenly self-conscious as hell.

"Right on." I wince. That sounded dumb. "Well, I, uh, yeah. I'm happy to do a girls' night with Cora on the days you have bowling."

With a hushed laugh, I unfold my body and stand. The couch and the table are so close I find myself standing between his knees. His green eyes glow like he's drinking me in for the first time, his stubble just the right length to lend him a slightly unpolished look.

"What's so funny?"

"You. *Bowling.*" I drag my front teeth over my bottom lip.

His eyes trace the motion and my skin itches. "You can crash here if that's easier. You could just… sleep over on those nights."

When I glance down, his fingers are clamped onto his thighs, bracketing where I stand between them.

I'm struck by the whiteness of his knuckles. The clear tension in his body. I wonder what he'd do to me with those hands if he just let go.

Next time you ask me that, make sure you are.

I clear my throat and think of West. I think of Ryan. I think of what a mess I am right now and resolve that no one needs my current personal life added to their plate.

Then I step around his knee.

"Oh, nah. I'll get outta your hair. I just want to check on Cora before I go."

"Rosie, wait." Before I can step out from between his legs his hands let go. They go from gripping that table to holding me in place. One big, strong palm on the outside of each thigh.

All the air freezes in my lungs, but the skin beneath my leggings sizzles with throbbing heat.

I can't look away from it.

His hands.

My legs.

It makes me want to step closer. But instead, I just focus on forcing myself to keep breathing and watch. He does the same. When I peek at him, he appears entranced. Motionless.

Seconds pass, but neither of us moves. My heart beats so hard it aches.

And then he finally sucks in a ragged breath and turns his eyes up to me. They're wild, and green, and brimming with heat. "Thank you. For all your help."

I offer him a simple, speechless nod. I feel his fingertips pulse on my legs, and that spurs me to step away from him. His hands lose contact, and I fight the urge to move back into them.

"I'll be right back," I whisper with a soft tremor to my voice. His head doesn't turn to follow my motion, but he nods all the same.

With a deep breath, I dash upstairs, deciding not to overthink what was a simple thank you. We've touched before. It's nothing new. And I can't go there right now anyway.

I wince as the floorboards creak beneath me letting out a sigh of relief when I poke my head into Cora's room. With her black sheets and bright red lava lamp, it really feels like Dracula's lair in here.

But I pull my hair down and drop the neon-pink scrunchie on her bedside table all the same before taking a moment to watch her. She looks downright sweet when she's sleeping.

She's pretty enough to wear any fucking color she wants. And as I watch her sleeping form, I make a silent vow to teach her as much.

When I turn to leave, I skid to a halt. Because Ford followed me up here and has caught me basically baby-gazing at his sleeping daughter. An expression has fallen over his face that I can't quite place. It's soft. Laced with longing.

We exchange no words, but as I pass him, his hand hovers over the small of my back. A whisper of a touch—nothing more.

He trails me down the stairs and goes for my jacket, holding it up with that signature bitchy look back on his face. Right where it belongs.

"I'm walking you home," he whispers roughly.

There's no *may I*, there's no *Rosie would you like*—it's just a fact. This is what he's doing, and I suspect if I told him not to, he'd ignore me and do it anyway.

So, I shrug and say, "Okay," before sliding my arms into the sleeves.

We step out into the cool night and turn toward the lake. I could take the main road, but step for step, it's probably three times as far. Plus, I love to pass by the water. Especially when it's dark out like tonight. When the soft lapping against the shore is the loudest thing within earshot and the crescent moon casts a shimmering reflection off the inky water.

There is water in Vancouver but not like this. Not water like glass. Not water that smells like fresh rain.

"You can leave me here," I say when we get to the fence line. "I may go hang on the dock for a bit."

Try to get my bearings.

But Ford doesn't pick up on my need for space. Instead, he nods and follows me onto the dock, hands shoved into his jean pockets.

I could tell him to get off my dock, stomp my feet,

fall back into our comfortable bickering, but I'm too tired tonight. There's a softness between us right now that I don't want to ruin.

And whether or not I want to admit it to myself, I like that he followed me out here.

We both stop at the edge of the dock. Side by side, taking it in.

"I missed this," I murmur.

He's quiet for a few beats, and then, "Same."

"It's so… uncivilized out here. It's hot, it's cold, there's snow, there's fire. Bears, cougars, leeches. I missed the heart-pounding excitement of being somewhere so untamed. We were so carefree when we were kids here, weren't we?"

From the corner of my eye, I see him give a stern nod. "The city gets monotonous. It changes you. You adapt. And you almost forget what this feels like."

My heartbeat quickens. I know he's talking about living in the city, but somehow my brain interprets it as more. I don't think I forgot what this place feels like. I was just so focused on being the bright spot for my family—the fun-loving, career-driven child—that I ignored any twinges of longing I had for it.

"Do you think you'll go back?" He rocks on his feet as he says it.

"Cora asked me the same thing tonight."

"Yeah? What did you tell her?"

"That this feels like home."

"The job is yours for as long as you want it."

I grin up at him. "Until I drive you crazy enough that you lose it and fire me."

He snorts. "Do your worst, Belmont. But we should make it more official. I'll file that résumé and you can send me your references. Then no one can ever say you got a handout."

I freeze. *References*. Why had I not thought of references?

I want to hug him for knowing I'd never want to be perceived as getting a handout. And I want to pull the tiny hairs at the back of his neck for reminding me that my references are royally fucked.

My breathing speeds up as my anxiety rises. Again, I'm forced to think about a split second in time, an unwanted advance that should be easy to get over. But I'm not over it. I hear that sharp intake of breath echo in my ears and am transported to that boardroom all over again.

"You all right?"

I hear the concern in his voice. Usually, I'd want to do everything in my power to avoid this kind of attention. To smooth things over and not be a problem for anyone.

Maybe it's too quiet, maybe I'm too tired, maybe I trust Ford more than I ever realized and that's why I've never felt the need to be perfect for him.

But I respond with a quiet, "No."

That one word has him turning to face me. "What's going on?"

Tears prick at my eyes, spurred by embarrassment. A heat in my chest that feels like it could choke me as it spreads to my throat. "I can't give you my references. Or at least not what should have been my best ones."

"Why not?"

His voice is harsh now, yet I know deep down it's not directed at me.

Has it ever been?

"Because I got fired." The words spill from my lips, and it's such a relief to confide in someone instead of walking around with it all bottled up and feeling guilty.

"Why the fuck would they fire you?"

I nibble at my bottom lip and tears gather on my bottom lashes. One blink and they'll fall. So I don't look at Ford. I keep my eyes on the water.

"My boss had a bad case of wandering hands, and I told him where he could shove it. I'm not sure of the company's inner workings beyond that point, but he clearly got to HR before I did. The company decided it was easier to let me go without cause than hear my side."

He says nothing, but I can feel his gaze on me.

I shrug. "So I can give you their contact information, but I doubt they'll have many nice things to say about me."

I blink, and two fat tears lurch over my lashes. I imagine the sound of them in my head. *Bloop, bloop.*

With a forced smile, I reach up to wipe them away.

Ryan hadn't known what to say when they fired me. I'd cried, and he'd assured me something better would come along.

Ford doesn't give me pretty words that do nothing to make it better. Instead, he reaches for me gruffly and tugs me against his chest. One strong arm clamps over my shoulders and the other wraps around the back of my head, like he's shielding me.

For the second time tonight, I feel his fingers in my hair. And for the second time tonight, I take a deep inhale of his heady, masculine scent.

For the second time tonight, tears fall.

And I don't stop myself from nuzzling against his chest. His cotton shirt soaks up my tears and I roll the silver chain hanging from his neck between my fingers. I feel the pendant against my cheek.

"I'm a mess. My life is a mess. I got fired. I've spent two years of my life with a perfectly decent man, and I don't know how to tell him I'm not in love with him anymore. I'm living in my brother's shitty bunkhouse and cooking on a hot plate. I eat chips every day. I'm swimming in a sea of student debt. I feel guilty all the time, for abandoning my life, for running away, for *failing*. And I'm so tired, Ford. I'm so fucking tired."

His stubble prickles at my scalp as he presses a kiss to my hair and nuzzles his cheek on the top of my head. "Just rest for a minute then, Rosie. I got you."

His words only make me cry harder.

I don't know how long we stand here while Ford lets me fall apart in his arms. Taking all my anguish so I don't need to carry it around myself.

His hand never stops stroking my head. Even when my tears run dry.

I feel spent. Dopey. Like I could fall asleep right here.

"Lately, I've wondered if I'd have been better off rising above the whole thing," I say against the safety of his chest. "Ignoring it."

I'm talking about the job, the assault, and he knows it.

His arms tighten around me, and his voice comes out like pure venom when he says, "No one should ever have made you feel like it's your job to rise above this. You're allowed to process however you need to, Rosie. But me? I'm going to ruin them."

Ford's rough words wash the anxiety from my body, and I sigh. "Please don't tell anyone. Only you and Ryan know. And I don't want to rehash this all."

He stiffens and his voice is chill when he asks, "And what did Ryan do about it?"

"I don't need anyone to do anything about it," I answer vaguely, burying my face against him even harder, like I have only once before in my life. I was scared then too. "Just telling you feels good."

His only response is to kiss my hair again and hold me for a few more seconds.

Then Ford lets me go and walks me to my door like a perfect gentleman. And when I crawl into bed, I don't replay any of his words. With that secret off my chest, safe in Ford's capable hands, I finally relax and sleep like the dead.

Because as much as I don't need a knight in shining armor to defend my honor, I'm relieved I have one who feels compelled to do so.

CHAPTER 17

Ford

I'm tired. Tired from a night spent researching Stan Cumberland and Apex Construction Materials—all of which I found on Rosie's LinkedIn profile. After I put the Rage Against the Machine version of "How I Could Just Kill a Man" on full blast in my AirPods, I went on a hunting expedition to find out everything I could about the guy.

I just dropped Cora off at school. This morning, she got to talk to her mom on the phone again. She found out we'll be able to go for a visit soon, and that news lightened her entire demeanor. Then she talked about Rosie the whole way to school. A literal stream of consciousness. I have never seen the girl talk more.

It affirmed the fact that we are probably both obsessed with Rosalie Belmont. The only difference is I'm not the one wearing her bright-pink scrunchie this morning.

Cora is.

I can't help but smile as I watch her bounce into school. Black and gray from head to toe, but with a blinding pop of pink to tie off the thick braid hanging down her back.

I think about watching Rosie go back to leave that scrunchie for Cora. A token of something I wasn't privy to. And I don't need to be. Seeing the way Cora smiled when she came down this morning with it in her hair was enough to know it meant something to them.

I spend the drive back to work running through the list of emails I need to respond to. The calendar I need to create based on a recording studio that has a constantly changing completion date. The inroads I need to make with different labels so that the music I produce doesn't just languish here in the mountains. The contracts I need to draw up, the orders I need to sign off on, the bills I need to pay for both the studio *and* the bar.

All that is to say, I spend the drive stressing out about all the things in my life I can't control. So naturally, when I walk into work, the first place my eyes go is to Rosie's desk. It's empty, which is just as well. She doesn't need me panting around after her when she already has so much on her shoulders. I hope she slept in.

But when I get to my desk, I know she hasn't. Because there's another torn page from her journal on my desk. I can't help but laugh when I pick it up and read the yellow Post-it note on top. It says, "Thanks for last night. You owed me one anyway."

Confused, I remove the sticky piece of paper and read on.

Dear Diary,

Today I broke my thumb on some vacation bitch's face. West had to drive me to the hospital because Mom and Dad were both working.

You'd think he'd be worried about me, but nope. He told me he was disappointed I didn't know how to make a proper fist. He told me I should have pulled her hair instead. I foresee some very questionable fighting lessons in my future based on the way he ranted about how the thumb never goes inside the fist.

How was I supposed to know? I've never hit someone. Happy, good girl Rosie doesn't hit people. Truthfully, I've never felt inclined before today.

I'm sad because I'm sure my upcoming volleyball season is fucked.

But I'm not sad I punched her.

I lied and told everyone she insulted Tabitha's family by making comments about Erika. I only said that because I knew no one would talk about it. That tale is one of those small-town stories that only gets whispered about behind closed doors.

The truth is, she said Ford could be hot if he lost the glasses and found a personality.

She must be stupid because Ford looks just fine, and his personality is good too. She's probably just embarrassed because he said something funny and she needed her airhead friend to draw a cartoon to explain it to her.

Plus, I'm allowed to rag on him. But I don't like it when other people do.

Heard she's fine. Which means I'll punch her again next time I see her. But with my thumb on the outside.

I must read it three times. It makes less sense every time. Based on the date, Rosie was seventeen and I was nineteen going on twenty when she wrote this. This was our prime bickering era. Her parents worked a lot, and West always included her. She tagged along everywhere with us. I'd have been the same with Willa had we been closer in age, but the five years between us changed that dynamic. And she was often off competing at horse shows in the summer while I bummed around in Rose Hill.

Bummed around in Rose Hill and tried my damnedest to keep from falling in love with Rosalie Belmont.

I'm still trying.

Which is why I shove any feelings about this journal entry down deep—where they belong—and toss the page into the top drawer of my desk.

I walked in here, bound and determined to give her the

space and respect she needs to work through this bumpy phase of her life. To support her in any way I can. And to smile when she spreads her wings and takes off again.

Because I'm a grown-ass man. A *dad*. I can be mature.

Which is why I slump down in my chair and make the phone call I've been putting off for far too long now.

A single swipe and my phone rings. Once. Twice.

"Ford!" My mom's smoky voice fills my ear and I smile.

"Hi, Mom."

"How's my boy?"

"Well, as it turns out, I have a daughter."

I decided earlier that ripping the Band-Aid off would be the best approach.

"And such a knack for delivering big news," she says.

I knew my mom would be the one to talk to. Where Dad would blow up and calm down eventually, Mom is the steady Eddie. That's always been our dynamic. Plus, the older I get, the less I want them meddling in my business. I know they mean well, but it irks me all the same.

"Figured it was best to just come out with it."

"I imagine if you'd done that, we wouldn't be having this conversation." She laughs, amused by her own wisecrack. Something I've grown accustomed to with a sex therapist as a mother.

"I donated sperm when I was nineteen."

"You always have been charitable under that crabby exterior."

"Mom."

"I'm sorry. No one prepared me for this conversation.

And that's really saying something considering the things I hear on a daily basis. Care to elaborate on why you were donating sperm? Based on the number of times I found you doing your own laundry with a bright red face, I assumed you were mostly making your donations at home."

"Fuck my life." I scrub a hand over my face, wishing the floorboards would give out and drop me down into a dark hole. "I needed money to buy my ticket to the Rage Against the Machine concert. Dad wouldn't spot me any cash."

Mom sighs heavily. "Well, you sure showed him."

My cheek twitches. That's the exact same thing Cora said.

"Right. Well, anyway, she's living with me right now. And will be around for the foreseeable future. So if we could not talk about her like she's a burden, I'd appreciate it."

That brings on some silence. Like the reality of it is really sinking in.

"I'm sorry. I didn't mean it that way. Have… have you crossed your t's and dotted your i's?"

I know this is her gentle way of asking if I'm being responsible from a legal perspective. I've got a lot of assets to consider now, as my lawyer reminded me repeatedly.

"I have. Her name is Cora. And, well, she wants to meet you. And Dad."

"Yes, this will be special news to break to your father." I can hear the amusement in her tone. "You conveniently called me at the time of day when you know he works out. Am I meant to let him know? Using your mother as a shield in your thirties is kind of cheap."

"You know how Dad is. He's like Willa. They fly off the fucking handle, and then they calm down and get to work. You know he'll be here wearing his World's Best Grandpa T-shirt in a matter of days. I just don't need him to call in the cavalry to save me from this, okay?"

She laughs now. "No doubt about that. Except we're in Portugal for another few weeks. Then we'll spend the summer in Rose Hill... You know, I'm really excited to meet her. Why don't you tell me more about her?"

I'm ready to launch in, already feeling the relief of talking to my mom. "So she's—"

"No. First, how are *you*? My boy. How are you holding up?"

I shrug in the empty office, and all it does is remind me of Cora. *How am I?*

I'm like Rosie. I'm a mess. But I'm keeping it together.

However, I don't tell her that. I opt for, "I'm all right, Mom."

And then I gush about my daughter.

Mr. Grant,

Just a heads-up that I'm helping Sebastian pick up supplies and will be back in the office shortly. But I wanted to touch base while I wait at the hardware store (so boring!).

I've been thinking a lot about merchandising opportunities and took it upon myself to have something drawn up. Attached here is a possible design for a company sweatsuit.

Based on the number of emails the info account gets from female fans I think this could be a great item to offer when the new website goes live. There are plenty of merchandising opportunities for us to explore but, as a woman, I can tell you that I would wear the hell out of this. Artists might like them too! We could even do them as Christmas gifts or something.

Please let me know if you have any thoughts or feedback.

All my best,
Rosalie Belmont
Business Manager at Rose Hill Records

Rosalie,

These sweatsuits are pink. The logo has flowers. And the name of the company isn't even listed.

Have a happy day!
Ford Grant
CEO and Producer at Rose Hill Records

Mr. Grant,

The pink and the flowers are pretty and feminine and directed at the people who will be purchasing. Maybe we can make a manly version for you with a big, lifted truck and those steel balls that some men like to hang from their back bumper? If you're interested, I would be happy to get that sample drawn up! You would look downright dashing in blue.

And I'm so glad you brought up the company name. It's not on there because I'm wondering if you want to go back to the drawing board on Rose Hill Records? I feel like everything in this town is called Rose Hill something or other. It's very on the nose, you know? Kind of... uninspired.

Looking forward to hearing your thoughts on this. If you're scowling at me upon my return, I'll know I've gone too far. But it needed to be said.

You're welcome,
Rosalie Belmont
Business Manager at Rose Hill Records
Located in Rose Hill, British Columbia (duh, obviously)

Rosalie,

I appreciate how enterprising you are. You can have the sweatsuit. Especially can't wait to receive my manly one for Christmas. It sounds exquisite.

But I'm not renaming my company.

Have a happy day!
Ford Grant
CEO and Producer at Rose Hill Records (and that's final.)

"I'm here! And I brought Sebastian!" Rosie announces as she waltzes through the door to the old barn, with my bowling teammate following behind.

Where she's all smiles, he's all frowns. But his frown isn't nearly as deep as when he scowled at Stretch last night.

Bash tips his chin at me and says, "Gonna take a look around," rolls up the sleeves of his thick plaid shirt and storms off like he's on a hunt for someone to fight with.

"He's charming, right?" Rosie whispers conspiratorially as she approaches my desk.

I lean back in my chair, like the extra distance between us will help me want her less.

Spoiler alert, it doesn't.

I steeple my hands beneath my chin and regard her. She's

doing that thing she always done where she acts extra chipper to smooth out any ripples. I've watched her do it with West as a teenager and now she does it so naturally I wonder if she even notices. It's like she thinks her problems aren't worthy of attention and solving because they might be inconvenient to other people.

And in that she'd be wrong.

Her glossy smile doesn't hide the skin around her eyes that's still puffy from her tears. My chest aches at the thought of her crying alone in that old dingy bunkhouse. And I can't even bring myself to scowl at her over the suggestion that I rename the company.

Aside from that, she's polished from head to toe. Hair ironed straight. Wide-leg dress pants in a camel color, topped with a soft, creamy sweater. A gold necklace dangles around her neck, and I remember the way her fingers felt gripping my chain last night on the dock.

My hand absently moves up to it, and I mimic the motion, realizing how close she came to the pendant. When her eyes pop down to my hand, I stop.

I clear my throat. "Sebastian? Oh yeah. All charm."

"If he's mean to you, let me know. I'll punch him. Thumb on the outside." She winks and holds up a fist before shifting on her feet. It seems we're both uncomfortable after last night but won't give voice to it. We *can't* talk about it.

I can't, at least. Or I'll say something I shouldn't. I'll have to stick to action.

She doesn't need another boss perving on her. And I don't want to be perv-dad-boss.

So, I fall back on an old faithful—teasing her.

"You sure? Looks like you still don't know how to make a proper fist. And you're no good to me with a broken hand."

She rolls her eyes. "There he is. Ford the dick is back."

I hate being a dick to her, but I just don't know how else to act. So, I grab the envelope in front of me and hold it out.

"What's this?" The tips of her fingers brush against mine when she takes it, and I cover the shiver that races down my spine by shifting in my seat.

"A signing bonus. Employment contract is in your email. I'll need your direct deposit information for future payments."

When she opens the envelope, her lips pop open, and her eyes go wide.

"No."

"I wasn't asking your permission, Rosie."

With a quick peek up she says, "Let me clarify: hell no."

"Hell yes," I reply impassively.

Her head shakes, but her eyes stay latched on the check, pinched tight between her fingers.

"Nah." She glares at me head-on now. "It's too much."

"No, it's not. I pay my employees well. Always have."

She shakes her head. "This is a start-up. It's not in the budget. I've been working on those spreadsheets. I *know*."

I tilt my head and give her my best are-you-fucking-kidding-me look. "Rosalie. It's in the budget."

"You don't give people with zero experience a signing bonus like this. I don't even have references."

My molars clamp down at the mention of her fucking references. "I do."

Her lashes flit rapidly, like she's trying to keep from crying. And god, I hope she doesn't cry. If she cries, I'll be up and out of this chair faster than you can say, *Stan Cumberland is dead.*

"I don't deserve this." Her lips wobble as she stares down at the check again.

"Rosalie." I say, and she takes a deep breath. Our eyes lock, and I give her a moment to get her bearings.

Then I tell her the simple truth. "You are worth every penny."

Her jaw pops as her teeth clamp down, and her shoulders do this little shimmy as she pulls herself up taller and one hundred thousand dollars richer.

I thought it was enough to help her situation without making it seem like a handout.

Truthfully, it didn't seem like that much to me. Which is bizarre and wholly out of touch if I let myself think about it.

To Rosie, it seems like this might be a lot of money. But from where I'm sitting, she deserves so much more.

"Ford, I—"

I lean forward, hanging on to her every word.

But that's when Bash comes stomping back, announcing, "You've got mold."

Rosie mouths a silent but carefully pronounced *thank you* as she clutches the check to her chest and wipes at the corner of one eye.

And I spend all day wondering what she was about to say.

CHAPTER 18

Ford

Tonight is a night I would have chosen to spend away from Rosie. I need to create a little distance. My train of thought constantly reorients to her, my eyes constantly search for her, my body turns in her direction without me even thinking about it.

It seems I'm attuned to her no matter what I do.

So it tracks that I was both thrilled and devastated when I walked in to Cora announcing she and Rosie were playing a game of Monopoly. I tried to leave them to it, but participation wasn't optional. Now I'm stuck spending my downtime trying not to stare at Rosalie Belmont.

My body doesn't seem to recognize that she is now my employee in an official capacity. But my brain does. My brain is *painfully* aware that not only is Rosalie Belmont my best friend's little sister, but she's also someone I can't cross professional boundaries with.

"Oh my god! *Another one?*"

At the kitchen table, Rosie rubs her hands together with an evil grin as she places yet another hotel on the Boardwalk. "Listen, little storm cloud, I told you I was good at this game. I always have been. Ask Ford. I kicked his ass at this game as a teenager."

My lips flatten. "No, you didn't."

"Ha! Yes, I did. It's actually incredible that you became as successful as you are with how truly terrible you are at Monopoly."

"I'm not terrible. I just have different priorities."

Rosie leans back with a smug look on her face, reminding me that when we're not at work together, it would appear all professional pretenses evaporate.

"Well"—she leans back in her seat while thumbing through the colorful play money in her hands—"from where I'm sitting, it appears your priority is losing."

I scoff and watch Cora's amused gaze bounce between us.

"It's a board game, not real life. I don't care if I lose fake money as much as you do."

Rosie stiffens. "What's that supposed to mean?"

As if she senses the shift in our interaction, Cora tries to run interference. "Well, I'm having a lot of fun watching Rosie clean you out."

I shrug and offer Cora a wink. "Me too. She's good at it."

Rosie's eyes narrow at that and she sets her stack of cash down. "Is that some sort of reference to what happened today?"

My brow furrows as I try to follow.

Cora stands. "I'm getting a snack. Who wants a snack?"

"I'll give it back if you're going to lord it over me, you know."

"What?" I whisper to Rosie, hearing Cora rifling through the pantry noisily.

Rosie matches my dropped voice, but there's anger in her whisper. "The advance. I'm not going to keep it just so you can lord it over me with snide, underhanded comments about me being good at cleaning you out. I have more dignity than that."

Shit. I hadn't given that money a second thought.

"That is not at all what I—"

"Hey, Rosie!" Cora calls, cutting me off. "Can you come reach this for me?"

With a shake of her head, Rosie pushes to stand and pads over to the pantry, shoulders taut and her head held high. She's miffed, but it doesn't prevent me from acknowledging how satisfying it is having her *here* in *my* house, walking around in bare feet like she's at home.

"I don't know what that even—"

"Ford?" Cora pops out of the pantry, innocent eyes meeting mine. "Rosie can't reach it either. Can you help?"

I sigh heavily and slide my chair out to help. I round the island and see Rosie up on her tiptoes, reaching for the very top shelf. A sliver of her bare stomach peeks out from where her T-shirt has ridden up. My eyes take in her narrow waist, the curve of her ass in tight acid-wash Wranglers.

"Here. Let me," I bite out more harshly than intended and step up behind her. As I reach above her, I will myself not to press too close.

I feel the rush of air before I hear the door click as it shuts. The small lock handle turning makes a soft clicking noise.

My body freezes, sprawled over Rosie's back in the darkened closet. The only source of light is what peeks in from around the door.

"Cora?" I ask firmly before Rosie's soft breasts brush my arm and my chest as she turns to face me.

"Cora, you did not just lock us in here!"

I grip the shelf above Rosie's head to keep myself from gripping her.

"I'll let you two out when you quit bickering about dumb shit. Listening to you two is exhausting. You both like each other. Start acting like it."

Rosie steadies herself with one hand on the center of my chest as Cora's footsteps recede.

"Cora! Get back here right now and let us out!" I shout.

Rosie giggles almost maniacally. The heat of her breath fans against my throat. She smells sweet, like Coca-Cola and the Fuzzy Peach candies she's been grazing on all night.

It makes me want to kiss her. Taste her. Here in the dark where no one would know.

A heavy silence descends between us. All I can feel is the awkward tension emanating from the woman pressed up against me... until she finally comes up with something to say.

"This giving you a serious case of déjà vu, Junior? Or just me?"

I swallow, thinking back to that night.

Seven minutes in heaven. A dumb teenaged game. And of course, as some sort of cruel cosmic joke, I got shoved into a dark closet with Rosalie Belmont.

My laugh is a low rumble. It feels like the surrounding shelves vibrate with it as I drop my head in defeat. "It's not just you, Rosalie."

Rosalie. Because I cannot call her Rosie right now. This pantry is too fucking small, and she's too fucking close.

"I really had to work the next day to convince West nothing happened in that closet." She laughs, quieter this time, as she recalls the story.

I swallow. "Nothing did happen. I recognized you right away." It was her scent, that heady perfume she wore back then—borderline overpowering—sweet like black licorice.

Her fingers thrum on my chest. She taps them like keys on a piano. "I know, but we did a good job of convincing everyone it did. Didn't we?"

I nod, even though I'm pretty sure she can't see me.

"I messed up my own hair," she says.

It's clear as day in my head. Rosie hushing me and dragging her fingers through her hair.

I start when the tips of her pointer and middle fingers touch my lips. My hand shoots up and I grab her wrist, but she doesn't back down. She dusts the pads of them over the top dip of my lip and whispers, "Wiped my cheap, sparkly lip gloss all over your mouth."

"I remember," I reply roughly, fingers wrapped tight around her wrist.

"I can't remember the flavor. I was constantly applying that garbage," she muses, fingers tracing again as a shiver races down my spine.

I don't even need to think about it. I *know*. I will never forget.

"Watermelon."

She sucks in a breath at my instant reply, and the tip of her nose grazes mine as her face tips up to mine.

Then my stomach burns, because I know I can't be doing this. I quickly drop her wrist and step back, feeling the metal rack behind me pressing into my shoulder blades.

She says nothing, but her breathing sounds heavier than before. More ragged.

"You let everyone think we made out in that closet," I say in a raspy voice. "You told them it was *good*."

I can faintly see the outline of her head nodding in agreement.

"Why?"

"Because people treating you like you couldn't land a girl bothered me. And that's exactly what I told West. How I got him off my ass about the whole thing."

"I *couldn't* land a girl."

The closet falls silent, and then, "You could. You were just too good for all the ones who were interested."

Interested? I'm not sure I even noticed them. All I saw was Rosie back then.

Still.

"I don't know about that."

"I do. I watched."

"Paying pretty close attention for someone who professed to hate me."

She hums thoughtfully. "What's that saying about keeping your enemies closer?"

"We're not enemies, Rosalie."

"Things might be a lot simpler if we were."

Her words hang in the air between us. I'm not sure what to make of them. I wish I could see her face right now.

"I wasn't making a reference to the signing bonus."

Her head moves in a brisk nodding motion again. "Okay."

"I wouldn't mock you about that."

"Only other things?" Her voice sounds almost hopeful as she asks the question.

I swallow. I only mock Rosie to cover for *other things.* But I also never tell her no. "Only other things."

"Okay."

"You're qualified for this job, you know? It's not a handout."

She scoffs. "Please, Ford. I practically begged you."

I shrug. "Be that as it may, I could pay you and not entrust any part of my business to you. But I haven't done that. You're an asset. Your work has value. And you'd be a fool not to take an opportunity like this. Let no one make you feel otherwise. Especially not me."

Silence descends between us. Perhaps I took it too far, but I hate seeing her second-guess herself like this. I hate how someone made her feel like her value was wrapped up in the way she looks.

"You confuse me," she blurts.

I chuckle dryly and scrub a hand over my jaw. "The feeling is very mutual."

"Do you think…" She trails off and I wait for her words, leaning her way to hear what she might say next. "Do you think under different circumstances you and I might have been—"

A click and a flood of light cuts Rosie off as Cora yanks the door open. "So? Did we work out our differences?"

I can't believe I'm being scolded by a twelve-year-old. I can't believe I'm wishing she'd lock us back in a dark closet together.

When I turn my attention back to Rosie, I'm struck by her wide eyes and her perfect cherry lips popped open. God, I so desperately want to know what was at the tip of her tongue.

More. Might we have been *more*? I wonder if that was her question.

It's one I've asked myself many times over the years. But it's never the right time to ask. There's always too much at stake.

And this moment is no different.

I don't look back at Cora when I respond with, "Yeah, we called a truce."

Then I leave the pantry before I can spend too long analyzing the confusion painted on Rosie's face.

CHAPTER 19

Rosie

I'VE SPENT THE LAST THREE WEEKS WORKING MY ASS OFF TO deserve the hundred thousand dollars Ford handed me, like it was a few bucks change to go buy a Slurpee at the corner store.

I create truly magnificent spreadsheets and projections and financial systems for Rose Hill Records.

I bring Ford a cup of hot tea anytime I make my own—especially since he stocked the kitchen at the office with my favorite blends from the Bighorn Bistro.

I help manage Bash and his timelines as the projects around the old-barn-turned-office-space carry on. In only a matter of a few weeks, he's transformed the place with new drywall and modern light fixtures. The painting has yet to come, but I can already envision how beautiful it will be. Fresh but rustic all at once.

I pick Cora up from school every day—sometimes with

Ford as a bitchy-faced chaperone—and try to play it cool when I see her wearing my scrunchie. We never talk about it, but she wears it daily, and it makes this pinching sensation pop up in my chest when I see it.

Ford and I are *friendly*. Too friendly. Too… bland. He keeps a respectable distance, never pulls my hair, and doesn't say rude things like he has no plans for us to fuck. In fact, he swears more around Cora than he does around me.

On Sunday nights, I have dinner with my parents, West, and the kids—on the weeks that he has them.

Every other Thursday, I do pizza and a movie with Cora while Ford goes to Dads' Night Out at the bowling alley. His team loses every time, but he always comes home smiling.

It's nice to see him smile.

And every day I watch him fall a little more in love with the young girl he never saw coming.

On this Friday afternoon, I have my earbuds in while I work on an email to different soundproofing specialists who might have time to work in Rose Hill for a stretch. I'm trying to keep myself from stressing about Ryan's impending visit this weekend. He messaged me last night and said he'd be making the trip on Saturday morning. *Finally*.

I've tried to get this meeting done and over with for weeks now. I even offered to make the nine hour drive myself. Hell, I could afford to fly back now. But he's had an excuse at every turn. And wanting to get it over with doesn't mean I'm not still dreading it. Losing sleep over it. It's going to be awkward and sad and I find myself obsessively running through all the gentle ways I can break the news to him. Practicing out loud to get the delivery *just* right.

I hate hurting people's feelings, and I know this will hurt for him. But I also know that touching Ford's lips in a dark closet came dangerously close to something I've always sworn I'd never do.

If it weren't a total dick move, I'd end it via text and go… I don't know. I probably wouldn't be doing anything that different from what I have been. Maybe I'd just enjoy my freedom.

Freedom.

I try to keep my eyes on my computer, but they keep drifting up to Ford and Cora. I wonder if being drawn to Ford the moment I think about freedom has some sort of deeper meaning.

I wonder what it means that I can't seem to stop looking at him, period.

Right now, he's showing her a record player that he unpacked today. Cora's curled on the leather nailhead couch that's pressed up against the wall, watching Ford open the record player with rapt attention.

They've been bonding over music every chance they get. The conversations are all Greek to me, but the way they both light up when they discuss a band they like is satisfying all the same. I've come to love watching them interact. I love the way Ford has thrown himself into being what she needs, and I love the way Cora has thrown herself into making the most of what has to be an incredibly hard situation.

I often feel like there's a lot I could learn from each of

them. Like the universe stuck me with them for that express purpose.

Which is why I pause the podcast on my phone, so I can listen in on them without looking like I'm eavesdropping.

"…who gave it to my dad, who gave it to me," Ford says as he lifts the machine's plastic lid.

"Why not your sister? Record players and names seem kind of sexist where your family is concerned, Junior."

Ford coughs out a laugh and my lips twitch as I drop my gaze back to my screen. Cora is the fucking best.

"I don't know. My sister got our grandfather's guitar. Does that count?"

Cora shrugs. "I guess."

I can see Ford thinking as he lifts the needle. For all his smug looks and biting words, he's a sensitive guy. I'm willing to bet that the possibility his family traditions are sexist will keep him awake at night.

He pulls a record out of its cardboard sleeve, pressing his tongue between his lips as he carefully places the needle back down.

"Will you show me how to do that?" Cora leans forward, watching him as though he's performing some super impressive procedure.

Me? I can't stop staring at the definition in his forearms. The way the veins in his hands bulge when his fingers flex.

"Of course." He flicks the needle up and steps back, gesturing her forward with one hand. "Come here, I'll show you. And you can listen to music on this whenever you want."

Cora looks shocked as she approaches. "You'd let me use it when you're not here?"

Ford shrugs. "Yeah, I mean, it will probably be yours one day. If you fuck it up, that's on you." He talks about how to line the needle up, but I'm not sure Cora is listening. She's watching him, adoration and confusion warring on her doll-like features.

Ford doesn't realize he just told her he plans to be around for the rest of her life, but Cora heard it loud and clear.

My eyes slice away, and I turn my podcast back on to keep from intruding. A few minutes later, I peek over again to see Cora back to sitting on the edge of the couch. Ford sits down too, and she edges closer.

The music's beat echoes through the office, and I vaguely hear Ford talking about Fela Kuti, an artist from Nigeria who I've never heard of. Cora listens, eyes wide as he speaks passionately.

The sight makes my stomach flip and my heart beat faster.

It's possible my ovaries twinge.

And when I hear a knock at the door, I shoot out of my chair to give myself a breather from the stifling sweetness of the moment.

I expect to be greeted by Sebastian's grumpy fucking face. Instead, I'm staring at Ford's little sister, Willa.

Standing right next to Ryan.

"Rosie, hi," Willa says, hands on her hips, wild mane of red hair flowing down around her face. We don't know each other that well. Sure, she spent time out here, but she was younger than the group of kids I roamed with in the summer.

She looks good. Sunkissed, well-rested, and thoroughly pissed off. "Sorry to barge in here like this, but I need to talk to my asshole brother."

I blink, trying to wrap my head around whether she flew here and rented a car or just drove from her home in Chestnut Springs, a small town one province over. I quickly recover when she tries to move past me and step to the side to block her entry into the office.

She moves to the opposite side to pass.

And I cut her off there too.

Cora and Ford are having a moment inside, and if she thinks she's going to storm in and lose her shit on him, she's got another thing coming. Willa has one eyebrow cocked like she can't believe I just cut her off. Twice.

"Hi, Willa. Maybe I can help you first?"

"Rosie, get out of my way. I have some words to exchange with the dickhead who failed to tell me he has a daughter."

Oh, she's *mad*.

I smile sweetly at her, completely ignoring Ryan. No fucking way am I letting her in here right now. She can have whatever sibling freak-out she needs with Ford—away from Cora.

"I'm so sorry. That won't be possible at this time. But if you wait a moment, I can go retrieve him for you."

"You've got to be kidding me. Retrieve him? I'll pull him out by the hair myself for not telling me I'm an auntie." She tries to step to the other side, and I block her again. "Rosie, what do you think you're playing at here?"

"Willa." I inject all the pleasantness I can muster into my voice. "I'm not playing at all. You're in my town. This is my place of work. He's my boss." I leave out that the little girl in there feels like she's mine in some ways too. "If you think you're going to barge in here and throw a tantrum because you weren't privy to something you feel you should have been, you're wrong. You can have your fit out here, and I'll bring Ford to you so he can watch."

Willa stares at me, and I stare back at her. I can see Ryan's head swiveling between us as we face off. And then… Willa *laughs*. She's smiling when she says, "I forgot what a bitch you can be."

"Years of practice with an older brother. We become well-honed, don't we?"

I give her a wink, and she sighs, dropping her chin to her chest. "I've been stewing the entire way here. I just ranted at your boyfriend here on the walk up to the front door. I'm gonna go"—she hikes a thumb over her shoulder—"pace around on the hill while you *retrieve* him. I bet he loves that you talk all fucking fancy like that."

"Yes. It's practically *Downton Abbey* around here." I give her a subtle curtsy and turn to Ryan as she rolls her eyes and walks away. "Ryan. You're here early."

His smile wobbles, and he seems uncertain. I'm not sure he's ever seen me like that. I've always been agreeable, studious, eager-for-a-fancy-city-job Rosie.

Rose Hill must bring out the feral side of me.

"I got an earlier flight, so figured I'd head straight here and surprise you."

I give him a wobbly smile back. He takes a few hesitant steps forward, opening his arms, and through no fault of his, I internally recoil.

I knew he was coming. *Later.* At this moment, I realize how badly I needed those last several hours to amp myself up. I could have practiced a few more reassuring things to say. Googled a few more synonyms for *it's over*. I had a plan to hit him with a compliment sandwich and now all the words flee my head, leaving me with only a full-body sense of dread.

I knew it would be uncomfortable seeing him again. But looking at him now, standing in front of me with open arms, makes me realize I may have underestimated just *how* uncomfortable.

The last man I hugged was Ford, and I melted into him.

When I raise my arms and step forward, the moment is plain awkward. My hips stay pushed back, and Ryan pats my back.

Fuck me, this is going to be painful.

When we step away, he's already peeking over his shoulder toward Willa. "You should go grab your boss. Then we can talk. You almost done for the day?"

"Yeah." I sigh. I don't want to be done for the day. I want to spend my entire Friday night listening to Nigerian funk while watching Ford and Cora talk about different instruments and complex drum beats and how to use a record player. "I can be done."

I turn and walk back through the entryway and round

the corner into the main office space. When I face the brown leather couch, Ford and Cora are both sitting straight up, staring at me with almost identical expressions on their faces. Thick brows, high cheekbones, and the same almost feline-shaped eyes—just in slightly different colors.

Their alarm is clear.

"So, you both heard all that?"

"Willa isn't exactly quiet," Ford deadpans.

My cheek twitches. "No, she isn't. She's pacing on the hill, waiting for you. And Ryan is outside."

"Ryan is here?" My gaze shifts to Cora, who asked the clarifying question I wish she hadn't. Her eyes are narrowed now. Arms crossed. Shoulders held up tight.

"Yes."

"For how long?"

"I'm not sure."

I'm not going to lie to her, but I'm also not going to tell her I plan on sending him packing before I've even told him.

When I glance at Ford, the intensity of his gaze scorches my skin. I feel the telltale itch that always comes when his eyes trace over me with that intense, almost displeased look on his face.

I used to wonder if I was allergic to him. It seemed feasible enough.

But in the past few weeks, I've come to realize that's not what it is at all.

"Well, I'm getting out of here," Cora announces, slapping her thighs as she pushes up from the couch. She marches right past me, avoiding eye contact. And when she gets to the front door, I hear, "Move it, fuckboy," followed by the door slamming behind her.

My eyes widen right as Ford clamps a hand over his mouth. His eyes shut and his shoulders shake.

"That was rude," I say with a chuckle, biting the inside of my cheek to keep from falling into a fit of giggles.

"Oh my god," Ford practically wheezes before running his hands through his hair. "How did I end up with you all? You're like a fire-breathing dragon. Willa is a rabid dog, and Cora is no better."

I smirk and cross my arms before giving a casual shrug. "Seems like you've got a type."

Now his eyes are back on mine, and he's not laughing anymore. My body warms as his eyes take a leisurely slide from my face down to my feet and all the way back up.

"Yeah. I do," he says.

Then he's up, his tall frame striding toward me. His big hand lands on the small of my back, making me squirm in my own skin as we walk side by side to the front door. He rubs his thumb in gentle circles, and I almost cry.

I don't know why. The pressure. The stress. The impending conversation I'm about to face.

Before we turn into the short hallway that leads to the entryway, Ford stops. One finger hooks into the thin leather belt wrapped around my waist.

A soft gasp leaves me as I come to a screeching halt and turn to face him.

"Are you okay?" His low voice is rough and gritty as it rumbles in the air between us.

All I can offer back is a nod. "Are you?"

His head tilts, and the motion brings to mind the calculated movements of some sort of apex predator. Reminding me, like he always does, of a lion stalking around a cage. Sleek and powerful and ready to pounce. The way he looks at me sometimes is almost animalistic.

A shiver runs down my spine as he murmurs, "No."

Such a simple word, yet it hits me in the chest like a ton of bricks.

When he turns and walks away from me, he takes my breath with him.

CHAPTER 20

Rosie

RYAN LOOKS AROUND THE BUNKHOUSE WITH AN EXPRESSION of shocked wonder on his face. "This is where you've been staying?"

The floorboards creak beneath his boat shoes, and he runs a finger along the condensation that's gathered into little pearls on the single-pane window.

I immediately feel defensive. He comes from more than me. More money. More property. More fancy vacations.

His parents bought him the condo in downtown Vancouver outright. Mine worked themselves to the bone to build something new for retirement on property they've been handed down through generations. Their idea of a fun vacation for us is camping in a tent.

Ford is supposedly a billionaire, a child of an A-list celebrity, and he's never made me feel as self-conscious of where I'm from as Ryan did with that one sentence.

"Yeah, Ryan."

There must be something final in my voice because he turns and stares at me. His overnight bag rests at his feet, his jaw is perfectly clean-shaven his blond hair slicked in a perfect little swoop.

If he were properly distressed, he'd have run his fingers through it and fucked it all up by now. Like Ford, who's constantly pulling at his hair.

"You're breaking up with me, aren't you?"

I sigh and my arms go limp at my sides. We're standing in the middle of this tiny cabin, staring at each other like strangers. Might as well rip the Band-Aid off.

I look him straight in the eye like I promised myself I would and blow past all the lines I've been practicing. "Yes. I'm sorry."

A couple of beats pass before he says, "I figured this was coming."

A sad laugh bubbles up out of me. "Now I feel worse."

"Don't." He cuts me off by holding a hand up between us. "I wasn't planning on leaving early today, but my boss looked at me like I had two heads when I told him my plans for the weekend. He asked me why I wouldn't just make a long weekend of it. Insisted I leave early and hit the road."

I grimace. "Romantic."

Now it's Ryan's turn to let out a sad laugh. "It's not. It's not at all. He said to me, 'Aren't you itching to see her?' and I told him I was. But, Rosie, it's been a month since you left, and I wasn't itching to see you. And I think I knew this was coming and have just been avoiding it."

"Why?"

His head tilts, and he gives me a sad look. "Have you been missing me?"

I bite down on my lip a few times, weighing my words. "Not in the way I should."

"That's why I've been avoiding it. I didn't want to hear that. But I've also had enough time to realize that while I'm happy to see you, I wasn't itching to see you."

A physical weight lifts from my body at his admission. The heaviness on my shoulders just—*poof*—evaporates. I feel like I've been carrying an elephant around on my back, and Ryan just pulled it right off. "I think… I think we had so much in common. You know? We were in the same program. Same classes. Same study groups. Same friends…"

He drops his gaze, understanding dawning on his face. "And you don't know what we have in common anymore?"

"Yes. I'm sorry," I say again because I really am. I'm sorry to see this chapter of my life end—it wasn't all bad. But I won't miss it and I'm not sad about the new one I've started.

"Rosie. Stop apologizing. It's okay. We were young when we met. We both grew up, and I think in that process, we grew apart."

I nod, expecting tears to well in my eyes. But they don't. I could tell him all the ways he went wrong. But I don't.

I'm sure he'd have a list for me too if we wanted to venture down that path. I'm not sure what else to say or do. So, I stick out my arm and offer him a handshake. He drops his watery eyes and flinches before slowly reaching forward to grip my palm.

Maybe a hug would have been nicer. But I don't want to hug Ryan. Leave it to fucking Ford Grant Junior to ruin hugs for me.

I've never endured a more painfully awkward handshake and I sigh in relief when it finally ends.

"Are you okay?" he asks, swiping the back of his hand over his nose.

"Yeah." His question takes me back to that moment with Ford before we left the office. Before he walked away.

"Are you?" I repeat the same words, but don't hang on to his.

Ryan smiles good-naturedly, but the watery eyes remain. "Yeah. I am."

I can tell he's sad, but if I'm being honest, I'm not especially worried about Ryan being okay.

Instead, I'm stressed by the fact that Ford isn't.

"I'd love to go pay your parents and your brother a visit while I'm here. You cool if I crash for the night? I'll take off in the morning."

"Yeah, of course," I lie. But I'm not cold-hearted enough send a grown man who is now wiping at his eyes back out onto the highway.

I might feel relieved about ending things with Ryan.

But that relief is eclipsed by feeling downright sick over Ford and that parting *no*.

CHAPTER 21

Ford

Cora went charging out of the office but clearly stopped short outside. I can see the uncertainty painted all over her face when her gaze snags on Willa in the distance, sitting on a stump beside the fire pit near the lake, stick held in her hand as she draws in the soot.

"Actually, I'll… take a lap around the property and let you deal with this first," Cora offers, voice just a little more timid than usual.

I gather her against my side in the world's most awkward half hug and squeeze her shoulder. "Whatever you want. She's not as bad as she seems. I promise."

Cora's eyes narrow like she isn't sure about that, but if I know my sister, she'll have Cora won over in no time.

"Why didn't you tell them all about me right away?" Her voice is small and her face downturned, so when I peek at her, I can't make much out.

I also can't tell her about my father's past—wouldn't even want to correlate the two. Plus, knowing Cora, she can hit Google and find it all anyway. So I share only a piece, something she'll understand.

"I'm just… I'm a private person, Cora. I'm close with my family in that I love them all very much, but I don't want them in my business. Willa used to work for me at my bar, and it was torture. Constantly all over my personal life. If she hadn't been such a killer fucking bartender, I'd have fired her ten times over so I could have a little peace. I grew up with the paparazzi around—having to consider every move I made and how it might look outwardly. I don't like that feeling. I needed processing time with you, and truth be told, I didn't want differing opinions or to worry about how bringing you into my life might be perceived. I knew it was the right thing to do, knew it was what I *wanted* to do. And now they can all just deal with it."

She peeks up at me from beneath a fringe of dark lashes and long bangs with a soft smile.

"It has nothing to do with them and everything to do with you and me, yeah?" I say.

She leans into my ribcage now, squeezing me back.

"Plus, they're all going to love you. I already knew that," I add for good measure, because it's true.

"Don't let her push you around, okay?" is all I get back from her.

I clear my throat to cover a laugh. "Okay."

And with that, Cora spins on her heel to walk away and I saunter toward my sister. When I get close, she doesn't look up—just continues using the tip of a twig to draw in the ash.

"What are you drawing?"

She sighs wistfully, lips tipping up ever so slightly. "Hearts."

I glance down and realize she's made a repeating pattern of them along that side of the pit.

"You seem calmer."

Her green eyes move up slowly from the ground and she drops the stick. "*Calmer?*"

"Looks like I thought wrong."

She stands and heat splashes across her cheeks. "Of course you thought wrong! How could you not tell me this?"

"The sperm donation part or the kid part?"

"I don't care what you do with your dick, Ford! But a kid? A niece? What the fuck, man?"

I bite at the inside of my cheek. "You know what went down with Dad. I wanted everything in place before I told anyone the news. I didn't want to be talked out of helping her."

"I wouldn't have talked you out of it."

"But you'd have told Mom and Dad. You've got a big heart but also a big mouth."

Her arms cross, and she works her jaw. "I don't know about that—"

"I don't owe you an explanation for everything that crops up in my life. Despite what you might think, not everyone is the open book you are. And I'm a grown man, not your kid. I told you all when I was good and ready."

"But you didn't tell *me*. You told Mom. And she's the one

who told Dad, who eventually told me. And it came up like they thought I already knew! That's fucking brutal, Ford."

My throat tightens and guilt lances through me. I got so swept up in Cora. In Rosie. In work. "I'm sorry, Willa. I should have phoned you and told you. You're right, that wasn't fair of me."

She freezes, and I see Cora pad silently up behind her, shaking her head at me.

"What did you just say?" My sister holds a palm up to her ear like she didn't quite hear me.

"That wasn't fair?"

A smug smile curves her wide mouth. "No, the other part."

My molars grind. I know what she's after. And I'm not sure I'm in a position to deny her right now. "Okay, fine. *You're right.*"

Cora huffs out a light laugh and Willa spins to take her niece in for the very first time. Silence descends between the three of us as the two of them watch each other closely.

Cora leans around Willa to look me in the eye. "Way to not let her push you around."

I scrub my hand over my mouth to cover my smile. "You two are real ballbusters, you know that? Must be hereditary."

Willa turns back to me with wide eyes and a stunned expression on her face. "Oh, no, Ford. She is *all* you." Her head moves back and forth between us. "Like… you as a tween but make it a girl."

Cora and I both roll our eyes.

"Truly unreal." My sister laughs the words out. "It's a pleasure to meet you, Cora," she adds, extending her hand. "I'm Willa."

Cora approaches to take her hand. "Yeah, I heard that part. The neighbors might have too."

At that, my sister throws her head back and laughs, then tugs Cora into a hug. One that has Cora looking completely taken aback.

When they pull away from each other, Willa asks, "What were you guys doing when I got here?"

"Listening to music."

"I like listening to music."

Watching them interact does something to my chest.

Cora eyes her warily. "What kind of music?"

Willa bites down on a smile, eyes slicing to mine for a beat. "All kinds. Can I join in?"

Cora brightens. "Really?"

A shrug from my sister. I might as well not be here at all. "Yeah. Show me what you like. Let's go hang. I'll even let Ford join us," she teases.

Then they turn away, back toward the office. All I get is a wave over Willa's shoulder, urging me along, followed by Cora blurting out, "Do you like Rage Against the Machine? Ford donated sperm so he could afford to go see them."

My sister laughs and turns mocking eyes back on me. "Now there's a story to pass down through the generations. Love that for Ford."

And just like that, friends are made and embarrassing

stories are told. I spend the afternoon watching them inter-act, soaking up the sight.

But my mind? My mind is *always* on Rosie. And obsess-ing over what the hell she and *Fuckboy* are up to right now consumes me.

It makes me something I don't think I've ever been.

It makes me jealous.

CHAPTER 22

Ford

WILLA AND I WALK INTO THE ROSE HILL REACH, A PUB THAT sits right on the water, and she looks around in wonder. "Damn, they really cleaned this place up. It used to be a total dump."

She's not wrong. It was a total dump when we were younger. *Just* dumpy enough that we all got away with drinking here before we were legal.

Now it screams elevated ski lodge. They have entirely redone the dock out front, providing a bridge out over the water to a massive floating patio. West and I met here for a beer the other day, and I couldn't help but take a trip down memory lane while we chatted.

"Wanna sit outside?" Willa carries on without me saying anything. "It's pretty nice tonight."

The dock reminds me of Rosie. Sitting there with her, getting pushed into the lake, holding her.

"Nah, let's sit inside. I can kick your ass at pool and buy you a drink." Cora seemed pretty happy to spend her Friday night with West and the kids, so I might as well take a load off. Try to shake this funk I've been in.

Willa snorts a laugh and starts in that direction without complaint. "You owe me a lot more than a drink. Buy me this entire bar, Ford."

"No."

"Come on! I see so few benefits to being the little sister of the World's Hottest Billionaire. I get radio silence, a secret niece"—she peeks over her shoulder at me—"who I'll admit is really fucking cool, and what? I bet you'll buy me shares in that genealogy testing company for Christmas."

That makes me laugh.

But the laugh dies on my lips when we turn into the section of booths near the pool table and I'm met with a set of crystal blue eyes I'd know anywhere.

"Oh, thank god!" Willa announces when she sees Rosie and *Fuckboy* sitting together in their booth. Looking at him reminds me I really need to talk to Cora about how sometimes we just insult people with our eyes rather than our words. Or at least behind their backs. "Some people who aren't Ford to hang out with."

My sister turns and sticks her tongue out at me while I just roll my eyes. This is our dynamic. We pretend we can't stand one another's company when in reality, we get along well. Since she got married and moved to Chestnut Springs, we do spend less time together. I'm not managing the bar in the city anymore, and she's not bartending. In fact, she has two kids now, and she's the one who barely reaches out anymore—even though she makes it sound like I ignore her.

I'm perceptive enough to see that she's living a life that doesn't involve talking to me on a daily basis. And it's a good thing. Her lack of contact means she's happy. Or at least that's how I interpret it.

"Hey, guys." Fuckboy says it good-naturedly enough. A friendly wave in our direction. He seems like a nice enough guy.

And I hate him. I hate every last thing about him.

Cora mumbled something about him looking like a douchey Ken Doll earlier. I couldn't place what she was talking about then. But now I see it.

He stands up and gestures for Willa to sit on the bench across from him and slides in next to Rosie.

Rosie, who is staring at me.

Rosie, who works for me.

Rosie, who has a boyfriend. One I thought she was on the outs with, but seeing them here, *together*, makes me realize I was dead fucking wrong. They seem too damn happy to be broken up.

That realization has my heart plummeting hard and fast into my gut. My stomach rolls and I grit my teeth to cover the corresponding nausea.

She might be West's little sister. She might be my employee. She might be taken.

But none of that stops me from wanting her almost obsessively. Working across from her day in and day out has my brain operating at a fever pitch to keep from crossing any lines where she's concerned. I'm unaccustomed to not getting what I want.

And I *want* Rosie Belmont.

It has become downright torturous pretending I don't.

I cut my gaze away from her and drop onto the bench next to my sister. As usual, she starts talking. Something about her kids, her friends, bull riding, hockey, and calving season.

Honest to god, no one can get a word in edgewise with Willa's monologuing. Even the server can't break her flow. I would usually find it annoying, but having to sit across from Rosie and Ryan while they're out together has me stewing like a petulant child.

I'm so jealous it *hurts*.

Without Willa filling all the space at the table, I'd say something I regret. Ryan, annoyingly, is a great conversationalist and asks engaging questions to keep the chatter going.

I try not to stare at Rosie.

And I fail.

Her finger slides up and down the exterior of the pint glass. Condensation drips down in the movement's wake. Her nails are hot pink. The same color she recently painted Cora's.

When I lift my eyes, I realize she's caught me staring. But it doesn't stop me. Now she's doing it too. We watch each other carefully for a beat. Then two.

Her lips part on a sharp gasp.

I try not to imagine her with the guy beside her. His hands on her. His lips on hers. I hate the flash of that image so much that my brain swaps those hands out for mine. On her waist. Tracing the column of her spine through the silky shirt she's still wearing. Fisting her hair. Giving it a tug like I have before.

But this time I don't let go. I tilt her head and drop my mouth to her neck. She moans in my ear. Wraps her legs around my waist.

A sharp kick to my shin from under the table startles me. And I find Rosie giving me a what-the-fuck-are-you-doing kind of glare.

I know that vision in my head can't be me. But it doesn't stop me from wishing it were. I adjust myself in my pants and go back to focusing on polite conversation, though the ideas running through my head are anything but polite.

"Tell me about your job," Willa says to Ryan.

He comes back with something about oil and gas and pipelines and finishes with, "But, ya know, I'm really just getting started with the company. Still working my way up."

That foray into the dark and forgotten recesses of my mind has me feeling more agitated than I already was.

I clear my throat. "I suppose that explains why it's been so hard for you to get away and see Rosalie."

Rosie's eyes look like they might roll right out of their sockets, but Ryan gives me a confused quirk of his head before saying, "Yeah. Totally."

"Do they not give you vacation days at your job?"

From the corner of my eye, I glimpse my sister watching the exchange, subtly leaning forward.

Ryan rubs at the back of his neck. "I mean they do. I was just saving them for something—"

I cut him off with a patronizing smile. "More important?"

He turns a pink hue, going bashful. "I mean, I don't know if I'd put it that way."

He doesn't seem all bad. I should back off and give the guy a break. But I don't. I smirk and give him my best asshole glare. "Really? I would."

I hear my sister try to stifle a snicker from behind her hand.

"Ford—" Rosie starts right as Ryan says, "Hey, man, not all of us—"

"Go to bat for the woman we're with?" I cut him off sharply, knowing he did nothing in the wake of her being assaulted at her workplace. "Yeah, I've noticed."

Ryan is bright red now, but he's clearly given up on defending himself. Might as well roll over and show me his tummy.

Rosie leaps to his defense. He doesn't deserve it. But she's such a good fucking person she does it anyway. "You're being a dick, Ford. I have vacation days in my contract, but some of us can't afford to just take time off willy-nilly. I was perfectly capable of going back for a visit too."

I tilt my head in her direction, hating that *she's* going to bat for *him*. "And yet you didn't."

She sucks in a breath, her shoulders rising toward her ears. "Can I please speak to you outside?" She elbows Ryan, who drops his eyes and moves out of her way. Too much of a pushover to stand up for his girlfriend. Too damn nice for a girl like Rosie.

"Oh, Ford, you idiot," Willa whispers while looking up at me with slack-jawed amusement all over her face. "You are down so bad for that girl."

All I offer back is a roll of my eyes as I slide off the burgundy banquette. Seems less incriminating than trying to deny it. After all, I need to pick Cora up from West's house after this fiasco of a night out, and Willa has a big mouth. I don't need her sharing this theory with my best friend.

That would be a goddamn disaster.

One disaster at a time, I think to myself as Rosie digs her nails into my forearm and drags me toward the door.

"I'll take the bill," I say politely to the server as we blast past her computer station. "Be back in a moment."

"He won't be back," Rosie mutters as she storms out the door. "I will leave his dead body in the parking lot and you can frisk him for cash."

"Charming," I murmur back to her.

"World's Deadest Billionaire will be the new magazine headline. The cover will be a picture of your face, and I'll be personally invited to complete the design by drawing devil horns and scribbling out your eyes."

"Shame that I'll be dead. I might actually be interested in reading that article."

The cool spring air hits us in the face and her nails dig deeper into my bare forearm. I should hate it, but it just makes me think about fucking all the venom right out of her while she scratches at my back with those pink nails.

A few purposeful steps and we're around the corner of the building. Standing in the dark. She's panting in fury, and

I'm breathless for a whole other reason. Her eyes are so blue they almost trend white in the dim light that filters around the side of the building. Patio lanterns strung around the property dot the darkness of the night with warm bright spots. The smell of lilacs permeates the air, emanating from the bush behind us, while the minerality of the lake water beside us adds a soft undertone.

I will forever associate this smell with the look of rage on Rosie's pretty face right now.

"You've got some fucking nerve! You know that?" She's mad enough to give me a soft shove. One hand on each shoulder pushes me up against the pub's pale-yellow vinyl siding. She doesn't stop her forward motion and closes the space instantly.

"Careful, I'm still your boss." I keep my palms flat against the wall behind me.

She barks out a laugh in my face and lifts her hands beside her head in frustration. "You're also the asshole I grew up around. And I know what a prick you can be, but goddamn it, Ford, that was too fucking far. He's already had a rough day. That was *mean*. A dick-measuring contest is unnecessary."

"I genuinely don't give a fuck about his day. My dick is definitely bigger. And I'm not concerned with my likability. I don't care about him. But I do care about you."

That takes her aback, but only for a moment. One swift blink and she's right back at it.

"Ford, you are going to walk in there, and you are going to apologize."

I cross my arms defiantly, leaning back against the siding in a way that appears a hell of a lot more unaffected than I feel. "Have fun scribbling my eyes out because over my dead fucking body will I apologize to him."

Her mouth pops open again, true disbelief lacing her every feature as her hands fall limp at her sides.

I can tell she's about to go on scolding me, so I cut her off before she can. I spit out the words I've been swallowing for the past several weeks. "He doesn't deserve you."

Her teeth clank as she slams her mouth shut. *"Excuse me?"*

I repeat the sentence even though we both know she heard it. "I said he doesn't deserve you."

Her cheeks flush, and her eyes are wild. She is *spitting* mad.

I fucking love her like this.

"Oh, what? And you do?" She bites the words out, stepping even closer to me. The tips of her shoes bump the toes of my boots, her breasts pressing against my forearms where they're now crossed against my chest.

"No, Rosie. But I'm not the type of man who will let that stop me."

I don't think. I just reach for her. One hand on her jaw, the other gripping her waist. Holding her like I could shake her in frustration—except I never would. Instead, I flip us. I turn her quickly so she's the one pressed up against the wall.

Her heavy breaths puff out against my skin. Her eyes flash down to the silver chain around my neck, but she makes no other move to escape me. "Oh, cute, now I'm Rosie and not Rosalie? What does that mean?"

Her words are a taunt; her eyes are defiant. I know her boyfriend is inside, and it just makes me want her more.

My eyes race over her face. Flushed cheeks. Twinkling eyes. The tip of her tongue on that full bottom lip. "Rosie, shut up."

She pauses at the use of her nickname again.

Then she straightens slightly before spitting, "Don't tell me what to do," back at me.

And I just shake my head at her, tightening my grip and shifting my hand over so I can brush a thumb over her damp lips. "Rosie, shut up because I'm going to kiss you right now unless you tell me not to."

I love that she doesn't go all soft on me.

Our gazes latch onto to one another. She tips her chin up.

And for once she doesn't say a fucking word.

CHAPTER 23

Rosie

WHEN FORD TUGS MY HAIR BACK AND TAKES MY MOUTH, MY knees go weak.

But he catches me. He holds me up. He presses his leg between mine, wraps his big palm around my throat, and kisses me senseless while I hold on to his hips for dear life.

The energy between us is intense, and yet he doesn't rush. His lips are firm, his tongue is soft, and his stubble rasps against my skin, sending sparks skittering over my body.

He savors me. He makes every touch, every point of contact feel like it lasts longer and goes deeper than should be humanly possible.

With Ford Grant kissing me, the world stands still.

I smell him.

I feel him.

I taste *him*.

My palms itch, so I slide them beneath his shirt. His warm skin and the light smattering of hair just above his belt buckle make me groan into his mouth.

He nips my bottom lip in response and dives back into working my mouth. My fingers inch up, exploring the ridges I peeked at the night when we sat together after his swim. He's tall, all lean muscle and masculine bulk.

I whimper when my hand finds the end of that silver chain. It's a talisman, a reminder of the night he held me. The night I so desperately needed to be held.

And no one was there except for—

"Ford," I breathe his name against his lips and hardly recognize my voice.

"I'm sorry," he murmurs back.

My smile gets cut off by another tug on my hair, and now his mouth is on my neck. Biting. Kissing. Licking.

"No, you're not." I roll my head back and press my breasts out toward him. I swear my body already knows what my head has had an impossible time wrapping itself around.

I expect him to laugh, but he takes his mouth off me, and I want to stamp my foot. I want to plunge us straight back into that frantic moment of need.

I want to be consumed by him.

That wild look flashes in his eyes as he pulls away, only far enough to meet my gaze. We both know he's not sorry, so he doesn't confirm it—he just watches me for a moment. I'm worried he'll leave. Stop. Throw in the towel and walk away.

Instead, his voice comes out soft and deep—almost pained—as he murmurs, "No, I'm not."

And then he kisses me again. But it's different this time. It's soft.

The pads of his fingers curl under my chin, and then his knuckles stroke up over my cheeks. My chest aches with the sweetness of it, and I press myself closer to him. Wanting his heat, his touch, his protection.

Because no matter how much he infuriated me tonight, I'd be a fool not to recognize that the man kissing me right now would ride headfirst into battle with me. For me. He'd cut people down with his words. Scorch them with his glare. Humiliate them with his directness.

And after everything this past month has held for me, that makes me long for him in a completely unfamiliar way.

I grip his chain and press down on his leg. If I could crawl right into his lap and have him pet me like a fucking cat, I would. I'd purr for him.

The kiss slows, and I can sense his retreat before it's even happened.

"Ford, please don't stop."

He takes his hands off my face and props them on the wall behind me before dropping his head to the crook of my neck. My hands roam gently over the back of his head as he dusts kisses across the top of my shoulder, making my body break out in gooseflesh.

"I should."

"You shouldn't," I counter, raking my fingers through his hair like I've seen him do so many times before.

"I have to. You know this isn't okay."

"Why?"

His head turns up now, and he stares at me. My body trembles under the weight of it, and his eyes narrow like he's noticed. He doesn't miss a single thing.

"Why are you looking at me like that?"

His hands remain propped above me, and I'm practically riding his leg. He's caged me in, and I'm happy to stay right where I am. Even with his menacing green gaze boring into me.

"Rosie, I told you to make sure that you were single the next time you ask me that."

Oh god. He doesn't know.

"I…" I shake my head, gazing back at him. He kissed me. Consequences be damned. My voice shakes. "I am."

"What?" He pushes off the wall and takes a step back.

"I didn't think about you not knowing… *that's* why Ryan had a bad day."

Ford winces at the mere mention of his name and rakes both hands through his hair, only stopping when he's gripping the back of his head, elbows still up in the air. His lips are puffy, and his eyes are tortured. "Jesus. I had no idea."

"You kissed me anyway." I lift a hand to my lips and dust a finger over them. I swear I can still feel him there.

"I did."

"Are you sorry now?"

The silence between us is deafening. His jaw pops as his molars grind. And then, "No."

But he doesn't stay with me for long—he turns and starts walking away.

"Where are you going?"

"To apologize to Fuckboy," he calls back over his shoulder.

"Why? I thought you weren't sorry?"

He pauses, his hand pressed against the corner of the building, considering. His eyes slice back to mine, almost violently. My entire body tingles. "Let's call it my condolences then, because any asshole dumb enough to blow it with you when they've got you free and clear is having a bad fucking day."

"Are you going to come back after?"

Ugh. I hate asking that out loud. I sound *desperate* and so unlike myself.

Ford drops my gaze now, as if there's something terribly interesting about his boots. "That's the thing, Rosie. I've gone and made you my employee, and I know you need this job. There is nothing free and clear about us."

Then his fingers rap against the vinyl and he's gone.

Leaving me more confused about him than ever.

CHAPTER 24

Ford

I hear Willa before I see her. Heavy footsteps and a loud yawn precede her entry into the kitchen. My sister is not a morning person.

"Fuck, this place is really nice," she says as she peers around the kitchen. I can't help but feel a spark of pride. Before it was rough, a little run-down. Now it's all windows opening out to the lake, wide floorboards, wood-beam ceilings, and industrial light fixtures.

"It looks like a total dump from outside," she adds from behind her fist as she covers another yawn. "But that guest bed is to die for."

I scoff and shake my head while pointing her toward a full pot of coffee. "It doesn't look like a dump. I wanted to keep the reclaimed wood exterior."

She waggles her eyebrows at me. "Bet that was more expensive than just re-siding it."

All I give her back is an eye roll. It *was* more expensive. But those weather-worn vertical boards carried far too much character—far too many stories—to just tear down or cover up.

I like that the house is unassuming. I like that it feels like it belongs nestled in the wilderness of the Rockies.

"Can you leave me this place in your will? I love it. And we both know I'm going to live forever. I have too much energy to die." She approaches the long kitchen island with a mischievous grin, sliding up to its black stone counter. "You, on the other hand…"

"Nice, Wils. But I'm not dying." Though I feel like I might be after pulling an all-nighter.

She regards me over the rim of her coffee cup, taking a thoughtful sip. "No, but I'll put money on West killing you with his bare hands if he finds out you were making out with his baby sister last night."

Fuck. Did she see us?

I stare at Willa, willing my face to give nothing away. "Rosie is a friend and employee. Don't go making up stories."

"Oh yeah? Is pushing her up against a wall and shoving your tongue down her throat how you check your emails? Or was there a really important quote from a subcontractor hidden in there?"

Double fuck. She saw us alright.

I wipe a tired hand over my face. "Sounds like I should charge admission for how long you watched."

She laughs at that with a subdued shake of her head. "You can try, but I get a family discount."

My hand stays gripped over my stubble as I stare back at

my sister. "How does Cade put up with you?" As far as I'm concerned her husband should be nominated for sainthood.

She grins wider now. "He doesn't. He just holds on for dear life and comes along for the ride."

I can't help but laugh as I prop my hands on the edge of the counter and drop my head. I drove myself crazy all night long.

Should I? Shouldn't I? Could I? Why can't I?

"How is Cade? The kids?" I don't even look up at her as I say it. I can't.

"They're great. Life is great. I thought I was pissed at you for making me drag my ass all the way out here to rag on you before Mom and Dad could do it first. But honestly, this is just way more fun than I banked on. I love watching you be confused. It's very satisfying for me as the chaotic child with zero sense of direction."

My shoulders shake.

"You've never been more relatable."

I push up, my eyes meeting my sister's. "You're a true comfort, Willa. Thank you for the kind words."

"You don't need kind words. You need a kick in the ass."

"I know, I know. I shouldn't have done that."

Her eyes bug out and her coffee cup taps against the counter as she places it down a little harder than necessary. "Oh my god, Ford! You are so dumb. You've been in love with that girl since you were a teenager. You should absolutely have made a move."

I scoff. "I have not been in love with her since then."

"You have."

"That's not true, and we both know it. You were probably too young to understand that I mostly hated Rosie."

Or at least my cover was that I did.

Willa shakes her head and reaches for her coffee again, like she is profoundly disappointed in me. "You don't hate her. You never did. You hate that you think you can't have her."

"Deep. Except, I don't just think that. I know it."

"Who told you that? Did Rosie tell you that?"

I tilt my neck, feigning a stretch to buy myself a moment to choose my next words. "I've been friends with West for—"

"Pardon my French, but fuck West."

"I'm sorry?"

"No, seriously. You've never been weird about me dating a guy. Haven't walked around like you have some sort of claim over my body or my life."

"Never figured you'd meet someone nuts enough to take you on," I mutter just loud enough that she hears me.

"If I had told you I was dating West, what would you have done?"

I look her dead in the eye. "Invested in having a top-of-the-line bomb shelter built because the two of you together would certainly bring about some sort of nuclear event."

What I get in return is an exasperated eye roll. "Seriously, would you have been mad at West? Are you really telling me your best friend—who has held that title for literal years—wouldn't be good enough to date me? What would that say about you?"

My eyes flash to the staircase and I desperately hope this isn't the first Saturday morning Cora decides not to sleep in.

"I mean, yeah. It would have taken me a minute to wrap my head around it, because you both almost feel like family to me. But no, I wouldn't have been mad."

"Cool, I'm so glad I *almost* feel like family," she deadpans. Then, "So you wouldn't have felt betrayed?"

I run my hands through my hair, tugging, and then prop them behind my head. "No. I mean, maybe if you guys were sneaking around and not telling me."

She slaps the counter. "Well, good. There's your answer."

It's more complicated than that. Knowing the work situation Rosie just fled, knowing her financial situation, knowing I've hired her with a contract and everything… it feels slimy to go after her.

And as much as I see Willa's point, I still feel guilty where West is concerned.

"I think there's a little more to it than me knocking on West's door and telling him I'm in love with his sister." The words come out before I can stop them. Before I can think about them. Before I can process them.

"Oh boy. I really wish I could buy tickets for the coming weeks in Rose Hill. Sadly, the ranch is hella busy this time of year. So, I'm going to go hang out with my niece before I have to leave this afternoon. Maybe you should go for a swim or something. Figure your shit out."

Then she salutes me and walks away. She's at the base of the staircase, one hand on the wrought-iron banister, when she stops, spins, and marches right back up to me, placing her coffee on the counter.

"I know I tell you that you're awful and boring all the

time, but I don't mean it. You're a good man, Ford. Don't overthink yourself into unhappiness. Go after *exactly* what you want for a change. I love you." She wraps me in a rare hug—one I didn't know I needed.

And I hug her back. "Thanks, Wils," I murmur. "I love you too. That's why you're the sole beneficiary of my estate and holdings."

"Fuck yesss." She chuckles the words and squeezes me tighter. "But don't die yet, okay? Dying young would break your boring streak."

The door to the barn-turned-office creaks as I step into the space. Willa suggested a swim, but between the bar in the city, Gramophone, and this place, I feel like I'm drowning. So, working a couple of hours in an office that is finally almost organized is what will make me feel best.

The space has completely transformed over the past several weeks. Rosie wasn't wrong about Bash. He works efficiently, and he doesn't get in the way. We've had to work from my house for a couple of days here and there, when he's deep in refurbishing, but things have mostly come together painlessly—despite the constant frown on Bash's face.

The sliding barn doors have been retrofitted with glass and hung on new tracks. Built-in shelves have been mounted to the walls. New lighting wired. Even the exposed stone fireplace looks like it's been given new life.

But it's what's across from the fireplace that stops me in my tracks. Rosie is fast asleep, curled on her side on the leather couch. She's tucked her hands under her cheek and pulled her knees up like she might be cold.

I stand there, frozen, wondering what to do next. Deep down, I'm dying to slide in behind her. To curl around her and keep her warm. We could spend this entire Saturday lying together and listening to records.

Realistically, I know better. But it doesn't keep me from wondering what she's doing here, sleeping in the office. A quick glance at my watch tells me it's 7:00 a.m. and not an unreasonable time for her to wake up. So I make my way across the room, the gummy soles of my suede Gazelles quiet on the hardwood floors.

When I sit on the couch's far cushion, she stirs but doesn't wake. Her Birkenstocks lie discarded on the floor nearby, and on her feet are the kind of socks you'd use to make a puppet. Gray and white with a red line.

Only Rosie could make socks and sandals cute.

I reach for her, my hand wrapping delicately around her slender ankle. Thumb rubbing against the bone that protrudes there. It takes every ounce of control to not crawl into the crook of this couch and hold her. It would be warm and cozy and completely inappropriate.

I stifle a groan and glance up at her pretty face. Her lashes flutter and her lips curve softly before she rolls onto her back and forces her legs straight into a stretch. One that has her feet pushing down into my leg and her gasping out a startled breath.

Her eyes fly open, and one hand lands on the center of her chest as she regards me with a look of shock. "Fuck me. I was not expecting you to be sitting there."

"Sorry." My voice comes out rough, like gravel. "I was trying to wake you up gently. I came to get a few hours of work done."

Her hands cover her face, and she scrubs it a few times as though trying to get her bearings. "Why are you working on a Saturday?"

"No rest for the wicked." I continue caressing her ankle, even though it's now propped on my thigh. "You should know, you slept here."

Her hands move off her eyes but land on her cheeks, bracketing her face as she stares at me. Clear blue eyes like fucking arrows to my heart.

"Didn't seem right to sleep in the same room as Ryan."

I'm hit with an instant sense of relief.

The sentence hangs in the quiet office between us. We both know the meaning, but neither of us elaborates. We both know what happened last night, but neither of us says anything about it. I did apologize to him, but not for kissing her.

"When does he leave?" I ask.

Her tongue darts out over her lips, and she glances away before sitting up. She takes her foot with her as she retreats, and I find myself missing the contact.

"Today."

All I can offer is a nod. I don't know what to say. Knowing about him didn't stop me from kissing her last night. And knowing that they're over doesn't lessen my disdain for the guy.

There are a few good reasons I shouldn't have kissed Rosie Belmont last night.

But Ryan isn't one of them.

And I refuse to regret kissing Rosie.

Which doesn't mean I don't recognize that it can't happen again. One boss with wandering hands in her young career is probably more than enough.

She sighs as she twists her legs, feet landing flat on the floor as she rolls her shoulders out. "Ugh. Crashing on couches isn't as cool as it used to be."

"You could have slept at my house," I reply.

She responds with an unimpressed look. "Yeah, sure. That would have been great for the optics you're so concerned about."

I flinch and gaze away through the windows, watching the fog drifting over the lake. I think about West, but Willa is right—that could be managed. Most of all, I think about the fact she is officially my employee. I'm the one who drew up all the formal paperwork and now there's a power dynamic even though I wish there wasn't. And on the heels of the mess at her last job, I don't want to be another Stan in her life.

"I'm sorry about last night."

Rosie barks out a laugh and punches me in the shoulder. "I'm not, you dick." She stands from the couch and bends close, her hand on my shoulder as she whispers in my ear, "And I know you're lying."

When I turn to face her, our lips come close. Too fucking close. I drop my gaze to her mouth and watch her tongue slide out in a slow but subtle motion. I almost stumble, rushing to stand up too. Rushing to back away from her.

Rushing to keep myself from doing something I won't be even a little bit sorry for all over again.

"We can't do that again," I say.

"Oh, no?" She crosses her arms and tilts her head, twisting her lips like she's confused. The expression is totally fake. Her hair is messy from sleep, but leave it to Rosie to not give a fuck. She could wear a paper bag and still walk around like the princess who owns the place.

"No."

"You're telling me you're never going to kiss me again?"

I wince as if West might have an ear pressed against the door, then I mirror her position and cross my arms as we face off. "That's what I'm telling you."

Her eyes narrow. "What if I ask you to?"

"No."

"What if I beg you to?"

I can feel the flush on my cheeks and judging by the way Rosie's gaze flies to the side, she can see it too.

"No."

She nods, pressing her lips together as though she's impressed by my restraint. "All right. Whatever you say, boss."

As she slides her feet into the leather sandals, I start to panic. Because I know her all too well. She's determined and messy. And she doesn't back down. From her perspective, I just waved a red flag in front of her.

I didn't warn her off. I *challenged* her.

"Rosie. It's not safe."

She's at the door when she turns to face me, her hands pressing against the wood behind her. "What's not safe?"

"What happened last night. You and me. There's West. I'm your boss. You deserve a safe work environment. It's… not a safe bet."

She nods, but the motion is lined with agitation at the mention of her brother. "Right, well, I should go say good-bye to my *safe bet* before he leaves." She spears me with her blue eyes. "See you Monday."

Then she salutes me and walks out the door without another word.

I don't work at all. I throw on my swim trunks and torture myself in the cold lake, swimming between the new dock and Rosie's dock. And I swear I can feel her gaze on me the entire time.

CHAPTER 25

Rosie

IT'S MONDAY. RYAN IS GONE. WILLA IS GONE. AND I'M OBSESS-ing over stupid, bitchy Ford and how to act around him now that I know he wants to kiss me while also coming to terms with the fact that I *want* to be kissed by stupid, bitchy Ford.

My period is also due to start any day now, and I feel like my insides are trying to carve their way out of my body by way of my lower abdomen.

Basically, my headspace is trash, and my body is a traitor.

So, as any mature young professional would do, I resort to taking it out on my boss and harassing him via email. I tell myself it's allowed because he forced my hand by refusing to make eye contact with me from across the room.

Good morning, Mr. Grant Jr.,

I've officially heard back from three experts who

can come to complete the recording booth. Their prices and timelines are broken down in the attached spreadsheet with my completely unprofessional opinions noted in the margins. Truly, one guy cannot be trusted. He requested that I order him chicken wings for lunch every single day (which, fair, I'd love that too), but only the drumsticks, not the wings. It's alarming because the wings are clearly the superior piece of meat. To me, that proves he lacks any modicum of taste, and as such, I wouldn't let him near this place, because it's finally looking pretty great.

I hope you had an incredibly safe Sunday.

Making eye contact with you from across the room,
Rosalie Belmont
Business Manager at Safety First Records

When I hear the email ping from across the office, I try not to smirk. Instead, I pick up my agenda and doodle a dick on Monday, so it looks like I'm keeping track of something particularly important.

The sound of his fingers on the keyboard filters back to me, and when I glance up, his eyes are focused on his screen. I push the dick out of my way and decide to work on responding to the info email account for Rose Hill Records—most of which is barf-worthy fan mail for the World's Hottest Billionaire.

Good morning, Rosalie,

I appreciate your feedback on these options. I took a moment to scan the attached sheet. I believe that as my safety mascot and business manager, you are more than capable of selecting the best candidate for this job. Surely, the drumstick guy is a no—absolutely cannot be trusted.

Have a happy day!
Ford Grant
CEO and Producer at Safety First Records

P.S. I can see the dick you drew in your planner from here.

My eyes flit to where the planner has moved up toward the corner of my desk. Ford watches me openly now. I suppose he can see it with his height advantage. Or possibly because I made it extra bold by outlining it more than once. I shrug, turn the spiral-bound book toward me, add a sizable splash of cum erupting from the head, and hold it up to Ford.

He stares back at me blankly now, but I swear I see his cheek twitch.

I toss him a thumbs-up and get back to my email.

Mr. Ford Grant Jr.,

I'm so glad you enjoy my art. I call this piece "My Boss is a _____," ink on paper, by Rosalie Belmont.

Each droplet of the added jizz stream represents
the lies that he tells himself.

Yours truly,
Rosalie Belmont
Dick Manager

He snorts a laugh, one abruptly covered by a hand and dropped eye contact. We fall back into the tapping of our keyboards and fuck my life—today could not be more awkward if I tried. I catch myself looking at Ford, remembering him as a teenager.

Where I became sure of myself quickly, he didn't. Physically, he matured slowly, while at sixteen I could have passed for twenty-two. Emotionally, he seemed removed and often fumbled his words around people. As the son of a famous rock star, I think he could have gone one of two ways: life of the party or untrusting and withdrawn.

He was the latter. He learned how to protect himself by using his words and facial expressions as armor. It made him come off cool, maybe even superior, but I see now it was a display of discomfort.

Where I was popular and outgoing, he was *nervous*.

It's with that revelation in mind that I get to the inbox and sift through different emails. One is a request for his presence at a fundraiser and silent auction for a devastating wildfire in Emerald Lake.

Mr. Ford Grant Jr.,

Would you like to attend this event in Emerald Lake in just under two weeks' time? I believe being able to use your name for marketing purposes would be very charitable indeed. Who doesn't want to attend a stuffy event with the World's Okayest Billionaire?

Respectfully,
Rosalie Belmont
Dick Manager

I consider changing my job title again, but Dick Manager has such a wonderful ring to it, and the fact he didn't respond about my art has me irrationally annoyed with him. Even though he's working. And I'm supposed to be working. And I know my hormones are taking me on a roller coaster ride right now.

So, I send it the way it is.

Dearest Dick Manager,

Thank you for passing this along. You can RSVP for me and a plus one.

Have a happy day!
Ford Grant
CEO and Head Dick at Rose Hill Records

I blink at the screen and read the simple email over and over again. Searching for a hidden detail. Something I missed. Because who would he take to the event as a plus one?

I scowl at him, but he goes on working, blissfully unaffected. He gets up, puts a record on, and sits back at his desk. Looking carefree while I stew.

It's possible he'd take Cora.

That could be cute. But then I consider how intensely private he is and decide he wouldn't expose her that way. His parents were extremely careful with him and Willa, and I suspect he'd be just as protective of Cora.

I start to thoroughly mull over the question. I have no right to care. Even so, *he* kissed *me*. And now he's ignoring me like nothing happened because he's feeling guilty. I also realize he hasn't once answered my question about him being single.

It never bugged me before, but now it does. What if I have to sit by while he dates some hot model who wouldn't be caught dead eating a full bag of chips by herself on a rickety dock?

She'd probably be nice too—she'd probably be hardworking and smart, with a thousand degrees, in addition to being extremely hot. And that just makes me hate his imaginary girlfriend even more.

I find myself wondering if he'd have kissed me like that if—no, I know him better than that. He *wouldn't*.

I'm glaring at him now. Arms crossed. Cramps raging. Eyes like lasers.

My email pings.

Rosie,

Are you joining the dark side? I feel that if you
practiced enough, you could probably Force grip
me and choke me out with that scowl.

Have a happy day!
Sith Lord Ford Grant
CEO and Head Dick at Rose Hill Records

I see the email, but I don't respond. I cross my legs and
lean back, foot bobbing, as I pretend to act casual.

"Who is your plus one?"

I thought I'd sound curious and unaffected. That's how
the sentence sounded in my head. But I sound petty and
accusatory, and he must hear it because his head snaps up in
my direction. His slightly slanted green eyes make my chest
ache, while the blush on his cheeks makes me want to trail
my fingernails through his rugged stubble again. His cable-
knit sweater with a plaid collar sticking out from underneath
is casual-mountain-man sexy, not at all stuffy billionaire, and
I can't even deny how fucking hot he is—which annoys me
even more.

He took me from oblivious to acutely aware and then
he left me hanging. So right now, I hate Ford Grant more
than ever.

"What?" He appears suitably confused.

"To that event in Emerald Lake? Who are you taking?"

He blinks, and I stare. The music in the background is

the only sound, and the air between us bubbles like boiling water on a stove.

Then he stands, without a word, and rounds his desk. All swagger as he approaches me.

He has an obnoxiously smug expression on his face when he props his hip against my desk and says, "You."

My foot stops bobbing. He says the word so plainly that it almost doesn't make sense to me. Doesn't quite register.

His brow furrows and his eyes drop to my lips. It fucking kills me when he looks at my lips now because I know what he can do to them—to me.

"Me?"

His head tilts, and his gaze moves over my entire body. Like he's putting the puzzle together, reading my body language. Picking up every little clue.

This time when he talks, his voice is earnest, not biting. "Yeah, Rosie. I can't go to an event like that without my Dick Manager."

I bite at my bottom lip. My eyes sting a little, and I know it's not him or his words. I know my emotions are running amok because I'm one day away from my period starting, according to my tracker. I know he said nothing especially sweet, but the relief I feel is strong enough that I need space.

"Cool." I nod firmly, stand up, and head toward the door like the emotional coward I am. "Forgot my…" I forgot absolutely nothing, but I'm looking for an escape. "Sweater at my place. Be right back."

His brow furrows again as I turn and walk through the sliding barn doors. The ones that are wide open, because it's warm out today. I can hear the concern in his voice when he says, "I'll go grab lunch. Want anything?"

"Sure, whatever looks good," I call back, hustling off the front deck.

I take my time walking back to my place. I even sit at the end of the dock for a while, just simmering in all my feelings. Then I take a Midol, grab a completely unnecessary sweater, and head back to the office. Primed and ready for a fight.

But when I get back to my desk, there's no Ford to be seen. However, there is a tin takeout container of chicken wings on my desk with an array of sauces on the side.

No drumsticks. All wings.

CHAPTER 26
Ford

I CAN HEAR THE PHONE RINGING FROM OUTSIDE THE OFFICE.

And when I walk in, my gaze lands on Rosie as she lifts the receiver and says, "Good morning, Ford Grant Junior's office."

She looks me right in the eye as she does it.

But then she winces and blinks away.

I take her in. She's wearing a simple cap-sleeve dress, blue like her eyes, and covered in a small print of daisies with little yellow centers. She's paired it with off-white cowgirl booties. Her hair is natural and wavy—just a little bit messy.

She looks fucking edible.

"Gemma." Her voice comes out with a light hitch. "What a pleasant surprise."

Oh good, my mom.

"Oh, yeah, he's a great boss. No complaints." She nods, then laughs softly. "We both know I can handle him. It's really been fine. Fun even." Her eyes slice up to mine. They're filled with a hint of worry. Like she doesn't want me to know she's having fun working here.

She stiffens. "No, no nice, small-town girls have been sniffing around him."

Lord help me. I shut the door and head toward my desk. I drop my leather shoulder bag and flop down into my chair to endure the next several minutes of my loose-cannon mom plotting with my loose cannon... whatever Rosie is.

Dick Manager is feeling entirely too accurate, since she not only manages me but practically leads me around by mine.

"Yes, superior looks. And all those *moods*. Really, who can keep up?"

Now she's back to glaring at me. I can hear my mother's voice but can't make out anything she says.

I glance down, and there sits another ripped page from the chaotic mind of a teenaged Rosie Belmont. I pick up the piece of paper and read it.

> *Tonight at the beach party, I saw Ford try to talk to a girl. She was cute, and honestly, she'd have been overachieving if she landed him. He's growing into himself and was hands down out of her league. Still, he struck out so hard. It would have been funny if my secondhand embarrassment wasn't so far off the charts.*
>
> *He doesn't do himself any favors by being so*

damn sarcastic. And knowing Ford, whatever he said likely bordered on insulting, so I almost don't blame her.

His intelligence comes off mean sometimes. I like it. But I can keep up. Some people can't. He needs a girl who can challenge him. And I could tell this one wasn't up to the task.

Sometimes I think I should let Ford hate fuck me just so he can lose his (alleged) virginity. I may not have loads of experience, but probably more than him. Maybe he'd frown less if he didn't have to walk around with an untouched dick all the time. A little practice wouldn't hurt the guy. I could send him back to college knowing where a girl's clit is and that would basically be philanthropic.

A coughing fit overtakes me, and I cover my mouth, thumping a hand on my chest a few times to clear my throat—and catch my breath. When I glance up, Rosie looks like the goddamn Cheshire Cat with her lips curving up, knowing what I've just read. And for once, her cheeks take a turn flushing.

"I couldn't agree more. Getting laid would really take the edge off for him," she replies to my mother.

Fucking kill me now.

I scrub at my hair, messing up any semblance of style it may have had when I arrived.

Rosie's brows pop up. "So, when you orgasm, it releases endorphins? And those make you feel happy? Well, dang, Gemma. I'm no doctor, but I'm definitely going to prescribe him an orgasm. Buy him a magazine and send him to the back or something, ya know?"

I run my finger over my throat in a clear threat while I stare back at Rosie. It just makes her smile harder.

"Wait. Did you just say orgasms help with—" Rosie bites down on her lip and nods. "All right, well, you actually *are* the doctor, so I'll take that under advisement. Do you want me to hand you off to Ford?"

Rosie presses her lips together to stifle a laugh. "You just wanted to talk to me? How sweet!" Another nod, and then, "I'll let him know. Bye, Gemma! Oh, and say hi to Senior for me."

With that, she hangs up and stares at the receiver for a moment before turning her wide eyes on me. "Your mom is so cool."

"I'm glad you think that conversation made her *so cool*."

"They'll be here next week. That's what she wanted me to pass on to you."

I pick up my trusty blue Pilot felt-tip pen and chew on the end as I boot up my computer. Chewing on a pen is a nervous tic I haven't been able to rid myself of since high school. While I wrote. While I listened to music. It's part of my process at this point. I've just accepted it.

Based on the box of brand-new identical felt tips in my drawer, I've damn near embraced it.

"She also suggested that a"—she holds her hands up in

air quotes—"*release* might be beneficial for you and your moods."

"Yes, I heard that part. Thank you for reiterating it, Rosalie."

"Oh good, we're back to Rosalie. Because you don't want to fuck me, right?"

I click on the unopened emails in my inbox. I'm not reading them, but I can pretend that I am.

"Silent treatment. Very original. Well, in that case, should I set you up in the back? I could scrounge you up an old *Playboy*? I bet West has one kicking around. Or there are websites now where anything you want is at your fingertips."

Maybe she'll stop talking if I don't engage.

From the corner of my eye, I see her lean back in her desk chair. I don't need a full view of her face to know she's getting a real kick out of this.

"Did you like my journal entry?"

I point the pen in her direction but say nothing and keep my eyes fixed on my computer. Then I go back to chewing on it and ignoring her entirely.

But Rosie isn't having it. Her boots click against the floor. She comes all the way around my desk and leans against the edge, facing me.

Today's Rosie differs from yesterday's version.

Yesterday, she seemed distraught over me going to an event with a plus one. It was obvious to me that it would be her. Who the hell else would I take? Did she think I'd kiss her and run off with someone else?

Because no, I'd kiss her and get all up in my head over it. Torment myself. That's far more on brand for me.

I lean back in my chair, pen in my mouth, and regard her. No, today she seems hell-bent on torturing me.

"You're being weird," she says.

"Rich coming from you."

She crosses her arms and smirks, edging farther over until she's in front of me and I can't avoid her gaze.

"Did you ever lose that pesky V-card, Ford?"

I swallow. "I did, Rosalie. I appreciate your concern."

"To who? You know some of my dating history. Now I want to know about yours."

"I don't talk to my employees about my personal life."

"I'm not asking as your employee." After the words fly from her lips, we're left staring at each other once again.

Then she pushes my keyboard back, props her hands on the desk, and slides herself on it like she's settling in for story time.

She winces again, cheeks twitching in a pained grimace.

"What's wrong?"

"My body likes to warn me about my impending cycle by giving me the kind of cramps that could keep me in bed all day. Your mom said orgasms can also help with that."

I chew on my pen and zero in on the hem of her dress, the way it drapes so daintily over her crossed legs. I roll my chair back to create some distance.

"You should go home and rest, then."

She laughs and waves me off. "I'll give myself a hand later and see if it helps. But for now, I want to talk about you."

"Bash is going to walk in and wonder why you're sitting on my desk."

Her head tilts. "I thought you were checking your emails—he got called away for a fire. He's sending a painter to finish up the interior and will confirm a date and time. Now tell me about your dating history."

I cross my free arm to keep from reaching out and playing with that flimsy fucking hemline, pen tapping against my lips.

"I remember the night in that journal entry. I asked that girl if she was reading anything interesting. She told me she wasn't a big reader."

Rosie's eyes twinkle with mirth. She knows.

"And I believe I scoffed and said, 'Figures,' to which she gave me a dirty look and walked away."

"Your mom once told me that if I went home with a guy and there weren't any books at his house, I shouldn't fuck him."

I chuckle at that. "She's told me the same thing." I shake my head as I think about my mom. The advice she gives is outlandish and direct and… not wrong. "That night, when you drove us home, I asked you what you were reading."

Her eyes widen with interest. "I don't remember that part."

"You told me about a five-book fantasy romance series you were reading in very over-the-top detail. I pretended I was annoyed. But I went and put it on hold at the library as soon as we got back to the city."

Now her lips pop open. "Please tell me it was the Fever Series."

My mouth twists in a wry grin, and I push my wheeled chair closer. An invisible pull between us. "It was."

"Did you love it?"

I think back on reading those books. I mostly imagined Rosie reading them. Remembered the way her hands motioned as she drove and talked. West had passed out in the back seat, and I kept having to remind her to keep her hands at ten and two.

Her response was to roll her eyes and steer on the straight highway with her knee.

"Yeah, Rosie. I loved it."

"Oh. Back to Rosie, huh?"

"You said you weren't my employee right now."

I reach forward and flick a finger against her top knee. I don't know why I do it. It's childish and unnecessary and yet I can't stop myself.

Her eyes trace the motion, and then I smooth the spot with my hand before losing my brain entirely as I stand, grip her knee, and uncross her legs myself.

She sucks in a breath but otherwise forges ahead like nothing has changed.

"Okay. So, spill the beans." She leans forward a bit, her thighs falling open as she draws closer, her knuckles almost white on the edge of my desk.

I consider her question and nervously toy with the hem of her dress as I step closer. "I met a girl in my second year of college. She was smart and kind, and we had a good time together. I think we dated for two years."

Her nose wrinkles ever so slightly. "And?"

I move the hem higher on one side, exposing an extra inch of skin. "And I broke up with her after undergrad when she wanted to move in together."

"You didn't want to live with her?" Her voice sounds strained.

"No," I say simply.

"Why not?"

Because she wasn't you is what's on the tip of my tongue. But I say, "It just wasn't right. I didn't want to settle down," and lift the dress higher on her opposite leg as well.

Rosie swallows and nods slowly. "Okay, and then?"

I sigh and try to step away from her, but she nudges me with one booted foot. An unspoken challenge for me to stay in place.

Not one to back down, I swallow and move in closer again, my quads against her knees. And then I continue—talking *and* testing the limits with the hem of her skirt.

"Then I dated a woman for a few years while I ran Gin and Lyrics and worked on Gramophone with my business partners. But after the app went public, everything changed. That was a hard time for me. I learned a lot of valuable lessons about friends and relationships. Mostly that when unfathomable amounts of money are involved, people often change."

"In ways you don't approve of?"

I swallow, thumbing the thin fabric as a distraction. "I didn't want to give artists a platform only to rake them over the coals and pay them a pittance. I made my feelings on reducing their royalties known—rather publicly—and my opinion was not appreciated."

"And this relates to the girlfriend how?"

"I would like to be more than the number of zeroes in my bank account to the people in my life who I choose to trust."

"So, you didn't trust this woman?" Confusion paints her dainty face and I move to pull away, but her feet shoot forward and her boots hook around the backs of my legs, pulling me in closer. Keeping me from retreating.

The position leaves the dress draped down between her now-spread legs, covering any view I might have. It has her leaning back over my desk. It brings me closer than I should be.

Close enough that I prop the pen behind my ear and reach forward, my hands gripping her bare thighs as though that might keep her from pulling me any closer.

Then I tell her what I've told no one else.

"No. I learned I couldn't trust her. Or the people I went into business with. When I offered to personally fund artist royalties to offset the cut she became awfully concerned with 'our' fortune. "Obsessed, really." I scoff. "Like it would even have made a dent. Luckily, my one business partner, and former friend, is a big proponent of hoarding his cash and fucking people over. Jumping into his bed was a very convenient transition for her."

Rosie gasps and I watch a range of emotions play out in her ocean-blue irises. First comes shock, then sympathy, and then outrage. "I hate her," she spits.

My fingers pulse on her thighs and a low chuckle spills from my lips. I love her ferocity. Her loyalty. But I don't tell her that. Instead, I say, "I trust sparingly now."

Her top teeth nip at her bottom lip as she regards me keenly. "Do you trust me?"

I watch my hands on her bare legs. Moving them down over the tops of her thighs to the bend behind her knees and then back up to where they started. Then I finally meet her crystalline gaze. "Yes."

She sucks in a breath and nods. "Good. Tell me who else there's been."

"No one else."

She sputters. "Wait. What? That's it?" Disbelief drips from her tone as her fingers flex on the edge of the desk, grappling for control.

My stroking turns to massaging. My cheeks feel warm, and my dick is rock hard.

"It's adorable that you think fewer partners means I've had less sex." I tilt my face up to hers as I say, "It's also adorable you treat me like I'm still the bumbling teenager I was back in the days recounted on the pages of that journal."

She blushes, and I watch it spread down her throat. Pink skin cropping up over her chest, expanding beneath the neckline of her thin dress.

"Rosie," I continue, trailing the tips of my fingers over the backs of her legs. "I think you may have confused my self-control and sense of integrity with lack of experience or interest."

She makes a breathy little noise that sounds like a long drawn-out "Ha," as though she's having a good laugh at how dead wrong she's been. Her chin drops, and she watches my hands trailing over her skin. Gooseflesh pops up on the tops of her thighs.

"You're really telling me you've only ever been with two women?"

I move my palms up over the top of her thighs. We both watch my hands disappear beneath her skirt.

"Yes, but I've only ever really wanted one."

I hear her swallow. But she doesn't respond. That realization might take her a while.

"One I can't fucking have."

I flip her skirt up around her waist abruptly and she gasps. My eyes soak in the sight of her slender thighs leading up to the apex, covered in a plain white pair of boy shorts.

"Oh my god," she whispers as we both take in the sight before us.

She attempts to squeeze her legs together, but all it does is clamp me more tightly in place.

I don't stop touching her. Can't peel my eyes off the way my hands look gripping her thighs.

"One who's been driving me crazy. Wincing all morning like she's in pain."

All Rosie does is pant and watch me move my hands over her. Up the sides of her thighs.

I dip the tips of my fingers under the line of the shorts, not far enough to go anywhere. Just far enough to tease.

She whimpers.

I already know I'm planning to tear down whatever wall I tried to build between us just to get to her. Keeping my distance is downright excruciating, and thinking I can keep up with it is borderline delusional.

"Should I help you feel better, Rosie?" I growl out the words, frustration lacing each one. My thumbs brush up her inner thighs, painfully close to her pussy.

I shake my head at my utter lack of restraint.

"I told myself I was going to stay the hell away from you. But here I am, making you spread your legs for me on my desk and dreaming about fucking you senseless."

I thought I'd rendered her speechless, but now she rises up on her elbows and volleys back. "Might be hard to fuck me senseless considering you still haven't figured out where my clit is."

Now my eyes are on hers, reading the heat in them. The dare in them.

"Is that what you think?" I feel my body shift, rising to her taunt. My eyes narrow. My skin hums. I love that Rosie Belmont is a constant challenge.

"If I didn't know any better, I'd say you think it's in my thighs somewhere. Maybe I really should have helped you out all those years ago."

I smirk and pull the pen from behind my ear, eyes latched on her center. "Let's see what I can come up with."

I drop back down into my chair and roll myself between her legs. Using my teeth, I tug the cap from the pen and lean closer. Rosie pants as I splay a palm over her stomach, but when I peek up, her eyes are shiny and bright. Lips parted in anticipation.

So, I carry on.

I hold the pen in my right hand and make my first stroke. One downward line, diagonal, across her underwear.

"Oh god," she mutters, hips bucking.

I know I crossed her clit based on her reaction.

"Stay still, Rosie. I'd hate to fail this test."

I clamp my tongue between my lips and cross my first line with an upward one. I hear her hum, feel her legs shake as she struggles to stay still. Then I lean back to look at my handiwork.

When she glances down at herself, I hear a muttered, "Fuck," between her heavy breaths. A blue X is drawn over the pristine white fabric.

"X marks the spot," I grumble, both hands holding her thighs open.

"Yeah."

"You're soaking through your panties, Rosie," I say, flipping my pen around and dragging the dull, rounded tip of it up the line of her inner thigh.

"I know, I know." Her voice is breathy as I approach the seam of her underwear.

"Does that mean I got it right?" I take another peek at her flushed face, but all I see are green lights, the all-clear to keep going. "Tell me to stop, Rosie."

"Please don't stop, Ford," is her response. Because of course she has to drive me fucking crazy at every turn.

Without another thought, the pen dips under the fabric. It's barely a touch. I graze her pussy carefully, as though it's somehow breaking fewer rules than if I were to hook a finger into her panties.

Her head falls back, and I can't pull my eyes from her. The wall I've painstakingly built crumbles. Disintegrates.

When I pull the pen out, it's wet and shiny. I toss it onto the desk beside her and stand again, leaning over her body as I press against the pen mark with my thumb. Telling myself the flimsy cotton stretching between us makes this somehow less depraved.

But the truth is, nothing about this feels wrong. Everything about this feels *right*. So I go with it. I trust it.

I trust her.

"Admit it, Rosie." I press in firm, even circles. "I found it on the first try, didn't I?"

She arches her back now, hands gripping my shoulders as her eyes glaze over. She keeps her lips clamped shut and shakes her head defiantly.

I chuckle and switch to gentle upward swipes. Feeling the fabric beneath my thumb go wet. Feeling the hard point of her clit.

I know I got it right. And I know Rosie doesn't want to admit it.

But that's fine. I'll let her have it.

Her moans turn to breathless gasps. Her cheeks turn from pink to red. I switch back to firm, slow circles.

"Fuck, this is so good," she murmurs, eyes downcast as she watches me work her. "This should not be this—" I cut her off by increasing my pace.

"This is exactly how it should be."

Her gaze snaps to mine and she nods. Then her breathing quickens. I watch her big blue eyes go from hooded to widened. Her eyes have always been her giveaway. So I'm not at all surprised when she gasps, "Ford!" as her back arches off my desk and her lashes crash down.

She comes with my name on her lips. Then she collapses back onto my desk, panting, and slings an arm over her face while I continue to gaze down at her, all beautifully disheveled.

This will play on repeat in my head for years to come. A moment I've imagined for far too long. All I can see is how perfect she looked when she came. My new go-to fantasy when I need to take the edge off.

Which is what I need now. My cock is uncomfortably hard against the stiff denim. And Rosie is altogether too soft and pliant.

Too easily flipped around and bent over this desk.

So, I lean over her, grip her head, and press a quick kiss to her hair before I cross into a zone there'll be no coming back from. I worry about fumbling my words.

I worry about fumbling *her*.

The only girl I've ever really wanted.

I'm about to talk about this—about *us*—when my best friend's voice filters in from outside.

"Ford! Get your ass out here! I wanna tell you about today's delivery!" My stomach drops and we both freeze. West sounds downright amused. But I'm not.

Rosie's eyes go round as they meet mine. Time stands still for a few beats. And then we both leap into action. It's not a challenge since we're both still fully clothed.

I flip her skirt down, and she smooths her hair as I gently

guide her to standing. But a simple glance down at her face tells me I need to keep West from walking in here at all costs.

Rosie looks freshly fucked and my cock is doing its best to burst through my pants.

So with one firm nod at her, I adjust and stride for the door to cut her brother off and protect our privacy. This is *not* how he should find out.

I round the back deck and almost crash straight into him.

"Whoa." He steadies my shoulders with his hands, a mocking smirk on his lips. "Didn't expect you to come running quite that eagerly."

"Dick," I mutter, desperately hoping he doesn't bother looking down at mine.

West nudges his chin toward the office. "Let's go have a coffee. I'll catch you up on my day."

My jaw pops, and I peek back over my shoulder. "Can't. Rosie's working in there. Just let me grab my wallet and we can take a trip into town. I need to grab some things anyway."

"Yeah, cool," is all he says as he turns back to the parking lot with a pleased swagger to his step.

I march back into the office to find Rosie sitting primly at her desk like nothing happened at all. Her eyes move from my face to beyond me, clearly checking for her brother.

"Did he leave?"

I nod and walk to my desk—the scene of the crime—and grab my wallet that's still lying on top. "Yes. I'm going into town with him. I have… errands to run."

"Oh, *errands*?"

"Yes."

"Is that what the kids are calling it these days?" When I look across the room at her, she holds her hand up and mimes jerking off while tilting her head at me.

Normally, I'd chuckle. But I feel guilty.

I don't like running out on her after what just went down. But the truth is, the way my brain works, I need processing time. I need overthinking time. I need to get West away from her because what I really feel is obnoxiously territorial when it comes to her.

Rosie knows how I work. Understands me in a way I'm not sure anyone has before. She doesn't try to stop me—she just giggles and continues pumping at an invisible dick as a way of teasing me.

And when I get to the door, she calls out to me smugly, "You still missed the spot, Junior. Guess you'll have to try again sometime."

I turn back and glare at her, all mussed and totally full of it. She knows exactly how to press on my competitive streak. "Sure, Rosie. That would be a hell of a lot more believable if I hadn't just watched you come all over my desk."

CHAPTER 27

Rosie

FORD DOESN'T COME BACK.

Some girls might take offense. But me? With him? I'm just amused.

The man might be able to find a clit with spine-tingling accuracy, but I'd be willing to bet he's out there somewhere tugging on his hair and overthinking the hell out of things.

It's charming. Refreshing. I decide I'll sit back and watch him freak out for a while. If what he said about me, about wanting me, is true, then I don't need to pile on. If I know Ford—and annoyingly, I do—he's driving himself crazy right now while trying look like he has it all together.

One thing I've always admired about him is his sense of integrity. He's been a faithful friend to my brother, but also a faithful (if begrudging) friend to me in a lot of ways. He wouldn't take muddying those waters lightly.

Despite his aloof exterior, he's a worrier. And I don't

want to add to his worries. I just want… well, I want more orgasms on his desk.

So, at lunch, I head back to my shitty bunkhouse to make myself a sandwich and say hi to the mouse that I'm fairly certain has moved in with me. My mood is only buoyed by the fact my cramps have all but evaporated.

First, I change my panties. Then I pull out the turkey and bread. Once I make my sandwich, I toss a few crust pieces on the floor for the mouse, deciding I should pick a name for him, and then head down to my dock for lunch with a view.

I only get through about half when my phone rings from inside my purse. When I put my sandwich on my lap to answer, my turkey on rye falls into the lake. As it sinks, I stare at it sullenly.

Only at this time of the month could I cry over a lost sandwich. I just upended my life and mostly walked away with a smile. That night on the dock with Ford was the only time I cracked.

But that sandwich was really good. And I'm so hungry.

I don't recognize the number on the screen. Wondering if it might be a contractor, I answer and try not to sound pissy.

"Hello?"

"Rosie?"

I look down at the screen again, brows furrowing. "Cora?"

"Yeah." She sighs the word like she's exhausted.

"What's wrong? Where are you?"

I'm already standing. *Worried.*

Cora drops her voice to a whisper. "I got in trouble at school." I hear rustling against the receiver, like she's holding a hand up to block the sound. "I think the school called Ford. But he's just so uptight sometimes. And I just… Can you come?"

"Be there in ten."

I hear her sigh of relief.

"But, Cora?"

"Yeah?"

"Ford might seem uptight to you, but you gotta know that underneath all that, he's torturing himself over how to make everything right for you. With him, it's all in the actions."

"You think so?" There's so much hope in her voice.

Even though she can't see me, I nod as I head toward my car. "I *know* so."

If I thought waiting for pickup outside was a blast from the past, walking through the halls of my old junior high school is a full immersion in nostalgia.

Extreme nostalgia. A nonconsensual walk down memory lane. I liked school, but I preferred socializing. None of my best memories are here. Though I do spy the exact locker that witnessed my very first kiss.

I head straight to the office. It's familiar because I often had to walk from the school, across the field, and wait there for West to finish his detention while I chatted with the nice administrators.

When I round the corner, I see Ford is already here. Cora is sitting on a bench, her head dropped. A steady stream of tears roll down her face, and I immediately want to punch someone. With my thumb in the right position, because fool me once and all that.

I decide to hang back. Ford is crouched in front of her, his elbows slung over his knees as his hands dangle between them.

Would I even be me if I didn't take a moment to appreciate how good his dark-wash jeans look stretched tight over his round ass and muscular thighs? A flash of him between my legs, eyes burning, cheeks flushed, dick hard, hits me. Every time he catches his tongue between his lips, I melt. The way he concentrates on a person when they have his attention is like a drug. The way I felt with his eyes on me, his hands on me. There's an intensity, an intentionality to everything he does.

I can see why people vie for his attention. It's addictive. And I think I've been addicted to getting his attention since I was a kid.

I'm only just realizing I've had it all along.

Cora's lips move, and I can hear the deep baritone of Ford's voice as he responds. She looks so small, so crushed.

I know he's uncertain of how to act around her, but god, I want to give him a shake right now.

Hug the girl, you stunted idiot!

When he finally reaches out and rubs her shoulder, she crumples. And he finally does it.

He tips forward so he's kneeling before her, tall enough that it brings them face to face.

And then he hugs her.

He wraps his jean jacket-clad arms around his daughter and holds her while she sniffles against his arm.

My eyes water. This makes me want to cry much more than my drowned sandwich. I slide back around the corner to gather myself before facing them. I shouldn't have been rubbernecking, and I definitely don't want to walk over there and add my hormonal tears to their moment.

Because it is *their* moment.

I breathe deep and count to ten. I shimmy my shoulders, sniffle, and wipe at the corners of my eyes to make sure I haven't sprung a leak.

Then I step back around the corner. Ford is still kneeling, now wiping the tears off Cora's splotchy face, and it's not my eyes that explode. It's my ovaries.

"I don't want you to worry about this," he murmurs. "I'm always going to have your back, all right? Never question that."

Fuck me, I should have stayed around the corner a bit longer.

Cora catches sight of me and cracks a wobbly smile, which draws Ford's gaze back over his shoulder. His eyes widen, giving away his surprise at seeing me here.

Cora peeks back at him. "Sorry, I called her."

Ford looks between us, and I can't quite place his expression. If I didn't know any better, I'd say it was longing.

I offer an awkward wave, followed by a high-pitched, "Hi."

Remember me? The girl with the blue ink on her panties?

"Hey," he replies, pushing to stand. And now he's wearing an expression I recognize.

Relief.

He's relieved I'm here and that lights a warm, gooey spark in my gut. I step forward, deciding it's safest to keep my attention on Cora. But when Ford reaches over and his big palm rubs a circle on my lower back, I still shiver.

I forge ahead, crouching to hug the girl I've come to consider a friend. "Hi, my little storm cloud. How are you doing?"

She sniffs, but nods against my shoulder. "Better now."

Now it's my turn to sniff as I try to ease the ache in my chest. "Good. Who do I need to kill?"

Her brows furrow as I pull back to look her in the eye. "You don't even know what happened."

I shrug. "You're upset. That's all I need to know for now."

She peeks up at Ford—his jaw is popping, his face murderous. "I think Ford is going to kill him first."

I scoff and wave a hand between us. "Please, no one can afford to bail Ford out. I'll have to commit the crime and Ford will need to bring the cash. That's what happens when you're the World's Okayest Billionaire."

Cora snorts a soft laugh, her lips twitching as she wipes the back of her hand across her nose.

"Mr. Grant?" A woman with short gray hair pops her head around the side of the door. "Principal Davidson can see you now."

He holds a hand up in a friendly wave, but as soon as she's gone, he mutters, "About fucking time, since he's the one who called me here."

I press my lips in a firm line to keep from smiling. Because Ford is *mad*, and I always get a flutter in my chest when he's bitchy like this. It's probably diagnosable, but I don't care.

"I'll stay with you, Cora," I say.

"No." She shakes her head. "You go with him. I'm fine."

"Cora—" Ford tries to protest.

"No," she cuts him off. "Go together. Good cop, bad cop or whatever. I'm all good."

I look at Ford and shrug.

He rolls his eyes. "Fine, whatever. Who am I to resist? The two of you run my show already."

As he turns away, I catch up and lean in. "Are you going to introduce me as your dick manager?"

He slants his head in my direction, not making eye contact as we step into the front office. "I don't know," he whispers on our way past some cubicles. "Are you going to introduce me as your clit manager?"

Caught off guard by his crass joke, I bark out a laugh just before we stop outside an office door that is labeled *Principal Davidson*.

I steer us back into neutral territory since eye-fucking him while getting told off at the principal's office seems bold even for us. "What are we walking into here?"

Ford stops and turns to me. "Cora and I have been listening to samples together. It's kind of become our thing. I told her she could pick an artist out of the stack, and I'd try to work with them. That she could consult and be part of the process."

"Oh my god, that's adorable. You might actually be the World's Most *Thoughtful* Billionaire."

"Rosie. Focus."

I give a swift nod. "Right. Okay."

"So, she picked Skylar Stone, and we're working on scheduling something."

My brows shoot high. "Wait. *The* Skylar Stone? Country bombshell Skylar Stone?"

"Yes—"

"Oh my god. She's so hot. I hope I get to meet her. Like there is nothing *okayest* about her."

"Rosie." He widens his big, frustrated green eyes at me.

I salute him back. "Right. Focus."

He goes on, speaking quickly. "Skylar has been having a rough go in the media lately. Apparently, during a current events conversation in Cora's social studies class, her teacher made a disparaging comment about Skylar, which in itself is inappropriate. So, Cora got a little fired up and insulted him. All caught up?"

"Yes. Let's go cut a bitch."

Ford shakes his head and turns away. Hand on the small of my back again, he leads me into the principal's office.

Principal Davidson looks exactly as I expected him to. A little round in the middle, a little bald on top. The lenses of his glasses have smudges and there's a coffee stain on his tie. I actually feel kind of bad for him. He seems run ragged, and Ford is going to eat him alive.

"Mr. Grant." He reaches forward to shake Ford's hand. Then he turns to me. "Mrs. Grant."

I look at Ford.

Ford looks at me.

A small giggle catches in my throat, and I decide not to correct the man. Instead, I offer him a sweet smile and reply with my good cop opening, "So lovely to meet you."

Ford is already shaking his head as he sits in the chair facing the desk. He stretches his legs out in front of himself, just far enough to embody a bored king on his throne.

I want to straddle him.

"Okay." The principal clears his throat and knocks his hand against the desk. "So, we had an incident today with Cora."

"She already told me all about it." Ford's voice is pure steel.

"Right, well, sometimes the details get lost in translation with children."

Ford continues glaring. "She's twelve. And I trust her."

"Be that as it may, she called her social studies teacher… What was it? Let me have a look at his report here in my email." The man clicks, peering over the top of his wire-rimmed glasses, which tells me the prescription is off. "Ah! Here it is. In front of the entire class, she referred to him as a, and I quote, 'chauvinist piece of shit.'"

I snort and rush to cover my mouth, pretending to cough. But I'm no actress, so I'm fairly certain I fail.

Ford steeples his fingers beneath his chin. "Well, is he?"

"Mr. Grant…" The principal is sputtering now, clearly taken aback by Ford's lack of horror. "We surely can't have students speaking that way to teachers in the classroom."

"Then you surely should not be trusting chauvinist pieces of shit to enlighten the minds of impressionable children."

I cut in. "May I ask what preceded Cora's comment? That might help, you know, shine some light on the situation. Because while I agree that she certainly can't speak that way to a teacher—and we will talk to her—I'd love to get some context why you think she might have said it."

Mr. Davidson nods along, clearly more appreciative of my approach than Ford's. "In the report, it simply says they were having a conversation about current events and discussing different magazine articles."

I cross my legs and hook my hands around my knee as I tilt my head. "And?"

"She insulted her teacher."

"Some people deserve to be insulted. Sounds to me like this man might be one of them," Ford bites out.

I can feel him vibrating beside me. I reach over and place a palm on his thigh to calm him.

As any good cop wife would.

"So, you have a report detailing the ins and outs of what Cora did, written only from the perspective of the person she allegedly wronged?"

"He's a professional."

I just smile now. The situation hits too close to home on the heels of my last job. The way things are so easily swept under the rug to protect the person in power.

Then I use my most sugary voice. "Yes, well, as you know, sometimes the details get *lost in translation with professionals*."

Ford cuts in again. "He told the class, after reading an

article about a famous young woman who froze in front of a camera and couldn't speak, that women just aren't cut out to handle pressure the way men are."

My jaw drops and I flop back in my seat, giving up on being good cop. Is bad cop, bad cop a strategy?

"Wow, this guy really does sound like a chauvinist piece of shit."

Ford's head whips my way, and now it's his turn to chuckle.

"We... I'll have to look into that." The principal pulls his glasses off in a tired manner and scrubs his hand over his face. "I was going to speak to you about a suspension, but—"

"Take a hike, Principal Davidson," Ford all but growls.

The man sighs and flops back in his chair. He's tired. Overworked, underpaid. Probably sick to death of everyone's shit. I give Ford a little squeeze, my hand still on his thigh.

"How about she switches classes?" I offer.

"We're short-staffed."

I scrunch my nose.

"There's what? One month of school left?" Ford asks and the principal nods. "How about we take the curriculum home with us? We'll teach Cora what's left. She can study in the library or here in the office during that period. And she'll take the final exam when the time comes."

Principal Davidson hems and haws about it being unconventional but eventually agrees—as if he had a choice once Ford made up his mind.

Once the meeting ends, Ford takes my hand and we step

outside. "You think Cora will be okay doing the rest on her own?"

Ford scoffs. "She's not on her own. And she's really fucking smart. I know she'll be just fine. But if I could buy a public school just to fire that chauvinist piece of shit I would."

Then he walks me through the office like he really does own the place.

And when we get out into the hallway, he's still holding my hand.

CHAPTER 28

Ford

"You sure you're okay to go to school today?"

Cora looks at me from the passenger seat, the brick building visible through the window. She went the day after the whole current events debacle, but she seems awfully quiet today. Even what's become a regular morning call with her mom didn't perk her up like it usually does.

"Yeah."

"You just call me or Rosie if something goes wrong. You know we'll drop it all to be there for you."

"I know." She fiddles with her fingers in her lap.

"You can come hang out at the office if you need a day off."

"No, I should go."

"I've seen your grades, kid. If you need a mental health day, you can take one."

She nods, nibbling at her lip. Usually she'd have a snarky, funny comeback, but she seems subdued today. "You've got bowling tonight? I get movies with Rosie?"

Good god. *You've got bowling tonight* is a sentence I never thought I'd hear.

"Yup. And we can go visit your mom this weekend. We'll take a trip into the city."

"Yeah. I'd like that. And I should probably mow the lawn while we're there."

I give her shoulder a gentle squeeze. "You don't need to do that. There's a company taking care of the house."

Her brows lift. "There is?"

I nod.

"We can't afford that. You should call them off. It's okay if the grass gets a little long."

"Cora." I take both her shoulders and turn her toward me. "I know you had to pick up a lot of loose ends for a while there. But now, you just need to be twelve. Go to school. Give me dirty looks. Hang out with your friends."

Her cheeks rise, and she peeks up at me from beneath the fringe of her black bangs. "Consult on an album with Skylar Stone?"

"That seems less typical for a twelve-year-old. But yes. Once the booth is ready, we'll get her out here. Okay?"

She nods back, serious. "Okay." Then, "Thank you for having my back."

Oh god. She looks like she's going to cry. She and Rosie are going to be the death of me.

"I'm always going to have your back, Cora. No matter what happens. With you. With your mom. You're kind of stuck with me now. That all right with you?"

She blinks rapidly and nods. Then she drops her gaze

and her voice comes out a little watery when she asks, "So you're not mad at me?"

I feel like I've been struck. "Why would I be mad at you?"

"Because you got called away from work because of me? Because I got in trouble at school? I've never been in trouble before. I don't know why I just blurted it out. Did I embarrass you? You seem… tense since then."

My shoulders sag as I take her in. This little girl who's been so grown up for so long. "Oh, Cora. I am so far from mad at you. I'm mad that an adult charged with educating you said what he did. I'm mad we live in a world where people think about women that way. I'm sad Skylar's being mocked when no one knows what's going on with her." I scrub a hand over my scruff and up into my hair. "I'm tense because I feel like I'm juggling a million balls and dropping the most important ones while trying to get it all done. And I'm nothing if not a perfectionist."

"What are the most important ones?" She asks it with so much hope. It breaks my heart.

"You. You are the most important one." And that's what gets me. This girl *needs* me, and I feel like I haven't been as present as I should be—as I could be.

"What about Rosie?" She says it innocently enough, but I'm not oblivious to her subtle comments. And clearly, she isn't oblivious to whatever is going on between us, either. The handholding might have been a dead giveaway, but I wasn't ready to let her go. We felt like a team in the principal's office. And after so long going it on my own, refusing to trust anyone, it felt really fucking good to trust Rosie.

And unlike other people in my life, I know she would never let me down.

"She's very important to me too. But don't tell her that. It'll go straight to her head."

Cora smiles shyly at that answer and returns her gaze back down to her hands. I barely hear her when she says, "Can I have another hug?"

It feels like she reached into my chest and cracked my rib cage right open. I just grunt, not especially trusting myself to speak, as I gather her into my arms from across the console. I squeeze her tight, but she squeezes me tighter.

"I miss my dad every day," she whispers against my shoulder. "But I'm so glad I have you now."

Then she grabs her backpack and leaps from the car like she's being chased. I wipe at my nose and chuckle when I watch her peek over her shoulder with a tiny wave. That hot-pink scrunchie the one spot of color in her outfit.

When she's gone, I'm stuck driving back to work. Worrying about Cora. And obsessing over Rosie and her white fucking panties.

It's all too much. I like things orderly. And my life is now full-on chaos.

As I pull up to the office, I can't help but smile. The old barn has transformed into a really cool space. Everything I envisioned and more. The stone chimney and barn-wood exterior have been preserved, but everything else is shiny and new.

Double-paned windows with black trim. On the side of the building, the sliding doors lead to a sprawling deck facing the lake. A new front door faces the parking lot, black with an ornate antique knocker and a keyless entry lock. The walkway leading to it is accented with trimmed garden beds. Rosie took it upon herself to plant bulbs for god knows what. Knowing her, she may have planted weeds just to piss me off.

Now, I just need the actual studio. The booth. The sound equipment. And I'm thinking a few tiny house-type cabins so artists can use the space as a retreat.

As I'm envisioning houses with old barn siding just beyond the tree line, my eyes land on a truck I don't recognize.

Curious, I march in through the open sliding doors. And come to a screeching halt as I'm confronted with a feeling I haven't known well until recently.

Hot. Sharp. Instant.

Jealousy.

Rosie sits at her desk while some guy in white, paint-splattered coveralls and a backward hat leans against the edge with hearts in his eyes. Practically flexing his biceps and giving her his best-in-show spiel like a big, dumb Labradoodle drooling on her desk.

"Good morning!" I announce my presence with a level of faux friendliness that makes Rosie shoot me a suspicious look.

"Hi?" she greets me with pure confusion.

"Who do we have here?" I march right up to the guy with my hand out, ready to death grip the hell out of his.

He takes it and I fake a smile as we shake hands. "I'm Scotty. Bash sent me up to work on painting some walls."

"All right, Scott. Bash gave you a rundown? Or do you

need me to give you one?" I edge in front of him, as though I can block Rosie from his view.

He chuckles. "Oh, nah, man. Scott is my last name. Derek is my first. But everyone calls me Scotty."

Scotty. I almost roll my eyes. What is it with men in this town who introduce themselves using a nickname when they have a perfectly professional-sounding first name?

"Okay, Derek. Do you need a rundown?"

He looks confused, his almost-baby face scrunching up. "Oh, no, I'm good."

"Okay, great." I cross my arms and stare at him.

His gaze flits over my shoulder to Rosie, then back to me. "Okay, great," he repeats.

And then he's off, walking back out to actually do something he's supposed to.

"That was entertaining," Rosie pipes up from behind me. She's smiling when I turn to face her, but it drops quickly.

"What's wrong?"

"Nothing." She turns and starts clicking on her computer. "How was Cora this morning?"

"Are you still in pain?" I watched her walk around the office gingerly all day yesterday, and today I'm done with it.

"Why? Are you going to give me another orgasm to help?"

"If you ask really nicely."

That has her eyes snapping up to mine. "Well, Aunt Flo is here, so you probably wouldn't want to."

I shrug. "That's what showers and dark towels are for."

Her blue eyes go comically wide. "What did you just say?"

"Rosie, I'm a grown-ass man. Your period doesn't scare me."

She blinks back at me, pure shock painting her face, and carries on like I didn't say that to her at all. "It's just the first couple of days that I feel like shit. Same old. I'll be good as new by tomorrow."

"Go home."

She snorts, eyes back on her screen. "No. There's nothing wrong with me. You already overpay me. I'll work. You just don't want Scotty making googly eyes at me while I sit at my desk."

I don't want *Scotty* anywhere near her, but I won't admit that. "No, I don't want you working while you're not feeling well. This isn't an emergency room. Nothing is so pressing that you need to torture yourself being here. And I pay you in line with industry standards and an amount befitting your level of education."

She sighs, sounding exhausted. "Ford, women have been working through their periods forever. Stop micromanaging me. When I get home to my shitty bunkhouse and pet mouse—who I think I might name Scotty—I will eat junk food and lie in bed feeling sorry for myself like a big girl."

Pet mouse?

She really needs to stay at my place.

I turn away, knowing a losing battle when I see one. But not before I toss over my shoulder, "Just because women have been working through their periods doesn't mean they should be."

"Knock that off," she mumbles to my back. "Nice Guy Manager doesn't sound nearly as cool."

I can't help but chuckle as I reach into the pocket of my leather jacket and pull out my keys.

"Where are you going? You just got here!"

"I have an errand to run." I toss her a wink as I stride out the doors. "I'll be back later."

"Wait! Is *running errands* code for masturbating again? Was it awkward with West there?" She shouts it loud enough that *Scotty* fumbles his paintbrushes out of the back of his truck.

Her laughter fills the air, and at least that means she's happy.

And even if it's at my expense, I'll take it.

When I return that afternoon after running errands, Derek Scott is still checking Rosie out. I swear the guy is part owl. He can be facing the wall opposite her and somehow turn his head about ninety degrees.

I find myself wishing he'd turn it a little too far as I flop back into my chair. Then I open my email and fire one off to Rosie.

> Rosalie,
>
> We should work at the house. These paint fumes aren't healthy.
>
> Have a happy day!
> Ford Grant
> CEO and Producer at Rose Hill Records

276

I don't look up when her computer pings. And when I hear the *whoosh* sound of the incoming email, my stomach flips. So lame.

Good afternoon, Dr. Grant,

I think the paint fumes are helping my cramps. So maybe they're healthy after all! Scotty seems fine. So who's to say?

All my best,
Rosalie Belmont
Business Manager and Natural Health Consultant
at Rose Hill Records

P.S. How were your "errands"? Did you stop by the bank and make another donation? Bet you didn't even need a magazine this time.

She giggles as I read it, and I catch Scotty drool while gazing in her direction.

Nurse Rosie,

Scotty does not seem fine. He's a grown man who introduces himself by a nickname that his friends probably called him when he was the high school quarterback here in town.

> Get your laptop and say goodbye to the stray puppy dog so he can finish his work.
>
> My errands were fine. I didn't use a magazine the first time, and if I were to do it again, I wouldn't need one either.
>
> Have a happy day!
> Ford Grant
> CEO and Bation-Master at Rose Hill Records

This time I get an unladylike snort out of her before she looks up and mouths across the room, *Bation-Master?* I knew she'd like that one.

She throws her head back, laughing.

Then she goes back to typing, and I wait with bated breath to see what she comes back with. I swear the tips of my fingers tingle when her email shows up with bold lettering in my inbox.

> Dearest Bation-Master,
>
> OMG! Do you really think he was a quarterback? 😍
>
> Also, if you didn't use a magazine, what did you think about?
>
> Wait, I bet I can guess.
>
> Was it three commas on your bank account balance?
>
> No. Hmm.
>
> Owning a private plane?

Oh! Or a yacht where all the staff have to wear matching polo shirts in a specific country club color, like "salmon" or something equally bland.

No need to respond. Just blink twice from your throne over there if one of my guesses is correct.

All my best,
Rosalie Belmont
Business Manager to the Bation-Master at Rose Hill Records

When I finish reading, I look up at her. Unblinking. Then I pick up *the* pen and tap it against my mouth like I'm thinking hard. Her eyes catch on it and recognition kicks in.

That's when I bite down on it and send her an honest email back.

Rosie,

I thought about you.

-Ford

When I chance another look, her cheeks are flushed, and her eyes are fixed on the screen. I chew on the pen harder, waiting for her to say something or to react in some way. But her phone vibrating on the wooden desktop steals her gaze.

Worry flashes on her face, and she reaches for it abruptly.

"Cora? You okay?" Her mouth pops open and closes a few times. "All right. Do you want me to—" Her eyes flash up to mine, and I'm already standing, walking over to her desk. "Okay. I mean, he's not dumb. He's going to know something is up."

Alarm bells ring in my head as Rosie and I face off.

Cora.

"Yep. Just stay where you are. I'll be right there."

She hangs up and I'm immediately on her. "What's wrong? Why didn't she call me?"

Rosie is up, packing her things. Grabbing her laptop. Heading toward the door in a true rush. "She begged me not to tell you. But you should be happy. I think I'll go work from your house today, after all."

I follow her out onto the porch. "Rosalie, so help me—"

"Ford." Her eyes are serious as she searches my face. "She might need a little privacy in the coming days, and you're going to need to respect that. But I need to get into your house and grab her some fresh clothes. If you can't figure out what's going on based on all that information, then you are dumber than Scotty looks."

Oh god.

I felt unequipped this morning, but now?

"Figure it out yet? Ya girls are all synced up. So be cool, Dad."

I bristle to cover my shock. "I am cool."

She reaches forward and yanks *the* pen out from behind

my ear where I propped it. "Not when you do that. Plus, I think this pen is mine."

She turns to walk away, but it doesn't stop me from landing one parting shot. "Sure tastes like it."

And again, we go our separate ways to the sound of her laughter.

CHAPTER 29

Rosie

"Okay, and it's just going to stick to your panties like this."

I pass the pre-applied pad back under the stall door in the school bathroom as Cora shoves her less fortunate pair of jeans into a plastic bag. I've handed her everything under the stall door after checking multiple bathrooms for her throughout the school like a total creep.

"I'm so embarrassed," she says tearfully.

"Why? We all get our periods. It's very normal. Welcome to the next, like, forty years of your life."

"In class?"

I wobble my head as I consider that. "No, not everyone. But statistically, based on the age of people who get their cycles and the number of hours they spend per day in class, it definitely wouldn't be unusual."

"I don't think anyone noticed."

"Probably not. Plus, if someone was looking at your butt, Ford might kill them."

That draws a sad little chuckle as the sounds of her righting herself in a fresh set of clothes fill the otherwise empty bathroom.

"Rosie?"

"Yeah?"

"There's just… there's a *lot* of blood. Are you sure I'm okay?"

I lean against a sink and glance over my nails, trying not to laugh. Because it's not funny. But it is a walk down memory lane. "Oh yeah. The first couple of days are often quite heavy."

"How can you just… talk about this so casually?"

I try not to think about Ford. Showers. Dark towels There's a man who talks about it casually. "Well, when it happens for one week out of every month, it eventually loses its shock value."

"Oh my god. How am I going to handle having this *every month*? It's so awful."

"Don't fret, little storm cloud. It's not so bad. I'll show you more when we get home."

"Okay," she says quietly before the sound of the toilet flushing fills the space.

When she comes out, she looks embarrassed as hell.

She reminds me so much of Ford that it's hard not to smile.

"Come here." I open my arms, and she shuffles forward. Her face drops against my chest and her arms go around my waist as I envelop her in a hug.

"Thank you, Rosie."

I realize she probably thought her mom would be here for this occasion, and that just makes me squeeze her harder.

"Of course. Told you I'd always be here."

"Can I skip the rest of the day?"

"Hell yeah. I'll sign you out. Everyone at the office thinks I'm Mrs. Grant anyway."

She laughs as she pulls away. "Would you ever want to be?"

My brows furrow. "Be what?"

"Mrs. Grant?"

Oh god. The way kids put you on the spot is so brutal.

I deflect with a wink and say, "Who wouldn't?"

Luckily, that satisfies her because she nods, slips her hand into mine, and doesn't let go as we walk out into the hallway.

"I'll take you home. But first, we'll make the stop that my mom made with me the day I got my period. I always told myself I'd do it with my daughter when her big day came."

We both know I'm not her mom. But neither of us points it out.

In fact, all she does is give my hand a squeeze.

When we walk into Ford's house after our short shopping excursion, he's sitting at the kitchen counter staring at his laptop screen, pretending to work.

I can tell he's pretending because beside him is a pile of what I would refer to as *period products*.

Pads of every shape and size.

Tampons of every shape and size.

Midol.

A hot water bottle.

I sigh and glare at him. So awkward.

"I thought you weren't going to tell him?" Cora throws her hands over her face like she can hide behind her palms.

I rub her back, bending at the waist to face her. "I didn't. But, honey, adult men are well aware this happens to women every month. It's not a global secret or anything. And you live with him, so like… he was going to figure it out."

"Stop talking. I want to die."

When I peek up at Ford, his eyes are wide. He's a tall, green-eyed idiot who does not know what to do right now. I tip my head toward him, signaling that he shouldn't just sit there like a statue.

He unfolds himself from the stool and takes long but tentative steps toward Cora. Then he crouches down in front of her, giving my calf a squeeze that sends butterflies erupting through my stomach. His other hand cups the pointed end of her elbow.

"Cora, I'm going to go bowling like a small-town weirdo tonight and leave you and Rosie to it. I'm not trying to make you want to die. I'm just trying not to drop any balls, remember? I didn't get to know your dad, but it sounds like he was a great man. I think he'd want me to make sure you had all the things you needed. Your mom would too." He points at the counter. "And that's what I went and did to make myself useful, because I'm nervous and fumbling and trying not to fuck this all up with you."

His voice hitches as the words come out, and I reach for his shoulder. It leaves us all huddled at the entryway to the kitchen. All connected by touch. By experience. By time and space and, shit, DNA.

Cora peeks at him from between her hands. "You're not dropping any balls, Ford."

He nods back at her. Squeezes her elbow. Then he stands abruptly and whispers roughly against my ear, "There are glass bottles of Coke in the fridge and the pantry is stocked with boxes of Old Dutch sour cream and onion chips. I flew them in for you. That was my errand. Have fun."

I gasp because I told him *weeks* ago those were my favorite snacks. A cut above.

He smiles against my cheek and presses a firm kiss to my hair before striding away like he's being chased.

"I'm going bowling." He swipes his keys off the counter and makes a very Ford joke in an attempt to leave us both laughing. "I'll see you period princesses later."

And it works. We're both in stitches when the front door clicks shut.

I wake up to the feeling of knuckles brushing my cheek. When I open my eyes, Ford is sitting on the coffee table. Just like he did once before.

"Hi," I murmur, shifting but not really bothering to right myself. I feel safe enough around Ford that being laid out in front of him isn't alarming in the least.

"Hey." He takes his hand away and I instantly wish he'd put it back.

"How was bowling?"

"Fucking awful. Bash was away, and he's pretty good. West thinks getting team shirts and coming up with a name will somehow make us better. Crazy Clyde told me about the time aliens abducted him. So at least that was entertaining. And the beer was good."

I smile sleepily. "I want to meet Clyde. You smell like beer."

"It was West's night to drive."

West. I'm hit with guilt over not having seen him much lately even though I'm living on his property. Everything between the three of us is so different from when we were kids.

Ford sounds downright tortured when he whispers, "Rosie, I don't know what I'm doing."

"With what?"

His eyes search my face.

"With work. With Cora. But mostly with you. I don't know what to do with you. West is… He's such a loyal friend. Possibly my only true friend. Such a long-standing part of my life. And you work for me now, and that…" He runs his hand through his hair, mussing it just the way I like. "That makes everything so much worse in my head. So much more complicated."

I stare back at him. Reading the indecision that consumes him.

"I stepped away from running Gramophone because my

business partners became people I didn't recognize. Actually, I didn't step away. I was ousted from the board and left as just another shareholder. We were college friends, and we founded that app with the best intentions. We founded that app because we loved music. Or at least I thought so. But money changed their goals, their outlooks… their loyalty."

My throat aches. My chest hurts. "Ford." I reach out and squeeze his knee. "I'm so sorry that happened to you. I had no idea."

His warm palm lands over mine. "Been too embarrassed to tell anyone. I guess it was nice that they agreed to say I was leaving my role to start a new venture."

I sit up, ready to punch someone for making this man, who brims with integrity and reliability, feel so low. Both hands on his knees now, I lean forward. "That was not *nice* of them, Ford. It was a cover for themselves. Fuck them."

He sighs. "I know. But I still… The pressure to keep up with my perfect record. To found another successful company so I don't look like a fool of a trust fund baby. I just… Remember when you told me you were tired?"

I nod, gathering his calloused hands in mine.

"I'm tired too, Rosie. Everything inside me feels so fraught, and I just want to get it all right."

"You're doing great. I don't tell you enough, but you're incredible. Your life has been turned upside down in so many ways. And here you are, excelling. Persevering. You aren't the titles those magazines give you—hell, you aren't even the titles I give you. You're a *good* man who is doing his best. And your best is more than good enough."

"But Cora—"

"Is going to be fine."

He just glares, so I carry on.

"Listen to me. Your taste in music is mediocre and your fashion sense is mountain-man-but-make-it-expensive. Your bank account is so full that you don't even know what to do with it."

"Great, thank you," he says dryly.

"A lot of the time, your vocabulary consists of grunts and bitchy, one-word answers."

"You should see how big my dick is, though."

I roll my eyes and forge ahead, trying not to get tripped up by the mention of his dick and how annoyed I am that I haven't seen it yet. "You grew up rich with a celebrity father. You founded a world-famous music-streaming service. Your bar is where musicians get discovered. You're about to work with some of the planet's most talented artists. I bet you donate to charity."

"I do."

"But from where I'm sitting, she's the best thing you've ever done."

That strikes him silent.

"I mean, look at her. She's smart, she's funny, and she's so damn special. Give her everything you've got right now. She needs you. Nothing is more important. The rest can wait."

He's still staring at me. Knees on his elbows. Face drawn. Hands over his mouth.

"I don't know what's going on between us, Ford. But there's something, no point in denying it. And yeah, it's messy. And complicated. And confusing. And I also worry that if things go sideways, it could be really bad. For both of us and for everyone around us. Especially Cora. And since I basically played a part in her conception—"

He groans and scrubs both hands over his face. "I already regret telling you that."

"Yeah, and it's even in writing. But anyway, stop over-thinking it. Let's just carry on like nothing happened. Go back to being frenemies who don't... exchange pens. This thing is so new, it never even got any legs, so nothing needs to change. I'm a big girl. I'll be fine."

I wonder if he can hear the lie in my words. I won't be fine. But there's too much at stake. I don't want to hurt his and West's relationship, and I especially don't want Cora to get attached to the idea of something that might just be a blip on the radar. She doesn't need anything else in her life that isn't permanent.

"I worry about you," is all he says. And I can hear the anguish in his words.

"Why? I got a really great make-out session behind the bar and the world's okayest orgasm out of the deal."

He drops his head between his knees now. Like he's on a plane, preparing for a crash landing.

I chuckle. "Sorry. I didn't mean to make you cry over it."

"Rosie. You kill me."

"That was funny. Why aren't you laughing?"

Now his head tips up. Eyes glowing neon, like they defy the dim light in the living room. "There's nothing funny about the way I want you."

I swallow, and my gaze snags on the silver chain that has slipped out from behind the V-neck of his T-shirt.

The pendant is dangling between us, in plain sight. I've felt it before in my hand but never really processed what it was. I reach for it and feel the familiar smooth metal of the key that's attached, warmed from resting against his skin.

"That's…"

He looks bashful now, like it's a struggle to hold my gaze.

"That's my diary key."

Ford nods.

"From like… ten years ago."

Another wordless nod.

"You kept it? All this time?"

"I figured I'd see you again one day. I just… I've worn it for so long that I'm attached to it. And the lock broke when you tossed it out the window, so it really wasn't necessary anymore. I just didn't say anything."

He wore the key to my diary for ten years.

My chest aches. My mind spins. This man has been keeping me close to him for a decade. Breaking speed limits to get to me. And I never noticed until now? What is wrong with me?

I want to hold him, I want to kiss him, I want to tell him I'm sorry for not seeing him. But that key can't change what we just agreed to—what we both know is best. I don't want to be another complication in his life right now.

Maybe one day. When the timing is right.

So, I offer him a nod of my own. Accompanied by a watery smile. "You're one of the good ones, Ford Grant Junior. Keep the key."

Then, refusing to let my resolve wither under the intensity of his stare, I add, "Thank you for the boxes of chips and bottles of Coke. You're a very thoughtful boss."

He winces at the title.

But he still says, "You're welcome," and walks me home like the gentleman he is.

And it takes everything I have not to beg him to come in. To be a little less gentlemanly just for one night. But I don't.

Turns out it's better this way because as soon as I close the door, I cry, and I'm not even totally sure why.

I've always hated Ford Grant—or at least that's what I tell myself.

And that's what I cling to all of Friday and the entire weekend.

It's the only way I'll get through.

CHAPTER 30

Ford

Rosie,

Decided to pull Cora out of school for today and head back to the city. She's good this morning, just seems extremely sensitive. Figured a change of scenery might do her some good. Her mom is ready for visitors now, and we're going to spend the weekend together. I hope you're okay to hold down the office until next week. Might not make it back until Tuesday.

—Ford

Good morning, Mr. Grant,

Thank you for the heads-up. Of course, I'm more than happy to hold down the fort here.

I hope you all have a fun weekend together.

All my best,
Rosalie Belmont
Business Manager at Rose Hill Records

Rosie,

To clarify, Cora and I are going to spend the weekend together. Not her mom and me. We're going to visit her mom, and then Cora and I are going to the zoo. Do some things like that. Maybe go up the Calgary Tower. Check on her house.

If you need anything, you can call. Anytime.

—Ford

Good morning, Mr. Grant,

No need to explain. You are welcome to spend your weekend with whomever you'd like.

Say hi to Cora from me.

WILD LOVE

All my best,

Rosalie Belmont

Business Manager at Rose Hill Records

Rosie,

We're safe at our hotel in the city. Cora says hi back.

Is everything okay?

Your emails are very formal. Blink twice if you've been possessed? Or kidnapped?

I'd feel better if you just insulted me.

What are you planning to do this weekend?

—Ford

Mr. Grant,

Thank you for the update. My emails are merely professional. And I have nothing but good things to say about you as my boss.

As your business manager, I think it's worth mentioning that keeping your company signature for work-related emails is best.

If anything requires your attention, I will inform you.

All my best,

Rosalie Belmont
Business Manager at Rose Hill Records

Rosie,

This isn't work-related, and you know it.

—Ford

Mr. Grant,

It would be easier for me if you could behave as though it were.

See you next week.

All my best,
Rosalie Belmont
Business Manager at Rose Hill Records

I'm not sure how I'll feel when I walk into the office on Tuesday morning.

I've spent the weekend getting to know Cora better. Getting to know her mom, Marilyn, better. Sharing experiences with the daughter I never expected and realizing I can't quite imagine my life without her.

She's fucking cool. Really cool. I would still think that even if we weren't related.

I've also spent the weekend worrying about Rosie. A pit hollowed itself out in my stomach when I walked away from her bunkhouse last Thursday night, and I haven't been able to shake that sick feeling all weekend. I should have gone after her.

I let her walk away too damn easy.

No matter how much fun Cora and I had. No matter how much I overate at Peter's Drive-In. No matter how exhausted I was from walking, biking, and waking up early to swim. I couldn't shake that sick feeling.

Like I went out, but may have left the stove on.

Like I just got to the airport, but may have left my passport at home.

I feel like I went to the city with Cora and left something incredibly important behind.

A piece of myself.

I only managed to get any sleep with my hand wrapped around the key at the end of my chain.

She told me I was one of the good ones, but that doesn't count for much when I feel so damn awful.

So, when I walk in through the open sliding barn doors, I expect to feel relief. I plan to lay it all out in an organized and logical fashion when the right moment presents itself. To tell Rosie there's nothing complicated about the two of us if she doesn't want there to be. That I don't care about the mess. There's no one I'd rather be messy with.

But when I walk in to see Scotty leaned up against Rosie's

desk, laughing his way through some dumb story about his weekend, all logic flies out the window. She's wearing a dark purple pencil skirt with a matching blazer and a pair of nude stilettos, like this is the damn city or something.

Never have I seen her dressed so formally for work since she started here with me.

Never has a pencil skirt looked so good on a woman.

I turn my eyes on my desk, breezing into the space and doing my damndest to avoid staring at her. From my periphery, I see Rosie shift over to peek at me, around the painter guy. He doesn't bother acknowledging my presence, or he's so busy staring at her that he hasn't noticed me.

I have no doubt she feels the animosity rolling off me. She's always been especially attuned to my moods—she's always been one to call me out on them too.

There's been no tiptoeing where Rosie Belmont is concerned, and I decide I'm done tiptoeing too.

I sit woodenly against the edge of my desk facing them, cross my arms, and clear my throat.

When Derek Scott finally turns, he shoots me a predictably dopey smile. "Morning—"

I match it and cut him off with, "Derek, your work here is done. You can leave."

"What?" In his defense, he sounds genuinely shocked.

"You have five minutes to pack up your things and get out of my office."

"Dude. Man. I was just taking a quick coffee break. I'm getting back to it right away."

I pin him with my coolest glare. I'm well aware I'm being

a dick, but right now I don't care. I'll paint the place myself so long as it stops him from ogling her. "Derek. Dude. Man. You're fired. Get out."

Behind him, Rosie leans back and crosses her arms. It does nothing but accentuate the swells of her breasts. Even the way her tongue pokes at the inside of her cheek in annoyance distracts me.

The guy mumbles something about being almost done, but I don't drop Rosie's stare from across the room when I address him. "That's fine. I'll pay you for the entire thing. Just leave."

He scoffs and keeps mumbling to himself as he packs up his paint and ladder and whatever else he left lying around. Rosie and I face off like we're having a staring competition while he does. She looks like she's going to kill me, and I hope she tries.

I hope she gets right up in my face and gives me a piece of her mind.

"Later, Rosie," he says as he takes one last long look at her before stepping through the wide-open doors.

"See you around, Scotty." She doesn't drop my gaze when she says it, and I see him cast a curious glance my way.

Then he leaves. Fucking finally.

And we face off.

"Welcome back," is how Rosie breaks the silence. She stands and smooths her hands down over the front of her pencil skirt. In the next moment, she's moving across the office, heading straight for the doors. With a tug, she slides one side closed. "You're in fine form this morning," she adds before closing the other as well. "Real charming, boss. Charging in here like a feral dog, pissing all over the place."

"Why are you closing the doors?"

She strides toward me, looking tall and powerful and royally pissed off. "So that I can tell you what a raging dickhead you are without risking anyone overhearing me."

My head quirks. "Oh, okay. Are we keeping things work-related now? Or is there a chance this rant you're about to go on is personal?"

She steps closer, the pointed toe of her shoe almost butting against my leather boot. "Don't pull that shit with me, Ford. You forget how well I know you. You fired a capable painter because you're acting like a jealous little boy. You can't behave that way in a town this size. It's a bad look. Just get this tantrum out of the way so we can get back to work."

I say nothing, so she sighs, hands on her hips, chin dropped like she's as tired as I am. "I thought we turned over a new leaf." Her eyes flit, only for a moment, to the chain around my neck before she licks her lips and adds, "I'm busy. And so are you."

I stand and glare down my nose at her with a dark chuckle. All she does is tip her head up. Doesn't give me an inch.

"You might have turned over a new leaf in a matter of days, but I've been watching this one grow for years. I don't think I'll be turning it over at all."

She rolls her eyes. "Ford—"

My hands dart out, land on her waist, and tug her against me. "Don't *Ford* me, Rosalie."

"Oh, we're back to Rosalie. That's at least a step in the right direction. Maybe that means you're over wanting to fuck me and we can—"

I press a finger to her mouth, startling her into silence. And then I speak very, very clearly.

"I'm never going to get over wanting to fuck you. And something tells me you won't care what I call you when I do."

Her eyes widen like she's about to say something, and I press my finger down harder. Watching the flesh of her lips give way beneath it.

"You told me nothing would change." She nods along. "Except everything changed. You changed. I changed. *We* changed."

She stops nodding—stops breathing.

"Because I spent all weekend *tortured* over you." I spit the words out in frustration. "I was supposed to be having a great time, but all I could think about was *you*. I've been obsessed with you for years, and I don't even know if I fully realized it. I've heard about you through the grapevine—looked you up online. I've gone a decade without laying eyes on you, satisfied that you were doing what you wanted to be doing. But it never felt like this weekend did."

She smirks now, challenge flaring in her eyes. "Good. I hope you were miserable," she says against my digit. "I know I was."

My hand shifts and I grip her chin. "Stop playing that game with me. We're not kids anymore."

"What game?"

"The one where we pretend to hate each other."

She tips her chin up defiantly. "You do hate me. That's our safe place. You have to hate me. It's easier that way."

I shake my head, molars grinding. "I definitely don't hate you, Rosie. Not even close. But I can fuck you like I do if that's what you need."

Her chest rises and falls, eyes ablaze. Gaze searching. The moment is fraught, like the seconds before a race starts.

Finally, her brow quirks. "Do you need a formal invitation or something?"

And those are the words that have every obstacle between us evaporating on the spot.

I flip her around roughly and step in close behind her as I bend her body at the hips. Her hands slap loudly in the quiet office as her palms hit the flat surface of my desk.

"Stay like that, Rosie. Claws where I can see them."

She gives the computer screen on my desk a nudge to make room for her spread fingers and it goes crashing to the floor.

I laugh. "Brat."

Then I'm gripping the hem of her tight-as-hell pencil skirt, tugging it up over her smooth thighs. Shoving higher so it's bunched around her waist. Her black thong outlines the globes of her ass.

I grip them hard. I know she can take it.

"This ass has been haunting me, *Rosalie*. That formal enough for you?"

All I get is a flip of hair and a flash of a flushed cheek as she glares at me from over her shoulder. "Fuck you, Ford."

I smirk. The one I know does nothing but piss her off. "You're about to be, Rosie."

I yank her panties down to her thighs and kick her feet apart so she's spread for me. I pause, taking her in. The black underwear stretched between her legs. The way her stilettos accentuate her calves. The glare she's still giving me from over her shoulder.

Her brow arches. "Do you need me to explain to you what to do next?"

I work on my belt with one hand, using the other to rub up over the column of her spine beneath her shirt and jacket, forcing her down onto her elbows. My hand continues its perusal, across her shoulder, a tight squeeze at her throat, before I hook two fingers into her mouth.

I shove my jeans down, working on my boxers as I lean over her body and whisper in her ear, "No, I think I prefer you with your ass up and your mouth stuffed."

Her lips close around my fingers and her teeth bare down in warning. My dick comes free, and I don't waste any time lining us up and running the tip over her to test how wet she is.

I groan at the contact, then growl against her neck, "This pussy is fucking soaked. Just like I knew it'd be."

Her hips shimmy and I hear her muffled, "I hate you," from around my fingers.

I don't take it personally. It's always been like this between us. We say one thing and mean another. So I answer, "I hate you too."

She's already hot, worked up, and pulsing beneath me, but now she widens her stance and arches her back, urging me on.

I push the head of my cock into her, and we both groan. I pull back out and her chin tips forward on a desperate whimper.

"More."

"You're awfully eager for my cock, considering how much you hate me. Aren't you, Rosie?"

I press my lips down on my tongue as I swipe myself through her wetness again, waiting for her to retaliate for that comment.

And she does.

She bites down hard on my fingers, but I don't remove them. I dig the fingers of my other hand into her hip and thrust forward, impaling her on my full length.

"Oh god," she moans, and I watch her fingers curl against the desk.

"Should I stop?" I grit out, trying to get myself under control.

"Mmm," she hums around my fingers. Her bite transforms into a firm suck.

My breathing goes ragged when I look down and see myself inside her. When I feel her clenching around me. "So fucking tight."

I want to touch her. Feel her.

I remove my fingers from her mouth with a wet popping sound and press between her shoulder blades, pushing her lower as I lift her hips.

My eyes follow the motion as I draw out and slide myself back in.

"Ford," she murmurs, and her eyes flutter shut from where she's laid out flush against the desktop.

"Should I stop?"

"Don't you dare."

I thrust again, hand roaming. Her back. Her hair. My fingers link with hers.

I grip her ass, I pull her hair, I fuck her like I hate her even though I don't.

"Is this what you needed, Rosie? Someone to fill this tight little cunt? Fuck all the fight right out of you?" My words come out choppy, breathless, as I pound into her. The desk scrapes the floors as we push it forward. "You going to settle down once I make you come on my cock?"

Her ass shakes with the force of my thrusts, and she chuckles. "You going to stop following me around like a sad puppy once you finish flopping around back there?"

I slap her ass and watch a handprint bloom on her pale skin. The hint of a tan line from last summer just beside my mark. She moans and rolls her forehead against the desk. I grunt on a forward thrust, getting off on the way she squirms. Loving the way she bites back. "That was mean, Rosie. And no. You're stuck with me. Give me all that bitchy attitude. It just makes me love you more."

The words slip out before I can stop them. They hang between us, heavy—an elephant in the room. I slow my motions as silence descends between us.

She finally lifts her head and looks back at me over her shoulder. Eyes glazed, cheeks glowing. I expect her to hear my words and run away. To move us back into familiar territory. Put us back on even footing.

But her voice comes out hushed when she says, "Okay, now I want you to flip me over and fuck me like you love me."

CHAPTER 31

Rosie

I DON'T KNOW WHY I EXPECTED MY REQUEST TO BE MET WITH a laugh or a smirk or an eye roll. That's how Ford and I operate—that's us. Being honest? Being *nice*? It's new and uncharted, and I don't know what to make of it.

But he does.

He doesn't miss a beat, helping me to my feet and turning me to him. His chest is hard against mine, his hands are gentle on my cheeks, and he kisses me like he can't get enough. It feels like he wants to be touching me everywhere he can.

Kissing. Stroking. Undressing me. He whispers my name against my skin like a prayer, and before I know it, I'm naked, seated on the desk, and he's dropping to his knees before me.

My knees part and I revel in his sharp intake of breath as he pauses to take me in. The way his rough hands slide up the insides of my thighs before hooking my legs over his shoulders. And the way his eyes flash up to mine as he drops his head closer to my core.

I feel exposed and vulnerable as he stares, just looks at my spread pussy for a few beats. Eyes twinkling like I'm the most exciting thing he's ever seen.

I almost combust on the spot when he growls, "Oh fuck yes," before lifting his gaze, smirking his stupid, cocky smirk, and then kissing my clit. A deep groan rumbles in his throat as he tastes me for the first time and my eyes roll back in my head.

I'll be replaying that noise in my head forever.

He starts slow, but neither of us has any restraint. Our fervor is on a constant upswing. My hips push forward, begging for more. His tongue presses into me, and my fingers grip his hair yanking him closer.

I broke every speed limit to get to you.

His teeth graze along my pussy, and my head tips back.

There's nothing funny about the way I want you.

His fingers slide in as he sucks, and my legs clamp around his neck.

It just makes me love you more.

He twists every ounce of pleasure from my body, his free hand blazing a trail of heat up over my stomach, strumming my nipple as he works me over.

"Ford!" I gasp his name as my orgasm hits me like a freight train. Hard, fast, and relentless. My body shakes as I come apart around him. I hold him just as tight as he holds me.

When the waves subside, he pulls out his fingers and

stands over me, hand cupping my cheek. "What I meant to say earlier is I'm fucking obsessed with you and I have no idea how to handle it."

At those words, I reach forward, wrapping my hand around the root of his hard length that juts out above the waistband of his underwear. Every hot, hard inch of it. It's huge, and I know I'll be feeling it tomorrow.

His head drops as he kisses my cheek. It hits me that I'm totally naked and he's not. I'm fully exposed, and he's not.

Except maybe he is.

I shed my clothes, and he shed all his barriers.

I run his head, the pearl of cum beading there, over my pussy and moan at the feel. His hands graze up over my ribs, and he holds my breasts reverently. Cupping. Squeezing. Then twisting on my nipples as I swipe him across my already sensitive clit and murmur, "What else? Tell me more."

I want him to feel just as naked as I do.

"What I meant to say earlier is I've dreamed about this."

I drop my head to his chest and breathe him in. *So have I.* The thought filters through my mind and I recognize its truth.

"What I meant to say is I missed you like crazy this weekend."

I nod, my forehead resting against the damp base of his throat while I guide his length back into me. "I missed you too."

He sucks in a shuddering breath as he fills me. My shaking legs take their place around his waist this time as he clears off what's left on top of his desk. It all goes flying as he lays me back and slides in to the hilt.

He moves, slow and achingly tender. I feel every inch, every ridge, every vein. He fills me so completely I almost can't stand it.

My hips move with him, and my skin breaks out in a light sweat.

We don't talk—we don't need to. We both know.

We understand each other so damn well.

"Rosie. Rosie." When I sit up to hold him, he chants my name against my neck, and I shiver. He sounds so undone. All for me. My nails rake down his back. "This is…"

My legs clamp him more tightly as he fucks me with increasing abandon, and I whisper against his skin, "Perfect."

Our eyes catch and something passes between us. Understanding. Agreement. We both know this is perfect. Him. Me. Us. Nothing has ever felt more right.

His jaw flexes as he pumps slowly into me, searching my eyes. He's always watching my eyes so closely. I usually find it unnerving, but right now it does nothing but make me want more from him.

So I lie back on the desk, let my legs fall open, and start to play with myself while Ford takes me in. That expression of reverence—borderline disbelief—back on his face in full blinding force. But then I bite my lip and pinch my clit and his expression turns downright wicked.

It's that cocky grin and slow bob of his Adam's apple that tips me off. He pulls out and then slams in hard. Again. And again. Steady, even, powerful strokes that shake my entire body.

Ford fucks me senseless on the top of his desk. Scattered

office supplies and a shattered computer surround us. But all I see is him. He looks like some sort of avenging god working me into a frenzy. Flushed cheeks, disheveled hair flopped over his forehead, veins bulging on his forearms while his abs flex with every thrust.

I think I could come just from savoring the view I get by lying with spread legs beneath his hard, heavy body.

His hands hold me open wide, and his eyes stay locked on mine. And when I fall apart again, he watches me like he's committing another moment to memory.

He's always staring at me like this. Like he worships me.

Then he drapes himself over me, fusing his lips to mine, and pumps into me until I feel him finish. I feel everything. Every pulse. Every kiss. Every touch.

If this is how it feels to be fucked like Ford Grant loves you, I want him to love me forever.

I hold him close. Hugging him to me even he's still inside me.

I can feel his heartbeat on my chest and his harsh breaths against my neck.

"You know what I hate the most about you, Ford?" I ask.

"What's that, Rosie?" He pants my name, runs his nose up the line of my neck, and tightens his hold on me.

"That hating you is downright impossible."

My voice cracks on *impossible*, and with that, we both know that I don't hate Ford at all.

In fact, it might just be the opposite.

CHAPTER 32
Ford

HATING YOU IS DOWNRIGHT IMPOSSIBLE.

The sentence plays on repeat in my mind as I carefully replace every single piece of Rosie's clothing. Putting them back on her is almost as erotic as taking them off.

My cum drips from her as I slide her panties back into place, and I take a base sort of satisfaction in swiping it up over her clit. Making her gasp.

Then comes the skirt.

The gentle hum of the hidden zipper that seals the tight, plum-colored fabric around her waist.

The way she holds my stare as I tuck her blouse back into the waistline.

The graze of my knuckles over the swells of her breasts as I rebutton her blazer.

She tries to toe her shoe back on, but I crouch and gently slap her foot away. Sliding the soft leather over each foot myself. Running a hand up the back of her calf and pressing a kiss to her knee before looking back up at her.

Her hand reaches for me, the tips of her nails trailing through the lock of hair that has fallen over my forehead.

"I'm sorry about your computer," she says softly, with a little twist to her mouth, like she's not sorry at all.

My eyes slice to the floor where my Mac lies, its screen hopelessly shattered. I grin back up at her. "Worth it."

Her cheeks flush pink, and she turns her head away, almost shy. "You're the first person I've ever had sex with without using a condom, so I should be all clear in that department. I'll get checked to be sure."

I suppose someone as allegedly intelligent as me should have been concerned about that. But she's turned me into a caveman, because all I hear in that sentence is that I'm the first man to fuck her bare.

"Same," I grit out, feeling my cock go hard for her all over again.

"I don't want you to think I'm trying to trap you with a baby, so I should also tell you I have an IUD." Her brow wrinkles. "Probably should have told you that before too."

I stare back at her. "I wouldn't feel trapped with you."

Her cheeks go even darker, and a heavy silence descends between us.

It's then that I hear the slamming of a car door from the driveway out front. My head flips in that direction and so does Rosie's.

Déjà vu.

She tugs at the bottom of her blazer, smoothing her hands over her hair.

"Who the hell would be here?" I try to straighten myself, but I don't especially care about anyone seeing me a bit disheveled. Instead, I look at my desk and everything scattered around on the floor.

"Maybe Scotty came back," she quips, the way she does when she's trying to smooth out any awkwardness or intensity. She's been doing that since she was a kid. West would get in trouble, and there would be Rosie, sitting at the dinner table, trying to lighten the mood while everyone else ate anxiously.

"Maybe he wanted lessons in how to properly—"

"Ford?"

I freeze and so does Rosie. Our gazes meet and now it's my turn to flush pink. Because that is not Scotty.

Rosie recovers first, slipping her professional mask back on. "Senior! Is that you?"

She strides away, down the hall toward the front door, and out of sight, still smoothing her clothes. She's walking a little gingerly and maybe a nicer guy would feel bad about that.

But I'm not a nicer guy, and I get off on knowing she's sore after what we just did.

"Rosie?"

Oh god. My mom too? I prop my hands on my hips and stare up at the ceiling's wooden beams. My dad will be oblivious to the mess in here.

But my mom?

Dr. Gemma Grant, Sex Therapist, is going to know exactly what went down in this office.

"Gemma! Hi! It is so good to see you two."

I can hear the heavy whooshes of hugs being exchanged. I should walk over there and greet my parents, but I'm stuck staring at the ceiling. Wondering how I got to where I am.

A kid I never saw coming.

A girl I've never been able to forget.

My parents showing up at the worst possible moment.

"Wow, it looks incredible," my mom says, sounding genuinely impressed.

"Ford has been hard at work," Rosie replies breezily. Not the least bit out of step. Like she greets parents with cum in her panties every day. "And Scotty too, his favorite tradesman."

Of course my mom picks up on that. "Does that mean he hates him?"

Rosie laughs, and I hear three sets of footsteps as they make their way down the short hallway to the main office area.

They stop short when they see it looks like a bomb went off, and I'm standing in the middle of it all.

My dad looks how he always does—silver-haired and suave. His hair color and a few extra lines beside his eyes might be the only giveaway for his age. Otherwise, he's still rolling around in jeans and fitted T-shirt with a long necklace like he and I are the same age.

My mom's hair is still bright red, just like Willa's, though I suspect she gets a little help in that department these days. It's chopped at her chin but styled a little wild and wavy. She's tall and lean, like she always has been. And is wearing an—admittedly—really cool jean jacket with floral embroidery up the sleeve.

She's also wearing a smirk.

"Son, the fuck you doing?" My dad says it with a deep chuckle, head pivoting to take it all in.

I shoot him a temperamental glare because I'm having a hard time believing that the last thirty minutes actually happened.

But not Rosie.

Rosie pats my dad on the shoulder and renders a light laugh. "You showed up on the heels of a temper tantrum."

Oh, I'm going to kill her.

My dad's brows furrow, and Rosie pins me with a wink. "You know how billionaires are. Something doesn't go their way, and suddenly they're pitching a fit. Stomping around. Breaking shit."

My dad laughs at that, hugging Rosie to his side. "You're a firecracker, Rosalie. I've missed ya."

But it's my mom who's staring at me with that knowing smirk on her face and a slightly arched brow. Because my mom knows I'll stew and pout and snipe when I'm pissed off, but not break shit. That's a Willa move. "How fortunate that Rosie knows how to handle Ford's newfound temper."

My dad is still chuckling good-naturedly when he steps forward to wrap me in a hug. And as I look over his shoulder at Rosie, my mom bumps the little vixen's shoulder with her own and quietly says, "Peeing afterward helps prevent infection."

And now I smile, because Rosie, who thought the tantrum joke was real fucking funny, is now staring at me.

Red as a beet.

When the doorbell rings at three o'clock sharp, I know my parents mean business. I told them I needed to get Cora from school and give her a heads-up they were here. I told them we wouldn't be home until three and that I'd call them.

I swing the door open, and sure enough, there stand my parents. I hold the frame in one hand and the door in the other, blocking them from waltzing in like they own the place.

"I told you I'd call you."

My dad scoffs. "You don't have a great track record in that department these days."

"Well, Dad, your track record for going overboard is still firmly intact, so I guess we're both consistent."

His brows drop low and my mom presses her lips together to stifle a laugh. She always gets a kick out of watching the two Fords butt heads.

"Kid, you have no idea. I've got my World's Best Grandpa T-shirt on under this button down."

"You do not."

"I do." He grins and lifts his shirt to unveil the tee that Willa bought him when her daughter was born.

"I told him he was coming on a little strong and needed to cover it up until we got a feel for Cora."

My gaze bounces between my parents. I can feel the

excited energy wafting off of them. And truth be told, I'm not sure how Cora will react to their presence—to their enthusiasm. They're a lot to take in sometimes. I've overheard her conversation with her mom. They're calm and mature, and there's no mention of peeing after sex or only fucking guys who read.

"Okay, listen. We need to lay down some ground rules first." I tug the door closer in behind me and watch my mom's eyes widen as my dad's roll.

"She has a mom, and she has a dad. Just because they're not here doesn't mean you can barge in and act like we're some sort of replacement family. If she wants to call you by your first names, deal with it."

My dad nods and my mom smiles.

"I also don't want to hear a single word about that time a woman made up a paternity story to scam you. It's in the past and has no bearing on Cora. Talking about that will just make her uncomfortable."

I'm met with murmured responses of "Yes" and "Of course."

I rake a hand through my hair. "And just… be cool. Okay?"

"Aye, aye, Captain!" My dad salutes me and I go back to glaring at him. "Any further directives?"

"Yes, Dad. She likes music, but please don't spend the entire time talking about your washed-up band. No one enjoys that as much as you do."

He chuckles, pinching my cheek like he did when I was a boy and forcing me to turn away while tamping down a smile. "You're a mouthy little shithead, you know that?" he adds, breezing past me. And only now do I notice he has a guitar case in hand.

My mom passes next, patting me on the chest. "It's adorable to see you so paternal. Whatever role you plan to play in her life, she's lucky to have you."

I turn and watch my parents waltz into my house, marveling at the updates and discussing their favorite touches. They don't notice Cora observing them from the landing on the stairs. I can see her clearly—peering from around the corner. Our eyes meet and she gives me a tentative smile. A subtle tilt of her head.

I wink back at her, tipping my chin toward my parents.

Which is all it takes for her to come all the way downstairs and bravely announce herself. "Hi, I'm Cora."

They both turn to take her in and much like Willa, they stop for a moment, eyes wide, mouths dropped open. I guess we do kind of look like each other.

"Hi, Cora. I'm Gemma," my mom rushes out, stepping closer with a friendly smile.

"And I'm—"

"Ford Grant Senior. Guitarist from Full Stop."

His lips twitch as Cora's eyes drop to the guitar case at his side.

"You still know how to play that?" I cover my mouth with my fist to keep from laughing.

He scoffs at her question. "Of course. But do you?"

Her eyes go comically wide as she shakes her head. I close the door and walk into the open living space to stand near my dad.

"Thought it might be fun to show you. Taught Willa myself too."

"You're going to let *me* play *your* guitar?"

He shrugs. "I mean, yeah. Why not?"

"I just… that feels like it belongs in a museum or something."

I lean close, give him a nudge with my elbow and stage whisper, "She means because you're old."

"No," Cora says almost breathlessly. "I mean because that guitar is iconic."

Dad turns an obnoxiously pleased smirk in my direction. "Ah, Cora. You and I are going to get along famously. I bet even my World's Best Grandpa T-shirt won't lose me cool points."

A starstruck laugh bubbles up from her throat as my dad pats her on the back and leads her into the living room.

That expression doesn't leave her face all day long. In fact, it only intensifies when she learns a simple tune and my dad gifts her a pick.

I wish Rosie were here to see her.

CHAPTER 33

Rosie

THE FIRST THING I DID WHEN FORD TOOK HIS PARENTS OVER
to his house was pee. And then proceeded to laugh hysteri-
cally into my palms while sitting on the toilet.

Only me.

Only Rosalie-the-hot-mess would get railed by her life-
long frenemy and new boss and then get walked in on by
his parents.

If I weren't so amused by the whole clusterfuck, I'd want
to lie down and die of embarrassment. But as it stands, I'm
kind of invested in seeing how this all plays out.

Call it a morbid sense of curiosity.

I re-create our moment of insanity in my head as I
wander back to my place in a happy sex daze. In the shower,
I close my eyes and pretend my hands are his, roaming my
body.

The way he switched from hard and domineering to soft

and worshipful gave me the best kind of whiplash. My body aches with the memory of him.

When I step out, I apply body lotion and murmur his words back to myself.

You're fucking perfect. I missed you like crazy this weekend. I wouldn't feel trapped with you.

In the past, sentiments like that might have triggered an alarm. I've never been one to get easily attached. But with Ford, they don't read like cheap pickup lines. They don't make sirens go off in my head.

All I feel is a warm, floating sensation low in my belly. Like tension unfurling, soothing all the anxiety. Washing away that pesky itching sensation I always feel in his presence.

"Ah!" I jump when I see my roommate, the little brown mouse, scurry across the floor and run under my bed. "Seriously, dude," I grumble, tugging on jeans and a sweater, feeling like I need to get out and walk, or be around other humans, or something—pace a circle or some shit. "You don't need to run out and startle me like that. Just be cool. Strut out like you own the place. I'm too soft to evict you anyway. I'll just make sure my brother doesn't find out about you."

I hear the light patter of him scurrying across the floor. He pops out on the other side of the bed, heading for the kitchen.

"I should name you Ratatouille."

I watch it. Little, round ears. Beady, black eyes. I should take issue with a mouse in my space, but I just… don't.

"Good point," I say to absolutely no one. "You're not a rat. I get it. I do. What about Scotty?"

Now that would be entertaining. I laugh at myself as it creeps along under the lower ledge of the cupboards, and I find myself watching it. Little nose sniffing, whiskers wiggling as it searches for crumbs.

Crumbs it finds—because I put them there.

"It would be nice if you could keep your poop outside. I'm getting a little tired of vacuuming and washing the floor every day."

A knock at the door draws my attention away, and I walk across the open bunkhouse to yank it open. I was expecting West, but Ford is standing right in front of me. Filling all the space with his imposing height and broad shoulders.

His hair is damp, and he's wearing a brown cable-knit sweater. The white T-shirt underneath peeks out, and I glimpse the flash of his silver chain disappearing beneath the layers.

He props a hand on the top of the doorframe, leaning in a bit closer. "Hi."

My eyes travel back up to his. And what I see there is... nerves. He looks *nervous.*

"Hi." I smile softly, take a deep whiff of him, and reach forward, hooking one finger around the chain and pulling it out. I brush my thumb along the tarnished key and shake my head. I still can't believe he held onto it for all these years.

"Who were you talking to?"

"My mouse," I reply absently.

"Your mouse?"

"Yeah, Scotty."

I peek up at Ford and his grumpy, heavyset brows. The

high peaks of his model-like cheekbones. No wonder they named him the world's sexiest billionaire. The monetary status is just a gimmick for a face that is most definitely magazine-worthy.

"You named the mouse, who is living in your house, Scotty?"

"Yeah."

A tendon at the edge of his jaw pops. "Why?"

"To piss you off."

He rolls his eyes at me in his signature bitchy way. "You think I'm going to be jealous of a mouse?"

I lean against the doorframe, stare up at him with wide, innocent eyes, and shrug.

We have a stare-off, which is nothing new, but there's an added heat. An added knowing.

"You're infuriating," he grumbles, and then he drops his head to kiss me, and I smile against his lips.

This kiss is different. It's not edged in anger or frustration or overbearing tension.

It's achingly sweet. Not soft, but drawn out. Again, his knuckles stroke along my cheek, and a shiver races down my spine. I step closer, wanting to be wrapped up in him.

Again.

All night.

All day.

If Ford were a blanket, I'd pull him over my shoulders and walk around like I was wearing a cape.

His tongue swipes against mine and his hand settles on my throat. "I came to invite you to our bonfire tonight." His breath is damp against my lips. "But now that I know Scotty has moved in with you, I think you should pack your bags and stay with me instead."

The tip of my nose runs over the stubble at the edge of his sharp jawline. "That might raise some eyebrows on the professional front. You fuck me once and move me in with you?"

He lands one hard kiss against my lips before pulling away and stepping back. "You know I don't give a damn what people think of me. You can stay in the guest room if that's more professional for you. I can fuck you just as easily in there." He hits me with a cocky smirk, stepping farther back as though he's preparing to leave. "Because we both know it wasn't only once. It was just the first time."

I bark out a laugh, grinning back at him. "I'll think about it."

"If you choose a mouse named Scotty over me, I'll be offended."

"I meant the bonfire. I'd be an idiot to choose Scotty over you."

I half close the door on him, pleased with getting the last word in. But then I open it again and see him staring at the bunkhouse with a boyish smile on his face.

"But Ford, we need to tell Weston."

I expect the smile to drop from his face, but it doesn't. "I know."

It's from behind the closed door I hear him call, "See you tonight."

Because he knows me well enough to understand, I don't need to think about it at all.

I hope Ford doesn't want to have sex with me tonight because I ate far too many hot dogs and s'mores. I'm so full that all I want to do is go to sleep.

Possibly right where I am. I'm already wrapped in one of Ford's blankets, after all.

The fire is warm, my cheeks hurt from smiling, and the glass of wine in my hand tastes way too damn good.

West just ruffled my hair—more of a noogie, really—and took off with his feral daughter and bookish boy.

Gemma and Ford Senior took off a few minutes later. And Ford just walked Cora back up to the house. Being there to see Cora connect with grandparents she never knew she had was a highlight of my life. She watched everyone chat and laugh and tease each other with wide, starstruck eyes.

I could have watched her taking it in all night long.

My little storm cloud glowed bright as the moon.

And now it's just me, my food baby, a glass of wine, and the stars.

I feel myself doze. A loud crack from the fire startles me awake and I shake my head. "Get it together, old girl," I murmur.

Not wanting to fall asleep and spill red wine all over myself, I push to stand and walk down the slope toward the lake. Toward the dock. It's my favorite place to sit.

Morning tea.

Peaceful lunch.

Bedtime wine.

It faces due west, which means it's a spectacular place to sit at night. It's chillier down by the water too, something I clearly need to stay awake right now.

I pull the blanket tighter around my shoulders and stare out at the inky water as I mull over the day's events. The boards shake before I ever hear Ford's approach.

He crouches behind me, but I don't turn to look at him. I keep staring out at the other side of the lake, now dotted with lights from a home opposite mine.

I swear I can feel his annoyance even though I haven't turned around.

I smile into the cool night.

His hand wraps around my ponytail, and he gives it a gentle tug, pulling my head back. Forcing me to look into his eyes, their green almost black in the darkness.

In the past, this has always felt playful. Flirtatious even. But tonight, it makes my stomach flip and my blood pump faster. It's downright commanding.

"Are you ignoring me, Rosalie?"

"Yes."

"Why?"

"Because I like fighting with you."

His head quirks in an almost feline way. A shiver races down my spine. It reminds me of the look he gave me earlier, right before he flipped me over and fucked me on his desk, just like I wanted him to.

"Do we fight, or do we flirt?"

I wink at him, my head still tilted back. "With us, I think they're the same thing."

He shakes his head like I irritate him. But I know better. Now I know he's always put on an act when it comes to me. To us.

And the kiss he bends down to press against my mouth all but confirms that.

When his fingers soften on my hair, he sits beside me, our bodies pressed tightly side by side. Not at all like the night I told him he would have to move closer to share my chips.

I hold my glass over to him, and he takes a deep swig.

"Tonight was a fun night," I say, cutting the silence. "Cora is so…" I trail off, shaking my head. I can't quite put into words what she is to me. So much like her dad that it hurts, so pure, so self-aware, so awake. I don't know her parents at all, but I know they raised a good one under less-than-ideal circumstances.

"Cool," Ford provides, taking another sip.

"Yeah. She's really cool."

"I'm gonna be sad when she goes back to her mom."

I go still. I don't know what I was expecting him to say, but it wasn't that. We didn't get much of a chance to talk about their trip since we were… otherwise engaged.

"You think she'll go back?"

He gives a firm nod. "She's a good mom. A good person. Good people get clinically depressed. She'll recover, and I'd never want to interfere with that. Cora belongs with her."

I drop my head to his shoulder. "I think Cora will always be in our lives now, in some way. And if her mom is as good as you say, she wouldn't keep her from you. Not after the way you've been there for them."

I hear him swallow, his body moving as he nods again.

"Stop hogging my wine, Junior." My hand makes a grabbing motion and the vibration of his deep chuckle rolls through me as he hands it back.

"You said *our lives*."

The wine is full-bodied and bursting with cherries as it spills over my tongue.

"Good listening. Gold star for you." I nuzzle closer, hinting that I want him to drape an arm over me, but his fingers clamp around the edge of the deck.

"Do you think you'll stay here in Rose Hill?"

That question has me straightening and turning to assess his profile. "Why wouldn't I? I have my family, a job that I actually really like—and I'm not just saying that because you're technically my boss—and a place to live."

"With a mouse."

"*Scotty*," I correct him, which earns me an eye roll. "My boss overpays me, so I could probably get my own place. A rental maybe."

I can tell he's tense. I can tell the post-sex haze has lost a bit of its luster.

I can tell he's worried about everyone leaving, even though he'd never say it out loud. I don't think he'd want me to point it out to him, so I reassure him in the best way I can think of.

"Can I sleep at your house tonight?" That question gets his attention, and he turns an unreadable face to me. A light crease forms between his brows, like he can't quite figure me out.

And that's good. I like keeping Ford Grant on his toes.

Which is probably why I add, "Main floor guest room. We'll keep it professional with Cora around."

CHAPTER 34

Rosie

THE PROBLEM IS, I DON'T WANT TO KEEP THINGS PROFESsional. I said it because it felt like a thing you should say when you start fucking your boss. Now, I'm lying in bed wearing Ford's shirt, food baby forgotten, wishing he'd sneak down the stairs and crawl in with me.

I try to talk myself out of it so many times. We already almost got caught once. But my body doesn't care—and neither does my heart. I want his hands in my hair, his warm skin against my own.

Which is why I creep through a dark house and up the stairs, keeping to the edges to avoid any creaking that might wake Cora. One peek into her room at the top of the stairs and I see her sprawled like a starfish. My lips curve up at the sight and then I very, very gently shut her bedroom door before padding down to the primary bedroom at the opposite end of the hallway.

The door is closed and no light shines from beneath. Some people might hesitate to march into Ford's bedroom.

I am not one of those people. I twist the handle and walk right in. His curtains are open and ambient light from outside filters in through the massive windows. The door clicks shuts behind me and I walk across to the king-sized bed. Much like Cora, he is all long, muscular limbs stretched out in the middle.

Unlike with Cora, I don't turn away.

I press one knee onto the mattress and crawl in his direction. His breaths are deep and the entire bed has a faint sandalwood smell. I think I'd settle for just lying here beside him, breathing him in.

Instead, I kneel at his side. Soaking him in, so relaxed. He looks younger—more carefree—like this.

With one hand, I trail the tip of my fingers over his lips—just like I did that day in the closet. I'd been on the verge of asking him if he ever thought we could be more. It seemed unfair to me in that moment that one of the best men I've ever known was standing right in front of me, telling me how valuable I was, and that I couldn't have him.

But now the only question I find myself asking is *why the hell not?*

His big strong hand flies up, steely fingers wrapping around my wrist. "Rosie."

It's not a question. He *knows* it's me.

"Hi."

"What are you doing?" he asks from behind closed eyes.

"Touching you."

His lips curve up in a sinful smile. "I thought we were being professional."

"Right," I whisper. "It's just that I thought about it and decided being professional is overrated. I want you to touch me too."

For only a moment, I'm taken back to that day in the boardroom. I told Stan that if I wanted him to touch me, I'd tell him.

Ford may be my boss on paper, but nothing about our relationship is reminiscent of *that*. Nothing between us is dirty—not in that way. Nothing about us *needs* to be a secret if neither of us wants it to be.

A raspy chuckle spills from him as his green eyes open and dive into my own. Chills erupt from the back of my neck, racing down my spine and over my arms.

"And you kept all your clothes on earlier, which felt distinctly unfair to me. So, I came looking for you."

"And you found me."

My teeth sink into my bottom lip as I nod.

"So what now?" he asks from beneath a quirked brow.

"I don't know." I suddenly feel nervous. I snuck up here with no plan, only knowing I wanted to be close to him. "Do you want me to leave?"

He stares at me extra hard now. It's borderline unnerving. The weight of his stare. The way my stomach flip-flops under his attention. I've never felt this way before.

"No, Rosie. I want you up here." His voice is soft and deep as he reaches for me. Broad hands circle my waist and I squeal as he hauls me on to him, so I'm straddling his torso.

"Gonna need you to be quiet, baby," he murmurs as his palms slide up over my quads, tips of his fingers dipping inside my underwear at my hips.

All I can do is nod, lick my lips, and watch how good his hands look roaming over my body.

"N-now what?" I practically stutter.

"Now you're going to hold on tight to that headboard, sit on my face, and try to keep your mouth shut while I make you come."

Before I can respond, he's moved me up, yanked the gusset of my panties to the side, and has his tongue in my pussy.

I gasp and fall forward, holding the headboard like he instructed, more out of needing something to hold on to than because I'm good at following directions.

My head falls back when his teeth graze my clit. He palms my ass and holds me close, like he's eating his favorite fruit. His eagerness does nothing but drive me even more wild.

"Hmmm," I hum, trying to cover for the string of expletives currently sitting on the tip of my tongue. My thighs shake with the strain of holding myself over him and his fingers dig in hard.

He pulls away, only to grumble at me in that deep tone.

"Rosie. I said be quiet. And stop being polite. I told you to sit on my face." The hand gripping my underwear yanks me down hard so that I'm fully seated.

He sucks my clit and my body bows into him. His hand slides up from my ass, over my hip, stomach, and up to my breast, where he gently caresses me. Holds me. *Touches* me.

He gives my nipple a good, firm twist that has me gasping and grinding against his mouth. All the response I get is a deep satisfied growl against my core as he continues to lick, and suck, and tease.

I ride him shamelessly. He told me to stop being polite, and so I do. I lose myself in the sensation, the feel of his skin on mine. The smell of him wrapped around me.

There's something empowering in asking for what I want. To be touched when I want. And I'm drunk on that— drunk on him—when everything inside me clenches. When that pressure builds so quickly, so intensely, I can't hold back... I shatter.

I feel like I blow apart into a million little pieces. My skin is hot, my eyelids feel heavy. And as much as I try to stay quiet, I can't.

His hand shoots up over my mouth and I slump into it, using his arm to prop me up while I cling to the headboard.

"Ford," I whisper as he moves me down. His limbs are moving and there's fabric rustling around me, but I'm too incoherent to keep up. "Ford."

"Rosie, baby. I told you to stay quiet."

My brain is too addled to care. "More." I fold myself over him, dropping my head into the crook of his neck and kissing him there. My teeth graze over the lobe of his ear as I realize he's removed his boxers while I blacked out.

"More?"

I nod, feeling his Adam's apple move against my forehead as he swallows. "More."

His hands move firmly, all business, as he removes my underwear. Then he sits up, leaning against the headboard and taking me with him.

I can feel his hard length propped against my ass as he positions us.

His eyes stay on my face as he reaches down to grip the hem of *his* shirt. The one he gave me to sleep in when he walked me to the guest room door and told me it might help me miss him less. Right before he smirked that annoying, I'm-right-and-you-know-it smirk of his.

He wasn't, though. Which is why I'm here.

My body coils with anticipation again as his gaze rakes over my bare skin.

His hands roam slowly yet purposefully. Over my arms, my collarbones. Reading me like braille. I think he's always been able to, and I just didn't know it.

"I'm not sure you can handle more, Rosie." He kisses my chest as my hands move in tandem, feeling him in a way I didn't get to earlier. "You're not very good at keeping quiet."

"I'll be good," I murmur, grinding my pussy back on him and feeling his steely length pulse against my ass.

My hands end up at the key around his neck. The fact he even sleeps with it on makes me smile.

And when I peek at his face, I can see the ghost of a smile on his lips too. But it's a different type of smile.

His fingers bump against mine as he takes the key from me. He lifts it between us. "Open wide."

"What?" As I whisper the word, he takes the key and presses it between my lips, flat on my tongue.

"Hold that there. Don't let it go. Or I'll stop."

My eyes widen, but I nod. It tastes metallic in my mouth, but suddenly his lips are on my nipples and my hands are raking through his hair. When he moves too far, the chains tugs at my lips, but I clamp them together.

I don't let go. Because I desperately do not want Ford to stop.

He reaches between us, urging me up onto my knees. I move obediently, and in return, I am rewarded by the sensation of his cock sliding against my pussy.

Back and forth. Back and forth. My eyes flutter shut as he tortures me. One hand grips my shoulder while the other is fisted around his length. I swivel my hips, feeling his crown notch inside me.

"Goddamn, Rosie. You're even better than I fucking dreamed," he mutters roughly. Then he shoves himself in, and I'm glad I have something in my mouth to keep me quiet. Because no one and nothing has ever felt this good.

My eyes snap open as my body adjusts. The light sting of him taking me so roughly for the second time today has blood thrumming through my veins at a rapid pace. My heart pounding even harder than before.

We stare at each other. His cock is buried deep inside me, his key now warm against my tongue.

My key?

Our key.

"Move, Rosie. Show me how bad you want it."

My pelvis undulates because I do want it. I lift and I drop back down, feeling every thick inch of him as I do. Reveling in the way his eyes widen before taking on a more hooded appearance.

What starts off slow and deliberate comes apart at the seams. Hands that were searching are now gripping. Breathing that was even is now choppy. Everything is hot and damp as we writhe together in silence.

We don't need words. They wouldn't do justice to something that feels like this anyway.

"You're gonna come on my cock now, aren't you, Rosie?" he growls roughly, breathlessly, against my ear. My body shudders in response. "I can tell. Your eyes give it away, even in the dark. Then every muscle on you goes all tight. You ride me so damn hard. So eager. So warm. So fucking tight."

I'm so full of *him*. His words. His body. It's too much, and right when I'm about to go barreling over that edge again, he pulls the key from my mouth and kisses me soundly, swallowing the sound of me screaming his name as I come.

With a fist full of my hair, he pumps into me hard. Spilling himself, filling me up thoroughly right my orgasm rocks me. Flays me. Leaves me slumped in his arms, desperately trying to catch my breath.

I don't know how long we stay like that. Me straddling his lap, his cock pulsing inside me, clinging to each other and kissing. Slow, languid, deliberate kisses that make my throat ache with their tenderness. Eventually they slow and Ford rolls me off him carefully.

Always carefully. Even when he's rough with me, he's so damn intentional. I feel nothing short of pampered with him. And when he gets up to retrieve a warm washcloth, the point is only driven further home.

"What are you doing?" I breathe the words, trying to stay quiet as he comes to kneel between my splayed legs.

"Taking care of you."

The warm cloth swipes over my swollen core and I let out a soft moan. "You don't need to do that."

He continues wiping me gently. "But I want to."

I'm struck silent by such a simple sentence.

I lie in Ford's bed, letting him take care of me. And when he's finished, he lifts the covers, crawls in behind me, and holds my body against his all night long.

CHAPTER 35

Rosie

I WAKE UP ALONE.

I reach for Ford before my eyes have even opened but find his side of the bed cool. I tell myself there's a good reason for him being gone already.

Namely, that his daughter is at the other end of the hallway.

I let my hands trail over my deliciously sore body as I recall last night. My skin hums and I know I could get myself there just by recalling the feel of him and all the things he does to me—says to me.

I take a quick peek out the window to see the morning looks just as beautiful as I thought it would, based on last night's sunset. A sunny morning always invigorates me. So I roll myself out of bed, feet landing on cold floorboards, and eyes finding the overnight bag that I thought I'd left in the guest room.

At the end of the bed, ripped jeans and a plain white tee with my long, caramel-colored cardigan are laid out—Ford clearly went to the guest room so I wouldn't have to walk through the house wearing only his oversized T-shirt.

I get dressed and do a quick finger comb through my slightly wavy tresses and then head downstairs, ready to start my mission of finding Ford. I can smell bacon, and I decide that if Ford is making a full fried breakfast on a regular week-day morning, I'll definitely take up residence in that spare room.

Except I draw up short when I hear voices. *Plural.*

And when I peek into the updated farmhouse kitchen, I pause. Cora is still in her pajamas—black, of course—at the island with a sketchpad splayed out in front of her. Gemma is seated beside her, looking through it eagerly as she explains each page. And Senior is cooking up a breakfast that has me concerned about his future cholesterol levels.

It's charming as hell. It makes my heart swell and my stomach growl.

"Good morning," I singsong as I enter the kitchen.

"Rosie!" Cora shoots up and runs to me, wrapping her arms around my waist in a hug that knocks the wind from me.

It's not that I don't like big hugs—I just wasn't expecting it. Gemma smiles with a subtle warmth toward me, a look I return before dropping my gaze to Cora's head. Where I'm taken aback once again. By a high ponytail wrapped up in my hot-pink scrunchie. No low braid. Just my hair tie and my go-to lazy style.

It makes my chest feel all warm, and I bend over to drop

a kiss on the top of her head. "Good morning, my little storm cloud."

"Morning, Rosalie," Ford Senior says from over his shoulder. "Cup of coffee?"

"Oh, babe, don't pretend." Gemma scoffs as she sips from her own mug.

My eyes dart between them. "Pretend what?"

"Ford already went to the office to bring back your favorite tea. It's right there." His mom points at a pink travel mug that I've never seen before.

I decide it's mine instantly. I also decide to play this off super casually in front of Ford's parents because… *awkward*.

I can't believe he nailed me like he did last night and took off before I woke up *and* left me in a house full of his family to do the walk of shame. But I bite down on my annoyance and put on a faux-happy face to maintain the façade.

"Cool, thanks." I saunter across the kitchen, wearing a carefree smile, and pick up the mug. One flip of the stopper and the aromatic scent of sweet rose petals drifts up. I know exactly where Tabitha harvests them. On the other side of the mountain, there's a stretch of wild rosebushes, and when they bloom, the perfume wafts throughout the valley.

It's my favorite time of the year.

"So where's Ford?"

"I'm right here, doll," Senior teases as he flips the bacon.

"No, the moody one," I volley back with a wink.

Gemma scoffs. "Oh, trust me. You spend forty years with that one and you'll realize he's no better."

He turns around and grins at her. "You'd be bored

without me, and you know it." His wife tries to stifle her smile and goes back to flipping through Cora's sketchpad.

Cora watches the interaction with a look of wonder on her face, and I think of how deflated Ford sounded last night at the prospect of her leaving. I desperately want her reunited with her mom. I desperately want her to be deliriously happy and well cared for.

But I hope she still comes around. Because Ford won't be the only one who's gutted when she's gone.

I stand here, staring, realizing no one has answered my question.

Finally, Gemma takes note of my hovering and, with a roll of her eyes, says, "He's at the office. We're going to take Cora to school today, so he decided to get an early start. Cora, why don't you go get dressed?"

I swallow, trying not to be annoyed by the fact he had me over and got the hell out of Dodge first thing in the morning. Leaving me to hang out with his *parents*.

My head bobs in a soft nod and I hold my cup in a toast. "Thanks. Have fun at drop-off."

I turn to leave and stifle a laugh when I hear Cora mutter something about how all the perv dads will be disappointed. She sounds very satisfied, and it makes me smile.

But only for a beat, because then I'm shoving my feet into my Birks and stepping out into the crisp morning air. I take a deep whiff. Pine. Mineral. And I swear I can almost smell the roses.

The dew on the grass wets my toes as I make my way across the property toward the barn. I can hear music blasting, and I don't know the song, but it sounds angry and frantic enough to be something emo-teen Ford would listen to.

When I step in, I come to a screeching halt. I don't know what I was expecting to see, but it wasn't *this*.

The muscles in Ford's back flex and ripple as one toned shoulder moves up and down the wall with a roller in hand. His bare feet stand on a white cotton drop sheet, his jeans rolled up just enough to show the line of the tendons in his ankles.

He's tossed his shirt over the back of his desk chair. Socks stuffed into the boots that sit by one of the wheels. Desk perfectly tidy. All proof of our clash yesterday erased. Unless you count the missing desktop.

It's not like I expected him to leave the office messy, but something about how easily he made everything right again irritates me. Like nothing happened.

I take a few steps farther in and prop my ass against the edge of his desk, sipping my tea while I watch him work. He's so tall that he doesn't need a ladder to meet the lines where Scotty had already cut in. His hair is messy, and now that I'm looking closely, I notice streaks of auburn at the front from time spent in the sun.

It did that when he was younger too. Would be a deep chocolate brown at the roots and gradually trend lighter and slightly redder as the summer wore on.

But his build is all different now. I can't help but appreciate the way he's filled out. The way he went from all limbs to all... *this*.

I savor my tea and follow his motions with my eyes,

each stroke matching the beat of the music. It's like my own personal striptease. A manly one, where he fixes shit.

And when I tire of him not paying attention to me, I knock the little metal cup that holds all his identical blue, felt-tipped pens onto the floor.

He starts and spins, clearly startled by the sound. A thin line of paint follows his arc as it sprays across the floor.

"Rosie." He scowls. "What the fuck?"

I smile. "Good morning, boss."

He lets out a beleaguered sigh, eyes tracing the paint splatter, but he says nothing about it.

"Thanks for the tea," I shout over the music, walking over to the record player to drop the volume to a more reasonable level.

Ford keeps a close eye on me as I do it, then grumbles, "You're welcome," before turning back to the wall.

"Whatcha doin'?"

"Painting."

I snort. "Oh my god, really?"

"I'm starting to agree with Cora about the perv dads. If I can't find someone who isn't a perv painter, I'll just do it myself."

"Very manly. You talk a big, tough game for a guy who slunk out this morning before I even woke up."

He continues giving me his back, like a dog I've pissed off or something.

"I'd have gone again if you'd been there. Almost just did the job myself," I add, layering a teasing tone into my voice. "You chicken, Junior?"

His free shoulder rises and falls in a shrug. "I don't know where we stand with everyone knowing or being public. Or whatever. West is completely in the dark. And then they showed up and I... I'm trying to respect your wishes to keep things professional."

I roll my eyes and drop my head back before making my way closer to him. "Ford, you've been riding my ass for years. You fucked my brains out last night." I smirk as I say the words, knowing they'll get under his skin, and I'm rewarded with a sour scowl from over his shoulder. "You really gonna get all respectful on me *now*?"

"I've always respected you." He crouches to glide the roller back and forth over the paint tray.

"Fine, but you've never tiptoed around me. We've always gotten in each other's faces. What's with the"—I step closer, my wet sandals crowding the space near the paint as I wave a hand over him—"weird pacifist approach? It doesn't suit you."

"I told you. I'm just trying to respect your—"

I use my toe and upend the tray, watching the palest blue ooze out over the drop sheet. "Respect my wishes a little less."

"What the fuck, Rosie?" He shoots up, towering above me. "That's going to soak right through this sheet and stain the floor."

"Good. It will give you something to do while you live out this new World's Handiest Billionaire era of yours."

"I had a plan for my life. You—" His jaw pops and his hand flexes tight on his narrow hip.

"Take all your plans, tear them up, and scatter them to

the wind?" I ask as I lift each foot to take my sandals off. Unlike his neatly stowed boots, I toss mine across the office, making him flinch. Then he nods tightly, agreeing with my assessment.

I step right into the pooling paint and it squishes between my toes as I shift my feet back and forth. I give him one raised brow.

"Guess what, Ford. Sometimes life gives you lemons, even when you didn't order them. And you can either make lemonade, or storm around stressing about how yellow isn't your color."

"That's not what happened."

"I'm not lemons?"

"No, you're…" His hand swipes through his hair, but his eyes stay trained on my toes. The pink polish on my nails disappears beneath the thick blue liquid. "I had come to terms with the idea that you would never happen for me. You were a memory, not a goal."

My head tilts as I absorb his answer. The longing in those two sentences hits me right in the chest. I reach for him, fingers hooking around the brown leather belt that props his jeans up, pulling his bare feet into the spreading paint.

"Ford, what if you stopped trying to control everything for a minute?"

I take the roller from him and drop it at our feet right as I slide a hand up his chest, over the warm, firm skin and a smattering of hair. My fingers wrap around my key and give the chain a firm tug. The clasp gives way, and now I'm holding this little piece of us in my hand.

This little piece he's held on to, an ode to the girl I once was.

I drop it into the paint at our feet, and he sucks in a hissing breath.

"What if you stopped worrying about the girl I used to be and started seeing me for the woman I am instead?"

"Rosie—"

"No. I'm not a memory. I'm not a goal. I'm not out of reach. I'm not the same girl who threw that diary out your car window. And I'm not going anywhere." I point at the silver glinting between our feet. "That was us *then*." I tug at his belt.

First the buckle. Then the leather.

"This is us now," I murmur as I work the button on his jeans. The zipper.

I don't know who needs to hear it more. Him, the man who's stuck in the past where I'm concerned. Or me, the girl who finally feels sure of herself and her choices—because they feel *right* and not because they feel mandatory.

A girl who knows what she wants for herself.

His jeans fall to the floor, and I fall to my knees. Right at his feet. Right in the paint.

I lift my chin high to meet his bright green gaze. So wild. So unusual. I can't help but marvel at the way he looks towering over me, all man, radiating so much tension.

"We're messy. And we challenge each other. And let's be honest, who the hell else in the world would ever tolerate us? Keep up with us?"

My fingers wrap under the wide elastic of his boxers, and

I tug roughly. His cock springs free right before me. Big and perfect and hard.

I lick my lips.

"Rosie, what are you doing?"

His palm strokes the top of my head, and I grin up at him. "Playing in the paint." My eyes drop to the head of his cock, mere inches from my lips.

"Yeah?"

Fuck. He's so beautiful. I want to leave my mark all over him. I want him to play *with* me.

"Yeah," I murmur, my breath becoming choppy. I crouch slightly to plant my hands in the paint.

Then I reach up and grip his thighs hard.

Leaving my handprints all over him.

CHAPTER 36

Ford

I watch Rosie on her knees at my feet. Doing her best to piss me off. To make a mess and draw me into it with her.

I like things orderly, but if I had to be messy with someone, it would be with her. All day long.

I smirk. She's not wrong. Who else would put up with her dumping paint on their floor and stamping it all over them?

And what does it say about me that her constantly challenging behavior only makes me want her more?

"You're out of control, you know that?" My hand slides down her cheek as her hands continue to make a mess on my legs. I press my thumb to her chin, popping those plush pink lips open. "You secretly get off on—"

"Ford, stop trying to start a conversation with me and get your dick in my mouth."

I let her finish her sentence. Of course it had to be something snarky and demanding.

And of course it works. It always works.

So, I give her what we both know she's after and shove my cock into her mouth, watching her pretty, blue eyes go wide as her lips latch on. Her fingers curl, gripping at my quads as they flex beneath her palms.

"Is this what you were after?" I pull out and slide back in. Her tongue swirls around the head before sucking me back in.

She nods, and I let my hands rest on her head. My eyes close, even though I desperately don't want to stop staring at her.

She looks fucking perfect.

Playful and mischievous and covered in pale blue paint. Demanding my attention, not letting me retreat the way I normally would.

I watch her struggle, knees sliding in the liquid as she grips at my legs and works my length hungrily.

My fingers tangle in her hair, and I smirk down at her. "Had a wet dream about this once."

Her eyes heat, and she pulls back just far enough to say, "Show me."

"I was mad at you that night. I fucked you like I was mad at you too."

She gives me a saucy wink. "Just think about what a pain in the ass fixing this floor will be."

I shift my gaze around the office. Pens scattered. Paint seeping off the drop sheet straight onto the restored hardwoods. It doesn't make me *mad*, but it makes my eye twitch.

It irritates me. I fist my cock and swipe it across her lips, watching them flatten to the side as I do.

"It will be easy enough for me. I'm going to make it your job to fix them. You break it, you buy it, Rosalie. I'll toss you some sanding paper, sit at my desk, and watch you work on your hands and knees all day long."

She raises an eyebrow in challenge. "That'll be the fucking—"

I shut her up by filling her mouth. "Just like you're working on your knees right now." I stroke her silky hair. "I bet you can't take the whole thing."

Challenge flashes in her eyes.

"Bet you'll tap out before I can fuck your throat the way I did in that dream."

She tilts her head back and opens her mouth wider, and I don't overthink it for once. I fist her hair and slide myself inside. Tight lips. Hot mouth. She swallows when I hit the back, as though trying to make room for all of me.

"Too much?" I ask, with a little curl to my lips, knowing it will piss her off.

She pushes forward, taking more, making a light gagging noise as she does.

"Yeah, too much. Knew it would be."

She lets out a deep humming noise around my cock, and I watch her reach down into the paint. She holds that hand up and shakes it out over the floors, splattering light blue into the open space in the middle.

A dark laugh bubbles up inside me. "Rosie, you brat," I growl as I slide out and back in, a little harder this time.

She has the gall to laugh while my cock is shoved in her mouth. When she does it again with the paint, I give up on holding back.

I fist her hair, hold her head still, and fuck her mouth roughly. She meets me with every stroke. Even when her eyes water, she looks eager beyond compare.

I'm obsessed with this girl. Always have been, always will be.

She hums contentedly as I thrust and then I'm there. Ready. Finished.

"Rosie, open your mouth and stick out your tongue. I want to watch you swallow my cum."

She pulls off with a wet, popping noise and obeys my command. I wrap a fist around my cock and groan as I rest the tip against her lips and let each shot paint her tongue white.

I'm winded, watching raptly, and she stays just like that, looking so fucking good. I feel like I could bust all over again. Her wide eyes stay locked with mine. She's watching me like I'm everything to her.

It's intoxicating, and I couldn't give less of a fuck about my ruined floors.

I rub the head of my cock over her parted lips one last time, smooth my hand back over her hair, and say, "Swallow."

Her lips close, and I watch her throat work as she does. Her tongue darts out over her lips like she's searching for more before she lets out a quiet, "Mmm. That *was* a good dream."

I shake my head in disbelief at what just went down between us. Afraid to hope that it might happen again.

It feels… too good to be true.

I guess that's why I drop to my knees, gather her against me—paint be damned—and kiss her like my life depends on it.

To convince myself that this thing with her might actually be real.

CHAPTER 37

Ford

"I can't believe you want to *practice* bowling," West teases before taking a deep swig of his beer. "Usually, you look like you'd rather tie a brick around your ankle and jump off the dock."

He's not wrong about that part.

And I don't especially want to practice bowling.

What I want to do is come clean with my best friend in a public place where there will be cameras. Just in case he tries to beat the shit out of me for spending all morning in the shower, scrubbing paint off his little sister.

Of course, we did more than scrub paint, and afterward, I felt like I was sneaking around. Hiding her.

I don't want to feel that way with Rosie, and I don't want Rosie to think she needs to be hidden.

"Just haven't seen much of you lately," I say. "Thought we'd hang out more once I moved here."

West grins and props an elbow against the table while we wait for our lane to clear out. "It's almost like we're two grown-ass men with shit to do."

I huff out a laugh. "True story."

"I'm always extra busy this time of year. People bring their young horses up for starting. The kids are wrapping up at school. I think that's why I look forward to Dads' Night Out so much. I get one night every two weeks where I can kick back and be myself. Without marking it somehow, I think I'd just work and parent and do chores around the farm without stopping. Forces me to look up now and then, ya know?"

I take a sip of my beer and nod, considering his perspective. Somehow, I hadn't thought of bowling nights that way. After all, I waltzed into town as a workaholic bachelor with no dependents.

But now that I've got multiple businesses on the go, an almost-teenager, and a maybe-relationship, I can see where he's coming from. I can see life getting away from you. The fact I've barely seen him since Cora joined the family is proof of that.

"You know..." He scrubs at the stubble on his chin, flashing the tattoos on his knuckles. "If you really hate bowling, I can try to find someone to replace you. Starting to feel like this is a prison sentence for you. Maybe you just wanna bring a book and read at our table or something."

I bark out a laugh. "Why the fuck would I do that?"

The look he gives me screams that he thinks I'm an idiot. "You pulled that shit all the time when we were younger. I didn't give a shit then, wouldn't give one now either. I know you and I are different. I'm cool, and you're a huge dork. But it works."

I roll my eyes. "West, you're not that cool. And being friends with me is safe because if you had a friend who was too similar, I think that might trigger the apocalypse or some shit."

His shoulders shake as he takes another drink. "Dude, I'm getting old. My wild streak is bowling and staying up late enough to watch *Saturday Night Live*."

"We both know you just watch the Skylar Stone episode on repeat."

He reaches across and punches my arm playfully in response.

I know I'm putting off telling him what I came here to say. I just don't know how to segue into the conversation. I'm not asking for his permission—I'm just trying not to blindside the guy after decades of friendship.

I don't excel at subtle conversations.

I rub my thumb up and down the chilled pint glass, gathering the courage to spit it out. "So, speaking of the apocalypse…" I peek at him from the corner of my eye. He's watching me, but I keep my gaze plastered forward on the lanes, trying to act casual. I take a deep gulp of my cloudy IPA before spitting it out. "I'm in love with your sister."

West doesn't move, but I see him nodding, tongue swiping over his bottom lip.

The silence between us stretches out. One beat. Two.

The loud thump of balls hitting the lanes and the

crashing sound of pins falling a few seconds later tell me West has been staring at me for far too long.

My stomach sinks, and my cheeks heat. I finally turn my head, and I can't quite read his expression. It's hard to say with West. I've seen him smile and crack a joke before driving his fist into someone's face.

"Listen—"

He cuts me off, and I don't know what I was expecting him to say, but it definitely wasn't, "Yeah, I know. I've met you before."

I rear back as my brows knit together. "What?"

"Like I just said, you're a huge dork. And Rosie is an oblivious hurricane. You might be the only two people in the world who didn't already know this."

If I weren't focusing on keeping my jaw clamped shut, it would hang open.

I prepared myself for him to say a lot of things, but this… this was not one of them.

"I think we might be a thing."

Wow, that sounds really dumb.

West snorts a laugh, and I feel like he's laughing *at* me more than *with* me.

"Dude, if you don't get off your ass and properly date her, I'm going to pitch you to *Forbes* as the World's Dumbest Billionaire. After everything you've gone and done for that girl? Come *on*."

I blink. And I blink again. I thought I was going to be the one blindsiding him. "You really flipped this shit around."

West gives me his best unhinged smile, thumping a fist

against his cupped palm. "Did you think I was going to break your pretty face, Ford?"

"I…" I scrub my hands through my hair, my elevated heart rate slowing now that I've gotten this off my chest and cleared the air. "Honestly, man, I didn't know. You're kind of unpredictable."

He sips. He nods. I can see the wheels turning in his head.

"Nah. The only person more protective of her than me might be you. However, I have a couple of requirements."

My head falls back, and I look up at the ceiling, ready to get the third degree. Which is why I laugh when he says, "First, you're going to stay on the bowling team. And when I get team shirts made, you will wear yours with a smile."

I chuckle. "Fine. But not the smiling part."

West waves me off. "Second, you will help me come up with a sweet name for the team so we can start kicking Stretch's ass."

I groan and laugh into my palm. The relief of getting this over with has me feeling borderline giddy. "Fine. All you had to do was bring up kicking that guy's ass, and you'd have had me."

"Okay, so I'm just going to toss some ideas and you can say yes or no."

"You already have ideas?"

West stands and paces. He never was a sit-still kind of guy. "Dude, I'm a lonely bachelor. I have to do something after the kids go to bed."

"Looks like you used up all your game when you were younger."

His mouth pops open. "Okay. *Now* I'll hit you."

I make a rolling motion with my hand, thrilled that there's no awkwardness between us. No damage to our friendship.

He bounces on the balls of his feet, a little too excited to be having this conversation with me. "The Bowling Stones," he spits out, followed by a dramatic pause.

"No."

"What! Really? I thought you'd love that one."

"Yeah, no."

"Okay. What about… 4 Guys 12 Balls."

"Fuck no," a dry voice grumbles from behind me. I turn to see Bash, beer in hand, pulling up a stool at our high-top table.

"What are you doing here?"

He shrugs. "Got back yesterday. West called today for a practice. Figured, why the hell not?"

I spin on West. "I didn't know other people were coming to our practice."

West shrugs, brushing me off. "I wasn't expecting this to be the moment you declared your love for my sister."

"Rosie?" Bash's brow furrows, and I prop my elbows on the table, dropping my head into my hands. "Explains why you fired Scotty. That kid thinks with his dick," Bash mumbles before taking a deep swig.

"Okay, enough about Rosie. Back to team names."

I ignore West. "Bash, are you going to wear a team shirt?"

He shrugs, face impassive. "Sure. I don't care. Not concerned about how I look in a magazine. Would rather beat Stretch."

God. I'm so petty. I swear all anyone has to do is mention beating Stretch, and I totally pivot.

"Okay." West holds his hands up like he has something amazing to announce. "Here's another one. Bowls Deep."

"No," I say, right as Bash quirks a brow and asks, "How old are you?"

"Okay, fine. Gutter Gang?"

"That makes it sound like you're all a bunch of rats that live in the sewer," a feminine voice cuts in.

When I turn, I come face-to-face with the woman who's always at the town bistro where I buy Rosie her tea.

"Tabby!" West lifts his hands up in greeting.

The name rings a bell. She looks familiar, and I suspect I should remember her from summers spent here as a kid. But it's her hand, wrapped tight around a mountain of a man's bicep, that draws my attention.

"Overheard your phone conversation earlier, West. You need a fourth for your team?"

West glances back at us. "Oh yeah, forgot to mention that Crazy Clyde is in the hospital. Kidney issues. Had to go check on him. Assure him they weren't making up his diagnosis just to harvest his organs."

Bash grumbles and shifts in his seat. "Who the fuck would want Clyde's organs?"

"Right. Well, here. This is Rhys. Take him." The tiny woman shoves the man forward like he's nothing, even though he's got at least an inch or two on me and is built like a football player.

He's on the scruffy side, with long, dark hair and a beard.

But it's his eyes that are the darkest. I'm not easily intimidated, but if I was going to be intimidated by someone, it might be him.

West clearly suffers from no such feelings. "You're one big bitch, aren't ya?" he says as he claps the guy on the shoulder.

"You can say that again." Tabby scowls at the guy's back, and he stiffens at her words, though he doesn't turn to face her.

"You ever bowled before?" West carries on.

"No," the guy grits out, clearly annoyed by the situation.

"You a dad? We can always get you a cat or something if you're not. Then it will still count as Dads' Night Out."

"You're going to make this guy a cat-dad?" Even Bash sounds floored by West's confidence.

"Not a big cat guy," the guy responds. "And I'm not really a dad either."

Tabby barks out a laugh. "Rich." Then she turns on West. "He *is* a dad, whether or not he wants to admit it. And for what it's worth, I think you should name your team the Man Children."

With that, she spins on her heel and marches out of the bowling alley.

"You're a real ball-buster, Tabby. I appreciate that about you!" West calls back to her as she leaves.

She flips him the finger over her shoulder.

And that's when Bash chuckles to himself over the rim of his pint glass. "There it is."

"There what is?" West asks as he turns to face us. The "big bitch" is still just standing there like a pissed-off mountain.

Bash shakes his head. "The team name."

I watch West process, moving his lips silently, trying it on for size before breaking out in a grin. "Hell yeah, boys. Welcome to The Ball Busters!" He claps once. "Let's get practicing. This is gonna be an every-other-week thing. Get us in fighting form. Bust Stretch's balls."

I straighten and scoff. "I'm not practicing every other week. That amounts to bowling weekly."

West's lips pull back and he hisses like he's about to break some bad news to me. "Oof. Sorry. It was the last requirement to date my baby sister."

Bash shakes his head and turns toward our now-empty lane, waving our new angry teammate along. "Let's go, new guy."

When I pick my beer up to follow, I glance at my best friend. He looks so excited that it's damn near impossible to be annoyed.

He claps me on the shoulder as we follow the others to the floor and tips his head toward me as he drops his voice to say, "I'm so fucking happy for the two of you."

CHAPTER 38

Rosie

Rosie,

Reminding you that the fundraiser is tomorrow.
It's black tie, so I took the liberty of having an outfit
delivered to the hotel in Emerald Lake for you.

—Ford

Good morning, Mr. Grant,

Your emails without all the formal shit are
substantially less entertaining. If you ever want
to get in my pants again, I require you to be witty
and borderline mean.

What did you order me? What if I don't like it?

All my best,
Rosalie Belmont
Reality Check Manager at Rose Hill Records

Ms. Belmont,

You mostly wear skirts. So, I'm not bothered by that statement. I'll just bend you over and fuck you in that.

And I ordered you a dress and a pair of heels. You often wear fuzzy socks with Birkenstocks, which only proves that you have poor fashion sense and can't be trusted to dress appropriately for an event of this caliber.

Have a miserable day!
Ford Grant
CEO and Fashion Police at Rose Hill Records

Mr. Grant,

I'll wear the dress. But you can pry my socks and sandals from my cold, dead hands.

All my best,
Rosalie Belmont
Dick Manager at Rose Hill Records

Ms. Belmont,

I'm heading to the office from school drop-off. I expect you to be down on all fours sanding that paint stain when I arrive.

Have a miserable day!
Ford Grant
Overlord at Rose Hill Records

When Ford walks in, I am, in fact, *not* sanding the floor. Since yesterday, I've cleaned up the tray and drop sheet as best I can, but I'm not doing manual labor in my lace skirt and silky blouse.

He can go fuck himself if he thinks that.

My expression must be a dead giveaway because he takes one look at me, scowling at him from behind my desk, and smirks.

"Figures," he says as he strides toward his desk and drops his bag on the chair. He proceeds to the mess of blue paint on the floor and props his hands on his hips, staring down at the stain on what were perfectly polished floors. "You ruined my floor, Rosie Posie."

"Sorry, obedience isn't my strong suit," I needle him from my desk as I lean back to watch him.

His head tilts, and he gives me a dry glare. But the way he moves with such fluid grace is disarming. A simple head tilt exudes power and I feel myself shiver as his eyes trace my body.

"If I wanted someone obedient, I wouldn't be chasing after you."

I flush, not accustomed to comments like *that*. Comments where he speaks so freely about wanting me. It's a thrill. An addiction.

It makes my stomach flip and my head flustered.

So, I change the subject.

"What time are we hitting the road tomorrow? My car or yours?"

Now he's back to smirking.

"We're not driving, Rosie."

I hold a finger up as he prowls toward me. I left his bed mere hours ago, but I'm not sated. I already want to go back. Feel his weight on top of me. His teeth on my skin. His cock stretching me.

I lick my lips and swallow before crossing my legs and wondering how I went so damn long being oblivious to the way he looks at me. Ten years of living, ten years of perspective, and now it feels like the most obvious thing in the world.

I went from a man who barely glanced up at me from the cat videos on his phone to one who can't look at anything *but* me.

"Oh." I try to recover. "Are we going to ride there on the Death Star?"

"Don't be ridiculous. The Death Star is a space station, not a ship. But we are going to fly."

My brows furrow. "There's no airport here."

"Not a public one."

I pause as I work it through, my eyes widening as I realize what he's saying. "Oh my god, you really did jack off while thinking about a private jet."

"Maybe to thoughts of you on my private jet. And now you will too." He smiles, striding closer, all confident swagger until he towers above me and bends at the waist. His lips are dangerously close to mine when he says, "Wait until you see my yacht."

And then he kisses me breathless with a whispered, "Good morning, Ms. Belmont. I knew you'd be wearing a skirt."

"Fuckin' gross. Leave a sock on the door or something," West announces as he steps into the space. He lets out a low whistle as he turns on the spot and gazes around the office. "Dang. I can't believe this is the same dusty barn. I really gotta get over here more often."

"Looks good, right?" Ford straightens and walks toward his best friend.

They hug with a firm, manly back slap. I smile as I watch them. I wasn't sure how telling West would go, but the text I got from him last night was all the confirmation I needed. It said, *If I could build you a boyfriend like a Build-A-Bear, he would come out as Ford Grant.*

That was it. The only thing he said.

I wrote back, *Weird, but thanks.*

And then we didn't say another word about it.

I think that all went about as well as it could go, so I decided not to mess with a good thing.

"So, I just wanted to check your size for the shirts I'm ordering—"

"What shirts?" I ask.

Ford's head snaps in my direction and his eyes narrow. "No one likes an eavesdropper, Rosalie."

It's such a childish remark, and so *him*, I can't help but bark out a laugh. "Hiding something, boss?"

West laughs, looking highly amused. "Yeah, our boy here agreed to wear team shirts at bowling in exchange for dating you."

"It wasn't in exchange! It was a gesture of good faith between old friends."

Ford wearing a team bowling shirt is so quintessentially *not* him that the mere image sends me into a fit of giggles. "Oh my god. *Please*. I can't wait to see you guys. This is so deeply satisfying. Is there a cheering section at your games?"

Ford presses his fingers against his temples, massaging in slow circles like I give him gray hair.

I have no doubt that one day I will.

It's then that West pipes up, "Oh, man. Who messed up your floors?"

We all glance over at the giant smudge. The dark wood peeks through in several spots. I sort of… swished the drop cloth around in the paint when I cleaned it up, so it now looks like a giant swipe across the floor with a smattering of droplets around it. I wish I felt guilty about it.

Ford freezes but keeps his fingers pressed against his head.

I decide to throw him a bone.

"Oh, that? It's modern art. All the rage in the city right now. Sort of… an… asymmetrical focal point for the space."

It's straight-up bullshit. But I hope my brother is removed enough from all things art and all things city to buy what I'm selling.

West's hands land on his hips, head nodding as he examines the *art*.

And when he says, "Cool. I kinda like it," I let out a deep sigh just as Ford clears his throat to cover a laugh.

"Have you told Cora you own this thing?"

From his ridiculously cushioned seat, Ford furrows his brows at me. "Of course. How do you think we got to Calgary?"

"Wait." I raise my hand that isn't holding a flute of champagne, gesturing for him to stop. "You *flew* to Calgary? That's… that's like a simple three-hour drive!"

He rolls his eyes. "Don't I know it. I thought it would be a fun treat, but Cora bitched at me the entire time about how bad for the environment these flights are. I'm sure she'll tell my parents all about it while she spends these couple of days with them. But we need to be back in time for Sunday. She's having an end-of-the-year get-together with some school friends at my parents' place, and I don't want to miss it."

I stifle a laugh because I can totally see Cora giving him shit—while the entire Grant family hosts a party for her at their massive lake house.

"Well, this is truly over-the-top."

He shrugs. "Get used to it."

I smile shyly and slug back the rest of my champagne. I don't know how this became my life.

"All right, what's this fundraiser for again?"

"You're the one who fielded the invite."

"I know, but I was just looking for reasons to harass you via email. You're lucky I didn't forward you the one from *People* magazine asking for a rundown of your dating history for an article they were going to do."

He huffs out a soft laugh, shaking his head. "What did you tell them?"

"That you were a virgin and a hermit and in an exclusive relationship with your yacht. They asked why you're never seen in public with women, and I was like… have you tried taking a boat that big out on the town? Just plain cumbersome."

Now I get a glare.

"Okay. I didn't respond. I just deleted it."

He nods. "Good. And it's a fundraiser to rebuild after last year's big forest fire. They reached out because I told Bash he could give the organization my email."

"Well, that was alarmingly nice of you."

"Rosie, stop running your mouth and get your ass over here." He pats his lap, and old Rosie wants to tell him to go fuck himself.

But new Rosie gets up, straddles her boss' lap, and kisses him eagerly while smiling, because she is indeed wearing a skirt.

"Are you sure it's all in? Don't close the door until you're *sure*. If this gets damaged in any way, I think I'll barf."

Ford drops his head in through the open car door. "If you barf on that dress, you'll damage it. Hold yourself together."

"Ford, this dress is worth as much as I make in a month."

His brows scrunch together. "Is it?"

"Yes."

"That's appalling," he says as he stands. "Remind me to give you a raise when we get back home." He slams the door and rounds the vehicle to the other side.

When he slides in, I start to protest yet another raise, and he pulls his phone out to check if there are any messages. "Don't even open your mouth to argue with me about this, or I'll shove something in it to keep you busy."

The driver starts the engine, and I press my lips together as I stare out the window over the arid mountains and sloping vineyards that lead to the lake's edge, trying not to laugh at how rude Ford can be and how scandalized this poor older man looks.

Rather than take the seat behind the driver, Ford slides over into the middle and buckles himself in next to me without even glancing up from his phone.

Ford's thumbs tap endlessly as he sends message after message. He hasn't said it out loud, but I can tell he's nervous about leaving Cora. He texted his mom asking about her, and she told him to take a Xanax and go enjoy himself. Based on how quickly his fingers are flying over the screen, that was the wrong thing to say.

I reach for him and slide a hand over his muscled thigh. He looks edible in a tuxedo. I'm so used to seeing him in jeans, chunky sweaters, and rugged plaid shirts that I nearly fainted when I walked out of the bathroom to see him in this midnight blue getup.

Then when I saw the receipt for my dress in the trash bin, I almost passed out all over again. The dress is… otherworldly. I feel like a glowing Greek goddess wrapped in dusty, pale pink silk. The neckline dives deep, and the fabric gathers at the waist, where it ties in a knot, the ends of the sash tumbling to the floor like waterfalls. It has long sleeves, but the wrist cuffs stretch high up my forearms, dotted with round silk buttons.

The dress screams femininity and the nude suede pumps with ankle straps and a bow over the toes don't hurt either. I'm wearing simple gold hoops and my hair is half up in loose waves. This dress needs nothing else.

I've *never* been this dressed up before. But even I wouldn't ruin this outfit with socks and Birks only to piss Ford off. It would be an affront to all that is right in the world.

I squeeze his leg gently, trying to reassure him that Cora will be fine. "She's going to have a blast with them."

"I know." He sounds tense, and my lips twitch. Watching him in dad mode is a kink I never knew I had. Like, Ford was hot before, but make him all concerned and hyper-protective of a little girl who I'm also a huge fan of, and he becomes downright irresistible.

"They raised two really amazing humans." I squeeze again. "She'll be lucky to spend time with them too."

He doesn't respond to that—just slides his hand over the silk covering my leg and mirrors my motion.

"I feel like a princess," I murmur, watching the setting sun over the peaks of Emerald Lake.

"You are one."

I sigh.

The things he says are just subtly elevated. He doesn't tell me I *look* like one. He tells me I *am* one. Such a simple differentiation, yet so profound.

We ride in silence the rest of the way, taking in the low-lying mountains and arid landscape. Where Rose Hill is craggy and wild, Emerald Lake has a certain polish to it. A college town rich with wineries and orchards. It's a place where NHL players and politicians keep their summer houses.

It's small enough to be charming, but ritzy and close enough to Vancouver that it plays host to an event like tonight's.

When we pull up in front of the lakefront resort, it's brightly lit, with tall pillars and a grand entrance.

I feel like I should be working here, not attending an event. I keep that thought to myself and just soak it in, leaning into the firmness of Ford's strong body at my side, lending support.

The tips of his fingers graze my neck as he reaches across and pushes my loose hair behind my shoulder. His head inclines toward me. It feels a bit like that moment in the movies where Dracula is about to bite the girl, but there's also something really horny going on.

"You ready?" he whispers against the shell of my ear before dusting his lips across the curve of my neck.

"Honestly, if this dress wasn't so pretty, I'd tell you to take me back to that absurd suite overlooking the water and rip it off."

He smiles against my neck. The way his lips tip up and the light dusting of stubble on his face tickles my skin. "I can still do that, you know."

I whip my head to him, giving his chest a little shove. "If you ruin this dress, I'll break up with you."

Break up.

My eyes widen because I feel like I just prematurely slapped a label on us.

God. How many girls must try to attach themselves to him? And who could blame them? I'm there too. I have puppy-dog eyes for childhood dickhead, Ford Grant.

I flush and turn away, scrambling out of the car before he can make fun of me. Although I ask him to do it all the time, I don't know if I'm strong enough to take his mocking over this particular slipup.

The driver holds the door open, and Ford says nothing as he slides out behind me. He just presses his hand to the small of my back and guides us toward the red carpet near the entrance.

CHAPTER 39

Ford

DOES IT MAKE ME A DICK THAT I'M GRINNING OVER ROSIE'S slip of the tongue?

Maybe. But I made peace with who I am a long time ago.

She's got her head held high, the light shimmering on her collarbones as she walks at my side, refusing to make eye contact.

I think the most satisfying part is that for all her sass and confidence, it's something as simple as implying we're together that has her freaked out.

That's my move. I'm the one who blurts things out and then has to retreat awkwardly or say something mean to cover for it. So I'm not sure what she's all stressed about.

It's almost like she hasn't been paying attention.

If she had been, she'd know I've wanted this for a long fucking time. Wanted *her* for a long fucking time. So, yeah, she can bet her sweet ass we're together.

I slide my hand over her silk dress, savoring the feel of her lower back and lack of panty lines, before I slip it over her hip possessively as we follow the red carpet around the corner toward the courtyard. It's a sweeping paved area on the lake with twinkle lights strung through the palm trees that aren't remotely indigenous to the area. Set back is a pair of big sliding glass doors that open into the ballroom.

I'm about to direct us off this over-the-top red carpet when a bright flash stops us in our tracks.

I *hate* having my picture taken without permission. It's an intrusion I've faced my entire life. My dad did his best to keep Willa and me out of the spotlight, but the success rate wasn't one hundred percent.

But I also know how to play nice in front of the media. Learned that from my dad too. My fingers dig into Rosie's hip, so she turns toward me. Her hand slides up over my chest until she's clinging to me. And I just hold her against me tighter.

The photographer smiles at us, and a blond woman wearing a sequined red dress with a recording device pops up from behind him. "Ford Grant, what a treat to have you here tonight supporting the Emerald Lake Wildfire Recovery."

I give her a thin, practiced smile. "It's a pleasure to be here. Or it was until they photographed us without permission."

The woman blanches but swiftly regains her composure. "I'm so sorry. Would you like me to have the photo deleted?"

Rosie's fingers circle at my chest, a warning to *be nice*, I'm sure. But she knows better. I am nice; I just don't come off that way sometimes. I can practically feel her rolling her eyes at me. She'd say I'm being a dick.

"No, I'd just like to be asked first."

That strikes everyone silent while the woman works her head around how to proceed. "Can we get a photo of you for the paper?"

Rosie starts to cover for me. "Oh, that's not necessary—"

"That would be lovely." I give her a real smile.

The woman counts down, and this time, we're facing the camera, Rosie still tucked tight against my side.

The photographer turns to show us the shot on the screen, and we look so damn good together that I swallow, covering the emotion that swells in my chest.

"And who are you out with tonight? We'll add it to the description."

Rosie goes stiff. I don't know what she's expecting me to say, but something tells me it's not, "Oh, this is my girlfriend—Rosalie Belmont."

I walk into the party with a speechless girlfriend on my arm.

And I've never liked having my photo taken more.

The night wears on in a blur of boring conversation and forced enthusiasm. I think that's what I hate the most about any of these events. Everyone is so fake. They all have their own agenda. The vast majority of them couldn't care less about rebuilding after a devastating fire.

The lives upended.

The insurance claims denied.

The livestock lost.

The effect on the environment.

The list goes on, and the more I think about it, the more the tragedy of it drains me. The more the ass-kissing and lobbying bugs me. Because this event is for lobbyists. City contractors. Construction moguls.

This isn't about the fire—it's about their best interests. It's what everything tied to money becomes. It's exactly what happened at Gramophone. A bunch of men in suits around a table deciding to cut the rate they pay artists to give a little extra to shareholders.

I'm bitter and disillusioned by it all.

It's why I disappeared into the mountains. To Rose Hill. To Rosie.

The only bright spot of the night is watching her work the room with such… aplomb. She smiles, and it's genuine. She laughs, and it makes everyone nearby smile.

Even though we haven't addressed it between us, I introduce her to people as my girlfriend, and she presses closer every time.

I find it impossible to take my eyes off of her. The shimmer of the pale pink silk sliding over her skin mesmerizes me. It's borderline sensual the way her painted lips press against the edge of a champagne glass and the way her throat bobs as she swallows it is enough to make me blush as I'm transported back to that morning in the paint.

Needless to say, she *glows*, and everyone sees it. Everyone is drawn to her, just like they always have been.

Rosie at a lake party. Rosie playing beach volleyball. Rosie hiking. Rosie at the fucking grocery store. I've watched her effortlessly draw attention for most of her life, and I'm not even sure she realizes how organically she does it.

"Rosie, is that you?" a woman's voice says, filtering in from our right.

I turn, and Rosie's hand glides across my back as she steps in front of me while keeping as close as possible.

"Faye?" Her eyes light up when she takes in the dark-haired woman, who appears to be a bit younger. "Hi!" She almost squeals as she wraps her free arm around the woman's neck. I press my lips together to cover the smile because I have a feeling the champagne is affecting her volume control.

Gin did the same thing to her when she was younger.

Rosie holds her back. "How are you? What are you doing here?"

"I quit working at Apex and came out here to do my master's. Journalism. Just here putting some time in at a local paper before classes start in the fall." She holds up the press pass lanyard around her neck with a grin.

Rosie smiles the most genuine smile in the room as she holds the woman back to look at her. "Good for you. Oh, this is…" Rosie peers back at me, lips twitching in a mirror image of my own because I've been the one saying this out loud all night. And now it's her turn. "This is my boyfriend, Ford."

Faye's eyes move to mine and bulge a little. "Nice to meet you," she says demurely, reaching forward to shake my hand.

"Likewise." I try to smile, but I'll never be good at events like these or pretending small talk invigorates me.

Her gaze turns back to Rosie, and she clears her throat. "I have to get this off my chest. I'm just so sorry about what happened." Her hand waves between them. "At the office. With Stan."

Rosie's smile dims. "Yeah, me too."

"It's like everyone speculates about what went down, but they're too scared to say or do anything beyond gossip at the water cooler."

I feel Rosie tense and my molars clamp as the woman rambles on.

"If it's any consolation, that place is in shambles. Most likely going to go under. Shit was spiraling alarmingly fast when I got out."

Now I stiffen.

"What a shame," Rosie deadpans.

A few beats of silence hang in the air, chatter around us rising to the forefront, then both women burst into a fit of giggles.

"What was happening?" Rosie asks, while dabbing at the edges of her eyes.

Faye steps closer, dropping her voice to a whisper. "They kept having to move offices. I don't know if it was a money thing or what. They got an immediate eviction notice and sent everyone to work from home while they sorted stuff out. Then they moved to a whole new building and got evicted again. Rinse and repeat. I'm sure it was draining the coffers."

Rosie's mouth falls open, and she blinks a few times. "I mean, there must be contracts in place to prevent that?"

My jaw pops and I try to act casual as I glance around the room.

Faye shrugs. "I think so, but even legal costs can add up. It was all very mysterious. Nobody knows why. Heard through the grapevine tonight that it just happened again."

Rosie's posture is straight and stiff as her head turns to me, slicing me with a scathing look. One that stills me.

Rosalie Belmont is smart as a whip.

Smart enough to figure me out. I just stand by and watch her solve the puzzle at hyper-speed.

"Shit. That's…" She shakes her head and looks back at Faye, recovering quickly. "Well, Stan's empire falling apart… couldn't have happened to a nicer person."

They both laugh while my heart thuds heavily in my sinking stomach.

The two women laugh and play catch-up for the next few minutes. And when Faye finally leaves us, Rosie returns to my side, slides her fingers through mine, and grits out, "Time for you and me to have a chat."

"About?"

"In private," is all she says as she leads me out of the room, finally wearing a smile that matches the fakeness of all the other vipers slithering around us.

And even though I don't wear a fake smile, I realize I might be one of them after all.

CHAPTER 40

Rosie

"HERE?" FORD ASKS AS I DRAG HIS INFURIATING ASS OUT OF the event.

"No. I don't want some asshole snapping a photo of me reaming you out and running a headline about you being the World's Most In Trouble Billionaire."

He *smirks* at my response. "At least that title has a little character to it."

Do I want to tear his head off? Yes.

Do I want to protect him at all costs? Also yes. I swear, if that blond reporter writes something mean about him, I'll pull her extensions out.

I ignore him, hail our town car, and scoot to the opposite side.

Of course this charming idiot does what he did before and slides into the middle. I've always known Ford to be unapologetic and firm in his beliefs, and the way he's reacting now is proof of that.

We ride in silence, hands on each other's knees, the view out the window blurred by the dark night whipping past on the mostly empty roads. The minute the town car comes to a stop in front of the opulent boutique hotel, which sits on a cliff overlooking the lake, I fly out the door. The driver is flustered by not being able to open it for me, but I barge past him, the swish of silk accompanying the tapping of my heels against the brick walkway that leads to the front doors.

I hear the low mumble of Ford thanking the man, who I'm sure will go home and tell his partner about the strange couple he drove tonight. I head straight for our room without a glance back. Ford's low chuckle as he takes long strides to catch up with me rumbles across the back of my neck. Just the sound of him makes my hair stand on end.

I'm mad at him right now, but my nipples pebble all the same.

Fucking Ford Grant.

I stop at our door, and he's already caught up, thanks to his fitness and obnoxious height. He swaggered up while I stormed out, and he still caught me.

It's annoying.

The veins on the top of his tanned hand catch my eye, highlighted by the midnight blue of his tuxedo jacket. He swipes the card, opens the door, and follows me in.

As soon as the door clicks shut, I spin on him. "Explain yourself."

His tongue presses against his cheek, and he props a shoulder against the wall, unperturbed by my agitation. "What part? I told you I was going to ruin them. You told me you wanted to forget about them. All I did was follow through and respect your wishes."

I suck in a breath, transported back to that night on the dock when all those truths spilled from my lips while tears spilled from my eyes.

He absorbed every last one.

"I thought you were just…" My hands wave around as I search for the words I want to use. "I thought you were just talking a big game."

His head tilts in that signature Ford way, making heat pool low in my body. "That's the problem, Rosie. You've spent too much time around men who talk a big game but don't possess the will to follow through."

I swallow and everything inside me clenches.

"Stan has been learning a very valuable lesson of late." He takes a brief peek down at his Rolex. "In fact, your friend was right—he learned another one just a few hours ago."

"What's the lesson?" I ask in a hushed voice, taken aback by Ford's brazenness. By his brutality.

"That he has no power. No pull. That everything he has is easily taken away. He's getting a little taste of the way he made you feel."

I'm shocked. And I wonder why. I've always known Ford was like this—cutting and vicious and *good* down to the marrow of his bones.

This vengefulness is new to me. It should upset me, but… I find myself in awe of a man who would go to such lengths for me.

He looks like a predator. With his nonchalant voice and

shy demeanor, he's one you'd never see coming. And yet here he is, a cat playing with the mouse as he kills it slowly. And I'm strong enough not to blink away.

I feel stronger than I ever have before. Even in my frustration with him I'm finding myself. Drawing lines in the sand for how I will and will not live my life. Good girl Rosie has been replaced with a version of Rosie who knows that life isn't black and white. That people grow and change and recreate themselves.

There's no title for this Rosie. It's just me, stepping into a version of myself that makes *me* happy.

I finally have a grip on those tendrils of control I lost somewhere along the way. I can feel them weaving themselves back into my bones. I stand a little taller as the realization works its way through my body.

"How are you doing it?"

I feel *good* as I stare back at Ford. I feel equal to him in a way I never have. Talking about this openly makes me feel like we're really a team. A *great* one.

"You really want to know?"

I roll my lips together, considering his question. Maybe it's better if I don't know every dirty detail. "Give me the abbreviated version. One that doesn't implicate me."

He nods firmly and slides his hands into his pockets. I don't think he even realizes how beautiful he looks right now in the darkened room. The light filtering in from the window gives him an iridescent sort of glow. "I've recently started investing heavily in Vancouver real estate."

My eyes bug out and my chin juts forward. "You're *buying* the buildings?"

"It's a good investment."

My voice rises in time with my disbelief. "No, it's not! Those high-rises have got to be worth millions! That's *ridiculous*."

I shout and he just smirks. "Tens of millions. Per building."

All the blood drains from my face. *Tens of millions.*

"Ford. All this because… You can't… you can't spend that kind of money on me! You can't spend that kind of money on playing games, *period*. It's irresponsible. I'm not worth—" I scream at him only to cover for how nauseous I am over the thought of all those zeroes.

"*You are worth every fucking penny!*" he shouts, arms flung wide. "I'm careful with my money. I'm downright philanthropic. But this? This isn't a game. I'm in love with you. This is pocket change compared to what I'd be happy to spend on you. There is no price too high to watch this asshole pay for every moment of misery and self-doubt he caused you."

With two long strides, he's standing in front of me, body vibrating with rage. His hands land on either side of my neck, forcing me to look at him as his thumbs trace reverently over my jaw.

His eyes glow with intensity as mine fill with tears. "Hear this, Rosie. You are worth every penny. Every fortune. Every investment. Every risk. You are priceless to me."

One stray teardrop rolls down my cheek when I blink, and Ford watches its slow descent with a sort of fury I've seen on his face before. One I'm realizing I've misplaced over the years.

I misread Ford's expressions when I thought I infuriated him.

He was infuriated. But for me. Not with me.

"Do you understand?" He practically growls the words and I dip my chin in agreement, sniffling once.

"I think so."

I spent a lot of time wondering why the boys in my life never felt an inclination to stand up for me, and now I'm face-to-face with a man who's made it his mission to do it. Even in the throes of passionate argument he makes me feel more secure than I ever have before.

It's... overwhelming. It's heart-rending. It's *safety*.

Our gazes collide, and with one hitched breath, I crash into him. Kissing him. Clutching at the lapels of his jacket with such intense need that it almost hurts.

My chest aches as his lips claim mine, his big hand cradling my head like I'm the most precious thing in the world.

We cling to each other, but it's not enough. It's not close enough. Raw enough. I don't know what to say to him, can't find the words. All I know is I want to be cocooned in him. In his protection.

It feels like after so many years of going it on my own, working so hard to make something of myself, to stay out of trouble, I have somewhere soft to land. Somewhere I can let the worst, bitchiest, most unlikable, sock-and-sandal-wearing version of myself show and still be loved.

It's a kind of devotion I've never known.

It's a refuge I never let myself dream of.

The sandalwood in Ford's cologne is heady and

intoxicating, the expert stroke of his tongue against mine a wildfire through my veins.

"Take this off. Now," I bite out between kisses, unwilling to pull back enough to talk.

Ford groans into my mouth as I work at his shirt buttons while he shrugs off his jacket. I rip the last few, not caring. If he can spend millions playing games, he can buy a new shirt.

I'm struck dumb all over again when I see what's around his neck. The silver chain and that goddamn key. Pale blue speckles of paint mar the metal. And all the air leaves my lungs.

"You fished that out of the paint?"

"Of course. I plan to wear it forever."

Then my hands are on his bare skin. My fingertips memorize every ridge as I count every ab. I move up to his pecs, moaning as I flick a finger over his nipple and it hardens. Just like mine.

I pull back to admire him, the silvery light highlighting his toned body.

"Fuck. I'm going to keep pushing you into that lake for years to come just so you keep swimming." He breathes out a soft laugh. "Lose the pants."

He keeps his eyes on me while he undoes his belt casually, making me wet in the process. His slacks fall and I swiftly remove his boxers and wrap my hand around his steely length.

Ford hisses through his teeth as I twist my palm around his girth and dust the pads of my fingers over the straight line of his collarbone. I marvel at how angular everything on this man's body is. His nose. His jaw. His brow.

He's a painful sort of handsome. Not pretty or soft. There's no boy-next-door appeal with Ford. There's a wickedness to him. Sharp jaw, wide shapely lips, cunning eyes.

"I'm sorry I never noticed," I murmur, thinking back to all those summers we spent at each other's throats. How different it all must have looked through his eyes.

He was just my brother's dickish best friend who always had some snide remark to make. But he was there for me at every turn.

I was oblivious.

"I'm sorry I never told you," he murmurs, reaching between us with deft fingers to pull away the sash at my waist. Once loose, all it takes is a simple shrug of my shoulders for the plunging neckline to give way and the stunning silk garment to tumble into a soft pool of dreamy pink fabric at my feet.

The rush of cool air has every fine hair on my body rising. Like every fiber of me is reaching for *him*.

"Ford, I—"

"Rosie," he cuts me off, but his voice is gentle. It holds a tremor as his gaze sizzles over my skin, and he delicately removes the daisy-shaped pasties that cover my nipples. "I think we should take a break from talking with our mouths. There are more important things I'd like to do with mine."

His head drops to my chest, and he sucks my nipple into his mouth with a guttural groan. My head tips back, my hair tickling my spine, as I'm plunged into the sensation of being worshiped by Ford Grant.

The tug of the sticker on my right breast sends a sharp jolt of pleasure straight to my groin as he continues to work the opposite nipple.

When his dark mahogany hair moves over to the other one, I stumble, my heels tipping me back until I'm pressed against the wall.

I grip his strong shoulders as his lips drag torturously over my body Then he drops to his knees before me. With his hands splayed over my rib cage, he trails his tongue between my breasts, skims his teeth over my stomach, and nips at the soft spot just beneath my hip. I shiver and lift my body to meet him.

He leans back slightly and stares at me. My core. My stomach. My legs.

He uses one thumb against one side of my pussy and spreads me.

"Ford…"

"Rosie, shut up and let me admire you."

My breaths come sharp and choppy as he swipes through me, spreading the wetness up and over my clit. A shiver racks me every time, but I can't peel my eyes from the look of intense focus on his face. It's the same one he gets when I see him listening to a demo with big noise-canceling headphones on.

His forest-green eyes slice up to my face. "I like seeing how wet you are for me. Proof that this is real."

Then he drops his head between my legs, turning the attention he just gave my rock-hard nipples to my pussy.

My head tilts back against the wall as his tongue works

me. His stubble scrapes against my inner thighs. He sets my body ablaze with every stroke, every firm press of his lips. I rock against his face, but he doesn't pull away—he takes it one step further. Lifting each of my thighs over his shoulders, spreading me and diving in deeper with a hungry snarl.

I feel out of my body. Like I've exploded into a cloud of bliss and could float away if it weren't for the man between my legs, gripping my thighs and feasting on me like I'm the best thing he's ever tasted.

The coiling sensation at the base of my spine takes hold. A tugging between my hips.

"Oh god. Oh fuck," I murmur, fingers raking through his hair. Toes curling tight against the base of the stilettos still strapped around my ankles.

I see my release shimmering before me, like heat waves on a hot day. So real I could reach out and touch it.

But Ford pulls back, and it ebbs away. I groan and thump a fist on the wall beside me before peering down at him.

At his *smirk* and glowing, almost otherworldly eyes.

"What are you doing?" I whine the words.

"Watching you." His focus flashes down to my spread pussy and back up to my face.

"Less watching. More of what you were doing before."

He lowers one leg off his shoulder and then the other as he leans back on his haunches, looking altogether too pleased with himself.

"Not yet."

My eyes widen, a flash of frustration streaking through me. "You're torturing me."

Ford chuckles, low and deep, and it makes me sway on already unsteady legs. He stands and stares down at me. "You've been torturing me for years."

He gives me a quick kiss and I can taste my essence on his lips. It brings me a base sort of satisfaction to know that he tastes like *me*.

He reaches down and lifts me like I weigh nothing. I imagine for a man his size, that's probably true. He man-handles me with ease, carrying me farther into the dim suite.

"If you learn anything tonight, it should be that I get off on playing with my food before I finish it," he whispers against my ear.

When he drops me on the bed, stepping up so that his knees bump against the edge of the mattress, my legs come together.

"Spread your legs, Rosie."

My chest heaves with heavy, excited breaths and I let my legs fall apart for him. I feel like I could combust under the weight of his gaze.

"Too dark to see." I glimpse his profile, the outline of his body as he rounds the bed and flicks on the bedside lamp. A golden glow fills the space, accentuating every shadowed dip on his body. I glance up at where he stands near my head and watch as he takes a moment to let his eyes roam me. Spread out for him. An appreciative groan rumbles in his throat and my entire body clenches in anticipation.

Then he tugs two pillows from against the headboard and steps down the side of the bed so he towers over my splayed body.

"Flip over, Rosie. Get on all fours."

I'm too mind-numbingly turned on to bark back at him. I'm pliable. Needy. I do exactly as he tells me.

"Yeah, baby. Just like that," he mutters as I turn onto my knees and lift my ass in the air. One big hand caresses the closest globe appreciatively while the other slides the cool pillows beneath my stomach.

Then his attention moves lower, a teasing swipe across my clit before two fingers push inside me, scissoring and stretching me. I turn to glance back over my shoulder. To catch sight of his solid body looming over mine as he plays with me.

I pant, mouth popping open as I soak up the view, as he keeps working me relentlessly. Then I feel a slap against my cheek. I look back up at him and he's fisting his cock.

"Open up, Rosie. Put that mouth to use."

There's no hesitation. My lips are already parted and he takes full advantage by sliding himself into my mouth while he fucks me with his fingers. I rock back and forth on my hands and knees, pushing toward him at both ends. Surrounded by *him*.

I moan shamelessly, overwhelmed by sensation. He plays me like a maestro, standing beside me, filling me in so many ways.

I suck eagerly at his length, arching my back and clenching around him when he adds a third finger and growls, "Such a tight, needy little pussy."

My head bobs. Because, yes, I am so needy right now.

He smooths a hand over my hair. "If your mouth wasn't stuffed full of cock right now, would you be asking for more?"

I hum and nod, still working at his length. But he pulls away all the same and presses my back. It's a light pressure, but my arms buckle beneath me so I'm down on my elbows.

"Hips up, baby," he directs and I'm immediately lifting my hips, knees digging into the soft mattress as I melt into the pillows beneath me and feel my heel-clad feet dangle on the edge. I let Ford position me exactly as he wants me. His hands gentle and domineering all at once.

I whimper when he steps back and moves to the end of the bed, his knees bumping against my ankles as he steps close.

The Egyptian cotton sheets are silky between my fingers when I grip them. Cool and soft and too damn nice for the ways we're about to deface them.

"Stop pretending to be shy and spread your legs, Rosie. I want to see that tight little pussy drip for me."

"Fuck you," I whisper, but there's no venom; in fact, it comes out more like a plea. And there's no fight. I let my knees slide across the sheets, feeling my wetness seep out as I do.

His satisfied groan does nothing but confirm it.

"That's what you need. To get fucked. I can see that much." His words rumble over my spine, and I feel his heat as he comes to stand behind me. "It's what I need too," he adds as he runs the bare head of his cock through my folds. "What I've always wanted."

He carries on teasing me, his words slow and measured. Totally unhurried.

"So, I'm going to enjoy this. Watching you make a mess

for me. Fucking you. Making you come until your legs give out and the only thing keeping this ass up for me are those pillows."

He slides in fast and hard.

Palms on my ass, cock shoved snug inside me.

"Yes," I moan, arching my back and pushing into him.

His fingers flex.

"Wish you could see the way you look stuffed full of me, baby. So fucking right."

"Yes." I move my hips against him again. "So fucking right," is my hushed response, repeating his words.

His movements start out exacting and measured. Every thrust in just as painstakingly even as each glide out. I know he's watching me take him. And that turns me on. Knowing he can't look away, knowing he's getting off on the view of me stretched around his cock.

I turn my head to meet his emerald gaze. I bite my bottom lip and clench around his overwhelming thickness. An unspoken challenge that he recognizes with a growl. With fingertips that dig into my ass and measured strokes that border on punishing.

A smile touches my lips as he fucks me into the bed. Our skin slaps as he pounds me hard enough that I lose purchase. I give in and let the pillows take my weight while Ford forces me to see stars.

I get lost in him.

His hands.

His body.

The way he plays mine with such mastery.

It's a blur, a high I'll never be able to re-create.

I shatter, screaming his name, and my legs give out as he showers me with kisses. He works his way up my spine, thrusting once, hard, and then follows. Erupting before draping himself over me. Our damp bodies pressed together, heaving through sharp, ragged breaths. He brushes his nose against the shell of my ear. A touch that somehow overflows with tenderness.

A touch that makes me turn my head and whisper what I've known for some time.

"I love you, Ford."

He just nuzzles against me again and responds with a quiet, "I've always loved you, Rosie."

CHAPTER 41

Ford

I WAKE UP WRAPPED AROUND ROSIE LIKE I'M A CHILD snuggling with my favorite teddy bear. Her torso curves into mine, my legs framing the backs of hers. I've got an arm draped over her shoulder and my hand covers hers completely, our fingers linked.

She smells like the lilacs that grow down by the lake, and she feels like heaven.

She feels like home.

She feels like she's finally *mine*.

I shut my eyes and nuzzle down into her neck, trailing the tip of my nose over the shell of her ear. Breathing her in, letting her hair catch in the bristled stubble on my chin. I want so badly to drift back to sleep, to spend all day like this.

But there's a subtle buzzing going on somewhere in the room. Annoying, like a fly buzzing around my head. Intruding on our peace just enough that agitation flares inside me. And then concern takes hold as I think about Cora and whether anything could be wrong.

She's mine but not. Bearing the burden of safeguarding her until her mother recovers is an immense pressure. And it's that stress that pulls me from the warmth of the bed and the comfort of Rosie's sleeping body.

She stirs as I search the room. We were in such a frenzy last night that I'm not sure where our phones are. Her tiny, pearl-encrusted clutch is dropped by the front door, but when I touch it, it's not vibrating.

The buzzing stops, then picks up again, and worry flares inside me. I turn, heading toward the pile of clothes that are actually an expensive tuxedo. The jacket is tangled up in the pants, and my fingers scramble to separate it as the noise grows louder. I lift the jacket and shove a hand into the inside pocket, my gut dropping hard and fast when I see my lawyer's name flashing on the screen.

The heavy, gasping way I suck in a breath has Rosie's eyes flipping open as every worst-case scenario flashes through my mind. Which is why I'm equal parts relieved and surprised when I pick up with a "What?" and Belinda answers with, "Why are you ignoring your calls? Weston Belmont got arrested last night, and I've been trying to get ahold of you for hours."

Rosie sits up in the bed, not bothering to cover herself. She's stunning. All warm and rumpled and wearing a bite mark on her left breast from last night.

It's a shame she's about to be really fucking mad at me.

While my lawyer chews me out about how I need to

get my ass to Vancouver and help my friend because some asshole named Stan is hell-bent on pressing charges, I soak Rosie in, not fully listening.

Pleading with the universe for this to not be something she holds against me for too long.

"Got it," I say back to her. "We're on our way." I hang up and take in the confused expression lining Rosie's face.

"What's going on? Is Cora okay?"

My heart thuds heavily against my ribs, knowing what I'm about to tell her and feeling even more in love with her for asking about Cora before anything else.

"Cora is fine. But…" I scrub a hand over my stubbled jaw and let loose a muttered, "*Fuck*."

"Ford." Rosie tugs the sheet up over herself, like a layer of protection. Like she's already anticipating some sort of blow. "What's wrong?"

"West got arrested. We need to go to Vancouver."

She rears back ever so slightly—this wasn't what she was expecting. We both know her bother has stayed out of trouble since having kids. They seemed to soothe some of that reckless abandon in him. That ferocity.

But now *I'm* the one who pushed him too far.

"For *what*? And why the hell was he in Vancouver?"

She pushes up onto her knees, gathering the sheet higher, almost wrapping it around herself, reading my face—my body.

"He was helping me."

Her face is blank, eyes wide like saucers. The silence in the room crescendos.

"With Stan."

She stays eerily still, staring—no, glaring—at me as splotches of red expand on her chest and travel up her throat, unspoken words forming in her heart and moving up to her vocal cords so she can hurl them at me.

Angry, pissed-off words. Because I *know* I shouldn't have involved West in this.

"You…" Her voice is stony, a troublesome sort of calm. "You told *my brother* about what happened with Stan?"

I drop my phone on the desk beside me and take a step toward her, but she holds a shaking hand up to stop me.

"No. You're going to stay right there."

I swallow heavily and stop my forward motion before lifting my arms and raking my fingers through my hair. "Rosie, I'm sorry. We weren't together at that point. When I told him, I still… I figured we were going to be what we'd always been. Nothing had happened between us yet. I never knew we'd be where we are now."

"I…" She glances around the room now, a breathy, disbelieving chuckle lurching from her throat, followed by a pained groan. "I told you that in confidence." Her eyes slice back to mine, pinning me to the spot. "You are the *only* person I've told that to other than Ryan. And something has *always* been happening between us. We've always had secrets."

"I'm sorry." It's all I can say, and I'll say it over and over again. No matter how many times it takes.

"You told me you wouldn't tell anyone. And then you decide that of all the people in the world to tell, my *brother* seemed like the ideal candidate? Who else? My parents?

God." She drops her face into one hand while the other clutches at the white sheet. "How humiliating."

"You have *nothing* to be humiliated about." I spit the words out like venom.

She looks back up at me, face drawn, hands limp at her sides. "Fine. So why exactly is my brother facing charges?"

My molars grind. West and his fucking temper. "I don't know the details. He hit Stan. I thought he would be okay just being the one to hand-deliver the eviction notices. He wanted to do something and was getting a kick out of tormenting the guy. But apparently Stan came at him this time, and you know how that goes over with West."

She shakes her head at me, like she can't quite believe what I'm telling her.

"You know we've always been partners in crime."

She scoffs. "Yeah, when you were kids playing ding-dong ditch or getting booze underage, it was fine. You guys are adults now, and you can't just play this off like you are two teenagers getting into trouble. This isn't… Ha!" She barks out a laugh. "I'm sorry. I'm just having a really hard time wrapping my head around how someone as intelligent as you can be so deeply oblivious. He has two children who need him, Ford. He doesn't have billions of dollars in his coffers. You can't use him to do your dirty work just because he's always been a little rougher around the edges than you. You keep your hands clean and play chess while West takes the fall? If you're as good a friend to him as you claim to be, how could you have put him in this position?"

"That's never how I meant it. We were working together as a team."

"Right, well, one of you is sitting in a police station and the other is lounging around in a thousand-dollar-a-night boutique hotel room. Forgive me for missing the *team* aspect of this venture."

My throat dries as I wrap my head around what she's saying, finally seeing the entire situation from a perspective other than my own. Beyond my tunnel vision for revenge on a man who wronged someone I love.

"I didn't think—"

"No." She stands and the sheet drops, leaving her entirely naked as she walks to me. "You didn't think because you are privileged beyond compare." Her arms fly out wide. "You have power you don't even recognize. Money. Clout. A name you complain about but wield like a weapon. And that's okay. You should make the most of what you've got. But goddamn it, Ford. At least recognize it. Own it."

I blink. Stricken by the rawness of what she's telling me.

"That day? In that office? Stan stole my power. It was for a split second, and maybe it should have been easy to brush off, but it changed *everything* I worked for in my life." She snaps her fingers, and I flinch. "*Poof*, gone. It was a stark look at how truly insignificant I was. It made me question my value."

My throat aches. It contracts so tightly on itself that I'm unable to find my voice.

"That was *my* story to share. When I was good and ready. Or my secret to keep for however long I wanted. And I entrusted it to you."

"Rosie—"

Her head shakes sharply. "No. I don't want to hear it. I know what you were trying to do, I do. But Ford…" Her fingers comb through her wavy hair as she blinks away. "You guys aren't teenagers with grudges against some small-town boy who dumped me anymore. The dynamic with us isn't what it was when we were kids. And I know he's your best friend, but if you and I are ever going to be anything, I need to be the one who comes first, Ford. I need that loyalty from you, even over him. I won't settle for less."

Her voice cracks, and she blinks her tears away. Head held high as she turns back toward her overnight bag, rifling through it for clothes.

I watch her dress in guilty silence, realizing what I've done. Undermined her trust and tried to play god. Pulling strings I have no business pulling, no matter how virtuous my cause or pure my intentions.

Keeping secrets I shouldn't, while spilling the ones I should.

"Rosie, I'm sorry. I'm so fucking sorry."

She ignores me and, now dressed, continues packing her bag. And I just stand here in my boxers, the morning after the one night I had everything I could ever want, watching it all go up in smoke. And I'm the asshole who lit the match.

I finally give voice to what's been turning my stomach for the past several minutes. "Are you coming with me?"

She straightens, duffel in hand, and walks straight up to me. "No. I am booking my own flight to Calgary, and then

I hope Tabby or someone will pick me up and drive me back to Rose Hill."

"But we could—"

Her pointer finger jabs me in the chest, and her eyes sparkle with unshed tears as she goes toe-to-toe with me. "No. You are going to walk in there like Ford Grant Junior with your big swinging dick and World's Hottest Billionaire title, and you are going to make this *right*. You break it, you buy it. Go be a *team* or whatever you little boys are calling this shit."

My molars grind as I give her a firm nod. I'll give her anything she wants to make this right.

"I'm going to go make sure my niece and nephew have someone to pick them up when their week at their mom's place ends. And I hope to god Mia doesn't have any second thoughts about sending them to a guy who flies off the handle while playing Dog the Bounty Hunter for kicks."

I swallow and her eyes search my face. Anger flashes through them, and a plea lurks beneath it in those blue depths. "Cora's end-of-school party is tomorrow." It's a silent command for me to be back with everything fixed. She grips my chin. "Make this right."

With that, she turns and walks out of our hotel room.

But not before calling back over her shoulder, "And also, I quit."

Then the door clicks shut on me.

CHAPTER 42

Ford

GUILT HAS BEEN MY CONSTANT COMPANION THE ENTIRE flight into Vancouver. Rosie's take on everything I have—my power, my privilege—hit me like a freight train.

The ultimate wake-up call. Because I don't think a single other person in my life has ever laid it out like that. Willa is swayed by the ease of our upbringing, whether or not she realizes it. Our struggles are not the same as other people's.

Struggles, yes. Because we all struggle. But it's so much more nuanced than that.

And the more I think about it, the more I realize my dad was trying to teach me this exact lesson by not handing me the money for that ticket all those years ago. He could have afforded it. He could lose that hundred bucks in the wash and not notice it was missing.

But he wanted me to learn to notice it.

Instead, I found a workaround and carried on with my

life. My education. My last name. I know I haven't abused them or used them poorly, but I am guilty of being oblivious to the power they wield. The way they've set me up in life, even when it didn't feel that way.

On the drive to the police station, the reality of Rosie's words sinks in. I decide that I'm very comfortable with what I have and that I will use every tool at my disposal to make this right for West.

And I realize I owe him an apology. Because I *do* know better than to send him into this situation.

If West sees a cliff, he's gonna jump off it. If he finds a horse no one can stay on, West is gonna ride it. And if he runs into someone who needs punching, West is gonna punch them.

That's just him. And I unknowingly steered him into this.

I tug the glass doors to the station open and shake my head when I round the corner and see him having coffee with a cop at his desk. West's hands are gesturing and he's grinning as he tells the potbellied middle-aged man what appears to be a hilarious story.

The cop has one hand on his stomach, the other wrapped around a mug, and a wide grin spread under his gray mustache.

This is also very… West.

The man could charm the pants off anyone.

"Weston," I say as I approach, tilting my head when I see the way his knuckles are split.

When my friend of twenty years turns and hits me with his most mischievous grin, I know he's not seeing this the way Rosie is. Or maybe he is, and he doesn't care.

I tap a finger against my knuckles, a silent question about his bloodied ones.

He chuckles and gives me a wink. One I've seen him use to get himself out of trouble—or into it—for years now. "Nah, dude. You should see the other guy."

The cop shakes his head and pinches the bridge of his nose. "I'm assuming you're Mr. Grant?"

I swipe my tongue over my teeth as I reach a hand toward the cop. If identifying myself helps West get out of this, I'll do it. So, it's with a wince that I correct him. "Ford Grant Junior. Pleasure to meet you…" I glance at his name tag. "Constable Rollins."

The man takes my hand firmly, his shrewd eyes narrowing. "Ford Grant as in…"

West laughs. "Oh, right. I forgot to mention he's a *nepo baby*, as his daughter would say."

My eyes roll, but I don't respond.

Recognize it. Own it.

"Well, it's nice to meet you. Big fan of your father."

I smile and say thank you. This doesn't surprise me at all. Pretty much any middle-aged man is a fan of my dad and his band.

"You can take your friend here."

My eyebrows pop up. "That's it?"

West slaps my shoulder as he stands from his chair. "Yeah, just been hanging out and chatting here. First thing I did when they gave me my phone back was order a big box of donuts for these fellas for being so great to me."

My eyebrows scrunch. "You ordered cops donuts?"

West fires a finger gun at the man across from him and grins. "Funny, right? They loved them, though, so the stereotype's not wrong. The science is all here to back it up."

I stand staring, slack-jawed. Only West Belmont would get arrested and turn it into a jolly good time where he makes new friends by testing out an age-old stereotype.

Constable Rollins laughs softly, shoulders rising and falling as he stares at his donut—laid out on a napkin on his desk. "Please, I'll never get any work done with this clown hanging around. Take him. He's yours." The man waves a hand, shooing us away.

"That's it? No charges?"

He nudges his chin in West's direction. "Your friend here can show you the footage we just got maybe an hour ago. No charges."

I sigh in relief. But then the man pipes up again, "Well, except the ones he's pressing."

I arch a brow at West, and he just starts walking through the open station, boots clunking on the thinly carpeted floor as he makes his way toward the front door.

He smiles and gives *another* finger gun to the disheveled guy sitting on a bench by the front door.

The man sneers back at West. And that's when I recognize him.

Stan Cumberland.

I've researched him enough online to recognize him anywhere. Even beneath the purple eye that's swollen shut.

It appears that his wife is talking to the woman at the front desk. She turns to look at me, her face drawn and tired.

From head to toe, her attire screams wealth and luxury, and I have no doubt she never saw her Saturday morning playing out this way.

I feel bad for her, but not bad enough to stop me from walking right up to Stan, kicking the toe of his dress shoe with my "stupid expensive boots" as Rosie called them, and towering over him. "You touched the woman I love without her permission. That was a very. Poor. Choice." I bite the words out and don't bother lowering my voice.

His wife gasps from behind me, but Stan just scowls.

I turn to walk away but then stop to face him again as I lean against the push bar of the door. "The next time you consider laying your greasy hands on someone without consent, remember my face. Because I can afford to keep fucking with you for the rest of my life. And I'm just petty enough to do it."

And with that, I turn on my heel and leave the building before they can arrest me for uttering threats.

We're seated in the back seat of the town car I booked when I finally turn to my best friend, eyes fixed on his split knuckles. "I'm sorry."

"For what?" West asks, confusion lacing his voice.

I flop back against the black leather. "For sending you out to do this shit."

From my periphery, I see West nodding. It's several seconds before he responds.

"I know you fancy yourself really smart—but, Ford, I don't work for you, and you didn't *send* me to do shit."

"I told you something I shouldn't have and was well aware of how you'd react. I wanted a partner in crime, and I knew you wouldn't turn me down. You never do."

He laughs dryly, stubble rasping beneath his fingers. "That's because we're friends, not because I'm stupid. If you asked me to do something I wasn't prepared to do, I wouldn't have done it. And I think you might be underestimating how much I've grown since I was twenty. I didn't attack that weasel-faced motherfucker. *He* attacked *me*."

I glance over at West. "What?"

He hands me his phone as a black-and-white security video fills the screen. "That's what your fancy-ass lawyer found after talking to me. Turns out when you own the building, getting security footage is a breeze."

I hit play and watch West stride into the building's front lobby, wearing a plaid collared shirt, tattoos on display, hair slicked back. This is his version of dressed up. He's speaking to the woman at the front desk when Stan appears at the corner of the screen.

Stan's hands shoot up and flail frantically—he appears to be visibly agitated.

In response, West holds his own hands up, stepping away. Of course, I can see the shit-eating grin on his face, which didn't help diffuse the situation. Within moments, Stan has leaped at West.

He tackles him to the ground only because he takes West by surprise. He can't land a punch. West turns and shifts, and Stan punches the carpeted floor, looking like a petulant child throwing a tantrum.

Then he knees West between the legs, and I watch my friend double over on the screen.

"Oh fuck." I reach down and protectively cup my dick.

"Yeah. It's all right. I don't need to get a vasectomy now."

All I can do is shake my head as I watch West recover before hitting Stan *once*.

He knocks him out with one hit and leaves him lying flat on the ground.

"See? I was a good boy."

I chuckle. He's right. That's just self-defense. "Rosie would kill me for saying this, but… that was kind of awesome."

My best friend beams back at me. "We still got it."

"But you shouldn't have been there in the first place." I tip my head back against the rest. "We can't pull this shit anymore, West. It was funny when we were kids. The two of us against the world. But we're not kids anymore. The dynamic has changed. This…" My hand waves around the car. "There are too many real-life consequences. Bowling once a week needs to be the only dumb shit we do now."

"Wow, that sounds an awful lot like something Rosie would say."

I grunt and nod once.

"I know you think I'm dumb—"

"I don't think—" I try to cut in.

"I'm razzing you. Chill out. What I'm reading between the lines here is that it's you and her against the world now."

I roll my head along the headrest to look at my friend. "This is a weird conversation."

He blinks twice. "Are you... are you breaking up with me?"

I bark out a laugh. "You're an idiot."

West punches my shoulder playfully and then hisses between his teeth. "No, you are. I was married once, remember? Ask me why it didn't work."

"Why didn't it work?"

"Because neither of us especially wanted to be on the same team."

I see the wisdom in what he's saying.

"I like Mia as a person. She's a great mom. A good human. But, man, oh man, the way I would do anything but spend time with her. That's actually why I started bowling. Just grasping for a reason to get outta the house."

"Shit. That really is desperate."

He chuckles. "Get fucked, Junior. Bowling is the best."

We fall into a companionable silence, the tires humming along the road, and I get lost thinking about the people I want on my team. The ones who love me enough to tell it like it is. The ones who know me as more than just my name or my connections.

People like that are hard to come by.

A person you want to spend your free time with. A person you never tire of. A person who can be brutally honest with you because they want the best for you—not because they're trying to wound you, but because they feel safe enough to lay it all out.

That takes a special kind of trust, one that—the more I think about it—Rosie and I have always had. Where we can call each other on our shit, but never with any malice.

It hits me that no one has *ever* understood me the way Rosie does. It hits me that our trust is more than just surface level. It's forged in friendship. Bound in respect. Sprinkled with animosity, which I'm starting to think is really just longing for more. It always has been. Except now, it's our special brand of foreplay.

Nausea hits me as I think back on all the moments she's been vulnerable around me. The little moments in our friendship she's entrusted to me—the ones I've never told a soul about. Her diary. That key. That she called *me* to come get her that night.

I feel sick that I told West a secret that never belonged to me.

"So, she figured it all out?" West finally asks.

"I told her, but yeah. She's smart—she definitely figured it out."

"Are you… are you guys alright?"

I sigh heavily. "I believe I have royally pissed her off."

West doesn't say anything.

"I shouldn't have told you what happened. That was an overstep."

He nods. "Probably. But she'll forgive you."

"I hope so."

"She will."

"I was trying to handle it for her, not to embarrass her or make any waves."

West snorts and slaps his knee. "Way to make no waves, Ford. Expertly done, you awkward fuck."

My head drops back again, and I stare at the ceiling of

the town car, having no idea how to make this right. Rosie is angry, and she has every right to be.

And Cora will be too when she finds out. I'll be a mass polluter and a juvenile, lying dumbass for risking what I have with Rosie.

That sounds like something she would accuse me of.

So I make a few calls on the way home.

CHAPTER 43

Rosie

I FELT IMMENSE RELIEF WHEN MY BROTHER TEXTED ME TO confirm he was free and not charged with anything. And then I got another one.

Heading home. See you soon.

Home. He says it like we share the same one.

I'm staring at Ford's words when his mom blurts out, "He's a total goner for you. Whatever the reason I'm picking you up without him, I hope you know that."

I roll my eyes over to Dr. Gemma Grant as we approach Rose Hill.

Yeah, I called his mom. First, I love Gemma and I knew she'd come. Second, this seems suitably embarrassing to Ford for being such a royal dumbass.

Such a dumbass that his mom had to come clean up his mess.

I suffered through a few long-ass hours of small talk

and then she drops *that* on me right as we hit the town outskirts.

Swallowing, I turn in the passenger seat to face her. "Gemma, I adore you, and I respect your insight and knowledge on relationships and how important it is to pee after sex. And I won't even lie and pretend it wasn't a petty part of me that chose to call you knowing it would piss Ford off. But my brattiness has some limits, and divulging information to you about Ford and me is one of them."

The skin beside Gemma's eyes crinkles, and her lips tug into a very full smile as her hands twist on the steering wheel. "That was the right answer."

My brows furrow, and I stare a little harder at the woman beside me.

And like she can feel me considering her, she talks again. "Ford needs someone who puts him first, even when they're pissed off at him. And I can *tell* you're pissed off. Been watching you stew for hours. And you deserve that from him, too. That privacy."

I almost roll my eyes and tell her she should have this conversation with her son, but she keeps monologuing before I get the chance.

"I've been with his dad for decades and decades. And that man has infuriated me from time to time. But being in the spotlight is hard, and he and I made a promise to keep certain things between us. Because when you love someone, and you share the mistakes they've made with people who don't love them the way you do, you can't expect those same people to forgive them the way you do either. You can't unsay those things or undo that damage."

I flop back, letting out a heavy sigh. "That's really fucking wise, Gemma."

She chuckles and flicks her signal. "I went to school for a long time, been married to a Ford Grant for even longer. Seems like I should have figured out a thing or two by now."

"Are all Ford Grants this… frustrating?"

"I'm afraid he comes from a long line of frustrating men named Ford Grant."

"Well, if we have a boy, I refuse to name him that."

Then I start and turn wide eyes on her. *Fuck*. That was an obnoxious slip of the tongue.

The car is quiet for a few beats, and then we both burst out laughing.

"God." I scrub a hand over my face. "You gonna take back that part about me protecting our privacy?"

"No." Gemma is grinning like a lunatic as we turn onto my family's plot of land. "But I am going to take that slipup to mean you two are going to be all right."

She parks in front of my brother's house, and I sigh, reaching to unbuckle myself. "Yeah. I'll forgive him. Don't worry. Thank you for the ride—I really owe you one."

It's as I grab my bag and step out of her car that she leans across the console. "Hey, Rosie?"

"Yeah?" I bend to peek back into the vehicle.

"Make him work for it."

I grin now, tossing her a wink. "Oh, I plan to." Except

I'm not sure I know how where her son is concerned. I'm too far gone for him.

I need time and space to think. So I slam the door and head to my bunkhouse to feed Scotty.

He's probably starving.

Rosie: I picked up your kids and we are playing at your house until you get here. Beyond that, I'm not speaking to either of you man-children.

West: You're a lifesaver, Rosie Posie.

West: Just so you know. I didn't do anything wrong. Self-defense. I'm going to be the one pressing charges against him.

West: Don't be too hard on Ford. He's already got that emo James Dean thing going on. You're just making it worse.

West: I mean, okay. We fucked up. I'm sorry.

West: You are the only girl in the world I would send this many unanswered texts to in a row.

My first order of business is to pick up my niece and nephew. They make the switch at 3:00 p.m. on Saturdays, and as cool as Mia is, I'm not sure she'd appreciate knowing that West was locked up for assaulting a person.

A shitty person who deserved it, but still.

When we get back to West's house, it's warm enough

that we have a water-gun fight and I make sure to give them freezies *and* ice cream. Because fuck West for pulling this shit.

I time it perfectly. We're back inside watching cartoons when I hear Ford's G-Wagon idling outside and the slam of the door as West hops out. When he walks in the door, the sugar is just settling into their bloodstream.

"Daddy!" Emmy shouts from the couch before barreling over the back of it and launching herself into her dad's arms.

Me? I just stand watching him, arms crossed, wondering how the hell my parents got through raising him.

"Hi, Rosie." West grins at me.

I scowl back, shaking my head. My brother winces, and if he were a dog, he'd do that thing where his ears droop and his eyes go wide like big guilty saucers.

Then I give both sugar demons a kiss, grab the basket of laundry I did at his place over the last couple of hours, and walk out the front door.

"Where are you going? Wanna stay for dinner? I'll cook for you."

Kiss ass.

"No thanks. I'm going to go drink my dinner on my dock."

"*Your* dock?"

I look back at my brother, ready to be the one who assaults a person if he tries to tell me it's his. That dock has become my favorite place to sit, so he can fuck all the way off. I point down toward the water. "Yeah, West. *My* dock."

He tilts his head, brows furrowed. "Sis, that's not your

dock. That's not even *our* dock. That dock is firmly on Ford's property. I've seen land survey certificate."

"No, it's not. Ford told me it's mine."

West chuckles and shakes his head, leaving me standing at his door.

Dumbfounded.

Back at the old bunkhouse, I fold my laundry, unpack, and "accidentally" drop some crumbs on the floor while trying to make sense of this new development.

It irks me more than it should. Mostly because it makes it even harder to be mad at Ford.

I make my way down to the lake with a bottle of red wine in hand and my favorite Navajo blanket wrapped around my shoulders.

I know that if I can sit on the dock and watch the sun go down, maybe I'll be able to let this day go. Let all the grains of frustration I feel dissolve into the darkness as the light slips behind the mountain peaks.

Except when I get to the spot where the wooden boards meet the green grass, I stop. There's a small sign. A plain slab of wood with light blue paint slashed across it.

It reads *Rosie's Dock*.

I stare at it for several moments before realizing there's an envelope on the ground beneath it. My name is scrawled across it in Ford's alarmingly perfect handwriting. I swipe it up and rip it open. Inside is a deed to a small section of Ford's massive property. According to the map, it's long and narrow and reaches all the way up to the back of the property. It's a buffer between his land and my family's, and it's also the section that links to the dock.

All this time, this dock hasn't been mine at all. But when has Ford ever said no to me?

The paper rattles in my shaking hand, and it's with a swirling pit in my stomach that I walk to the end of the dock.

My dock.

I need the peace and quiet I couldn't find earlier with West's kids around to process the last twenty-four hours.

Quite possibly the last several months.

But when I sit down, Ford and his shredded arms are swimming in the lake. The sun hits his already-tanned back and droplets of water shimmer on his skin. His hair appears almost black while wet and plastered across his forehead as he tilts his head to breathe.

He's so beautiful, it almost hurts to look at him.

And I must be some sort of masochist because I also can't look away.

I don't know how long I sit here watching him. Long enough that all my anger, all my reasons for being disappointed, feel redundant and overwrought.

He *shouldn't* have told West what he did. Shouldn't have turned it into some sort of high school vendetta.

And yet, I know him well enough to understand his chest-beating alpha bullshit was well-intentioned. He'd never hurt me. Not on purpose.

I'm sad he broke my trust the way he did. But I also know I'll forgive him. *Tomorrow.*

I'll forgive him tomorrow because I don't want to be a

total pushover where Ford Grant is concerned. The man is far too accustomed to getting what he wants.

Eventually, he stops and surfaces, facing away from me. I watch the muscles in his back and shoulders bunch and release as he treads water, staring out at the same view I'm facing.

Except I have my eyes locked on him, not on the sky or the mountains. I find myself wondering how long I've been staring at Ford Grant.

I'm thinking it's been a long-ass time, but I was too oblivious to see it. Too convinced he was too cerebral for a girl like me. Too convinced he disliked me. Too convinced he was *just* my brother's best friend, and I was just their annoying tagalong.

I'm thinking that Ford and I have been in love with each other for years and just rationalized it to the point it felt unlikely, made up... *impossible*.

I suck in a breath, and he spins to face me, surprised by my presence. "Rosie." He breathes my name like it's the air itself. Necessary. Integral to his survival.

All I do is hold my glass up in a silent toast and swallow over the dry lump in my throat.

His face is drawn, and his Adam's apple bobs as he regards me. "I'm sorry. I'm so fucking sorry."

I nod quickly, blinking, wishing away the moisture that's building behind my lashes. "I know. The dock, huh?"

He nods. "Squatter's rights."

"Ugh." I blink away, wiping my eyes. Of course he has to be sorry *and* funny.

"Arranged for Cora's mom to come for a visit,—driver

brought her out here for the party tomorrow. So, she's setting up in the spare room."

And sweet. Triple whammy. Fuck my life. How am I supposed to be mad at this man?

I take a deep swig of the ruby liquid. Bigger than any wine connoisseur would approve of, but I'm hardly drinking for the tasting notes right now.

"That was thoughtful of you."

He nods, the sound of water swishing accompanied only by the song of a loon farther out in the lake. "Figured Cora might be less mad at me that way."

I turn my head. "Why would Cora be mad at you?"

"Because I…" His teeth clamp down, and a muscle in his jaw pops as he searches for the right words. "Because I hurt you."

I let my eyes work over him. This serious, studious, deeply caring man. "You did."

No point pretending he didn't. What happened with my job was not only a violation but also incredibly embarrassing. I wish West didn't know, or at least that I'd been the one to tell him, though I don't think he'd have been my first choice of person to tell.

I'll probably want to rehash that story one day. Might feel good to get it off my chest. Maybe I'll tell Cora when the time seems right. Let her know that her run-ins with chauvinist douchebags aren't over, but her calling it out the way she does might be the change we need.

But not yet. She's too little and Ford and I are too new. That being said, I want to be able to tell her I faced this obstacle head-on That I didn't run and hide. If she can call her teacher out, I can call Stan out.

"I'd like your lawyer's contact information."

He blinks.

"Why?"

"If West is going to press charges, then so am I. Plus, there's gotta be a wrongful termination case there."

A ghost of a smile touches his lips and a spark of pride flares in my chest.

"And I'm not going to air out every bump in our relationship to your daughter. I'd never do that. That's not how this works."

"How does it work?" He asks it earnestly, with such a quiet voice and downcast eyes. My heart cracks a little at the simplicity of his question.

He turns his eyes up at me, still treading water easily.

"It works like... I'm gonna lick my wounds for a day. Because you really pissed me off. But we're not kids anymore, Ford. I don't want to stay mad at you, and I don't want to tell other people about the mistakes we make. Give me tonight. I'll be back tomorrow."

I swallow. His mom's words come back to me as I sit here staring at a man who loves me enough to spend millions ruining a guy for touching my ass, one who will carve up his land just so I can have my dock. "Because other people might not love you the way I do. Might not forgive you the way I will. You and I? We're a team. I kind of think we always have been."

He blinks rapidly. There are already droplets of water on

his face from swimming, but if I were a betting woman, I'd venture a guess that at least one of them is a tear.

His voice comes out raspy, rough like sandpaper, as he reaches for the metal ladder attached to the dock to steady himself. He looks straight up into my eyes and I soak him in. "I think I told West because I was scared of what I'd do if I had to keep that to myself. It felt like a simple way to step back into the roles we always played. To keep him as my friend and you as his bratty little sister who we had to protect."

I chuckle. Joke's on Ford. I'll always be West's bratty little sister.

"To keep myself from falling head over heels for a girl who was not only off-limits but unavailable."

My heart drops in my rib cage as it hits me how tortured he's been over me.

"I was trying to do what was right. And I…" He rakes a hand through his hair, like he always does when he's agitated. "I fucked it up. I did too much. I kind of went off the deep end because of what that asshole did to you." He laughs dryly. "All those buildings. This dock. Coming back to this town. That ridiculous, messy paint spot on the floor of my brand-new office that I don't think I'll ever be able to bring myself to fix because nothing about it needs fixing. Conscious, subconscious, I don't know how or when—I don't even know if I was fully aware I was doing it."

A tear rolls down my cheek as I listen to him pour his heart out to me in an uncharacteristic fashion.

"Rosie, everything I do is for you. I know I'm not necessarily a safe bet right now, but I need to know—"

A safe bet. It's the second time he's said that, and I hate it. I'm shaking my head as I place the wineglass on the old boards of the dock and push myself into the freezing cold water. I plunge in with a sharp gasp and open my eyes under the green-tinged mountain water. I let myself sink for a couple of beats, enjoying the shock of the moment, letting the water wash away the tears that had welled in my eyes.

There are rocks beneath me.

Air bubbles above me.

And Ford in front of me.

His hands are on me, wrapping around my waist and pulling me to the surface before I even have time to kick my legs.

"What the hell, Rosie!" he barks at me the minute we breach the surface. He rapidly moves us to a place where he can reach the bottom, though I still can't.

His cheeks have turned a dark pink and his eyes are glowing, the way they do when he's mad. "Are you insane? That scared the shit out of me!" His jaw pops, and I give him a small smile in response. "Actually, don't answer that. I already know."

My soaked clothes are heavy, so I wrap my arms around his neck and my legs around his waist. His warm arms wind around me, and his hands grip my ass. "I left all safe bets behind, Ford. I don't want a safe relationship. I don't want a safe love." His eyes dance between mine, and I forge ahead. "I want messy and snarky and…" I peek back over my shoulder at the old barn, transformed into a new office, before turning my gaze back on him. "I want a wild love. I want *you*, even though you make me want to push you into the lake and break your computer and throw paint all over your pristine floors. I want this feeling I have with you where it hurts to breathe when you get too far away, where my skin itches uncontrollably when you look at me. Where thinking feels overrated because we both know nothing and no one will ever feel like this. Like us."

He nods and I watch one lone tear trickle down his already-wet cheek, mingling with the water that's already there. Like it never even happened. But I know.

"So I'm going to be mad at you for a few more hours. And then we're going to carry on. I'm going to be chaotic, and you're going to be meticulous. I'm going to drive you up the wall and you're going to insult me in that way that feels nothing like an insult and everything like saying *I love you*. And we're going to do this thing together."

I cup his cheeks and give his head a little shake. "Because who the hell else would put up with me?"

Then he drops his head to my chest and murmurs, "Putting up with you is my favorite thing to do."

At 11:59 p.m., I hear a soft knock at the bunkhouse door, and when I swing it open, Ford is standing there. One side of his mouth quirks up in a smirk while he casts his gaze down to the glittering Rolex on his wrist, stacked with beaded bracelets. Like those somehow make him more salt of the earth and less *I buy tens of millions in commercial real estate for shits and giggles.*

We say nothing for several seconds, and then he holds up his wrist, showing that the clock has officially struck midnight before crossing the threshold of the house.

He steps right up to me, gripping my chin and murmuring, "It's officially tomorrow and I'm fucking sick of being without you," before dropping his lips to mine. "I have a couple of things I need to tell you."

"Okay," I murmur between kisses. "Hurry and tell me so I can put your mouth to better use."

"I'm sorry," he breathes out. And I can hear the ache in his words.

Then, "I'm giving you half of Rose Hill Records."

That has me pulling away to look him in the eye. "No."

"Yes."

"You really have to stop waving your money around like this. It's obnoxious."

"Rosie, that business"—he points back toward his property—"is worth absolutely nothing right now. There's no client list, there are no contracts. There is some equipment that could easily be sold and two people who work really damn well together. Please. Be my business partner, and if the place goes under... well"—he rakes a hand through his hair and chuckles—"then I guess you're going down with me."

I swallow. Going down together. Feels like we already have. We're too intertwined to let the other one go. So I nod and scoff a watery, "Please, I'm exceptionally good at my job. I'd never let that place go under."

When my eyes land back on his earnest face, his gaze

traces over my features, searching for a silent affirmation. And he must find it because he nods.

I nod back.

Then we spend all night clinging to each other in that bunkhouse, and he doesn't even complain about my pet mouse.

CHAPTER 44

Ford

IF SOMEONE HAD TOLD ME SIX MONTHS AGO I'D BE STANDING in the living room of my parents' summer house with Rosalie Belmont's head tipped against my shoulder while my daughter and ten of her friends watch WWE wrestling, eat pizza, and drink root beer floats, I'd have told them they were out to lunch.

"Look at our little storm cloud," Rosie murmurs, her hand at my back, thumb hooked beneath my belt. "Hanging out in the same living room we used to. Isn't this where you and West played that mean Ouija trick on me?"

I cover my mouth with a fist. I shouldn't laugh over the memory of Rosie and a bunch of other girls screaming. But it really was funny. West snuck away and hit the breaker when things were tense. Frightened teenage girls ensued.

Rosie went from screaming in terror to hugging me. I held her tight and was glad West wasn't there to see.

"I don't remember that trick," I lie. It was definitely us.

"You're full of shit, Junior. I have it documented in my journal. I know it was you guys. West hit the power breaker; that's the only thing that makes sense."

My lips twitch. "Or you and your friends summoned an angry ghost. Who's to say?"

"Ford," she warns, eyes narrowing.

Dousing a smile, I shrug, because I don't want to incite her wrath when we've only just made up. I go back to focusing on Cora. Something we *can* agree on. "It's like a whole storm in here. Were these kids running around Rose Hill a few months ago? Or did Cora indoctrinate them all? It's a sea of black and gray. And why are girls this age watching professional wrestling?"

Rosie's body hiccups with a laugh. "Probably for the storyline."

My forehead scrunches. "What?"

"Kinda like how boys read *Playboy* for the articles."

I stiffen, head rearing back slightly. "No chance."

"Ford. There are tanned, manly men with big muscles throwing each other around. Yes chance."

"But she's—"

"Almost a teenager?" Rosie hits me with an expression that says, *Are you stupid?*

I swallow and look back at Cora, who has tomato sauce on the corner of her mouth and is pointing at the TV. "Oh my god. *Wild Side*." She practically moans the man's name. "He's my favorite. Never says a word and no one ever sees his face."

The guy is massive, with dark, wet hair and a terrifying black leather mask that covers his entire face.

Rosie chuckles and covers her mouth with her palm. "Why does nothing about her liking that surprise me?"

I just grunt, not ready to wrap my head around the idea that this sweet little girl who just came into my life is lusting over giant men in leather.

The doorbell rings, and Rosie swats my ass before walking away to answer it. "You stay here and glower, papa bear."

I roll my eyes as she departs, but I can't peel them away from her as she weaves through the living room, past the kitchen island, and down the hallway. There's a tug at the center of my chest when she moves out of sight. I want to follow her, to be close to her, even though I know she'll only be gone for a moment.

It's Marilyn who draws my attention back as she finishes chatting with my parents and sidles up beside me.

It's nice to have her here. A good surprise. Cora cried when she walked in yesterday, and that's when I left to swim—to give them some space.

"My husband used to look at me like that, you know."

I glance down at her. She seems better. Brighter. A lot healthier. I'm happy to see it, even though it makes my stomach drop. Because I also know what it means in the long run.

"Like the world might stop turning if I was out of sight."

I blush lightly. I know my ability to hide my feelings for Rosie has all but crumbled over the past few months. I'm not sure I was ever *great* at it, but I've definitely gotten substantially worse.

"I wish Cora could have seen him then. He was so vibrant." She blinks, and I look away, feeling thickness in my throat as I watch her recall her husband. "So healthy."

She's nodding when I glance back at her. "Have you enjoyed having her around?" she asks.

A soft keening sound gets caught in my throat. "Marilyn. You're killing me here."

She pats my shoulder in a motherlike way. "You're a sweet man, Ford. I like you a lot. It's a simple question. Has this been a burden to you? If I think about trying to repay you for all you've done, the weight of it is crippling. And I also know this isn't what you signed up for."

I swallow, hearing Rosie and West and his kids at the front door. "I'd sign up for this over and over again."

She smiles, and her lightly wrinkled skin bunches as she does. "I want her to have a vibrant, healthy, happy male role model in her life. I want her to have friends. And family. I want her to have *this*. This place—it's been so good for her in the wake of everything she's lived through. I see how different she is here, the way she's re-created herself. Grown into herself."

With a wave, she gestures around the house, eyes bright.

"I'm thinking..." She trails off, nibbling at her bottom lip as two men in leotards flop around on each other in a big square ring. "I'm thinking a change of scenery might help me re-create myself a little bit too."

I go still, glancing down at her. I suspect I know what she's hinting at, but I don't want to jump to any conclusions or make any assumptions.

"But I don't want to do something that infringes on your freedom or your plans. I don't—"

"I would love to have you both here." God, I can barely get the words out without sounding choked up.

Marilyn nods once, firmly.

"I can buy a house for you—"

Now she rolls her eyes at me, a little spark that reminds me of Cora. "Don't insult me. I'll buy my own damn house. You can track me down a Realtor."

My lips press together as I fight to stifle a smile.

"Hey, can we go out on the boat?" Cora calls out.

"Of course," is my instant reply.

But then she turns back to her friends and says, "Who wants to go boating? My dad says he'll take us!"

And she says it like it's the most casual thing in the world. *My dad.* We don't have a conversation or get all mushy about it—it's not her style. She's practical, and she's settling into a new phase of life like Marilyn just said. I don't think she's replacing her dad—and I wouldn't want her to—but it's nice to feel like she might be open to adding another.

I stare at her for a few beats, soaking the moment in, then clear my throat. Rosie's watery eyes meet mine from across the room, and I smile back at her as I say, "I'll get the tubes hooked up. You guys get changed."

Then I take my daughter and her friends tubing for the very first time.

Once the end-of-the-year party has wrapped up, Rosie

leads me back to the office. Her fingers link with mine, our soft footsteps on the grass turning to dull thuds on the wooden deck.

"You know we don't work on Sundays," I grumble. Because where I really want to go with Rosie is to bed.

She grins back at me over her shoulder, chin brushing over the thin spaghetti strap of her rose-pink sundress. Her hair falls in loose waves and flies out like a fringe as she spins on the spot. The look on her face is all trouble and whimsy and *I'm gonna be a brat now*.

It's a look I know well.

A look I've come to love.

And as she basks in the sun's warm rays, framed by the mountains behind her and a bed of brown-eyed Susans at her side, I'm struck by the overwhelming need to kiss her.

I stop in my tracks and tug her toward me. Her hand lands on my chest and I cover it with my own, wrapping the other around her body and gripping the back of her neck.

"That fucking look, Rosalie," I grumble, searching her face.

Her eyes are twinkling, and her smile is soft. "I have no idea what you're talking about."

It's with a frustrated groan and zero restraint that I drop my mouth to hers and kiss her. It's thrilling and consuming and what I've always dreamed of.

Kissing Rosalie Belmont whenever and wherever I want.

She whimpers into my mouth as I deepen the kiss, fingers gripping tightly at my shirt before she pulls back.

"Come on." Her voice is breathless. "I want to show you this. I think you're going to love it."

"Is it you naked and bent over my desk?"

She rolls her eyes and laughs lightly. "You may want to spank me for this first, but after that… yes." With a wink, she turns and swaggers into the office, looking so pleased with herself that I feel concerned. She leads me over the floorboards until we're standing right over the blue paint disaster.

"So, it turns out the trophy and awards store is open on Sundays. I grabbed it while I was waiting for pizza. Which reminds me, we need to take Scotty a leftover piece."

I'm about to complain about her attachment to the mouse when she points at the wall, and sure enough, there is an engraved gold plaque mounted right next to the floor.

It reads:

Wild Love

Paint on lumber

By Rosalie Belmont and Ford Grant

I stand staring at it for I don't know how long. I like things orderly. I like them precise and tidy. I'm exacting, and I'm sure my sister would call me uptight and neurotic.

And yet, I've never loved a mess more.

I have no words, so I pull Rosie into a rough hug, breathing in the sugary scent of her hair, savoring the smooth skin of her neck against my lips.

She nuzzles into me, and I don't know how long we stand like that, only that I eventually pull away, put my favorite Allah-Las album on the record player, and pull her down onto the deep leather couch.

We spend all evening wrapped up in each other, listening

to music, just like I've wanted to—since the morning after I first kissed her and found her sleeping here.

Just like I dreamed of before I even realized she was the dream.

EPILOGUE

Rosie

"What are you humming?" Cora asks as I put fresh towels on the shelf in the first-floor bathroom.

My brows scrunch. "I don't know."

"Was that 'Pumped Up Kicks'?"

I shrug. "Maybe? You and your dad are the ones with ears for music in this house."

It's been a month since the end of school. A month of us all living together.

It feels like playing house.

It feels too good to be true.

"You know that song is about a school shooting," Cora deadpans, her black bangs dead straight across her forehead.

I stop. Sometimes she's so abrupt and morbid that I need a second to catch up.

"Really?"

She nods soberly.

"But it sounds so happy. I was humming it happily!"

"Shaking your ass too."

I flush but refuse to be embarrassed. *I'm* the one doing chores after dark.

"Did your dad teach you this?"

She nods. "Just came from the office. Listened to a bunch of new stuff."

A slow smile spreads across my face. That has become a favorite pastime for them. They sit on that leather couch, drink root beer, listen to music, and talk about it. *In depth.*

Upcoming tours.

Synthesizers.

Auto-tune.

Guitar pedals.

I once walked in and found them watching a video where Jack White—who I was told is in fact *not* Edward Scissorhands—builds a guitar with an old board, a few nails, a piece of string, and an old Coke bottle.

"Well, that sounds exactly like the type of storm cloud conversation the two of you would have."

I get a petulant eye roll for that one, but it doesn't bother me at all. This week, Marilyn closed on a house in town. Ford didn't buy it, but he made the entire process his business. Dickering on price, organizing movers—I even overheard him tell Marilyn that he knows a good painter named Scotty that he could connect her with.

The same Scotty he fired for talking to me.

Petty bastard.

Either way, knowing Cora will be close is the cherry on

top. I foresee plenty of music sessions in the office for these two. The odd weekend at our place. A come-and-go-as-you-please arrangement is what it's looking like.

"Speaking of conversations I like to have—"

I snort. "Oh, this should be good."

"Have you ever done Bloody Mary?"

"What?"

Cora rolls her eyes like I'm dumb. "You know… Bloody Mary. Where you say it while you're turning and then see her in the mirror?"

"This is so on brand for you." I slap a hand over my mouth as the sentiment slips out, and Cora's eyes roll again. But she also chuckles.

"I want to try it. But not alone."

I nibble at my bottom lip. "Like, on Halloween?"

"No. Right now."

"Right now?"

She shoves me farther into the bathroom, facing the mirror. "Right now."

"You know ghosts aren't real, right?"

All Cora does is quirk a brow as my eyes drop to the one pop of pink over her shoulder. My velvet scrunchie. I'm gonna have to pack her stocking full of those at Christmas.

"Let's go, Rosalie. You chicken?"

I step up beside her, my jaw dropping. "Kid, did you just call me Rosalie and a chicken in one breath?"

She just forges ahead. "Okay. Let's do this."

I shake my head. "You need to get back to school. Some structure is good for hellions like you."

Our eyes catch in the mirror and we both giggle. That was a lie and we both know it. Summer has been the most fun. Cooking over the fire. Boating when it's hot. Cora has even learned to water-ski.

"So, we have to say Bloody Mary thirteen times. Getting louder each time. On the last one, she'll show up in the mirror."

"Ford is gonna think we're nuts."

She shrugs. "He already does. Plus, he went to West's. Okay. Go."

Wow. She is like… really hell-bent on this.

"Bloody Mary," she starts with a whisper, and I fumble the first one, trying to catch up.

Then I get the timing right. "Bloody Mary, Bloody Mary, Bloody Mary, Bloody Mary, Bloody Mary." We keep getting louder until I worry that someone is going to call the cops. "Bloody Mary, Bloody Mary, Bloody Mary, Bloody Mary, Bloody Mary, Bloody Mary."

We look over at each other before screaming the last one.

"Bloody Mary!"

Then every light in the house cuts out, and I scream, jumping what has to be a few feet off the floor.

Cora though? Cora is giggling. And I piece this together quickly. She and her dad are playing a very adorable joke on me.

But going from bright light to being plunged into darkness has my eyes struggling to adjust.

"Ford fucking Grant!" I shout, hoping, for his sake, he hears me loud and clear from wherever the electrical panel is in this house. "You are an overgrown child and I'm going to kill you for this!"

Cora laughs harder.

"Turn these lights on *right now*!"

I stomp my foot like a petulant child.

And then I start when I hear the amused rasp of his voice from right in front of me. "Okay."

I'm confused by how he's so close, but all that confusion evaporates on the spot when the lights flash on and I take him in.

Down on one knee.

Wearing a lopsided smirk.

And holding up a ring.

A huge cushion-cut pink stone set on a dainty rose gold band. Smaller white diamonds flank the center stone, arranged in a way that looks an awful lot like leaves.

His eyes remind me of leaves.

"We figured you had to have a pink ring," Cora blurts, practically bouncing on the spot.

From behind Ford, my brother appears. Smirking exactly like I bet he did the last time he played that joke on me.

"Rosalie Belmont—" Ford starts, but I cut him off.

"Don't Rosalie me. Are you seriously proposing after scaring the shit out of me the way you did as a teenager? You cannot possibly be doing this."

He grins that grin that makes my stomach flop. Followed by a wink that makes my skin itch. "Loved you then. Love you even more now. If we aren't driving each other up the wall, what's even the point?"

My eyes sting, and I blink away to Cora. Her hands are cupping her cheeks, and I'm not sure I've ever seen her appear so… adorably excited.

I cross my arms and lean in to take a closer look at the ring. I'm trying to appear casual, but my cheeks are hot, and my heart is thrashing wildly against my ribs.

I want to throw myself at his knees and beg him to *please* marry me.

But instead, I lean in close to him, sucking in the scent of his signature cologne, and murmur, "Maybe I should say no. Teach you a lesson."

Cora gasps, and West laughs.

Ford's eyes flash with amusement. "Sure thing. Say no. I'll chase you down, force this ring onto your finger, and teach you a lesson of my own, Rosie."

Now I smirk. "That actually sounds pretty fun."

Before Ford can finish rolling his eyes, I dart out of the bathroom right past him.

I fly out the front door to the sound of my brother's and Cora's laughter as Ford clearly tries to get his bearings. The minute I'm out the door, I burst into a full sprint, grass tickling my feet as I use the hill to my advantage, running down toward the water.

Toward *my* dock.

I can hear Ford's breathing behind me. A breathless laugh as he chases me down.

My footfalls rattle across the dock's wooden boards as I barrel toward the lake.

And he follows.

"You're trespassing, Junior!" I shout back at him, a sort of maniacal laughter lurching from my throat.

His long arm captures me around the waist as he hauls me to him, mere feet from the end of the dock. "Try to get rid of me then, Rosie. I dare you. I'm making everything that's mine yours anyway. I'm even renaming the studio."

My brows furrow.

"I wanted to name it after the town I've come to love. But…"

"But Rose Hill Records is kind of uninspired?"

Ford's eyes roll. "Yes, you've mentioned that."

"So, what are you calling it?"

He swallows and watches me so carefully. His tongue darts out and he presses it between his lips. It hits me that he's *nervous*. This man actually thinks I might not marry him.

"Wild Rose Records. After the girl I've always loved. But as my business partner, I need your input."

I blink. My heart thuds harder. *Fuck me*, that's romantic. Being considered my boss bothered him. Ethically *and* romantically. He flinches every time it comes up—especially with how I came to need a job in the first place.

He shifts his feet, waiting for me to respond. "I know it's not Rosie or Rosalie. But Wild Rosie Records sounds—"

"Kinda dumb," I finish for him as I sniff and slide my hands up over his broad chest. "I love it. I really love it. But I'm not giving you half my dock. I refuse," I toss back as he stares down at me, shaking his head, green eyes twinkling.

"Rosie, shut up and marry me," he growls with a touch of desperation in his voice.

Then he yanks my hand off his chest and shoves the ring onto my finger.

It's so us.

I'd laugh if I weren't so entranced by the way it sparkles when I wiggle my fingers.

"Yeah. Yes. Definitely. I definitely want to marry you. Very much."

He breathes out a laugh. "Thank god."

Then my fingers curl into the soft cotton of his shirt and I tug his mouth down to mine. He kisses me and I feel like I could float away.

But I don't.

I hold him tight… and pull him straight into the water with me.

Dear Diary,

Tonight, I had a bunch of girlfriends over. We were at Ford's parents' place because they're away tonight, which meant we could have the entire house to ourselves. I'm sure half of them only showed up because they're secretly obsessed with West.

Anyway, Tarah brought her Ouija board, and I was convinced it was super stupid. Obviously, ghosts aren't real. But then the five of us started playing, and I swear the piece moved. Of course, Ford had to walk in and see us playing it.

Just the easiest ammo for him to shit on me with.

So, I invited him to play with us, right? Thinking that if he were in on the game, it would neutralize his evil plans.

Except Tarah looked just a little too excited about having him join us. She moved over immediately to make room for him and smiled all stupid-like at him.

Which meant I was stuck kneeling, facing Ford and his annoying, condescending smirk while she stared over and made moon eyes at him.

As if Ford would ever be into a girl who likes Ouija.

Next thing you know, this bitch will be trying to read his tea leaves or his palms or the veins on his ballsack.

I didn't miss the way she got her fingers all over his, either.

Kinda made me hope that we *could* actually conjure a ghost. One that would break her fingers for me.

Anyway, we asked the spirits if one of us was going to die young (if I were a worse person, I'd wish for it to be Tarah) and then it slowly landed on YES.

Which would have been stupid except the lights cut out right then, and I lost my shit.

I played it off after, like I was cool. And I'd never admit it anywhere but here, but I was shit-scared.

I don't think I've ever screamed so loud in my life, but it was SO dark and SO sudden. I turned to run, but Ford was there. He must have stepped straight over the board, straight through the chaos of screaming girls, to get to me.

He reached for me, and I went. I clung to him.

He's a lot less scrawny than he used to be. I'm not sure when that happened, but his arms have muscles now. And he even smells good.

Okay, really good.

I should probably be mad because I'm sure West cut the electricity as a prank.

But instead, I… I don't know. It sounds crazy, but I'm almost glad he did it?

Ford held me until the lights came back on. He whispered, "I've got you," against my hair and I believed him.

I'd never admit it anywhere except on these pages, but I felt safe in his arms.

And I was disappointed when the lights came back on.

READ ON FOR A SNEAK PEEK AT THE NEXT BOOK IN THE ROSE HILL SERIES, *WILD EYES*

West

THE SUN IS SHINING, THE LAKE IS SPARKLING, AND THERE'S another fucking tourist on the side of the road trying to get a selfie with a bear.

Not just any bear either. A grizzly.

"You have to be kidding me," I mutter as I press gently on the brakes of my pickup truck and shake my head. I don't have a clear shot of the woman, but I see skin-tight jeans, a crop top, and a waterfall of loose chestnut waves spilling down her back in shiny ripples.

While the bear forages in the ditch behind her, she lifts one hand, gesturing to it wildly as she holds her phone up in front of her.

I pull over onto the side of the road and park in front of her Tesla. Because *of course* she drives a Tesla. And she has to be a good thirty feet away from it, like she's slowly edged herself closer to the animal.

When I finally roll to a stop, I just watch in pure, dumb-founded shock for a moment. During the summer months, you see this kind of city-folk stupidity in Rose Hill, and it never fails to blow my mind. It's like people go from having *see a bear* on their bucket list to having *get killed by a bear* on their bucket list.

I press the button to lower my window, because I don't want to startle the animal, and I also don't particularly want to get out of my truck. I enjoy living and my days of testing those limits are—mostly—behind me.

So, using the calmest voice I can I muster, I say, "Ma'am."

But she continues talking to the camera. Clearly record-ing herself. "It was just a casual drive down a scenic back road when *bam,* the most beautiful bear saunters down into this ditch behind me—"

"Ma'am!" I lean against my door and wave my arm to catch her eye. Maybe me photobombing her video will snap her out of it.

And it does. She spins on me with furrowed brows, fiery eyes, and a face I'd know anywhere.

A face most of *the world* would know anywhere.

Yes, country music superstar Skylar Stone is mean mug-ging me for interrupting her video. I suspect I know what brings her to town, but I don't bother with small talk at a time like this. I don't want to be the guy known for standing by while a hungry grizzly devoured a beloved starlet.

"What!" she says with her arms held wide, like she didn't just turn her back on an unpredictable apex predator. "I'm going to have to re-record this for my socials now."

"That's a goddamn grizzly bear. You need to get back in your car!" I hiss, hiking a thumb over my shoulder toward her car.

She shakes her head and continues glaring. "You know what I'm fucking sick of?"

"Is it living?" I bite out, right as instinct takes over and I step out of my truck. As much as I'd like to slam the door, I leave it open to avoid making any noise. "Because that's what it looks like right now."

She scoffs. "No. But I am fucking sick of people telling me what to do."

Her piercing gaze rakes down my faded black jeans, the ones caught on my scuffed charcoal Blundstones, before perusing back up to my plain white T-shirt. Her eyes hover over the hole that's ripped near the neckline and a small wrinkle crops up on her dainty nose. As though she's found proof that I'm not worthy of giving her advice.

I approach with caution, craning my neck to glance down the slope, where the telltale brown grizzly hump peeks out above the shrubs. I can hear its deep, satisfied grunts as it forages. Likely ripping berries off a bush as an appetizer before it comes up and tears the limbs off our bodies for the main course.

"I relate. I really do. But this may not be the hill to die on right now. Literally *and* figuratively. If we survive this, I will personally drive you to a zoo and film your social media content for you. And I hate social media, but I don't break promises."

She follows my gaze and then lifts her chin to face me

head on. Plush, heart-shaped lips purse tightly and hazel eyes narrow at me like missiles ready to launch. She hides her phone by crossing her tan arms.

Pure sass.

She reminds me of my six-year-old daughter, Emmy. Something that's only emphasized when she practically stomps one foot. The difference is, I'd have picked Emmy up like a football under one arm and gotten the hell outta here a solid sixty seconds ago.

"It's eating. It doesn't even know I'm here. And I've never seen a bear before." She practically whines the last part. Like I'm the bad guy ruining all her fun.

My jaw drops as I look this woman over. She's got diamond studs the size of blueberries in her ears. They're so big that if she was anyone else, I'd think they were fake. "Listen, I get it. There aren't bears in the city. It's an experience. But that"—I point at the bear—"is not Winnie the Pooh down there."

Her expression is strained as she glances longingly back at the ditch. It's as though she sees my logic, but so badly wishes she didn't.

I keep going, because it seems like the children's fiction reference really hit home. "Eeyore isn't trapped in a well. Piglet isn't off finding him a pot of honey. Just…pretend I'm Owl, and I'm giving you really good advice right now."

"But, there are *babies*."

She practically coos *babies*. She says the word with extra emphasis, like it should make this entire thing endearing. Like it makes her irrational behavior more logical somehow.

But anyone who knows about bears knows that things just got so much worse.

"*Please*," I say, trying a less forceful approach while also filling my voice with as much pleading as I can muster. With one arm held out, I fold my fingers over my palm repeatedly, gesturing her forward like I might a skittish horse. I've got lots of experience with those. All bluster, until they're not.

She must pick up on the urgent tone in my voice because her shoulders fall, and she swallows heavily as her eyes dart back and forth, seeming to weigh whether I'm trustworthy.

Finally, I get a nod and a tentative step away from the deep ditch. A heavy, relieved breath rushes from my lungs as she moves toward me.

But that relief is short-lived because right as she moves away, the bear follows her as though attached to an invisible leash.

I almost can't blame it.

She's alluring. There's something about her that makes it hard to look away. You can see it on-screen. Hear it on the radio. And it's even more pronounced in person.

"Okay, doll."

"Don't *doll* me—"

"You need to shut up," I say, while keeping my voice as even as possible. My gaze moves beyond her to the massive bear emerging from the slope, four-inch-long nails clacking as it takes its first steps onto the asphalt. The sound freezes Skylar in her tracks. "Walk toward me. Do not run. Do not look behind you. Stay calm."

ACKNOWLEDGMENTS

Wild Love was a joy to write from start to finish. I'm not sure I've ever fallen harder for a couple that I did for Ford and Rosie. Their banter. The longing. The way they could push on each other's buttons so precisely—that's a special kind of love.

A book—like a child—takes a village to grow into something that is ready for readers. Luckily, I have one of the very best villages a girl could ask for. So, I really need to thank everyone who helped me grow all these words on a page into what I consider my favorite book to date.

First, my husband. My constant source of book boyfriend inspiration and most supportive cheerleader. I can't imagine my life without you.

My son, my sunshine. My happy boy who makes even the worst days feel so much better. I love you to the moon and back.

My assistant, Krista. As of writing this, we've worked together for two whole years, and I just know there are many more to come. Thank you for keeping me organized and sane.

My friend, Catherine Cowles. The person I write with pretty much every day. I'll never stop thanking the universe for bringing us together. I don't have a sister, but you feel like one.

My girls, Lena Hendrix and Kandi Steiner. The cheer squad, the safe space, two of the most incredibly talented and kind-hearted women I know. This job would be a hell of a lot lonelier without you. Love you big.

My editor, Paula Dawn. This is our TENTH book together. I doubt I can write one without you and your brain. Retirement is when I say so. Thank you for all the notes in the margins.

My beta reader/proofreader, Leticia Texeira, and my beta reader Júlia. The time you ladies spent on this book with me helped make it what it is. The voice memos, the suggestions, the constant hair-petting—you're stuck with me.

Aimee Ashcraft, who delivered what might be the most incredible content edit I've ever had the pleasure of digging into. Your feedback was utterly invaluable. No doubt in my mind that this book would not be as good as it is without having had your hands on it. Thank you.

My agent, Kimberly Brower. The woman, the myth, the legend. Lol. Jk. Kinda? But honestly, it's such an honor to work with you. Your dedication in unparalleled and I'm so fortunate to have you on my side. But also, please never take me for tea.

My editor, Christa Désir, and the entire team at Bloom Books. You all worked so hard on this book and I am forever grateful. Thank you from the bottom of my heart for taking a chance on me. I literally pinch myself every time I see my books in stores.

My editor, Rebekah West, and the entire team at Piatkus and Hachette. Thank you, thank you for believing in me and for sharing my books with the world. Seeing them in the hands of readers from so many places is such a thrill.

xo,
Elsie

Can't get enough of Elsie Silver?

Don't miss the Chestnut Springs series.

Fall in love with Wishing Well Ranch, today.

'Elsie Silver's writing is a true revelation!'
Ali Hazelwood

Available now at

PIATKUS